LUIGI PIRANDELLO was born in 1867 in Agrigento, Sicily. The son of a prosperous sulfur dealer, he studied philology, earning a degree at the University of Bonn. The young student also translated Goethe's *Roman Elegies* into Italian. In 1893 Pirandello settled near Rome and began his literary career, strongly influenced by the regional naturalism of the Sicilian novelists Verga and Capuana. His work, however, became increasingly marked by highly individual psychological and philosophic overtones, colored by a deepening skepticism and pessimism. In 1904 the family sulfur mines were flooded, and Pirandello was forced to earn his living teaching in a girls' academy in Rome. About this time his wife suffered a mental collapse; until her death in 1918 Pirandello endured a nightmarish domestic existence. Nevertheless, by 1916, when he turned to the writing of plays, he had written over three hundred stories, several volumes of poetry and essays, and four novels, chief among them *The Late Mattia Pascal* (1904). His plays, reaching their peak of genius with *Six Characters in Search of an Author* and *Henry IV*, won him worldwide renown. In 1934 he was awarded the Nobel Prize; he divided his royalties among his three children. Luigi Pirandello spent the last years of his life in rootless wanderings throughout Europe. He died in 1936.

Luigi Pirandello

The Merry-Go-Round of Love

Translated by *Frances Keene*

and Selected Stories

Translated by *Lily Duplaix*

With a Foreword by *Irving Howe*

A SIGNET CLASSIC

Published by THE NEW AMERICAN LIBRARY

Contents

FOREWORD

PIRANDELLO is one of the honored names of European literature, but few Americans know anything about him. Literate persons are likely to be familiar with one or two of his titles: there is the play *Six Characters in Search of an Author* and then . . . well, there is the fact that he was a highly intellectual dramatist specializing in the interchange of appearance and reality. And usually that is about as far as it goes. For Pirandello has survived in our culture more as a name than a living force; he has not shaped our feeling or bent our thought as Kafka or Lawrence or Proust has. Look hastily into his plays and you may well accept the stock judgment that they are clever theatrically but lacking in range and depth. Pirandello the writer is not warm or lovable or magnetic; he bears no theories of social renovation or psychic rebirth; he is not a culture-hero promising, or threatening, to transform our lives.

Yet Pirandello is a major figure. Like Thomas Hardy, he managed in one lifetime (1867—1936) to complete two full-scale literary careers. He began as a writer of prose fiction, publishing several novels and hundreds of stories, and then he became a dramatist, composing over forty plays, several of them absolute masterpieces. (Actually the plays and stories overlap in time of composition, but it is useful to regard them as products of two distinct careers.) In 1943 Pirandello received the Nobel Prize.

Why then has he failed to capture or hold the imagination of American readers and theater audiences? Some reasons are obvious: the early translations frequently muffled his brilliance, there has arisen a false notion that he is a mere juggler of a very few ideas, and the liberal intellectuals have been hostile to him because of his membership, more the result of opportunism than principle, in the Italian Fascist Party during the twenties.

There are other reasons, more elusive and important. Seri-

ous twentieth-century readers turn to literature not so much
for the direct pleasure of seeing human experience represented fictionally or of savoring mastery of language and
form. We expect more from literature: we expect that it
discover norms of conduct, that it yield revelation as well as
portray reality. Almost unwittingly we find ourselves insisting
that the great modern writer be not merely a portraitist of
life but also a self-affirmed prophet, a moral revolutionist, an
agent of transcendence. The message of guidance that neither
politics nor philosophy nor religion now seems able to provide,
we look for in modern literature.

That message in precisely what Pirandello refuses to give.
He refuses on principle, for he does not believe there is such
a message, and he does not believe the writer would have
any business offering it even if it did exist. Pirandello is a
skeptic. His best work is characterized by unqualified doubt,
at times by an extreme relativism of perspective that can
be said to approach epistemological panic. He searches for ap-
proximate truths rather than a fixed salvation, and meanwhile
he offers little hope or solace. This skepticism, which in the
actual course of his writing often serves as an incitement to
humaneness, is the only "salvation"—modest and depressing
as it may be—that he would claim to offer. He never yields
to, though he often deals with, rhetoric and apocalypse, vanity
and program. The reader who comes to a Pirandello play or
story with the usual complement of anxiety will leave without having been disburdened. It is as if Pirandello were to
proclaim as his motto: "All ye who require miracles and
bromides, turn elsewhere."

There is more to it. Pirandello is a writer strongly marked
by the tone of his time, the tone of grayness that gradually
suffuses the culture of Europe during the late nineteenth and
early twentieth centuries. The energy of the immediate past,
a moment of bourgeois confidence, has begun to wane; the
energy of the immediate future, a moment of experimental
daring, has not yet quite appeared. It is remarkable how wide-
spread is this mood of twilight sadness, this feeling of psychic
depression. Pirandello, Chekhov, Gissing, Hardy, the early
Mann, and a bit later Martin du Gard—these writers are
very different from one another, yet all reflect in their work
the feeling that a great century of hope, work, and progress

has come to an end and that a littleness of spirit has over-
taken European life.

Perhaps this feeling is due to the intensified crisis of bourgeois society, perhaps to the triumph of scientistic ideologies,
perhaps to the decay of religious conviction, perhaps to the
growth of our dismal modern cities. For the moment it hardly
matters. What does matter is that in writer after writer who
comes to maturity at this time there is a weariness of spirit,
a shared conviction, as the great German sociologist Max
Weber put it, of being witness to "the disenchantment of the
world." The forms of social existence harden. Energy seems
to run down. Values crumble. The spirit of denial and cold
rationalization takes command. And Freud's dictum that civilization is purchased through the suppression of instinct and
pleasure must be regarded not merely as a theoretic specula-
tion or even a personal statement but as the expression of attitudes common to many thoughtful men of the time.

Nowhere is this tone of things more seriously—or austerely
—communicated than in Pirandello's stories and plays. The
stories are filled with glimpses of lonely city streets, barren
provincial towns, sluggish middle-class homes, stuffy Sundays,
and torn families. Pirandello is the poet of frustration, the kind
of frustration that seems inevitable and pervasive in civilized
existence. Few writers have ever dealt more honestly with the
tiresomeness and boredom of daily life, not as the emblem of
some "deeper" metaphysical condition but simply as an irreduc-
ible fact in itself. Finally, the vision of denial that dominates
his work is more frightening than the visions of horror that
would later appear in the work of the great twentieth-century
modernists. To stay with a writer like Pirandello takes strong
nerves, a gritted determination to see things as they are. The
reward, however, is a penetration into truth, not the whole
truth, but a necessary fraction.

II

Luigi Pirandello was born in Agrigento, Sicily, the son of
a moderately well-to-do sulfur dealer. Sicily figured as the
setting in a number of his early stories and one or two plays,
mostly as a scene of social brutishness and provincial depriva-
tion. It also proved important to his career in another way:

the dominant literary influence upon his early work was the naturalism of the Sicilian novelists, Giovanni Verga and Luigi Capuana.

As a youth Pirandello turned to philological studies, earning a degree at the University of Bonn and translating Goethe's *Roman Elegies* into Italian. He wrote some conventional verse, but his talent first came into evidence with *The Outcast,* a novel published in 1893. During this phase of his career Pirandello found life extremely difficult, at times insupportable. Because his family had lost its money in a mining disaster, he had to turn to the drudgery of teaching at a girl's school in Rome. His wife, an extremely jealous woman, finally collapsed into insanity, and Pirandello, with his characteristic muted stoicism, nursed her at home, a virtual prisoner of her whims and delusions. In the twenty years between *The Outcast* and the First World War he nevertheless managed to publish a great many stories and four full-length novels, including the very fine one entitled *The Late Mattia Pascal* (1904).

Only in 1916 did Pirandello begin to devote his major energy to writing plays. He had written one or two before, but there now occurred an astonishing outburst of creative speed: brilliant plays composed in a few days or a week. In 1921 his most famous play, *Six Characters in Search of an Author,* was produced, and the following year perhaps his greatest play, *Henry IV.* Pirandello now became an international literary figure, his work being performed in theaters throughout the world and the catchphrase "Pirandellian" applied, not always carefully, to a kind of cerebral drama that released the philosophical skepticism and the concern with social and personal identity that had been troubling serious minds in the West for some time. In 1925, partly through a subsidy from the Mussolini government, Pirandello started an art theater in Rome; later he took it on tour through the major capitals of Europe. Though now relieved of financial worries and the burden of his deranged wife, Pirandello himself seems to have found little pleasure in his fame: he had suffered too intensely in the earlier years, his personality had, it seems, become too dry, and he had too keen a sense of the ridiculousness of success to remain anything but the isolated spectator he had always been. There is an amusing late play of his translated into English as *When Someone Is Somebody,* which portrays a great Italian writer, clearly a version of Pirandello himself, who has become so thoroughly a national institution he is not even named but merely designated as XXX. The great writer tries, through a clever trick, to establish for himself a new public identity, but the pressures upon him, not least of all the pressures from his decaying body, are too great. In an astonishing final scene XXX slowly turns into his own statue, a mere stone. Shortly before this happens he explains to his young admirers the reason for his loss of nerve:

> You don't know what an atrocious thing happens to an old man, to see himself all of a sudden in a mirror, when the sorrow of seeing himself is greater than the astonishment of no longer remembering. You don't know the almost obscene shame of feeling a young and hot-blooded heart within an old body ...

Here is the true Pirandello note, and the man who struck it could not yield himself very easily to transient vanities.

This is not to say that he was at all a heroic man. During the twenties Pirandello joined the Italian Fascist Party, not, so far as one can tell, out of enthusiasm for its chauvinist braggadocio, but simply because he preferred not to make difficulties for himself. Like most people, Pirandello seems to have had no strong political convictions; he took the easy way out, partly from indifference and partly for advantage; I think it reasonable to suppose that his support of the Fascist regime in Italy had about the same sort of ritual expediency as the support certain Russian writers give to the Communist regime. In any case there is no close or direct relationship between his Fascist membership and the content of his plays. Not only are the plays quite nonpolitical, but the very style of thought they display is at odds with the anti-intellectualism and nationalist demagogy of the Fascists. In much of Pirandello's work there is a devotion to cerebral intensities, an anxious concern with reflection as a value in life, and this is in no way lessened by his having to conclude that human thought seems to him hopelessly rutted in subjectivity. Whatever the practical or personal reasons for his support of the Mussolini regime—and they are to be seen as reasons, not justifications—Pirandello's major plays are the work of a *European* writer, a "good European."

"Under Fascism," writes Eric Bentley, "Pirandello's play-writing entered a third and more problematic phase. . . . Pirandello withdraws into a strange, subjective world of his own . . . or, as he would probably prefer to say, tries to create myths." At the end of his career, far from merely repeating himself as hostile critics have charged, Pirandello was still an unsettled writer; he abandoned the philosophical comedy that marks his greatest achievement and turned to a semi-allegorical, almost dream-like mode of composition. Some of his late plays, such as *The Mountain Giants* and *The New Colony*—difficult and obscure but extremely impressive—indicate that, far from yielding to the chiliastic vulgarities of totalitarianism, he remained a skeptic to the end. In *The New Colony* the skepticism is tempered by a strong humaneness, as Pirandello shows the effort of a group of smugglers and toughs to start a utopian community and its subsequent disintegration in petty disputes and human failings. He writes with considerable sympathy for these colonists, and his critique of their utopian impulse is anything but scornful: there is nothing here, so far as I can make out, that can be described as fascist either in tone or outlook.

In the concluding gesture of his life Pirandello clearly dissociated himself from the secular and religious institutions of his world. "When I am dead," he gave instructions, "do not clothe me." (The Fascists would come to bury him in a black shirt, but be denied by his will.) "Wrap me naked in a sheet. No flowers on the bed and no lighted candle. A pauper's cart. Naked. And let no one accompany me, neither relatives nor friends. The cart, the horse, the coachman, *e basta*. Burn me . . ."

III

Pirandello's stories are in the main tradition of nineteenth-century European realism. Except for those set in Sicily, which have a distinctive regional flavor and something of the pained intensity that can be found in the work of a writer returning to the miseries of his homeland, they are stories that often seem close in manner and spirit to the writ-

ings of the French realists and naturalists. Ordinary social
life forms their main setting. The weariness of middle-class
routine, the sourings of domesticity, the familiar cruelty of
city life provide their characteristic subjects. Like Flaubert,
though with less fanatic insistence, Pirandello cuts himself out
of his picture. He does not speak directly in his own voice; he
neither comments nor preaches; he allows the action to unfold
according to its inner necessities. His prose is neither elevat-
ed nor familiar, for he cares very little about "fine" writing,
and when he does engage in a rhetorical flight, it is usually
for ironic effect or in behalf of the elliptical characterization
required by the short story. He composes in a middle style,
denotative, austere, and transparent, the style of an observer
who achieves sympathy from a distance rather than through
demonstration.

Far more than we have come to expect in the modern short
story, Pirandello's stories depend upon their action, which
sometimes contains enough matter to allow a great deal of
expansion. It is not hard to see why some of the stories would
later become the basis for plays: they read like compressed
scenarios, full of quick notation and economies. It is also
characteristic of Pirandello's stories, I think, that while one
remembers the general tone and atmosphere of his "world,"
one rarely keeps in mind the features or voice of a particular
character. In so masterful a story as "Such Is Life," it is the
ambience of frustration and disappointment, the final sense of
human entanglement, that stays in one's mind far more than
the characters themselves.

There are rarely Joycean epiphanies of insight or Chek-
hovian revelations through a massing of atmosphere. Pirandello is more somber and subdued, more committed to the
necessities of the ordinary. The function of his style is to serve
as a glass with a minimum of refraction or distortion; and
whatever we may conclude about his ultimate literary purpose must come, not from a fussing with details of metaphor,
but from a response to the line of the action. In this respect
Pirandello the story writer is not quite a "modern" writer.

There is still another way in which he is not quite a "modern" writer. Though in his plays he breaks with the psychology
of nineteenth-century literary realism, abandoning the premises of a fixed individual character and of the knowability of
human relationships, his stories do not go that far. The stories

remained accessible to educated persons of his generation who had been brought up on rationalist assumptions. Such readers may have found them excessively bleak—for one does not leave Pirandello in a mood to embrace the universe—but they had no difficulty in grasping their import, as later they would with the plays.

Pirandello himself has provided a valuable summary of his major themes:

> . . . the deceit of mutual understanding, irremediably
> founded on the empty abstraction of words, the
> multiple personality of everyone (corresponding
> to the possibilities of being to be found in each of
> us), and finally the inherent tragic conflict between
> life (which is always moving and changing) and
> form (which fixes it, immutable.)

Most of these are already visible in the stories, though the theme of "multiple personality" is fully realized only in the plays. But Pirandello's treatment in the stories is by and large a conventional one—he would save his experimentalism for the plays. The stories, that is, deal with the difficulties of communication among human beings, the radical isolation of the self as it confronts its public guises, the tragic absurdity of trying to fix the flow of existence in perceptual and behavioral schemes. Yet even as they deal with these matters, the stories do not threaten the reader with a vision of the human lot as beyond comprehension or as open to so many meanings that there must follow a paralysis of relativism.

Pirandello has a sharp eye for absurdities, but this is still far from the view that life is inherently absurd. There may be anticipations of existentialism in his stories, as there may be in many writers of his day who were oppressed by the loss of nineteenth-century convictions; but precisely the writers, like Pirandello, who do seem to have anticipated the existentialist stress upon the utter insecurity of life prove in the end to be the ones who resist its full display. And this, in turn, has some relation to the fact that they were raised in a culture where Christianity retained a portion of its historic power: for if the faith no longer survived in full radiance, men still responded to its call to duties, burdens, and limits.

Pirandello's stories are controlled by his sense of middle-class life. Fantasy, playfulness, sexual abandon, religious emotion, any sort of imaginative transcendence—these seldom break through in the stories. A full tragic release is rare.

Much more characteristic are stories in which the final sadness arises from an acceptance by the characters that they will have to live on, performing their tasks without hope or joy. In a five-page masterpiece, "The Soft Touch of Grass," a bereaved and aging man is mistakenly suspected by a girl of having lewd intentions. Overcome by a conviction of the hopeless confusion of things, he goes back to his room and turns "his face to the wall." The phrase could serve as Pirandello's literary signature.

In "Such Is Life," a work that would do honor to Chekhov, a hopeless marriage, long broken, is hopelessly resumed. This story, written with a hard austerity and unrelieved by a single rebellious gesture, stays painfully close to experience. Its power depends upon Pirandello's decision not to allow his sympathies or convictions to interfere with what he sees. At the end the central figure is left with "an ever-present torment . . . for all things, all earthly creatures as she saw them in the infinite anguish of her love and pity, in that constant painful awareness—assuaged only by fleeting peaceful moments which brought relief and consolation—of the futility of living like this. . . ."

Reading these somber stories, one is struck by the accuracy of Eric Bentley's description of Pirandello's feelings and motifs. Bentley has in mind the plays, but what he says could, with some muting, be applied to the stories:

> Pirandello took from the *teatro del grottesco* or from his own fiction the antithesis of mask and face, the mask being the outward form, the face being the suffering creature. . . . His material is the flux of suffering; his art stops the flow; its stasis is at once its glory—in immortalizing the moment—and its limitation, since life, being essentially fluid, is inevitably misrepresented by art.
>
> His characters are effective not in direct relation to [his] conceptions, but because these conceptions enable him to suggest beneath the Mask of the physical presence the steady ache of suffering humanity.

IV

There are some humorous stories, too, such as "The Examination," in which a good-tempered glutton is diverted from

his studies by friends tempting him with shares of pleasure.
One smiles at the end, for Pirandello manages it with suavity
and tact. But it is a humor of sadness, and it brings little
gaiety or relief. About the pleasure of simply being alive
Pirandello has little to say in his stories, certainly nothing
to compare with his one marvelously lighthearted play *Liolà*,
in which youthful energies bubble without restraint or theory.

What I have been saying may seem to be contradicted by
the brilliant long story, *The Merry-Go-Round of Love*, which
appears here in English translation for the first time. Tradition-
al Italian humor, which delights in the undoing of a miserly
schemer and in the longevity of an old man whose death
everyone desires, seems to come alive once again in Pirandello's pages. (It is a humor somewhat similiar to that of recent
Italian films: a ridicule, both merciless and tender, of those
who would live beyond their physical and psychic means.) Yet
as the action unfolds there is a gradual darkening of tone, and
the earlier comic absurdities give way to grotesque obsessions,
so that finally the story comes to seem a revelation of the way
energy itself, the very life-principle, can become a malicious
affront to human life.

Only the stories set in Sicily have a certain buoyancy, not
because Pirandello glosses over the misery of his homeland
or indulges in peasant romanticism, but simply because here
the human drama plays itself out with quick violence. Men
rise, men fall; but they do not know the dribbling monotonies
of an overrationalized mode of existence, as do so many
characters in Pirandello's urban stories.

Behind Pirandello stands his master, the Sicilian novelist
Giovanni Verga, from whom he learned to disdain Italianate
grandeur and rhetoric. Reading Verga's great stories one feels
they are not so much "made-up" fictions as communal fables,
the record of a people born to catastrophe. Reading Pirandello's stories one feels they have been wrought by a man increasingly estranged from a world he knows intimately.
Pirandello does not achieve the virile spareness of Verga; no
one does. In Verga everything is subordinated to the decisive-
ness of the event; in Pirandello one must always be aware
of psychological motives, even if these seldom appear on
the surface of the story, and then mainly as a film of
melancholy. Verga's happenings are more terrible than Pirandello's, yet are easier to take, since in Verga men howl as
they suffer. Only a few decades separate the two writers,

but the distance between them reflects a deep change in spiritual temper, a loss of zest and will.

Writers, like the rest of us, do not choose their moment of birth, and it would be absurd to "blame" Pirandello for the depressing atmosphere of his fiction. So quick an intelligence must have been aware of the difference in the literary possibilities open to Verga and himself, and he must have realized that most of the advantages lay with the older man. But no serious writer chooses his subject; he can only choose whether to face it. And that Pirandello did with courage, honesty, and skill. His stories live.

LOST AND FOUND

CRICKETS trilled all through the calm September evening along the narrow beach cluttered with heaps of sulfur. Until the middle of the last century, this had been an inlet and the sea pounded against the walls of the expanding town. When the inlet filled in, forming a narrow, sandy strip of beach, it was quickly appropriated and loads of sulfur were dumped there.

Who could tell what would become of Vignetta a hundred or two hundred years from now? Meanwhile, for the inhabitants it was almost a city. The port handled most of the commerce of the island, though it still had no dock. Two long stony arms curved into the sea and were joined in the middle by a slender wooden bridge, called the Old Jetty. This modest span had the honor of accommodating a kind of harbor office and the white tower of the main lighthouse.

All day long the place was in a hubbub. Every morning at dawn the town crier woke everyone with a roll on his drum: "Men of the sea! To work!"

Carts loaded with sulfur had already begun to screech on their axles. They had only iron mountings and no springs and they jolted over holes in the big, dusty road, crowded by teams of skinny donkeys harnessed and loaded with sulfur in two baskets balanced on either side.

Sicilian boats with big triangular sails half-raised crowded into shore where scales were set up to weigh the sulfur before it was loaded onto the backs of the men of the sea. Sacks fastened to bands around their foreheads hung down and protected their backs. Barefoot, in duck pants, they waded into the water up to their waists to transfer their loads of sulfur to the waiting boats. When these were full, the sails were hoisted high and the boats conveyed their cargoes of sulfur to the merchant ships anchored inside or just outside the harbor.

All this activity took place on the beach .

In the town, on the main thoroughfare, other carts arrived laden with sacks of barley, wheat, and beans.

"Ho there! Weighers!" the porters hailed.

Sacks from each cart were taken down and emptied onto large burlap dropcloths spread out on the road. Barley and wheat were measured by *tomalo,* a Sicilian measure used especially for dry grain. The sacks were then refilled and carried into a warehouse, always well protected against humidity. Five *tomali* made one sack, and twenty *tomali* made a *salma.*

"Count one! Count two!" the weighers cried with every twenty *tomali,* in trailing singsong voices.

So it went until sunset, with only a brief respite at noon. In the evening, after all that noise, quiet reigned over the town. The crickets took over and thrummed their song along the beach among the heaps of sulfur; occasionally a watchdog barked. Meanwhile the surface of the harbor lay quiet as a lake, and a dark forest of masts huddled under the protecting light of the beacon, whose green flash was reflected in the black water.

Beyond the little port, the open sea extended all the way to the horizon in the moonlight, forming a wide semicircle with Punta Bianca to the right and Monte Rossello to the left.

Overlooking the quiet sea from the terrace of the Pirinzi villa, Signorina Rita listened to the avowals of her friend, Anna Cesaro. Her eyes wandered over those pale lips and slightly uneven teeth, causing Anna to lower her own eyes as she spoke and her voice to sound more muted and tremulous than ever. Sometimes Rita's eyes narrowed a little in sympathy, which disturbed Anna even more, and her trembling fingers plucked at the lace on her sleeve. Rita gave a little sigh and turned up her eyes.

"This morning, at last, I had my revenge," said Anna.

"Yes? What did you do to him?" asked Rita without the slightest curiosity.

"I closed the window in his face," Anna replied.

Rita sighed. In her heart she felt very sorry for her friend, who was so hopelessly in love with Mondino Morgani, the young doctor of Vignetta. Morgani was tall—six feet two at least—and as thin as a rail. He had hair the color of straw and bright blue eyes. His nose was thin but so prominent that every time he laughed it went white and the skin stretched so tightly it nearly split.

Poor Dr. Morgani, how could he return Anna's passion when he did not even suspect it? Or so Rita thought, and the timid confidences of her friend made her suffer for her. The poor girl was so misled that she did not realize how ridiculous her gestures must look to someone she wanted as a sweetheart —closing the window in his face, indeed! Poor thing—whatever for?

Being tied to the small town of Vignetta because of her father's sulfur business had altered Rita's naturally gay, easygoing disposition. The contrast here between the vastness of nature, the sky, the sea, and the depressing insignificance of the inhabitants was too strong. Her father was occupied all day with his business affairs, her mother with her housekeeping, so that Rita, left entirely to herself, fell into the habit of daydreaming. She had no friends in Vignetta except Anna, who was insignificant too, in her way. She found nothing and no one to interest her in this town. Aimless, almost lifeless, she consciously allowed the best days of her life to slip away one by one.

Anna lived in more modest circumstances than Rita. Her father, Rosario Cesaro, a strange sort of man, had died four years ago. He had thrown his all into sulfur holes in his mania to discover sulfur in the surrounding hills. He opened up those hills, dug holes as deep as six hundred feet, and found nothing but water—water, which meant the installation of pumps to drain it off, then subterranean tunnels to deviate the stream. He fed thousands and thousands of lire into those gluttonous holes without ever realizing any return.

Anna met Dr. Morgani at the unfortunate time of her father's last illness. After his death, her mother, her sister, and her brother-in-law were in mourning and paid little attention to Anna. She was now eighteen and had been in delicate health since childhood.

Mondino Morgani had been practicing medicine for only three months, and Signor Cesaro was his "first death." It was true, he had been carried off by an incurable disease, but nonetheless Mondino felt a kind of remorse over his death.

During her father's illness Anna grew so thin that her

small nose and slightly receding chin seemed to shrink back in alarm beneath those extraordinarily large green eyes under the flame of her thick, unruly red hair. Because of her long, slender neck, she seemed almost as tall as the doctor. When she coughed, Mondino glanced at her narrow chest and bony shoulders.

My God! he thought. That girl is tubercular.

He immediately took her under his care. He himself went to the kitchen to order broth and carried it up to the young girl's bedside.

"No, it's impossible," she said. "I can't, Doctor."

"Do me this favor. Look, just this little cup! Make an effort and it will go down."

"I swear to you—it's impossible."

"Do it for me. See, we'll try one spoonful . . . this little one."

"Oh, goodness."

"Another one, like a good girl."

"Enough. I can't take any more."

"Listen, I don't intend to budge from here until you drink this cup of broth."

Anna gave him a look with those big green eyes which said clearly, "I will do it just for you." Then she closed her eyes and swallowed.

"Good! That was fine. Now I can go feeling a lot happier! See you this evening, signorina."

From her little bed, Anna followed him all the way to the door with her eyes, then she dived under the covers, sighing happily, completely carried away, kissing the pillow with yearning lips.

Mondino even went so far as to sample some bitter medicine himself first, to get his new patient to take it. What doctor would ever do a thing like that? And the way he talked to her—and coaxed her!

Rita hinted to her friend that she doubted he could be in love with her. Poor Anna! She fished around in her memory. No, no. She was not mistaken—not at all. Those carnations in full bloom—yes, the beautiful plant of red-streaked carnations she kept on the window sill of her room! Dr. Morgani liked flowers very much, and during his calls he could never take his eyes off that plant.

"What beautiful carnations! May I, signorina?"

"Of course, Doctor."

He picked a flower with his long, thin fingers and put it in his buttonhole.

When Anna was up and around again, in gratitude to the doctor she presented him with the luxuriant pot of carnations. Dr. Morgani never wore any other flower in his buttonhole as long as the carnations were in bloom.

Was this not significant, too?

Rita thought to herself: That precious fool of a doctor; he's been basking in it. And on the whole she was right.

However, it should be said straight off that Mondino had no intention of hurting Anna. He really considered himself the most irresistible young man in Vignetta. By nature courteous and polite, he was without affectation, so what could he do about it? All the girls lost their hearts to him, thinking he was courting them. But, on his word of honor, there wasn't a word of truth to it. If they lost their hearts, they were free to do so—he even liked it—but he. . . . Moreover, Signorina Cesaro—a charming girl, no denying it—should realize that he had a very noble, lucrative profession in hand, that his parents were rich, and that she, poor little thing, had no dowry. Of course, when one is in love, one does not consider such things; however, parents usually did. He would not mention her figure—let that pass. Mondino had his own ideas on the subject: "Beauty is not important in a wife. It is enough that she be intelligent and virtuous." But what was the use of discussing it? For the moment, he had no intention whatever of getting married.

Every time he was called to the Cesaro house, he snorted like a tired horse.

"Ouf! That girl takes sick just so she can have me near her."

But once there, beside Anna's narrow bed, the provocative touch of that slender wrist trembling between his fingers, the burning look in those big green eyes pleading for mercy troubled even Mondino Morgani. He was embarrassed and could hardly put two words together—two words of Greek from that store of medical terminology in which he excelled.

"Has she any fever, Doctor?" her mother asked.

Mondino wanted to reply in exasperation, "There's one thing certain: If she hasn't, she soon will have."

II

"Look . . . look. He's turning around!" Anna nudged Rita's elbow on the railing of the terrace.

"Do be sensible, Anna," Rita chided, pretending not to see him.

Below, Mondino Morgani passed slowly along the beach, looking up deliberately at the terrace of the Prinzi house where the two friends were leaning. He passed like that every day at the same hour, always looking up at the terrace even when Anna was not there.

His look made Anna very happy. She thought it was directed at her.

"See . . . see. . . . Now do you believe me?"

"No, I don't," said Rita dryly, looking out to sea.

"Why not? I assure you . . ." Anna insisted timidly.

"I am suspicious. I believe only facts. If I were you, I'd be wary."

"You know something? Have you heard something by any chance?"

"No, nothing. I speak from experience."

"And yet . . ." Anna sighed, on the verge of tears.

Rita, looking at those pale, trembling lips and large, bewildered eyes, was sorry she had put her thoughts into words.

"Pay no attention to what I say. I'm feeling depressed today. No one knows about this better than you do, and if you say . . ." She interrupted herself to suggest, "Let's go down and play the piano. Come on."

Mondino Morgani passed by the terrace again.

Anna caught sight of him just as she was about to follow Rita, and she stopped with one hand on the railing, looking at him deliberately.

Mondino went by as straight as a stick without acknowledging her glance.

Did he see me or didn't he? Anna asked herself tremulously. Or was there someone in a window nearby?

She looked around but saw no one, and thought of what Rita had said. Suffering torment, she went down the steps of the terrace.

Rita was playing Coop's "Longing" fervently. Anna had hardly come into the room when she looked around, but kept on playing.

"He came back, didn't he?"

"Yes . . . but he didn't see me."

"Ah, he didn't turn around!" Rita remarked with a strange little smile at the corners of her mouth. She took her hands from the piano to pick up Anna's hands, looking into her eyes.

"If this is meant as a joke, he'll have to deal with me," said Anna, interpreting her friend's look and biting her lower lip.

"What can you do to him?" asked Rita with a shrug, the same smile still hovering on her lips.

"Oh, if he thinks I'm anything like the harbor captain's daughter, that big flirt with all her carrying-on, or that fish, Sarina Scoma, who bills and coos on the public square with the officers, or——"

"My dear," Rita cut in, "where men are concerned, *they* are always right. You love him, don't you?"

Anna went on biting her lower lip.

"All right, then, suppose he starts flirting with someone else, suppose he even marries her, leaving you flat. What can you do?"

"We haven't come to that yet," Anna objected. "In any case, I must rid myself of this uncertainty."

Rita sighed. Unfortunately, she was not at all uncertain.

Mondino Morgani felt perfectly sure that at the flick of his finger all the girls of Vignetta would throw themselves out of the window crying, "Take me! Take me!" Only one resisted him: Rita Prinzi. And there was no doubt, at least in Dr. Morgani's mind, that she was the most beautiful, the most intelligent of them all. Educated as a lady, she played the piano, embroidered, spoke French, came of a respectable family, and had a reasonable dowry.

And so back and forth he passed beneath her windows.

Rita saw very well what was going on. He thinks he has only to open his mouth like a frog, she thought, looking after him. Well, this fly won't fall in, my dear!

She went indoors so as not to give the fool any illusions. Oh, poor Anna!

At last Mondino was convinced that he was only wearing out good shoe leather and decided to take the plunge. "I'll pluck the loveliest rose of Vignetta! Goodbye, bachelor life! Goodbye, little secret affairs!"

But her answer was a curt "No!"

No? Why no? Why? Mondino asked himself. It gave him no peace. How can it be no? In despair, he walked up and down in his bedroom, hands behind his back, quite forgetting the cold, wearing only his shirt and slippers. That "no" was unexpected. How could it be? Their ages were right. Let's see, he thirty and she twenty-two—just eight years' difference. He was not deformed, nor so unpleasant to look at, really. For a man, he was of a good height, had a noble, lucrative profession, a good family from every point of view. "I don't understand it!" And he scratched his white, hairless chest under his shirt with cold, nervous fingers.

"I don't under . . . Ah-choooo! Ah-chooo!"

"God bless you, Mondino," his aunt called from the next room.

"Thank you," he called back.

He was catching cold. He put on his coat and began walking up and down again.

Could Signorina Rita be setting her cap for some prince? *For the moment, my daughter has no intention of getting married!* A fine excuse! At twenty-two. . . . When would she make up her mind?

He blew his nose loudly. For three days he did not leave the house.

"Mondino, a patient."

"Say I'm in bed with a cold."

"Mondino, they are calling for you from the Cesaro house."

"Signorina Anna? Be damned!"

He rolled over in his bed and pulled up the covers.

"The doctor has a cold."

III

It was a mortal blow for poor Anna. She learned about his

proposal to Rita from her friend's own lips through a trick of which no one would have thought Anna capable.

She had noticed a shade of bitterness pass over Rita's face and creep into her words whenever she referred to the doctor, where before there had been only pity. Why?

"I know that Dr. Morgani asked for your hand," she said to Rita, as if in answer to her friend's accusations against him.

"Who told you that?" demanded Rita with a frown.

"So then it is true!" exclaimed Anna, her face aflame.

"How did you know? Who told you?" Rita repeated in her embarrassment.

"No one. It was clear from what you just said."

"That I refused him?"

"Yes. Why? Because of me?" asked Anna, so emotionally upset that she looked as if she would faint any minute. "Oh, but if you did it because of me . . ."

"No," Rita put in haughtily. "In the first place you know that I never liked him, the old stick. But in any case I *would* have turned him down because of you."

Anna struggled in her heart with shame, love, jealousy, and humiliation. On the one hand, she felt like lashing out at the doctor with every kind of insult, and on the other, it hurt her to hear Rita say anything against him. She wanted to stop her friend from belittling the one she had so long deemed worthy of her heart, but pride restrained her.

"I have no dowry; that's the reason."

Rita tried to comfort Anna as best she could, deflecting all the ridiculous notions of revenge Anna proposed out of hurt feelings.

"Where men are concerned, as I already told you, they are always in the right. It is better not to love——"

"Yes . . . yes. It's far better," Anna agreed, sobbing.

Finally, when she had regained her composure somewhat, Anna went home. She wandered through the rooms all day in a daze, as if it was the menacing storm, whose clouds were rolling darkly above the iron-gray sea, that kept her from helping her mother with the household chores.

That night there was a downpour over Vignetta. Lightning flashed across the sky, and immediately afterward there was the crashing roll of thunder.

Anna stood before the open window, bewitched by the

violence of the storm. Rain lashed her face and drenched her clothes. She started with every flicker of that sinister light through the darkness over the raging sea. Crying, burning with fever, she imagined her unhappiness at this moment greater than that of any other living creature. She was wracked, trembling, and convulsed by her misery. Out at sea, in the middle of the storm—how fortunate were those sailors facing imminent death. To die ... to die ... a thousand times better to die!

The next day, when her mother came into her room, she found Anna in bed, the window open, and the floor still wet from the rain.

"Did you sleep like this? Are you crazy, Anna? Are you ill? Oh, Lord God! How do you feel? Are you feverish?"

In alarm the poor mother sent for the doctor.

"The doctor is in bed with a cold and cannot come," the servant said when she returned.

But he did come the following day.

Anna received him as though he were a stranger. She would not answer any of his questions, possibly because she feared her voice might betray her emotions.

Mondino turned to her mother. "Why did she stand in the rain? The window open all night! How idiotic!"

Anna clenched her teeth and closed her eyes, drawing a long breath through her nostrils. Then she coughed.

"Horrible weather! Look at me, and I did nothing foolish, Signora."

To underline the fact that he was suffering from a cold, Mondino blew his nose. Then he wrote out a prescription and left.

"I will be back this evening."

IV

Following Rita Prinzi's refusal, Mondino Morgani had an unforeseen series of utter failures. In quick succession he was refused by:

(1) The daughter of the harbor captain, Nannina Vettoli, rival of Rita Prinzi. She was twenty-four years old (twenty-one she said), dark haired, not pretty but winning, with a twelve-thousand lire dowry, her mother dead; she

spoke good Italian—not only the regional dialect—spoke fair French, and played the piano.

(2) Carmela Ninfa, eighteen years old, rather ugly—looked a little like a monkey—but had a twenty-five-thousand-lire dowry; both parents intact; French zero, Italian zero, piano zero.

(3) Sarina Scoma (even she!), twenty-seven years old, of dubious complexion under a pasty layer of make-up; fifteen-thousand-lire dowry; no education at all; spoke Italian by ear, though in her native dialect she was voluble enough.

(4) Giovanna Merca, the niece of Lawyer Merca. Her father was a leather dealer, but she always referred to herself as "Lawyer Merca's niece." No dowry, only her trousseau; she embroidered beautifully, played the piano, read trashy novels from morning till night, talked like a man, and was ugly—*but* she was Lawyer Merca's niece.

Nannina Vettoli refused him, or so he understood, because Rita Prinzi had refused him first; Carmela Ninfa because she was very short and he looked too tall beside her; Sarina Scoma because (at the moment) she was taken with an officer of a detachment stationed in Vignetta; Giovanna Merca because she was carrying on a feverish correspondence with a port official who had recently been transferred to Leghorn.

Mondino was almost driven out of his mind.

Apart from his person, apart from his family, was he a doctor, yes or no? Is a doctor of medicine, by rights, an important figure in a little town like Vignetta, or isn't he? Oh, it was quite evident that those girls had talked one another out of it—because, of course, apart from his person, apart from his family, where could they ever hope to find a better match? The girls' plot was all too plain in the marked displeasure shown by the fathers and the lawyer-uncle when they had to bring him a negative reply. He seemed fated to remain a bachelor.

"Good riddance!" Mondino would have cried, no doubt, if it were not for the fact that he *was* a doctor and was therefore obliged to call again and again at the Scoma house, or the Mercas', at the Vettolis' or the Ninfas'. To make the best of his amorous misfortunes, Mondino decided to look on the whole thing as the hand of fate turned against him, and using this excuse as a shield to hide his true humiliation, he would appear to harbor no grudge against any of the families concerned. But he was very gloomy.

Meanwhile Anna grew worse every day. Mondino's fears, based on her weak constitution, proved only too true. Sitting at her bedside, he felt more depressed than ever without knowing why.

Anna had brightened a little during her illness, as her tempestuous feelings settled into passive acceptance of her lot. However, from time to time a thought would return to stir them up.

She replied now briefly to Mondino's questions.

"How do you feel today, signorina?"

"Better, Doctor."

She said "better," but he well knew . . .

As the days passed, Mondino's visits grew longer and were more and more friendly. He talked with her mother and even managed to get Anna to say a few words.

After uttering a sad reflection on life or on the wrong concept we are apt to form of men or of society, he would smile bravely and sigh. Anna did not seem to be listening— but she was, most attentively.

Ah, the injustice of human nature, Mondino thought to himself. Here is this girl, dying because of me—and she really is dying, for there is no hope of saving her now. Yet I was unable to fall in love with her, the only one in the whole town I wouldn't have had to ask twice.

Suddenly he conceived the idea of asking her now; his spirit was low at the moment, and then he believed that, if nothing more, it might help her to die happy.

It would be an act of charity, he told himself.

Moreover, he owed it to her, because at one time he knew he had been a little too encouraging to the poor girl.

Rita Prinzi watched over Anna like a sister. She never left the sick girl's side, reading softly to her so as not to tire her and talking gaily to keep her spirits up. However, every time the doctor came she fled so she would not have to meet him.

One morning she was not quick enough, and as Mondino turned the doorknob, he heard a chair fall, yet he found Anna alone in the room.

"Am I disturbing you, signorina?" he asked from the doorway, leaning forward on his long, straight legs.

"No," Anna replied dryly.

"I thought I heard someone run out."

"Yes, Rita," said Anna.

"Oh," Mondino said with a wry smile. "Why does she run away? Am I so frightening?"

He sat down and took Anna's frail wrist between his fingers.

"I was wrong, signorina," he said, still holding her wrist, "to knock at certain doors where I should not have knocked, and I am sorry. If you could only know how deeply sorry I am, you would believe me. I wandered like a blind man, signorina. Now my eyes are opened, I hope not too late—if you will only believe in my repentance and forgive me."

His words took Anna's breath away, and little by little she drew her wrist from his hand.

"You should not be saying these things to me," she said without looking at him and in a voice that tried to be firm.

Anna's mother, called by Rita, now opened the door and came into the room.

"To your mother, then?" he asked, smiling toward her mother.

"What is it?" she asked, sitting at the foot of her daughter's bed.

"We were saying—or, that is, I was saying to your daughter—that she must get well soon because we need her—I especially. I even more than you, signora. I lost my way like a blind man, I told her, and I have found it again, here, beside this little bed. You do understand me, signora? Here beside Signorina Anna—what do you say to that?"

Her mother understood neither his words nor the bittersweet tone of his voice. She looked at him in surprise. Then finally she understood from the look he directed at her daughter as soon as he had finished speaking, and from the strained expression on her daughter's face.

She blushed and replied, almost stammering, "What? But I never imagined. I...I...I'm very happy. But you must have her answer from her own lips. Isn't that right, Anna?"

Anna, her face like wax, half closed her eyes.

"Then it's up to you, signorina," said Mondino, smiling, leaning over the bed expectantly.

"Well, then, *no!*" Anna said, opening her eyes with a frown.

At that "no" Mondino drew back, his face pale, a resigned smile on his lips.

"No!" he exclaimed. "You, too, *no?* Ah, you repay my sincerity badly, signorina. I did not believe..."

He broke off, passing his hand over his forehead and his eyes. Then he resumed, with a long sigh: "Never mind, Signora Cesaro, you have nothing to fear. This will not in any way affect my care of her. I will try to win, if not her affection, at least her esteem. Insofar as I am able, I will do my duty."

He immediately changed the subject with great tact, or at least that was Rita's opinion as she listened at the door.

V

Jesus—an authentic portrait taken from an emerald cut by order of Tiberius, Roman Emperor in the thirtieth year of the Christian Era. This gem, the inestimable value of which does not exceed its artistic merit, came, after many vicissitudes, to enrich the treasure of the Turks, whose Emperor later gave it to Pope Innocent VIII to redeem his brother who had been taken prisoner by the Christians.

Absorbed in thought, Rita sat at the foot of Anna's bed and involuntarily reread this inscription under a picture of Jesus hanging above it.

After her "no," Anna had taken a turn for the worse. Her condition rapidly declined.

"You should not be here, Rita," she said. "If I were you, I would be afraid to stay here."

"Of course not, Anna. You must be joking! You are better."

"Yes, of course—better."

She no longer had the strength to lift her arms and, with a bitter smile, called her friend's attention to this weakness.

Rita's parents had also advised her—nay, begged her—not to go to Anna's house any longer.

"Nonsense," Rita replied. "When the doctor himself tells me it is no longer safe to go there, I will not go. We have not reached that point yet."

Anna's illness had quickened her senses and especially reinforced her innate suspiciousness. She spied on her friend, convinced in her heart that Rita disapproved of her sharp refusal of the doctor's offer. Mondino's reaction was now one of brotherly attention—even in front of Rita. Why was it that Rita no longer ran from the room when Dr. Morgani came in? Instead, she turned to him with questions and asked his advice about Anna's care. Mondino evidently took some pleasure in answering her questions in his usual polite manner. And Anna gathered from Rita's expression that she no longer found him either displeasing or foolish.

Ah, how good, how very good he is, thought Anna deep in her heart, and how well he expresses himself.

At the same time, Rita confessed to herself: He is not as silly as I took him to be. And he certainly must have a good heart!

Mondino, on his side, was aware of these favorable reactions and carefully fostered them. Following this course, he felt certain of being safely maneuvered into port.

Anna foresaw it too and if, on the one hand, she had a feeling of jealous resentment against Rita, on the other hand, she forgave Mondino. She enjoyed hearing him talk so beautifully to her friend and noticed how he had already won her over. She wanted to say to Rita, "You see, he is worthy of being loved after all. Ah, now you think as highly of him as I did! Very well, go away. You do not stay here because of me any longer but only to see him and talk to him twice a day—I understand, perhaps even more clearly than you do yourselves. You show so much pity for me, both of you, because in that shared pity lies the path of your own love. Go away, Rita—for my sake and for yours—go."

But Rita did not go. She was impatient if the doctor was five minutes late, and went to look out the same window from which Anna had once leaned to watch Mondino go by. Rita, meanwhile, sincerely believed that her impatience was due only to her solicitude for her friend.

To discover just how far the understanding between them had gone, Anna pretended one day to be asleep at the time the doctor usually came to call.

That day her mother was not in the room because Anna had begged her to go to bed and rest after the long hours she had spent at her bedside during the previous night.

Finally Mondino arrived, and Rita quickly made a sign for him to come in on tiptoe.

"She's sleeping," she whispered when he was beside the bed.

Mondino looked down at his patient, then turned toward Rita and sadly shook his head.

"She already looks as if the end had come." Rita sighed.

Mondino nodded assent and then, a little embarrassed, said softly, "Now, signorina, listen. It isn't right for you to continue coming here. I understand that she is your dear friend. I am aware of your warmhearted impulses, but you must realize that . . . I am uneasy when I am away thinking of you here, constantly exposed to this danger. Do you understand me? Please go away after today—and don't come back. Will you promise? It is so unwise."

"I have already told her that!" cried Anna, suddenly opening her eyes wide on the two of them.

Rita and Mondino were startled.

"I said it was unwise," Mondino stammered, embarrassed, "not because of your condition, Signorina Anna, but because . . . because Signorina Rita is not well. She is worn out—and she suffers to see you like this."

"Ah, is that why? If that's all, then leave her alone, Doctor, because she is not suffering," said Anna, smiling bitterly. "I suffer—yes, I am the one who suffers. For pity's sake, let me die in peace. Don't either of you come back again. What joy can you have in loving each other here in the presence of death?"

Rita burst into tears, burying her face in her hands, and Mondino, confused, unnerved, could find no words to answer Anna. He went out hastily without daring to say goodbye.

About two weeks later Anna died.

For seven years now she has lain in the high-perched, lonely cemetery of Vignetta, among its bright flowers and its many cypress trees. It is as well for her peace of mind that she cannot know that Mondino Morgani and Rita Prinzi were married five years ago and now have two children, Coco and Mimi, as blond and blue-eyed as their father.

THE EXAMINATION

THE few guests of the Hermitage, isolated up there on top of the mountain, had been listening for some time to the donkey driver's voice as he made the exhausting climb up the slope to their retreat.

"Skee ... brr! Skee ... brr!"

In that stifling heat the continuous scraping of the locusts and shrill of the crickets was annoying enough without this. The guests wondered if that lopsided fellow, Natale, was bringing up a long-term fellow sufferer or just a passing visitor, and from time to time they leaned out the windows of the former convent which had been converted into an inn.

The convent was little changed. There were the same small cells, provided with a wretched cot so narrow it was impossible to turn over, a crude wooden table, a washbasin, and three or four rush-bottom chairs. The old refectory was still in use, and so were the long, dark, resounding corridors with their worn, gray stairs. But the little chapel adjoining the main building was always closed.

The guests tolerated this lack of comfort because living in a cloister had a piquancy all its own, and when this wore off, they did not want to admit it. It was Signor Lanzi who had had the bright idea of opening this so-called hotel; every year he promised that new quarters would be ready for the following season—built according to the Swiss plan, with a funicular railway.

"Yes," everyone agreed. "This would make a delightful place to spend a vacation."

"But when I've put my all into it and can offer you every convenience," Signor Lanzi would say with a sigh, scratching the top of his head, "you gentlemen will tell me that the prices are too high and you won't come, or you will think: If we have to pay that much, we might as well go to Switzerland! It'll make a better impression! And then where will I be with all my conveniences?"

Was there never to be a new building, Swiss-style, then?

Of course—the following year, for sure.

To entertain his guests, Signor Lanzi pointed out the exact spot where the new hotel was to be built and described it down to the smallest detail. It would be magnificent! They could almost see it there already, and each one came forward with advice and suggestions. Signor Lanzi also told them of the discussions now under way for the construction of a funicular railroad: The work was to begin next October.

"Bravo, Signor Lanzi! Natale with his good-for-nothing donkey is really a disgrace."

"Skee . . . brr! Skee . . . brr!"

Meanwhile, Natale's voice was coming closer.

Signor Lanzi with Quagliola, the former deputy, as bald and round as a barrel, and the redheaded professor, director of his own Tancredi Picinelli School, a thin, freckled, nervously polite young man, were walking on the terrace in front of the convent. Looking up, they saw the four other guests half leaning out their windows, waiting. There was blond Signora Ardelli, whose husband—"such a fine man"—came up every Saturday evening from town where he was employed; Signor Mesciardi, the lawyer, who was flirting with the signora; then Quagliolino, the son of the deputy, who had also tried to flirt with her like a silly schoolboy, to the detriment of his health; and last of all there was the little priest, Don Vine, who fled before temptation.

The donkey, reasonably enough, was the first to appear—then collapsed, ears dangling, eyes closed, his sides heaving as if he were all in. Natale rushed up, furious as a devil from hell, brandishing his stick.

"Up, pig! Up!"

A donkey should, it seems, feel insulted by being called a pig. But this one didn't. Realizing this, perhaps, Natale tried clubbing some sense into him. However, the donkey acted as if the blows were not meant for him. He only tried lifting one skinned ear to find out from which direction they came.

Finally, the new guest trudged into view, all out of breath. Lawyer Pompeo Lagumina, a nearsighted giant, was vexed because his glasses kept slipping off of his sweaty nose. The wide brim of his white canvas hat was limp with perspiration and flapped against his big face. Rushing up to the donkey, he shouted at Natale, who shrank back.

"I'll carry him myself, you brute, the way Morgante carried the monastery's horse!"

He really tried to lift the little donkey, to the general amusement of the onlookers.

"The man is a *mountain*, I tell you," whined the donkey driver apologetically to Signor Lanzi, indicating Lagumina.

"*I* came all the way on foot," Pompeo Lagumina shouted to Natale. "Why won't this donkey of yours stand up? He's even more of an ass than you are!"

"With that case full of lead," growled Natale.

"*Science*, idiot. They're books!" retorted Lagumina, shaking Natale by the shoulders.

"Ah, science! No wonder the donkey is weighed down," Quagliola observed, as Lagumina said harshly to Natale, "I won't pay you. You'll get no tip from me."

Signor Lanzi quickly interposed, "Do as you wish, Signore, but please come inside. You are in a sweat and might catch cold."

"Thank you. There's no danger of that," replied Lagumina, swelling his mighty chest. "Are you the proprietor?"

"At your service."

"Very kind, thank you. I would like to point out that I have not touched this donkey. I tried to mount it but my feet dragged on the ground. The beast simply collapsed under me."

"He broke the donkey's back," grumbled Natale.

"I'll break every bone in your body," thundered Pompeo Lagumina, turning on him with clenched fists. "Now, hold your tongue!"

From her window, Signora Ardelli burst out laughing. Lagumina looked up irritably and, seeing a lady, tried to pull the hat off his moist head, grinning like a big baby.

"I will say no more, signora, and leave everything to your good graces."

But Signora Ardelli had already disappeared from the window.

"I have come here especially to study," said Lagumina, turning once more to the hotel proprietor. His face suddenly grave, he commanded, "I require a room quite removed from the rest of the guests."

"Ah, here there are only poor monks' cells, made for study and meditation, signore," replied Signor Lanzi. "Come, I will show you."

"Gentlemen," said Lagumina with a bow, before stepping out like a grenadier and going stiffly off behind Signor Lanzi.

Signor Quagliola and Professor Picinelli glanced up to the windows where the others were taking in the scene. Mesciardi was rubbing his hands together, as if to say, Cheer up, the fun has just started.

"Did you say *lead,* Natale?" Quagliolino called down. "You were right."

"He killed my donkey for me, God damn his soul," Natale cursed, using his teeth as well as his hands to undo the cord around the load of books attached to the pack saddle.

Picinelli tried to urge the donkey to rise, but the poor beast knew only the language of a stick. Though he pricked up his ears at this friendly persuasion, he let them fall again, thinking, no doubt, He can't be talking to me!

A little later the guests at the Hermitage met under the trees to the east of the mountain for their midday meal.

Pompeo Lagumina, much refreshed after copiously dousing himself with cold water, his big face wreathed in smiles, sat down at his own table placed between that of Professor Picinelli and the table shared by the Quagliola. He was carrying a big book under his arm.

"Ah," he sighed, almost inaudibly, as he closed his eyes and placed the book on the table. "I really haven't a minute to spare."

All the guests were seated at separate tables, except for Quagliola and his son. Mesciardi, the lawyer, tried to listen to what the newcomer had to say, because he did not want to miss anything, but at the same time he wanted to keep his place near Signora Ardelli. He soon had an inspiration and, getting up, went over to Lagumina to present him with his visiting card.

"Since you are now a fellow monk . . ."

"Quite right. Thank you very much," Lagumina said.

Then he rose to distribute his cards all around with a great show of politeness. Names were exchanged, and Lagumina returned to his table.

"Although I am the senior member of this group," said

Quagliola, "your stature entitles you to the priority of the convent, lawyer Lagumina!"

"How happy I would be to accept it," Lagumina replied sadly. "And you may rest assured that—always with our Don Vine's consent—I would found a new order of Hermits, a band of jolly good fellows! But my time is precious. I am preparing for a difficult civil-service examination for Chief Clerk of the Council of State."

"No less!" exclaimed Mesciardi.

"Unfortunately, what can I do?" Lagumina sighed. "It's of vital importance to me. If I succeed—but there, I refuse to entertain a doubt as to the outcome. I have only a month at my disposal. When I think of it, my courage fails me."

But not his appetite. He devoured everything in sight, neatly putting away a large dish of risotto and talking uninterruptedly about his examination. His food disappeared so quickly that, foraging in his empty plate with his fork, he looked up with surprise at the guests, then at the waiter.

"If I'm not mistaken, this was very good. Shall we repeat it? Bring me some more. Ah, this mountain air! Too bad I cannot enjoy it—but it's a comforting thought that, for me at least, study has always been a consuming passion."

"Not to mention risotto," Quagliola remarked under his breath to Picinelli.

In fact, cutlets, chicken, salad, and the rest followed in quick succession. Don Vine, thinnish and fastidious, was simply amazed.

And the book? Patience . . . the end of the meal was at hand.

"How enchanting it is here!" Lagumina remarked as he got up, both hands under his belly, gorged and content. "Now, I think a little shade is what I need. Excuse me." Beaming, he took up his book and sauntered a short distance away to stretch out at the foot of a beech tree.

Today is Saturday. I've just arrived, he thought to himself, blissfully lighting a cigar. Tomorrow is Sunday. Best begin on Monday and give myself some time to get accustomed to the place and satisfy my curiosity.

He gazed into the distance at the ethereal blue chain of the Apennines.

"Ah, the spinal column of our Fatherland!"

What excellent ideas he had sometimes, without even thinking about it—in his moments of leisure—and what a strong picture that metaphor conveyed! He certainly had nothing to worry about for the forthcoming examination. He was nobody's fool. *The Apennines, spinal column of our Fatherland!* Had that thought ever occured to anyone before?

His head was not quite comfortable against the trunk of the tree. Slipping down a little, he rested it on his book and in no time was snoring loudly. At a signal from that terrible Quagliolino, worthy son of such a father, the other guests approached on tiptoe to gaze down at him.

"Shhh! He's studying," whispered Quagliola, holding a finger to his lips. "We won't disturb him. He's already before the Council of State!"

But Lagumina's sleep did not last long. Every Saturday afternoon the little group at the Hermitage gave the Honorable Ardelli a noisy greeting when he arrived from town. They made such a racket that Lagumina awoke with a start, and since he had been dreaming about the examination and was frightened, he immediately took the book from under his head and started to read, his eyes still puffed and red from sleep. Those idlers came over to him, bringing Ardelli, mounted triumphantly on the donkey. He was as round as Quagliola, but with the head of a Goliath.

"Here's our latest," said Mesciardi, pointing to Lagumina. "Ardelli, we would like to present our new Father Prior."

Lagumina got up, smiling. "I told you that I could not accept. You see me here wracking my brains. Good heavens, it's almost dark! I was so busy reading that I hadn't noticed."

"I must warn you, you'll ruin your eyes," said Quagliola with a show of sympathetic concern.

Sunday: true, he was determined not to lose a day, not even a single minute. But had he not promised himself, the evening before, to begin on Monday? Yes, first he needed to adjust himself to the mountain air. But, heavens, how late it was! Nine o'clock, already.

What a heavy sleeper! Tomorrow, Monday, I'll be up at five.

He dressed and, taking his big book under his arm, went down to the terrace.

What a crowd! So many women and girls, all in a holiday mood! They had arrived on little donkeys from the nearby villages. A swing had been strung between two trees. The girls were taking turns on it and everytime a young man gave a harder push, they let out joyful squeals of fright, feigning not to notice their flying skirts, but prettily displaying their legs in colored, openwork stockings.

Pompeo Lagumina turned away, frowning. He no longer had the right to look at girls. The one in his heart was enough. A responsible man, once he has given his promise, respects it. Near or far, it was his duty to be faithful even in thought. He invoked the thought of his modest little Sandra, who was eating her heart out for love of him at this very moment. She had waited two long years for their wedding, all the while contending with her sulky mother, who wanted her to marry her rich, stupid cousin Mimmino Orrei. Sandrina did nothing but laugh at him. Poor, poor Sandrina! But what else could he have done? His heart was as big as the ocean, so far as that was concerned. But as for money . . . Ah! Diogenes, yes, it was Diogenes who threw away the cup to drink out of the hollow of his hand. Perhaps Diogenes was not the right comparison. What would really fit him like a glove right now was that clerkship with the Council of State. Then her mother would consent, all right. But how could he study and prepare for the examination in the city when he had to spend so many hours a day at the Ministry of Industrial and Commercial Agriculture, and was always distracted in his free time by that terrible urge to see his sweetheart? Impossible. He needed to get away for a month, away from everything, off in a remote corner by himself. But then, he also needed the wherewithal!

When he thought of what Sandrina had done for him, it was a miracle Pompeo Lagumina did not burst into tears in front of all those people. The hard time she had, the things she went without to save a thousand lire, which she insisted on giving him so he could go away from her to study. Now everything depended on the outcome of the examination.

At this point Pompeo Lagumina quickly opened his book.

"Surely not here, with all this noise!" exclaimed lawyer Mesciardi, coming up to him, pointedly staring at the girls on the swing to annoy Signora Ardelli, who was all eyes for her husband that day.

"You're right," said Lagumina. "It's impossible here. Our convent seems to have been invaded with demons today."

And he laughed. There! Another beautiful phrase with a
classical ring. Decidedly, he had a flair for words. They
came to him just like that, as spontaneous as lightning. He
thought he would take refuge in the bush which covered the
steep slopes of the mountain.

What beauty! What shade! How refreshing!

"Ohhh . . . Ouch!"

Nothing much. He had taken a tumble, that's all. But he
had to be careful with that mess of leaves all over the ground
like a slippery carpet. It hurt a little at the base of his
spine. The book? There it was, over there by that tree. It
had slithered all the way down.

Lagumina was too frightened to let go of the bush. He hung
on with both hands while he stretched out one foot toward
the trunk of a tree below. Ah! Lucky thing his glasses were
not broken, banging against the tree like that. All right, he
would be more careful, but it was fun sliding down in little
spurts—Whee!—another . . . and   another . . . down . . . down
. . . from trunk to trunk . . . almost to the bottom of the hill.

Good for you, Pompeo! Now up you go!

Ah, the book? Heavens! He had forgotten it on the ground
up there—but where? How was he ever going to find it
again among all those trees?

If I don't find it, I'm ruined. Up . . . up.

He found it, fortunately, after searching frantically for
three hours. It lay open there on the dry leaves at the
base of a tree, bearing the visible token of a little bird.

"Dirty little thing!"

Pompeo climbed the rest of the way to the top, his face
aflame, dripping sweat, his clothes torn and disheveled, but
his appetite was unimpaired.

Monday: First of all, set up the books. It was five o'clock
on the dot, exactly the hour he had decided on. Pompeo
Lagumina rubbed his hands in satisfaction.

But that little table, it could never hold all the big books
he needed to have within easy reach. Still, a larger table
would never fit into the cell. What could he do? Ah! He had
an idea. He would set his packing case on two chairs beside
the table. There!

He diligently arranged the books according to subject matter, laid out paper to make notes, sharpened lead pencils as

well as red and green pencils for his particular signs, a memorizing device. Then, at last, he sat down to begin his assignment.

"Lawyer Lagumina! Lawyer Lagumina!"

Oh, those idlers again!

Pompeo Lagumina huffed and shook his fist furiously in the air. Let them sing out. They were a nuisance. Didn't they know he had not come here to amuse himself?

"Father Lagumina!"

"Father Prior!"

That prior business again. Yet if he didn't answer them, they might go on calling indefinitely, they might even imagine that he was still asleep.

He went to the window.

"Please excuse me, gentlemen. I've been at it since five! You know very well—"

"I know nothing of the kind," cried Honorable Ardelli, getting on the donkey. "I'm going back to town and I want all of you to come with me part of the way."

"Excuse me, I cannot come," Lagumina replied. "You have a very fine escort as it is. Leave me to my studies."

"I'll accept no excuses," said Ardelli. "We can't do without our prior."

"But Quagliola is the honorable prior."

"Then I, as prior, order you to come down and accompany our brother hermit," said Quagliola.

"Excellent," they all approved.

Mesciardi added, "Come on, Lawyer Lagumina. Don't forget that a little walk early in the morning is good for the mind. It clears the head."

"That's true," Lagumina agreed courteously—also because there was no doubt that a little walk . . .

He never should have said it.

"Come on down, then," they chorused.

He couldn't refuse now. He left the window, snorting, and went down.

"On one condition," he told them. "That we make it quick. I'll rely on you."

"Just the time to go and come back," they replied.

But all the way down as well as all the way back, they encouraged him to talk about the difficulties of his examination. He discussed it willingly. When they reached the top

of the hill, it was time for the midday meal. Pompeo Lagumina looked forlorn. He said he could not eat.

"A whole morning wasted!"

"What can you do about it now?" asked Mesciardi. "Be
patient. You can always study later on."

"But as you know, the morning is the best time for study,"
Lagumina argued irritably. "Let me go. Don't keep me."

"If you refuse to take a little nourishment," Quagliola
said with his usual placidity, "I'm telling you, you won't have
the strength to study. Isn't that true, Signora Ardelli?"

"He must eat," she said. "I hope he will excuse us for
not wanting to do without his pleasant company."

"Don't talk that way, signora!" Lagumina exclaimed, deeply flattered. "I would be so happy . . . if only I didn't find
myself in this . . . situation."

"We promise not to disturb you again," replied Signora
Ardelli. "Is that all right? Now please eat. Do me this little
favor."

In order to please the charming signora who pleaded so
insistently, Pompeo Lagumina ate. Eating and chatting, he
forgot his annoyance and did honor to his appetite. In fact,
after the meal he had difficulty getting up from his chair.
But now to work! No more excuses!

"Are you gentlemen going to sleep? I must go back to
my books. I hope you rest well."

And he went back to his cell. With all the good will in the
world he set out to study. But his eyelids were heavy and
he felt himself overcome by sleep. He tried to resist, but he
found it more and more difficult to concentrate on the page
before him. Little by little, as his resistance weakened, he
lost consciousness until his eyes closed of their own accord. With a sudden jerk of his head, he sat up in a daze.
Looking around him, he spied the bed. It was no use. There
was no holding out against such a meal in that heat. Just
a short nap—only for an hour.

When he woke up, it was evening.

"Lord! Look at that gloomy expression!" cried Quagliola
from the terrace as he caught sight of him at the window.
"What are you trying to do, kill yourself with work?"

"As a matter of fact, yes," muttered Lagumina, rubbing
his eyes and forehead as if he had really been hard at it

until then—not so much that he wanted to convince them as that he wanted desperately to convince himself.

"Come on down. We've already had supper."

"No. I'll be down later ... if I come," Lagumina said. "Now I must write a little letter."

He wrote his dear Sandra that he was alone up here with a huge dog who refused to follow the monks when they left the old hermitage. It was cold here in this Alpine solitude. He too felt cold in his spirit so far from her, and to console himself he studied without interruption. He even studied during his frugal meals, which were brought to him every morning by a boy from the nearby village. He ate in the old refectory, now completely deserted, while outside the wind howled through the trees on the mountaintop. The big dog watched him intently, his kind eyes deep as silent pools.

After reading his pathetic letter, Pompeo Lagumina wept. His lies were sincere because with all his heart he wanted everything he wrote to be true. Bundled up against the evening chill, with a lump in his throat, he went down to supper a little later.

Tuesday: That treacherous bed so filled him with fear after his experience of the previous day that he decided to go outside and study peacefully in the shade. No one would bother him there in the woods.

He selected a book and picked up his notebook and pencil to take along.

When he had installed himself, a stifled cry made him jump. Red in the face, his eyes glistening, Quagliolino suddenly rolled over on his stomach and looked up at him anxiously.

Lagumina smiled, but his voice was harsh. "Did I surprise you?"

"No. It's nothing," the boy said, lowering his eyes. Then he asked, "Did you see them ... over there?"

"No. I didn't see anything."

"Well, wouldn't you like to see the fine sport certain people around here have together?"

"Ah ... who?"

"Over there," the boy said, pointing.

His curiosity aroused, Lagumina crept over, and Quagliolino joined him.

"Shhh! Softly. Watch out for the branches. I don't know if they're still there."

"But who?" asked Lagumina.

"Don't you know? Mesciardi and Signora Ardelli!"

Pompeo Lagumina's eyes widened. "Are you serious? Has it gone that far?"

The young man sighed and nodded. Alas, yes.

"Ah, poor Honorable Ardelli," Lagumina remarked. "That's why they had a party yesterday to see him off"

"Oh, they have one every day," retorted the boy.

"Well . . . after all," said Lagumina, heaving a deep sigh, "it's a tempting spot, very treacherous. With nothing to do . . . in this season . . . man—*hic et haec*—is a beast, you know. A vile beast. He yields. There's not a man in the world who can resist. Take me. I came here purposely to study. Now with this news you have thoroughly upset me. It's terrible —not so much the betrayal, which we have accidentally discovered, as the confirmation it gives of man's common plight. The weakness of our natures exposes us to the mercy of chance. Propitious circumstances develop the germs of evil to a degree ranging from the smallest fault to the most monstrous crime. Ah, the evil in us is truly without end!"

He rambled on and on in this vein, dazzled by his own brilliance, intoxicated by the sound of his own voice, delighted with the profound ideas which sprang effortlessly to his lips.

The boy stared at him in astonishment, wondering what he had said to deserve all this. Swallowing his surprise, he asked finally, "Shall we go look for them?"

Pompeo Lagumina wanted to think over what he had said and tried to recapture his words, but was unable to. He felt discouraged. His mind seemed to work in flashes. Here he was standing before this boy who was staring at him like an owl, and there were times when he knew he was capable of stunning the whole world.

"Coming?"

"Oh, all right."

They combed the bush for several hours like two bloodhounds, stopping here and there, alert and suspicious of the slightest sound. Pompeo Lagumina felt moved by a heroic spirit, as if it were his duty alone to protect mankind from dishonor.

"Poor Ardelli!"

They searched far and wide but they did not find the guilty lovers. So another morning passed, and it was again time for dinner before Pompeo Lagumina had time to open his books.

Wednesday, Thursday, Friday . . .

As the days passed, all of them wasted for one reason or another, Lagumina was beset by humiliation and remorse on one hand and a mounting fear of the approaching examination on the other. On certain days his anxiety was so great that he could no longer remain alone in his cell. He had to escape and talk to someone to distract him from his torment. The sight of all those books, several of which he should have digested by now, became intolerable. All this information of legal, political, juridical, or administrative nature added up until it loomed like a mountain before his eyes. He escaped to the terrace, where the others sat gossiping idly under the trees.

"I need a breath of air. My temples are throbbing. My head is fairly steaming."

He rattled on for a while to numb his pain, then he fell silent, frowning. A few minutes later he went back upstairs to study, his jaw set. He opened his books and began to read, but at the first difficulty he encountered after only a few pages, he was plunged into despair. He fell prey to a restless remorse which gnawed at him like an irritating pain in his stomach; he turned an unreasoning anger brutally inward on himself. He wanted to slap his own face, claw it with his nails. With his elbows on the table, his head sunk in his hands, he moaned.

"It's not his fault, poor fellow," Quagliola remarked on the terrace below, first making sure that his son was nowhere about. "It's not his fault if Nature has endowed him with a body that demands only to eat and sleep. When he has eaten, come what may, he cannot absorb knowledge of any kind. His eyes close and—good night! Can he force them to stay open? When you can't, you can't."

Out of fellow feeling, he led the group under Lagumina's window and called to him, so that he might at least blame them for his lost time and so give him a pretext to steal from his martyrdom without compunction.

"I should study," the unhappy one told them every time he leaned out of the window.

"Yes, of course," answered Mesciardi, Quagliola, and Picinelli from the terrace, "but meanwhile come on down for a moment. Relax a little! Besides, we need you here to settle an argument."

Pretending to believe Lagumina when he told them of all he had accomplished that day, they said encouragingly, "Bravo, lawyer! Your goal is already in sight. Now take it easy."

Pompeo Lagumina was grateful for their kind words and the momentary relief. His heart swelled with tenderness, and a few tears glistened in his eyes behind their thick glasses. He could have kissed them. On the other hand, if he were forgotten and left alone in his cell, without being disturbed, he would grow angry and hate them. When he was not called, he leaned out the window to attract their attention and pricked up his ears, trying to catch a few words of their conversation.

"They might lower their voices," he muttered. "Beasts! Egotists! Amusing themselves—only right, of course, during vacation—but just the same, they could go farther off to do their talking. Must they be right here where they know a man is trying to work?"

And so the third Sunday of the month came around. The game of the Graces, a sort of lacrosse, was played on the hilltop with hoops and sticks which that tempting demon, Honorable Ardelli, had brought up with him—an innocent pastime for the poor brothers at the Hermitage. None of the young girls who came over that day seemed to catch on to the game, and even Signora Ardelli was unable to teach them how to throw the hoop with the two sticks and catch it again in midair. Pompeo Lagumina, whose attention was continually diverted from his book by squeals of excitement, leaned out of his window to glare at the girls. He would not even take a Sunday off from his books.

"I just want to see who is going to win," he said, going over to the window several times during the morning.

They made too much noise. He could not resist leaning out again at least to take part in the game with his eyes. His hands itched because, although nearsighted, he excelled at this game.

At last he cried out to one of the girls, "Not like that —no. Excuse me."

They all turned to look up at the window. Signora Ardelli sweetly begged him to come down and teach them how to play.

"Just for five minutes ... I warn you," he replied.

When he had been showing them how to toss that little circle of the Graces—ooop-la ... ooop-la—for about an hour and was perspiring freely, all the gay young girls burst into a round of applause.

It came like a bolt out of the blue!

Pompeo Lagumina, his hand half raised holding the sticks, was petrified. The hoop which had already been tossed landed like a crown on his head. They all laughed and he tried to laugh, too. He walked stiffly to the edge of the terrace, where Sandrina and her mother were standing quietly.

"What a wonderful surprise!"

"Liar!"

"Cheat!"

"What? No? Why?"

"Puppet!"

"Buffoon!"

"Sandrina, my own, listen ..."

"Go away!"

"For shame!"

They didn't give him a chance to speak. As soon as he opened his mouth, they fired point-blank, peppering him with insults. Then they turned and marched off down the mountain, without stopping for a moment's rest or even a sip of water.

Pompeo Lagumina closed himself in his cell and threw himself on the cot. He remained there for some time in a blank stupor which even frightened him at one point. Through that terrible nothingness, that suspension of consciousness, a grim idea occurred to him, and feeling lost and shamed, he did not know how to reject it. He thought that he had nothing to say in his own defense. He remembered Signor Lanzi telling them a few days before of the suicide of a poor *carabinière* the previous winter. He had thrown himself off one of the cliffs on the west side of the mountain. What a horrible death!

The laughing of the girls' voices on the terrace finally roused him and he was able to throw off the nightmare of that frightening thought. He rose from the bed and decided to write a long letter of explanation to Sandrina, in which he would propose to reconsider his drastic decision to kill himself if she would reply at once.

Naturally, the suspense of waiting made it impossible for him to study during those days. Under such conditions, who else could have done any better?

In dismal anguish he went down to the table at every meal and was not conscious of eating. Then he threw himself on the bed; after all, it was only in sleep that he could find peace.

Two days later the answer came—but not from Sandrina. Her mother wrote to tell him that his indecent behavior that day had been enough to convince her daughter that she was mistaken. She had finally given her mother the satisfaction of accepting her wise advice: she would marry her cousin, Mimmino Orrei, whom she had so foolishly refused. Henceforth all relations between her daughter, Sandrina, and himself must cease.

Pompeo Lagumina rushed down to the terrace waving the letter in his hand. At first he felt drunk with resentment, but soon his enormous body triumphed in its newfound freedom, as if a big stone had been rolled away from his chest.

"Rejoice, gentlemen!" he cried to his idle friends. "I don't have to pass the examination! Now I can accept the office. Waiters! What can you offer me today as Father Prior to this band of jolly good fellows?"

And he sang lustily:

> "Every Wednesday, a big turnout
> Of hare, partridge, pheasant and trout,
> Succulent beef and fat capon,
> Delicate fare to feast upon."

THE MERRY-GO-ROUND OF LOVE

I

"HE'S a treasure, yes, a real treasure, that Pepè Alletto!" And Raví would have been the last to deny it. But, between that and letting him marry his daughter, Stellina, no indeed! It wasn't worth talking about even in jest.

"Let's be reasonable!"

He would have liked to marry off his daughter in a way that met with popular consent, as he put it, and he went from one end of the city to the other stopping his friends and acquaintances to hear what they thought of the situation. All of them, however, reacted in the same way when they heard the name of the man to whom Raví intended to give Stellina. They were open-mouthed. They were stunned.

Raví found it hard to repress a gesture of irritation. He tried to smile and, spreading wide his hands, repeated:

"Just you wait. . . . Let's be reasonable!"

But who could reason with them? Some of them even went so far as to ask him if he was serious.

"Don Diego Alcozèr?"

And they would smother a laugh.

Raví turned angrily from such as these, saying:

"Excuse me, please. I thought I was talking to someone who could be reasonable."

For he had truly considered the pros and cons of the match, and he had arrived at the profound conviction . . . that it was a fine thing for his daughter. He had further convinced himself that he must bring the others around to his point of view, at least those who let him give vent to the irritation that was growing in him from day to day.

"You all wanted liberty, God knows! You wanted a king who would reign but not rule, you wanted everyone sub-

51

ject to the draft, you wanted a big army, bridges, roads, railroads, telegraph lines, electric lights in the streets—all wonderful things, I agree, and things I like, too. But they have to
be paid for, gentlemen! And what is the result? There have
been *two* results in my case: One—I have worked like an ox
all my life and I've been honest, unfortunately, so I
haven't been able to put by enough to marry off my daughter as she would wish—which would also be as *I* would
wish! Two—there aren't any young men. By this I mean,
there aren't any young men whom a foresighted father could
trust to insure the well-being of his daughter. Before they're
able to make their way, God knows what it takes! And
when they've made it, they expect big dowries—and they're
right. For, without having established themselves what father
would entrust them with his daughter? So? So a young girl
should marry an old man, I tell you, if the old man is rich.
There will be plenty of young men around after the old
man dies."

What was so laughable about that? He was talking sense.
Therefore:

"Let's be reasonable about it...."

If Don Diego Alcozèr had been fifty or sixty years old, no.
Ten or fifteen years of sacrifice would have been too much
for his daughter, and he would never have accepted the
proposal. But Don Diego was a good seventy-two! And
there was no need to fear difficulties of any kind: it would
be more like a simple adoption, after all, than a marriage.
Stellina would move into Don Diego's house like a daughter
—neither more nor less. Instead of living in her father's
house she would live in another house, with greater comfort
and as the absolute mistress of it. The house of a gentleman,
when all was said and done. No one dared question that
fact. So what sacrifice was she making? It was a matter of
waiting in one place or another, with the single difference that
waiting in her father's house was wasted time, since he
could do nothing for his daughter, whereas waiting at Don
Diego's for three or four years....

"Do I make myself clear?" Raví asked at this point, struck
by the force of his own reasoning and ever more deeply
convinced.

If someone reminded him that Don Diego Acozèr had already had four wives, what of it? Or rather, so much the

better! Stellina would not be such a fool (And here he made the horned gesture to ward off harm) as to let herself be buried by the old man, as the other four had done. With time and with God's help she, instead, would close her beneficent husband's eyes in peace, and then, *then,* would come the time for young men! Beautiful, rich, brought up like a princess, she would indeed be a prize! And the young men would gather like flies around a honey pot.

It seemed inconceivable to Raví that people did not agree with his reasoning. It was stubbornness, pigheadedness, to consider only the momentary sacrifice of her marriage to the old man. As if beyond this strand, beyond this sand bar, there were not the open sea and favorable tides! There, there was where one should fix his gaze.

Had he himself been rich enough to insure his daughter's happiness, no, sir, indeed he would not have given her in marriage to the old wretch! Stellina, at least for the time being, did not appreciate the good fortune that he was preparing for her—this was only natural and, in a way, excusable. But within a few years' time she would praise and thank and bless him, of that he was certain. He neither wanted nor hoped for anything for himself from the marriage. He wanted it only for her. And he felt it his duty as a father, as a mature man who had been tried and tested by the world, to hold his ground and force his inexperienced girl to obey. But he was deeply embittered by the disapproval of men of experience, like himself.

"In the name of the Father, the Son, and the Holy Ghost," Raví's wife, Donna Rosa, complained at home, making the sign of the cross with a gesture that was habitual with her and that she repeated every time she was annoyed or hurt to the depths of her limp, yellow flesh. "Leave him alone, can't you? Whatever Marcantonio does is well done, according to me." She said this to those relatives who came to her whispering how monstrous they thought the projected marriage was.

"It's a mortal sin, Donna Rosa!" Carmela Mèndola, the neighborhood gossip, wore herself out telling her. She almost strangled herself in her efforts not to cry out, and she gave herself resounding blows on her bony chest as she repeated: "If I say so in all conscience, it's a mortal sin that cries to God for vengeance!"

And, all upset, she untied and then tied under her chin the long ends of the big red wool scarf she wore on her head.

Donna Rosa pursed her lips, stuck out her chin, closed her eyes, and fetched a long sigh.

II

Don Diego Alcozèr was already being seen about town with his future father-in-law.

Marcantonio Raví, big, smug, and fat, with his flushed face close-shaved and his hand's breadth of jowl, with his legs that looked squat beneath his paunch and that carried him laboriously hither and yon, was the perfect foil for Don Diego. Alcozèr was thin as could be, small in stature, and ran along beside Raví with tiny, birdlike steps, holding his hat in his hand or carrying it on the head of his cane. This was, presumably, because he wanted to show off his one remaining strand of hair which he had let grow long and dyed an uncertain shade, almost rose. The hair was swirled about his head with studied care and hid his otherwise bald pate as best it could.

Don Diego had no mustache, nor even eyebrows—no other hair. His little eyes were unshielded, pale, and watery. His latest clothes were at least twenty years old—not because he was tight-fisted but because he kept them so neatly, free of wrinkles or dust, that they seemed freshly made.

This was what had become of one of the most irresistible lady-killers of the vintage of Ferdinand II, King of the Two Sicilies. He had been an accomplished gentleman, swordsman, and dancer. Nor had his merits been restricted to the fields of Venus and Mars alone, as he liked to put it. Don Diego spoke fluent Latin and knew Catullus and the greater part of the Odes of Horace by heart:

Tu ne quaesieris, scire nefas, quem mihi, quem tibi finem dî dederint . . .

Ah, Horace! Don Diego had derived his epicurean tastes from this, his favorite poet. He had enjoyed his life and he wished to enjoy it to the end. Therefore, he loathed solitude in which he often found himself disturbed by frightening fancies, and he loved youth, whose company he sought, philosophically putting up with the jokes and tricks young people played on him.

Here they were: he tapped the silver head of his cane on the table in front of the Falcon Café while Raví let himself slump into the creaking chair and, huffing and puffing, fanned his neck with his broad-brimmed hat while, with the other hand, he mopped the sweat from his flushed face.

"I'll have a barley-water, as usual," Alcozèr told the waiter.

Seated in front of the café, they resumed their conversation about the marriage—interrupted from time to time by the greetings Don Marcantonio distributed broadside to his many acquaintances, his voice loud and his gestures expansive.

"I kiss your hands! Your Grace! Your humble servant!"

Don Diego had not managed to call at the home of the prospective bride. Stellina threatened to scratch his face, to gouge out his eyes, if he dared show his face before her. Clearly, Raví had not mentioned any of these threats to Don Diego. He had only told him that a little patience was needed because, with young girls, you know....

"That's quite all right! Whenever you, or rather, whenever Stellina permits me ... *intra paucos dies,* I hope, *cupio quidem,*" Don Diego answered, calm and smiling. "Until then, you might take her this for today." And he took a little velvet box out of his pocket.

Today there was a bracelet, yesterday a little watch with its chain of gold and pearls, and before that a small ring with pearls and diamonds, an emerald pin, a pair of earrings.... These gifts cost Alcozèr nothing. Again, it was not because he was tight-fisted, but because he had so many jewels left by his dead wives: what was he to do with them? He sent them to his new fiancée after the goldsmith had polished them and placed them in new boxes.

Marcantonio Raví poured forth praise, exclamations of admiration, expressions of gratitude.

"But you spoil us, dear Don Diego. I am embarrassed ..."

"Don't be embarrassed, you ass! I know my way in the world and I know when gifts are necessary."

Don Marcantonio tucked the gift in his pocket and fumed with irritation at the obstinate attitude of his daughter, who seemed quite content to stay locked in her room, even refusing food, so long as she did not have to agree to the marriage.

Her mother was posted at the entrance to Stellina's room, like a sentinel. Their relatives, Carmela Mèndola, or some other neighbor would call and try to persuade her to take Stellina's side against her husband. But she retreated behind her usual gesture of the sign of the cross.

"In the name of the Father, the son, and the Holy Ghost! Don't put more wood on the fire, Donna Carmela. Haven't I enough troubles, as it is? See what a hell I'm in!"

"Aunt Carmela!" Stellina called from behind the door.

"Yes, dear child! What can I do for you?"

"Tell your Tina to come to the window. I want to show her something."

"I will, dear heart. I'll tell her right away, dear. Take this little package I'm slipping under the door. Eat it. You'll like it."

"Thank you ever so much, Aunt Carmela!"

"It's nothing, dear child. And you hang on. Just hang on. That's all it will take...."

Donna Rosa let them talk and do what they liked. And every day, as soon as her husband got home, she asked him the same question:

"Should I?" And she made the gesture of opening the door with her key.

"No!" Raví cried. "Let her stay there, wretched, wretched ingrate! Heart of stone! As if I weren't doing all this for her, for her own good! Look! Here's another gift, a bracelet.... Be sure that she sees it!"

Donna Rosa got up from her chair, closed her eyes, sighed, and, velvet box in hand, entered her daughter's room.

Stellina was seated on the floor near her bed, on a little rug, like a surly puppy. She grabbed the box from her mother's hand and flung it from her.

"Thank you so much! I don't want it!"

At this point, her mother finally lost her temper, too.

"Sixteen ounces of gold in that bracelet, you little idiot! You're not even good enough to look at it, no thanks to God for that!"

As soon as her mother had gone, Stellina rubbed her left elbow with her right hand and said, between clenched teeth:

"Go on, wear yourselves out!"

Then she straightened her clothing, rose from the floor,

wandered around the room a bit, and came to rest near the bureau, where she looked at the gift her mother had retrieved before leaving the room. Curiosity overcame her revulsion for the old giver.

She looked at herself in the mirror, lifted her hair high on her head, and smiled at her own reflection. Her fresh, amused little face was highlighted in the glass by two lovely, laughing blue eyes. With a smile on her face, she looked as if she were whispering to herself: "Rascal!" And she suddenly wanted to open all the other boxes to try on . . . at least the earrings . . . the earrings, for just a minute.

"No, this one's the ring. . . . It will certainly be too big. . . . Why, it fits perfectly! It could have been made for me!"

And she admired her small white hand with the ring on it, bending the hand first this way, then that, drawing it nearer her face or stretching her arm to its full length. Then there were her ears with the earrings dangling from the lobes, her wrists with the bracelets on them, and last the long gold watch chain on her breast. Thus bedecked, she went to the mirror in the wardrobe door and made herself a low bow:

"Until we meet again, Signora Alcozèr!"

And she burst out laughing.

III

"Well . . . it's all right. I'm in no hurry, my dear Marcantonio," Don Diego told Raví next day at the Falcon Café. "But, you see, it isn't on my account. It's because of the neighbors. Almost every night they serenade her under your windows with mandolins and guitars! You probably sleep so soundly you don't even hear them. . . . I know—happy young people. . . . How wonderful youth is! You know who they are? The Salvo brothers, with their cousin Garofalo and Pepè Alletto—guitars and mandolins."

"I swear, dear Don Diego, that I didn't know a thing about it, on my word as a gentleman! Can this be true? Serenades, you say? Just leave it all to me. You'll see this very minute that I . . ."

"Where are you going?"

"To look for those young fellows."

"Have you lost your mind? Sit down! Do you want to make me look an utter fool?"

"What do you have to do with it?"

"What do you mean, you idiot, what have I to do with it? We're just harming ourselves with all this hustle and bustle. I'm a person who does things calmly. They are young and they sing under windows: youth means joy. . . . Besides, didn't you tell me that Stellina knows how to sing? That's fine. I like singing. I brought the serenading to your attention only because of the neighbors who can't help but listen every night and . . . you know, evil tongues. . . . You should urge these young people to be a little patient, if you follow me. After all, your *puella* is already spoken for as a bride. But do it politely, calmly."

"Leave it to me."

"Without making a fool of me, understand!"

That very evening, Marcantoni Raví ran into Pepè Alletto on the street and, calling him to one side, told him:

"Dear Don Pepè, let me ask you politely to leave my daughter alone. If you don't, I'll be obliged to behave like the man who . . . well, do you see this stick? I'll break it over your head the first time I see you pass the windows of my house with your nose in the air."

Pepè Alletto looked at him with amazement, as if he had not understood. Then he stepped back and drew himself up:

"Is that so? Well, if I were to tell you . . ."

"That you are Ciro Coppa's brother-in-law, bow-wow!" Raví finished the sentence for him.

"*No!*" the young man said in a rage. "If I were to tell you that no one has ever broken any sticks over *my* head. . . ."

Raví started to laugh. "Oh, can't you see I'm joking? Tell me yourself, Don Pepè, how I should appeal to you. What do you want of my daughter? Since we're not animals, let's try to be reasonable about this. You are a nobleman, dear Don Pepè, but you haven't a cent. I too am a poor man, short of this world's goods. Poverty is no cause for shame. You know that I like you. Now come here, and let's be reasonable. . . ."

He put a hand under Don Pepè's arm and walked along with him, pursuing his argument:

"As for dancing, I know you dance as if you'd never done anything else in your life. I've heard you even dance with spurs on your boots. And you're said to play the piano like an angel. . . . But dear Don Pepè, this is not a question of dancing, if I make myself clear. Dancing is one thing, eating another. Unless people eat regularly, they can neither dance nor make music. Do I have to explain these hard facts to you? Just let me pull off this blessed marriage in peace. In fact, give me a hand with it. Why not? The old man is rich, he is seventy-two, and he's already had four wives. . . . Shall we give him three more years? Besides, the future is in God's hands. Tell me what you think the hopes of an honest father should be—the happiness of his own daughter, don't you agree? Oh, the man who is poor is a slave. Now tell me, can slavery and happiness be compatible? No. Ergo, first things first: money. Freedom is at home with wealth—they are compatible! And when Stellina is rich, won't she be free to do as she pleases and sees fit? So . . . what were we saying? Ah, yes, Don Diego. . . . Rich, dear Don Pepè! He is so rich that he could pave all of Girgenti with gold pieces, lucky man! Don Pepè, let me offer you something at the café."

Alletto was dazed. Not knowing what to make of Ravi's speech, he looked into his beaming face.

To tell the truth, he had never seriously aspired to Stellina's hand, nor had she given him any reason to cherish hopes—any more than she had to the many young men who swarmed around her. The girl attracted him, certainly, but he knew that, alas! he was in no position to take a wife, so he did not even consider the possibility.

Alletto lived with his mother, already in her seventies, who, in her loving obstinacy, still treated him as if he were ten. Poor sainted old woman! He was infinitely patient with her, in part to make up for all she had suffered with his father who had run through their fortune in a few years and then died of heartbreak. The only thing that had miraculously survived the holocaust was the old house in which he and his mother still lived.

Donna Bettina, of noble birth, was firmly opposed to Pepè's taking on any employment that his brother-in-law, Ciro Coppa, could perhaps have procured him through one of his many connections. Pepè was not, at bottom, too distressed by this. Work was not his strong point. It took him at least three hours each morning to complete his toilette. Habit! What could he do about it? His bath, care of his nails, then a careful hair combing, trimming his beard, brushing his clothes. And when at last he went out, late in the day, he looked like a proper milord. The old house in the Ràbato district jealously guarded the wretched secret of their obstinate sacrifices and harsh privations.

Ah, who knows, if he had been born and grown up in a great, pulsating city instead of in this sad, moribund backwater! His passion for music might have opened a way for him. An unknown force in his spirit told him so, the same force that drew him sometimes to his mother's out-of-tune spinet on which his fingers improvised minuets and rondos. Certain evenings as he looked down from the lonely path at the outskirts of town toward the great spectacle of the surrounding countryside and the sea spread out beneath, illumined by the moon, he felt himself seized by certain dreams, anguished by certain fits of melancholy. In that countryside lay a forgotten city, Agrigento, a city full of pomp, rich in marbles, sumptuous, yet soft from sophisticated pleasures. Now trees grew about the only two ancient temples that remained. Their mysterious rustling mingled with the continuous gurgle of the distant sea and with a sonorous, ceaseless tremolo that seemed to come from the bland light of the moon itself in the quiet of those abandoned places, but was in fact the song of the crickets in the midst of which could be heard, from time to time, the remote, sorrowful hoot of an owl.

But Pepè was almost ashamed of these strange moments of his, as if he feared that his friends would become aware of them, too. What a time he'd have then! No! Away with such fancies! Why waste time even thinking of them? Reality lay in the bleak, mean, monotonous round of everyday. That was the reality he must manage to adapt himself to.

What was Raví saying? What did he want of him? Evidently the good fellow imagined there was some sort of understanding between Stellina and himself because of which she would not agree to the marriage with Alcozèr. Well, why not leave him with that illusion? He promised to act prudently in future and to ask his friends the Salvo brothers and Gar-

ofalo to do the same. In exchange, he received an invitation
to the forthcoming wedding—in Alcozèr's name, too.

"You know, he's not a bad sort at bottom, poor fellow!"
Marcantonio concluded. "What can you do? He has a mania
about wives ... can't get along without one. But, God willing,
this will be his last! Shall we give him three years, give or
take a few months? I've told him, 'Dear Don Diego, we are
all mortal. Let the papers be properly drawn.' And I must
say he attended to it right away. I didn't have to say another word. On that point, as you might say, we're in the
saddle. I'm speaking not for myself, you understand, but for
my daughter. Well, well ... Stellina will manage as she sees
fit.... Weaknesses, Don Pepè: they say Don Diego is marrying again because, when he's alone, he's afraid of ghosts.
I believe Death appears to him at night on wings. And carries him off, Don Pepè! I'd give Him a hand to place him
firmly on His back.... The old man can't weigh more than
eighty-odd pounds.... At your service. I kiss your hands.
Not a word, though, Don Pepè, I beg you."

IV

About two months later the fiercely opposed marriage was
celebrated in Raví's house.

Don Diego wore—for the fifth time—his long-skirted, Na-
poleonic full-dress suit, a veteran of four marriages. Not because he was tight-fisted but because it was really as good
as new, although preserved all these years in camphor and
pepper in the walnut chest as long and narrow as a coffin.
Downstairs in his own courtyard his great geese did not
recognize him in this unfamiliar get-up, and they stretched
their long necks as they followed him to the main doorway,
hissing as if the devil were after them.

"Ha, ha! The ghosts of my dead wives!" Don Diego
thought, wrinkling his nose, and he turned to chase the geese
back into the courtyard with his hands, shouting, "Shooo!
Shooo!" as he ran.

Marcantonio Raví had papered the town with invitations,
still wanting popular approval at least as far as appearances were concerned. No one could make him accept the
fact that the disapproval of all his friends and acquaintances

was not due to envy of the good fortune that had befallen his daughter. And he had had a lavish banquet prepared, further to put the noses of the envious out of joint.

Don Diego was warmly congratulated. But he had not lived into his seventies for nothing: he greeted all these compliments with his usual cold little laugh.

Pity for Stellina—dressed all in white and bedecked with orange blossoms, in the midst of all the festivities— rose spontaneously to the lips of all the guests who, nonetheless, observed the conventions and offered her their congratulations. But they took care not to be too effusive for fear of causing the bride to burst into tears.

Raví soon felt a certain heaviness settle over the room. Stellina's expression cast a pall over the merry-making. Her father tried to liven things up a bit, urging on first this one and then that. Only Pepè Alletto, who had come with the three Salvo brothers, Mauro, Totò, and Gasparino, managed to act as if he were having a good time.

"Don Pepè, remember: Now it's up to you!"

Pepè heard in this ambiguous reminder the confirmation of his curious talk with Raví a couple of months earlier. He smiled, gazed at the meek little bride who seemed to him more lovely than ever in the pure white of her wedding dress, and said to himself, "Why not?" He went to the piano, sang and played, and urged the others to dance. Finally he managed to liven up the party. Everyone was grateful to him, and Marcantonio was most grateful of all. His head spinning with the happiness he himself had brought about, Pepè looked at the old bridegroom, Don Diego, with compassion. And he glanced at the others as if to say, "Feel sorry for him, poor old man. For the true bridegroom here will be I."

Toward the end of the party of which he had been the spark, not to say the hero, all the guests praised him so and admired so extravagantly the way he had organized the dances and played the piano that, at a certain point, he could not help blurting out, "I can speak French, too. . . ."

But the storm that had been threatening at last broke out unexpectedly. Don Diego wished to offer a glass of wine to his bride, as a gallant gesture. But the idea was unfortunate: his old hands trembled, partly because of the emotion of the occasion, and a few drops spilled on her gown. . . . Now, had the women seated nearby ignored the incident, Stellina would probably have been able to carry it off. But no! They all clustered around her, handkerchiefs in hand, and bent over to "clean" the spots. Then—only then—did Stellina burst into uncontrollable sobs and give way to a truly violent attack of nerves.

Now everyone gathered around her. Someone shouted: "Stand back, stand back! Give her air!"

Two young men lifted her in her chair and carried her into another room. Humiliated, Don Diego stayed where he was, glass in hand and shaking more than ever. Now the rest of the wine was spilling drop by drop onto the rug! Don Marcantonio tried in vain to restore order and to calm the guests by repeating; "It's the emotion, you know. Just the emotion!" No one paid him the least attention. Everyone was saddened by poor Stellina's fate. Her sobs and—what was even more painful—her convulsive laughter could be heard even from behind closed doors.

Pepè Alletto, pale and distraught, had collapsed on a chair and, his eyes half-shut, sat fanning himself with his handkerchief. Two tears certainly not inspired by wine coursed down his cheeks into his drooping mustache.

"What's the matter, Pepè?" Mauro Salvo asked his friend, seeing the sorry state he was in.

"Nothing . . . I feel . . . I don't know. . . ."

"Had too much to drink?"

"I feel so sorry for her," Pepè said, not even bothering to answer Mauro's crude question.

"You're right. Yes, you're right," his friend went on. "I'm sorry for her, too, but let's get going now. I'll walk you home. Everyone's leaving. . . ."

Salvo wanted to take Pepè by the arm, but Alletto withdrew, offended:

"I can manage quite well by myself. Leave me alone, please!"

"Overcome by emotion! Do forgive us. . . . Thank you for the honor of your company. . . . Emotion! . . . Good night and thang *you* . . . Forgive . . ." Raví said to this guest or that, distributing greetings, handshakes, bows, and salutations in the living room.

The guests left silently, slinking down the stairs like so many whipped dogs. Midnight had already sounded, the lamplighters had put out the street lamps, and the long street, deserted at this hour, was ill lit by a moon that seemed shielded by a thin veil of cloud.

"Who knows what a drama there'll be tonight!" sighed Luca Borrani, one of the guests, as he came out of the house rather noisily.

Pepè Alletto, who was just passing him with Salvo, caught the vulgar reference and yelled in his face, "Pig!"

Borrani struck out at him and replied, "Go on, you little virgin, you!" giving him a good shove.

Thereupon Alletto raised his stick and brought it down on Borrani's head. Suddenly he received a resounding slap. A devil of a scuffle followed: flailing arms and legs, shouts and imprecations, women's cries, lights and people at all the nearby windows, dogs barking, and lots of little clouds scudding across the sky.

"What's it all about? What's it all about?"

And the jostling throng went off down the street, calling out confusedly to each other. The people who had come outdoors leaving lamps in their windows stood about for quite a while, looking around them curiously and making conjectures and comments until the crowd of guests disappeared in the distant darkness.

V

"No, *sir!* The brute! I'll teach you how to handle such people. Just leave it up to me."

Ciro Coppa—solid, with a powerful chest and shoulders thanks to which he seemed even shorter than he was, a bull-like neck, a proud, dark face fringed by a short, curly beard that was thick and very black, a forehead made even higher by incipient baldness, great, dark, fiery eyes—was walking back and forth in his law office, one hand in his pocket while in the other hand he held a whip that he flicked nervously against his riding boot. The butts of two great pistols gleamed from his hip pockets and protruded outside his jacket.

Pepè Alletto had come to ask his advice. That very morning he had received a letter from Borrani. The letter declared that Borrani did not wish to challenge him for the insult and the unfair blow of the night before because members of the cavalry held that only cowards had recourse to such dodges as running about with a sword in one's hand. Instead, he wanted to warn Pepè that he would beat the hell out of him wherever he ran across him, even if it happened to be in church.

Pepè Alletto would have liked Coppa to call on Borrani and prevail on him, by whatever means he could, to withdraw the letter. Not that he was afraid. He was afraid of no one. But, you see, the possibility of coming to blows like a couple of young street toughs was not to his taste. Besides, he was so frail and skinny that Borrani, who was a colossus, could make mincemeat of him. And then, who had ever heard of kicks and blows between gentlemen. . . .

"Let me handle it!" Coppa had said, stopping in the middle of the room and pointing to the copyist's desk with his crop. "There's paper, there, and a pen and ink. Sit down and write. With one stroke of the pen, I'll settle his hash for you."

"You think I should answer him?" Pepè asked timidly. Ciro gave the desk a resounding thwack with the whip.

"I've told you to sit down and write, you fool! I'll dictate your reply."

Pepè got up uncertainly, and went reluctantly, to sit in the big leather chair at the copyist's desk. He rested his elbows on the desk and, head in hands, gave a deep sigh. Then he said:

"Excuse me, but . . . if you don't mind, I'd like to call your attention to . . ."

"What?"

"Well, my position is rather . . . how shall I put it . . . delicate. Last evening, to tell the truth . . . perhaps I . . . yes, perhaps I wasn't quite myself . . . for so many reasons. So I wouldn't want to compromise . . ."

"Compromise what?" Coppa exclaimed impatiently. "Did you receive an insult? Yes. And this is so incontrovertibly true that you hit him."

"And there's an end to it!" Pepè said. "He should have challenged me. He didn't. So . . ."

"So you'll challenge him!" Ciro concluded with a shrug.

"I? Why should I?" Pepè countered, stunned.

"Because you're an idiot, that's why. Because you don't

understand anything!" His brother-in-law was yelling at the top of his lungs. "Now sit down and write! You'll see."

Pepè, browbeaten, shrugged in turn. Then he asked, disconsolately:

"What should I put at the top of the letter?"

"Nothing, not a word of salutation!" Ciro replied, starting to walk up and down again, concentrating hard and pulling at his beard with two fingers. "Let's begin this way: *Your letter . . . your letter . . . is worthy of a person . . . your letter is worthy of a person who . . . should be confined to . . .* write! *. . . confined . . . con-fi-ned,* all in one word."

"I know!"

". . . to a jail or penitentiary comma *. . . instead of . . . instead . . .* with an *e-a . . . of moving about freely . . . freely among civilized men.* Exclamation point. Have it all down?"

"Civilized men! Yes, I have it."

"Paragraph. *But if you are . . . if you are a rascal* comma *. . . I am a gentlemen* semi-colon. *I will not allow myself . . . to be involved by you in another . . . another scandalous incident* period. Same paragraph. *And since I have had the misfortune . . .* exactly! *. . . the misfortune of soiling my hand on your* ah! *Head* comma *it is up to me . . . it is up to me* comma *in line with the respect I owe my person and my name . . .* are you with me? *. . .* comma *to raise you from the mud in which you would like to wallow* period. Same paragraph. *I am* comma *therefore* comma *behaving generously with you and sending you two of my seconds who have . . . who have full authority to speak . . . to speak for me* period. *They will return the letter . . . the letter you so basely sent me this morning* period. Have you got it all? Now sign it: *Guiseppe Alletto, Nobleman,* and not another word. Have you signed it?"

Pepè reread the letter, making every effort to give the words that sonorous, scathing ring his brother-in-law had given them.

"Fine!" Coppa approved. "Written as God willed it. Now an envelope, and write the address. I'll take care of having it delivered along with his letter to you. And don't give a thought to the matter of seconds. I'll find them for you right away. Don't even consider the Salvo boys or Garofalo. They're lightweights who won't come up to the mark in a thing of this kind. You go up to see your sister Filomena—poor thing, she's been feeling even less well than usual these last two days. If the doctor doesn't get her on her feet for me soon, I'll give him a good thrashing. Well, enough of this! I have to go to court, then a quick run out to the country to give that rascal of an overseer a dressing down. The land is as good as dead. By God, it doesn't yield enough to repay having it plowed up. What's the matter with you? What the devil's the matter with you? Afraid? ... You're looking at me like a perfect idiot. ..."

Pepè was startled by this frontal attack and rapped out, annoyed:

"Afraid? Not at all. Ciro, it's my head. I have a slight headache ... had one since last evening, in fact ... can't imagine ..."

"Why don't you say you were drunk? It would make a better impression," Ciro commented with mingled pity and scorn. "Go on. Go on up to see Filomena. Tell her I'll be back this evening. Just stay there and wait for the two seconds. Look lively, now, and don't be afraid!"

He took some papers from the drawer of his desk and went to court, his old slouch hat over one ear and his crop in his hand.

VI

Pepè found his sister wandering like a shade in the darkened rooms. She seemed old at thirty-four. An illness that the doctors had not yet diagnosed had been destroying her for the last several months, but she did not complain, considering this no more than a slight addition to the many woes of her life. She never complained about anything, if the truth were told, not even about being unable to see her mother who had broken with her son-in-law years ago. It would have consoled Filomena just to lay eyes on her! But Donna Bettina had sworn never to set foot in Coppa's house, and Filomena, because of her husband's fierce jealousy, could not only not go out of the house but was not allowed so much as to poke her nose out of the window. It did not matter to her anymore. The bitterness of total resignation could be read in her silent eyes, constantly absorbed by an undefined, unknown pain.

"Filomè, how do you feel?"

She shrugged her shoulders and lightly raised her arms as a reply. Pepè sniffed the stale air, then he went on:

"Couldn't we open the window a little?"

"No!" Filomena cried suddenly. "What if he should find out, God forbid?"

"He isn't here. He's gone to court, then he's off to the country. He'll be back this evening. . . ."

"Pepè, please, leave the windows closed. God alone knows how I long for a breath of fresh air. But I've reached my last days, Pepè. I feel that I'm not long for this prison. Thank God who is on earth as He is in heaven!"

"Don't talk wicked nonsense!" Pepè chided her, all upset.

"I'm only distressed because of the children," his sister's weary voice continued, "poor innocents. . . . For me it would mean liberation . . . and for him too, for Ciro. I'm not saying it spitefully, mind! You don't know Ciro; you people see only his defects . . . his fierce jealousy, for instance. . . . But he loves me, you know, in his own way. That's how he shows it! He shouldn't have married, that's all. He was born to lead another life . . . perhaps to be an explorer. . . ."

"Yes," Pepè agreed, "among jungle animals!"

"No, no," Filomena corrected her own words lovingly. "All I meant was that he should have had a life full of risks, a free, wild life. . . . You see how he is, he goes to extremes in everything, and in a small town, with the shabbiness of everyday life all around you, his exuberance seems even ridiculous at times. . . . He wants to right all wrongs. . . . And a poor weak woman like me, shut up here, can't help but live in a state of continual apprehension. . . . "

Pepè nodded agreement, and that nod was, at the same time, a gesture of sympathy for his sister. He looked about in the half-light and took note once more of the costly furnishings of the room. Inevitably, he said to himself, "He made you rich, but what pleasure did you get out of it?"

At this point, the little maid came in to tell him that someone was waiting for him downstairs in Coppa's study. Could it be the witnesses so soon? He quickly went downstairs. Instead, he found Don Marcantonio Raví, breathless and excited.

"Dear Don Pepè, what have you done? I haven't had a moment's peace."

"I did my duty," Pepè replied briefly, with a serious and sober air.

"However did this wretched fight start? And what's to happen now?"

"Nothing . . . I don't know. . . . But you may be sure that the young girl . . . the young bride . . ."

"You may go ahead and say young girl, Don Pepè! Oh, if you only knew. . . . All hell has broken loose at my house. Cries, screams, convulsions. . . . She absolutely refuses to go with her husband to his house. Last night, she stayed under my roof, understand? Young girl, indeed yes! And today was the same story. She doesn't even want to see him! Don Diego placed himself behind a door, and the things she let him hear! . . . Just think of it . . . I'm quite out of my wits. . . . All we needed was this added mess . . . this, this *duel!* Must you have a duel?"

"Yes, we must," Pepè replied, frowning. "We are men. . . . Besides, things have reached such a point that . . . "

"Not at all!" Don Marcantonio interrupted. "What's this 'we are men' talk? Whoever put that in your head? You were such a help last night, Don Pepè . . . and today, as a reward, you have to fight a duel?"

"Yes, I must," Pepè intoned with a grave and melancholy air. "Moreover, do you think it bothers me? It doesn't bother me at all. Nothing bothers me anymore. They can kill me, for all I care."

"The devil you say!" Ravi cried, almost with tears in his eyes. "It bothers people who care about you. . . . Excuse me for being so blunt, but you're a fool! Do you think everything's over for you? Just bide your time, don't rush things . . . let whoever enjoys dueling take part in duels, like whoever it was who put such an idea in your head. . . . Tell me the truth: wasn't it your brother-in-law? He was the one, wasn't he? I guessed it right away!"

He was cut short. Gerlando D'Ambrosio and Nocio Tucciarello, the two witnesses chosen by Ciro, were shown into the room. D'Ambrosio was a tall, blond man with a short neck, near-sighted with a long scar slashing the left side of his face from cheek to jowl. Tucciarello was stocky, bearded, thickset, with a willfully swaggering gait.

"Pepè, at your orders! Blessings on you, Big Marcantonio!" D'Ambrosio greeted them.

Nocio Tucciarello said nothing. Instead, he flicked one cheek in a half-smile and barely nodded his head.

"Do sit down, sit down," Pepè said eagerly, his eyes darting from one to the other.

"Many thanks," Tucciarello spoke for the two of them, repeating the gesture with his cheek and raising his hand slowly as a sign of refusal. "Dear Don Pepè, we must have a few words with you—with Don Marcantonio's permission."

"Should I leave?" Raví asked Alletto worriedly. Then he turned to the two recent arrivals: "I know all about it, gentlemen. In fact, I had come . . . "

Tucciarello interrupted him, placing a hand lightly on his chest.

"No need for another word. Dear Don Pepè, everything has gone as we wished. As soon as our friend saw us coming, he changed his mind. Yes, sir! He told us it had always been his intention of doing things the right way. 'We too!' we answered, of course. To cut it short, one brief meeting between the opposing seconds and everything was agreed upon: you will use swords and fight until the doctors cry quits. Are we agreed? Tomorrow morning at seven sharp Gerlando and I will be at your door. In order not to arouse suspicion, the carriage will wait for us with the doctor at the rise in the Passeggiata just outside town. From there we can go down to Bonamorone. Do I make myself clear?"

"Yes, yes. That's fine," Pepè hastened to reply, his vision clouded by his distress. He nodded over and over, "You'll be there at seven. That's fine."

"What the devil are you saying, Don Pepè?" Don Marcantonio shouted. "They're taking you to be slaughtered and you say, 'That's fine?' Gentlemen, you are either joking or you're mad. What are you thinking of when you plan to bring together two hot-blooded young men like this? I'm the father of a family, by all the holy angels and devils!"

"Leave the devil out of this, Don Marcantonio!" Nocio Tucciarello said calmly, his brows slightly puckered and his hand raised in a slow gesture. "When I have placed my good self in the midst of a question of honor, no one, not even the son of God himself, must interfere. If you have any commands to give me, I am at your disposal."

"What's that got to do with it, Mister God-Almighty!" Raví exclaimed. "I'm speaking with sound ends in view. What have commands to do with it? I'm your most humble servant, dear Don Nociarello! What I'm talking about is the duel. . . . We could all do without it. . . . Gentlemen, think of the consequences! When all's said and done, Don Pepè called a fellow a swine and got called a sissy. That's the truth, isn't it? He gave the fellow a blow with his cane and he got a shove in return: give and take, so far as I can see. The fight's over. Now why should you have a duel?"

"Ask the noble jurist, Ciro Coppa!" Tucciarello answered in the same chill way. "We have placed ourselves at the service of Don Ciro and Don Pepè, here present, who deserves our every support. Tomorrow at seven, then, and we kiss your hands."

The two seconds went off, followed by Don Marcantonio, who intended by hook or crook—and however humbly—to get Tucciarello to see his point of view.

VII

Pepè stayed on in the study, walking up and down and thinking.

"Let's see, let's see . . ." he said to himself, in an attempt to calm his frazzled nerves. But despite his efforts, distressing thoughts flashed through his mind and made him grimace. "All for a skirmish of no importance!" he exclaimed at last, exasperated.

Suddenly, surprised by the sound of his own voice, he looked about him for fear that someone might have heard him and twirled his cane furiously. He wasn't afraid, no, indeed, not he!

It was true, nonetheless, that he found himself in such straits—and at the risk of losing his hide for, after all, everything is possible—because of an act of idiocy. He could perfectly well have pretended not to hear Borrani's words. What did they matter to him, after all? What business was it of his? He had gotten mixed up in the business almost for a lark, and not because he had taken Raví's half promise seriously. Yes, but the crux of the matter was that, although it may have been a lark and he might have laughed the whole thing off, he was on the point of fighting a duel for that woman. And now, quite seriously, he began to acquire a certain right over her ... since he was risking his life for her. He had never held a sword in his hand. He knew nothing, absolutely nothing, about fencing. He saw Borrani, tall, strongly built, impetuous, standing before him with a sword in his hand, about to attack. Terrible! He felt faint and rushed from the study into the open air, eager to see people.

But, once in the street, it was as if his eyes were dazzled —he could make out nothing. Everything was confused, as if people and houses all trembled in the sun. He heard a buzzing in his ears. Instinctively, he hastened toward his own house. As he entered the Ràbato district by Porta Mazzara, the thought of his mother suddenly came to mind, and he felt tender to the point of tears.

"Poor, poor Mother!"

He found her wandering around the large rooms, a molted feather duster in one hand, a rosary in the other, as usual. She was muttering an Ave Maria and dusting, leaning up against some old-fashioned piece of furniture from time to time as if to tell it her prayers.

Donna Bettina had made an obsession out of keeping the house clean. So true was this that, if she heard the front door bell ring, she would call out even from the farthest room: "Clean your boots!" But she always maintained a dignified air, even when she was polishing the old furniture or attending to the meanest domestic chores, as if she was unaware of what she was doing.

She wore an enormous false braid about her head, made of her own hair when it had been dark brown. It lay in sharp contrast to the few gray hairs that were left above her brow. This braid was held in place by a square of black lace tied under her chin. The backs and palms of her small, white hands, heavy with rings, were protected by a pair of fingerless gloves, and her shoulders were covered with a black silk shawl so old that it had a greenish cast. Donna Bettina's constant preoccupation had been to conceal from others and bear with the greatest dignity her miserable lot in life—for example, she had made more than a few sacrifices in order to be able to afford the gold pince-nez that now bestrode her aristocratic nose.

Her face if not her figure still retained traces of her former beauty, a loveliness so exceptional that it had kindled many fires in the hearts of young men of her time. Even Don Diego

Alcozèr had fallen desperately in love with her, but with scant success. She was rich then, too, as well as of noble birth, and so beautiful! Married very young to Don Gerlando Alletto, she had been exposed to almost everything in her thirty years of matrimony. And she had forgiven her late husband all of it except for one thing that she could not seem to overlook: he had always called her jokingly, "Little Scrap." "Pure foolishness!" she would say. "Just because I was always small and slender."

Seeing her son come home interrupted neither her prayers nor her approach toward the big sideboard whither she was headed. Only after she had flicked the feather duster over the marble top did she nod questioningly at Pepè, thus making him a little sign with her head and her eyes that she wanted to know what was the matter with him.

"Nothing," Pepè answered.

And she smiled at him without stopping her prayers or the completion of her round of the house, molted duster in hand.

Pepè followed her with his eyes, finding it hard to curb the distress that made him want to run to his mother and hug her tightly to his breast.

"If I were not here for her to count on anymore!" he thought.

He well knew what a blow it would be for the saintly old woman. He felt full of remorse at the annoyance certain loving attentions of hers had usually provoked in him—her wish, for example, that he sleep in the same room with her as if he were still a little boy.

"Yes, yes. I'll always be with you, Mother dear!" he said to himself, and feeling that he could no longer control his emotion, he went to close himself in one of the rooms.

Several times during their meal his mother, seeing that he was not eating but was staring at her intently, asked him:

"What's the matter with you?"

"Nothing . . . nothing . . ." Pepè answered affectionately.

Then Donna Bettina raised a finger of one half-gloved hand and threatened him, smiling: "I know what's wrong," she said. "She got married, didn't she? She married that silly old man. . . ."

Pepè blushed, then sadly shook his head:

"No," he answered, "I wasn't even thinking about it. . . ."

"That's just as well," his mother said approvingly. "Don't think about it. . . . She was not for you. . . . Oh, you'll find the one who is for you, all right. For the time being, you would not want to leave your old mother alone, would you?"

Pepè could no longer control himself. He took his mother's hand in anguish and pressed it to his lips.

"No, no," he murmured, bending over her hand tenderly and kissing it. "Never, never, Mama!"

He rose from the table and, saying that he wanted to go back to Coppa's house to see if Filomena was better, he went out. Donna Bettina was upset at hearing her daughter's name. She no longer wished to have anything to do with her. When she had quarreled with her son-in-law because of the distress he caused Filomena, she had urged her daughter to leave the children with their father and return to her own home. Naturally enough, Filomena had refused to do this, and then her mother had told her that, as long as she stayed with her husband, she would consider her dead. Donna Bettina, her face somber, followed her son with her eyes without asking him anything.

It was late when Ciro got back from the country.

"Did your seconds come?" he asked right away, and wanted Pepè to tell him the conditions under which the duel was to be fought. "Swords, eh? I would have preferred pistols. Well, so be it! Stay to supper with us."

After supper, knowing that Pepè could not even handle a penknife, Ciro took him down to the study again to teach him a "foolproof thrust."

"I'm a little out of practice but, in an emergency. . . . Here!" he ordered, taking two whips out of a corner and handing one to Pepè. "Pretend it's a sword."

The lamp on the desk was lit, but its glow scarcely illumined the big room. Throughout the rest of the house, a tomblike silence reigned.

Pepè was at his most downcast—the whip in his hand and the blatant arrogance of his brother-in-law, who had taken an on-guard stance and lunged from time to time to give him little blows on the legs, seemed singularly inappropriate jokes. Meanwhile, Ciro was shouting at him impatiently, not realizing that the more he shouted the more firmly Pepè was rooted to the spot. Once more placing himself on guard in front of Pepè, he began to teach him the foolproof thrust. What with one feint and another, he really put his heart into it, grew angry, and cried. "This is like old times!" hotly attacking his poor brother-in-law. Pepè, protecting his head with his arms, bowed under the fury of the whistling whip lashes and called for help and mercy.

His sister arrived with a lamp in her hand.

"Help! Help! They are killing each other! Ciro! Pepè!"

"Keep still, you fool! Keep still!" Ciro shouted, breathless and radiant, leaving Pepè to his woes. "Can't you see we're joking?"

VIII

Raví had been waiting impatiently for about two hours, leaning on the iron railing that bordered the street leading out of town, his eyes fixed on a familiar point of the broad, green, undulant countryside that opens at the foot of the hills against which Girgenti seems to have stretched herself out. Every so often he would sigh, walk a few steps, or give the railing a good shake, but he did not take his eyes off the spot where the dark cypresses marked the graveyard at Bonomarone. And he muttered:

"Right down there, you devils! Birds of ill omen, you!"

The Passeggiata was deserted at that hour. A soldier at a window of the big gray barracks opposite was polishing a boot and whistling at his ease. Wagons loaded with great jars of water and pulled by weary donkeys passed along the dusty main road that ran below the Passeggiata, nor did the muleteers spare their beasts the weight of their own flesh despite the hard upgrade that led from the spring of drinking water down there near the cemetery. Don Marcantonio leaned over the railing and called out:

"Hey, tell me, did you see two carriages early this morning down there?"

No one had seen anything.

"Could they have gone some place else?" Raví asked himself distractedly. "Or did they come back to town by some other route? No, that isn't possible. This is the shortest way back. They must come back this way." And he pounded his big hands on the rusty railing.

"Oh, dry up!" he finally yelled at the soldier who had not stopped whistling at the barracks window.

Don Marcantonio felt as remorseful about the duel as if he had really been responsible for it himself, with the conversation he and Alletto had had shortly before his daughter's wedding. Hadn't that poor young man spoken up for Stellina, as if she were, indeed, his promised bride?

He would not admit, even after the disastrous outcome of the wedding feast and the violent scenes his daughter had made, that he could have been wrong in his "reasoning." He believed, rather, that the devil had had a hand in suggesting to Don Diego that he offer his bride a glass of wine, and then in setting Alletto and Borrani against one another.

"It was done to drive me to desperation!" Raví thought. "But I won't admit I'm beaten."

There was a lot of talk in town about the wedding party that had turned into a brawl. His name and Don Diego's were on everyone's lips. And Pepè's ridiculous phrase, "I can speak French, too . . ." was repeated with howls of laughter. The few drops of wine Don Diego had spilled on his wife's gown had already turned into half a bottle, and the strangest and silliest things were told about that now famous evening.

The day before the morning of the duel Don Marcantonio had noticed that people were looking at him scornfully. And they were not speaking to him. Well, bully for them!

"He who laughs last, laughs best! Give me two or three years and we'll see who was right."

Meanwhile, there he was—no two ways about it—waiting anxiously and with impatience for the outcome of the duel. He believed in playing an honest hand of cards, yes, sir! That dear, good, kind, respectful young man, Pepè Alletto, weighed on his conscience, and the time would come when he would be Stellina's husband, when Stellina had become the richest young woman in town. Then the two of them would be happy together, to spite the envious. And they would owe their happiness to him! "But why hasn't the carriage come back yet?"

Don Marcantonio could no longer keep his nerves in check, and he started down toward the big main road under the Passeggiata. When he reached the entrance to the bar-

racks, he spied a carriage at the end of the street. It was
moving toward town at a walk and was covered with dust.

"There it is!" he cried, and his heart pounded in his chest.

He started to run ponderously downhill, helping himself
with his arms as his short legs pumped away beneath his
heavy belly. "The wounded man is surely inside that carriage: it's going so slowly. . . . Who can it be? Who can it be?"

He drew alongside and reversed his course:

"Who's in there?" he cried, breathless, his hat in his hand.

Gerlando D'Ambrosio put his head out of the carriage, his
face flushed, and blinked from behind his thick glasses, his
face grim.

"Oh, poor Don Pepè!" Raví cried, striking his forehead
with the palm of his hand and looking inside the carriage.

Pepè Alletto turned a blank stare toward Raví. He looked
very pale, his jacket was draped over his shoulders, and his
open shirt revealed his bandaged chest.

"There's no room! Keep going!" Nocio Tucciarello told the
coachman furiously.

"Doctor, please tell me . . ." Don Marcantonio begged.

"Keep going!" Tucciarello shouted at the coachman.

"*Ecce homo!* Jesus among the Jews! Cutthroats! Brigands!"
Don Marcantonio, his arms upraised, called after the carriage.
He stood there, yelling and puffing in the middle of the
street, tears in his eyes and his legs trembling from the running he had done and from all the commotion.

IX

Pepè Alletto had suffered a great slashing blow from the
left shoulder well down the right thigh, requiring sixty-four
stitches to close the gaping wound. And during the operation,
he had fainted twice.

But Tucciarello and D'Ambrosio were not angry because
of the painful issue of the duel; they were upset by their prin-
cipal's behavior when he faced his opponent. It was not that
Pepè had made a cowardly showing, but as soon as he took
his sword in hand—"Holy Christ!" Tucciarello thought, biting
the tip of his mustache—he grew paler than a corpse. It was
a wonder that the sword did not fall of its own weight on his
body, as if the weapon were made of heavy bronze. A feint?

A parry? Nothing! He stood there, like a wooden puppet. . . . And then, of course, the other fellow made mincemeat of him at the first encounter. He was lucky not to have been struck on the head. Borrani would have cleft him in two, like a melon.

Ciro Coppa had already heard from Pepè's seconds, who had come back to town before the wounded man, how the duel had turned out. He had had a bed prepared for Alletto. Certainly, he could not let him be shipped home to his mother's house in such a state—the old lady, Ciro's mother-in-law, was over seventy.

Now, as he waited, he walked up and down with great strides and every so often muttered imprecations against women, the cause of all men's troubles. First, he had had a scene with his sick wife; who had shrieked, wept, raged, and finally fainted—all because a rabbit had wished to play the role of a lion. Idiot!

Then the servant girl came to tell him in a rush that the carriage was here.

"Let no one in!" Coppa cried, immediately envisioning a crowd of snoopers following the wounded man right into the house. "Let no one in except the doctor and his patient!"

And off he went, after the servant.

Pepè was carried in a chair from the carriage to his bed, and Ciro ran ahead to place his wife under lock and key.

"I want to see him! Ciro, for God's sake, let me see him!" Filomena begged him, weeping and pushing against the door with her hands and knees.

But Ciro had already run off to the patient's room to make him welcome, in his own fashion:

"You're the biggest fool on the face of the earth!"

"Shh, Counselor, shhh! He has a fever . . ." the doctor reproved him.

"Let no one come in!" Coppa cried in the doctor's face in the excitement of the moment, instead of answering him. And he repeated for good measure, "Let no one come in! I myself am going to stand guard at my own door. . . . Let him who enters beware!"

And once more off he went at a run.

"Pepè! Pepè! Let me see him! I want to see him! I beseech you . . ." his wife went on begging.

Ciro stopped all of a sudden, opened the door, and with his eyes bulging out of his head, yelled:

"Jesus, Mary, and Joseph! What do you want? I'll call them all down from Heaven for you! No, you can't see him, I told you. They are undressing him. He's naked. Let no one in!"

And it is true that he did not that day let in even the most intimate friends of his brother-in-law. Only a few of them were permitted to call on the following days, for by then there was no risk that the guests might catch sight of Filomena. Poor creature, the unexpected blow had worsened her condition and she had had to be put to bed.

That is why Marcantonio Raví and Alcozèr were allowed in to pay the patient a visit. They came together, the latter all smiles and good manners, the former upset, beside himself because of the bile that worked within him as in a furnace.

"Don Pepè! Dear Don Pepè!"

And he tried to kiss his hand, breaking into tears as if Pepè were stretched out there on his deathbed.

In fact, the wound was not dangerous, however long and painful it might be. Pepè complained to his two visitors only about having to lie still for so long, and every so often his eyes would search Don Marcantonio's for some news of Stellina.

Raví spoke of the interest his whole family took in Pepè's recovery, and Don Diego nodded agreement with the sentiments of his father-in-law. Had they all been interested, indeed? Then Stellina had heard about the duel? Pepè felt the liveliest joy at this, a joy only slightly marred by the curious smile with which Don Diego accompanied his steady nodding at almost every one of Raví's remarks.

"Do come back to see me," Pepè said at last. "I'll be laid up here for a long time, the doctor said. You can't imagine how much pleasure your visit . . ."

"Pleasure? For you? It's rather a pleasure for us," Don Marcantonio broke in. "I'd give my life for you, Don Pepè! God knows how I suffered when I found out. . . . Well, not another word. I can't speak freely here. Goodbye for now. I'll be back tomorrow . . . if they let me in. Did you know that, on the day of the duel, your brother-in-law left me outside his door? Left *me* outside, who'd have wanted to carry you in my arms to my own house to take care of you like a son? Enough of this! Until tomorrow, Don Pepè."

In fact, Raví returned by himself not on the following day

but a few days later, and he stayed a long time talking with
Pepè. He told him that he sent his wife every day to see Alletto's mother, Donna Bettina, and to give her news of him,
to comfort her, to keep her company, because the old lady was
consumed with rage and sorrow that she could not go to see
her son. Then he spoke to him about Alcozèr's handsome
house, about the way he treated his young wife—who had
finally given in—and about the visits he himself paid Stellina
every day in order to encourage her to be prudent and patient.

"Because, you see, dear Don Pepè, on the one hand, the
old man is aware of his position while, on the other, he loves
company. The result is people in the house, young men hanging about—do I make myself clear? Now although this pleases
me from a certain point of view because it amuses Stellina
and keeps her from feeling lonely, from another point of
view I don't like it at all because it gives rise to gossip. You
know how our town is. . . . Your friends go to visit, by the
way—the Salvo brothers and their cousin Garofalo, good,
high-spirited young men, all of them . . . and as for Stellina—
not because she's my daughter, mind you, but you know her
—a perfect angel! Just the same, would you think it wise to
put the dry straw so close to the flame? Well, enough of this.
It's no longer my concern. Now it's up to her husband, who
should have enough experience, wouldn't you think? Any-
how, you know the old saying, 'A fool is wiser in his own
house than a hundred wise men in the house of others.' "

"And what about Stellina? Stellina?" Pepè would have liked
to ask. "Does she laugh, and sing, and joke with the Salvo
boys and with Garofalo while I lie here, nailed to this bed
because of her?"

X

On what a Procrustean bed poor Pepè tossed and turned
from that day forth!

"Doctor, tell me, when can I get up? I can't stand it anymore."

But the doctor paid him little heed. He stayed with him
no more than a few minutes at a time, worried as he was
with quite another situation: he knew how serious Filomena's
condition was and he realized that Coppa would not admit

it. Instead, Coppa insisted that the doctor cure his wife as if, having suffered and spent money on her account, he felt he had a right not to lose her.

Coppa had scarcely closed his eyes all week and seated there beside her bed, ate a snack now and then only because she insisted, never taking his eyes from her face. In this way he really believed he was fighting off Death, and he would not believe that the enemy could carry off his wife before his eyes so long as he stayed there, steadfastly on guard, alert, armed by his own willpower. He listened to no one so as not to lessen by so much as a hair the violent tension of his whole being mobilized in defense of the sick woman.

If the doctor said something to him, he would invariably reply, "I know nothing about it. *You* make the decisions: you're the doctor. My place is here. I'm not making any complaints."

But finally the doctor demanded a consultation, and having been reassured by his colleagues that he had done everything possible for his patient, he declined all further responsibility. Signora Filomena's life was finished.

Ciro Coppa turned the doctor out of the house, cursing him. Then, feeling that his defense of his wife's life was less effective in that house in which medical science had been forced to give up the struggle with death, he went to the wardrobe and took out one of Filomena's dresses.

"Here! Get dressed. Quick!" he told her. "I'll cure you! We'll go to the country. You'll see: fresh air, walks in the open. . . . I'll show these charlatans how to save their patients' lives! Want me to help you get dressed? For God's sake, Filomena, don't give up now! Don't betray me. . . . You love me. . . . I. . . ."

Suddenly a great knot choked the words in his throat. His wife had slowly closed her eyes in pain at his desperate exhortations: two tears slipped from beneath her lashes and left their traces on her face. She made a sign for him to draw near her bed. Then the dying woman slowly put her arm about his neck and, with her trembling hand, caressed his hair.

"Do me one act of kindness," she murmured. "A priest. . . ."

Ciro, leaning against her breast, burst into furious tears as if grief, biting into him, had maddened him.

"Don't you trust me anymore, Filomena?" he roared between great wrenching sobs. Then, getting up abruptly, his face terrible in its torment, he asked her, "What sins can you have on your conscience to confess in the secrecy of the confession?"

"Sins? Who doesn't have sins, Ciro?" the dying woman sighed.

He rushed from the room, his hands yanking at his hair. He told the servant to call a priest.

"An old one! An old one!" he shouted and fled from the house so as not to be there during her confession.

He strode up and down beneath the trees of the Passeggiata for almost two hours, racking his brains to imagine what sins his wife might have had to confess to the priest.

What sins? What sins? Sins of thought, of course ... sins of intent ... but who had ever laid eyes on his wife? Sins of long ago?

And he walked with his hands pressed tight to the small of his back, his face contorted with jealousy, his eyes aflame.

Filomena died that night. Pepè wished at all costs to get up so that he might see his sister and kiss her brow once more. Ciro had locked himself in his children's room—they had been sent to stay with their grandmother—and he threw himself on one of the little beds, where he bit and rent the pillowcase so as not to cry out.

Next day, he told the maid to set the table and sent to his mother-in-law to ask for the return of the children. The old maidservant looked him in the eyes, fearing that he had gone quite mad.

"Set the table!" Ciro ordered, yelling at her. "And set a place for your mistress as well."

He wanted everyone, including Pepè and the two children, to sit down with him to luncheon.

"I'm the master here!" he cried, beating his fists on the table so that the glasses and silverware danced. "Yes, I'm master here! Think how upset Filomena would be if she knew that, because of her, her children went hungry! Let us eat!"

First, he served his wife, as usual, then the others. And wishing to set a good example, he raised the first spoonful to his lips. But no sooner had the soup spoon touched his mouth than he gagged, seized the napkin and stuffed it against his lips, bit it, and cried in a smothered voice, "Filomena! Filomena!"

But as soon as his startled children began to cry with him, bang! he pounded once more on the table.

"Quiet! I'm master here! Eat up, eat up! Children, don't upset your mother! She is here . . . to help you . . . she sees everything . . . and she suffers, dear ones, if she sees you don't eat for so much as a day . . . Eat up! Eat up!"

XI

Pepè made good use of his mourning for his sister and of his pallor after his long convalescence to look more "interesting" in Stellina's eyes, as if he had put on mourning because she had married another.

The first evening he was permitted out he called at Alcozèr's house in Via Porta Mazzara. As he went up the stairs, he felt his heart beating so hard that he had to stop every five or six steps to catch his breath. When he reached the next-to-the-last floor, he was cruelly hurt to hear Stellina's voice singing a love song, accompanied on the piano by Mauro Salvo: no doubt about it!

"Sing, ungrateful woman, sing!"

He leaned against the wall and covered his eyes with his hand.

Then there was a burst of applause and, in the midst of it, a long, silvery laugh. Pepè roused himself, climbed the last steps, and pulled the bell cord.

"Pepè!" Gasparino Salvo cried, surprised, when he opened the door. He went at once to give the joyful news to the guests in the sitting room. "It's Pepè Pepè Alletto! Pepè is here!"

Fifo and Mommino Garofalo and Totò Salvo rushed to the entryway. Don Diego, who had been dozing on the divan when the applause and voices woke him, rose to his feet as if stunned and looked at Mauro Salvo, who had remained seated, and at Stellina, who, one knee resting on the piano bench, let her hand linger on the keys while her eyes were held by the candle flame that burned beside the music rack.

Pepè entered to the noisy welcome of his friends and stood there, pale, tense, his eyes lowered, holding out his hand to Stellina, who offered him her limp, cold little hand while Don Diego, bowing and gesturing with arms flung wide, said to him:

"Bravo! Bravo! Here you are back with us at last! All well again? Congratulations. Sit over here by me."

Only Mauro Salvo said not a word to Pepè. He looked at him coldly from the chair in which he had remained seated, his heavy eyelids half-closed over his bulging eyes and his upturned snout of a nose looking as if, with obstinate pride, it were commanding the eyes to stay open.

Pepè stopped a moment, his glance resting on him. Then he turned to Stellina and asked:

"Am I interrupting?"

Don Diego raised his voice. "Whatever are you saying, dear Don Pepè? We are pleased and honored. We've waited for you many an evening, talking of you often. Isn't that so, gentlemen?"

Everyone agreed readily except Mauro Salvo—and Stellina.

"We were all saddened by the misfortune, the tragedy, you have suffered," Don Diego went on.

"Poor Signora Filomena!" Fifo Garofalo exclaimed, pushing his glasses up on the bridge of his nose.

A moment of silence followed on mention of the dead woman's name, during which Pepè gently shook his head.

"Poor soul, the fright I caused her was one more thing that hastened her end," he said.

"The fright you caused her," Mauro Salvo broke in savagely, his eyes lowering and his nose in the air, "was really caused—if what people say is true—by that brother-in-law of yours keeping her under lock and key so that she couldn't even go in to see you. That way she must have imagined you were at death's door. If she'd seen you with that little scratch . . ."

"Little scratch?" Mommino Garofalo broke in. "How many stitches, Pepè?"

"Sixty-four," Pepè answered modestly.

"Yes," Mauro went on, looking at the guests one by one from beneath his half-closed lids, "but certainly it wasn't a mortal wound nor even one to be frightened over."

"Quite, quite," Pepè agreed, in order to put an end to the

subject. "Well, be that as it may . . . but when I came up the stairs just now, I heard Signora Stellina singing a love song. . . . So you see I did really interrupt you all."

"What, again? But I've told you it isn't so, dear Don Pepè!"

Don Diego then told Alletto how they passed their evenings at his house, throwing in here and there an occasional reflection on the idiocy of life and the cursedness of old age. *Sic vivitur, sic vivitur. . . .* Company was more essential to him than bread, but of course he meant by this the company of young people! He had no use for people of his own age. Just the same, looking and listening, listening and looking . . . that wasn't much to be left with, alas. But he made his peace with it.

As he talked, Don Diego had about his lips that ambiguous smile Pepè had noted during the visit Alcozèr and Marcantonio had paid him. But this time the smile seemed intended for Mauro Salvo, toward whom Don Diego's eyes were frequently directed. Pepè was mistaken to be upset by this, however, for Alcozèr's little smile had a far more recondite meaning than Pepè's jealousy could attribute to it. It was true that Don Diego had been aware of Mauro Salvo's love for Stellina from the first, but for his own ends he had congratulated himself on this love rather than feared it. Mauro was ugly to look at and crude of manner: Stellina would never have paid him the slightest attention. Instead, the old man feared Pepè, protected by his brother-in-law and now enhanced by the prestige afforded him by the duel he had fought over Alcozèr's wife. Yet he had waited impatiently for the evening of Pepè's return, for, from that moment on, Stellina would find herself between two fires. The two rivals would mount guard over each other while he himself could rest easy and safe. This expedient would insure him the right to enjoy without risk the company of the other gay, heedless young people, and this was the cause of old Alcozèr's smile.

Little by little, the conversation picked up, and even Stellina took part, though she looked apprehensively from time to time toward the balcony where Mauro Salvo had withdrawn while the others were talking and the doors of which he had quietly closed behind him. Now he was out there with his back to the sitting room, his elbows on the iron railing, his head in his hands, looking at the black country-side in the moonless night.

Don Diego had been aware of his disappearance even before Stellina, and at a certain point he wanted him back in the sitting room again.

"Come on in, for goodness' sake! Do you want to catch your death in the night air?"

"I have a fearful headache," Mauro excused himself gloomily, coming in and closing the balcony doors.

Don Diego, in whose lashless eyes flickered the smile his lips would not betray, looked at him for a moment and then told him affectionately:

"Yes, yes. It shows in your face, poor fellow. Well, take heart! Don't be downcast!"

XII

During one of those evenings, they agreed to make an excursion to the temples. They were to meet at seven in the morning.

Don Diego had persuaded Pepè to join the group despite his mourning, and the Garofalos and two of the Salvo men had also urged him to come. When he agreed, Mauro excused himself, saying that he could not come.

In fact, he was the only one who did not turn up at the appointed hour. Don Diego felt that he had lost an arm and tried, with the excuse that the weather was not sufficiently fine, to put off the excursion. It was true enough that the sky was overcast: the autumn rains had not yet started. But the young friends and Stellina declared that the morning couldn't be better for an outing so that Don Diego had to give in in the end.

Stellina looked pleased; she teased Fifo Garofalo, who had worn a cloak and swore he felt cold. Pepè saw her laughing and smiled, as if he were a mirror held up before her.

When they reached the top of the Passeggiata, there was Mauro Salvo leaning his elbows on a stone post of the railing, his chin in his hands. The first to catch sight of him was Stellina. She caught her lower lip between her teeth, then, putting a finger on her lips, took Pepè's stick from his hand and, on tiptoe, ran to the spot where she could slowly tip

Mauro's hat askew with the walking stick. Mauro turned around, furious, but he was confronted by Stellina, who silently threatened him with the stick, her face as scowling as his, while the others laughed.

So he too joined the group. They were all laughing, and Stellina seemed the gayest of all. Don Diego looked at the six young men and his wife and beamed with pleasure at their lightheartedness, holding himself back as he dawdled behind them down the slope.

"Take it slowly, fellows. Easy does it . . ." he would call out from time to time, thinking that the road ahead was long and that the years weighed on him. At such moments, he would raise his eyes to heaven and his mouth would turn down at the corners.

The sky to the east was clouding up steadily. Over there on the horizon, on the blanched escarpments of the Crocca, fog rolled in threateningly. Perhaps it was already raining there. From nearby, a fresh breeze had blown up which seemed to wish to rally the exhausted trees with the news that the rain they longed for was on its way. In the scorched countryside bristling with stubble, there were other signs of the approach of rain—the joyous singing of larks and the chatter of magpies.

When, at a turn in the road, the group came upon the old Norman chapel of San Nicola surrounded by scrub pine and cypresses, Don Diego, who had felt a few drops on the back of his hand, warned them:

"Friends, let us stop here. I don't think it wise to go on toward the temples in this weather. Please take my advice— I am not old for nothing!"

"Not a word of truth to it!" they all objected. "A passing cloud! It won't rain!"

"Friends, I'll regret this," Don Diego averred. "But have it your own way. Let youth be served. On with the dance, young friends!"

After San Nicola, the road dropped more steeply, and they all gamboled along swiftly under the threat of rain. Soon they were within sight of the magnificent Temple of Concord, still intact and light as air on the brow of its hill, with its superb peristyle open to the view of those almond and olive woods that are called—in memory of the ancient city that once rose on the spot—the woods of civilization. Beyond the temple is the plain of San Gregorio, with a view of Agrigentum, and further still, in the distance, the limitless clouds, pregnant with rain, and the tops of the colossal cypresses rising above the almond and olive trees vibrated like banners alert to guard the ancient temple.

The joyful shouts of the young people echoed strangely in the austere silence among the age-old columns. Stellina, poised on the top step, from which one rises to the summit which is almost entirely destroyed toward the front of the altar, called for help. Mauro Salvo ran quickly to her assistance and pulled her up by the hands.

Fifo Garofalo, an archaeology buff, had draped himself in the picnic table cloth and had pulled his slouch hat down over his head:

"Come, oh profane ones!" he shouted, leaping up on a large stone in the midst of the temple. "The irreverent, too, are welcome! No, wait . . ." and he jumped down from the stone. "Let Signora Stellina act as a shade. There! Raise your arms . . . that's it. Oh, profane ones, adore the Goddess of Concord! I, the officiating priest, cry out to you: 'Let us pour out libations and pray. . . .' No, no, wait a minute!"

Everyone except Stellina, who was posing as a shade, had rushed toward the picnic basket a servant had brought.

"Hey, you, Pepè," Fifo went on at the top of his lungs, "you are my assistant. Ask those present, 'Who are you who make up this gathering?' "

"People who are starving," each one replied in his own way, including the shade, Stellina.

"No, it won't do! You have to cry out at the top of your lungs, 'Men of good will!' And if you don't say it loud enough, no one will believe you. Come, come, proffer a stainless wafer to our would-be Goddess of Concord. . . ."

"And strike a match!" Pepè added, looking up at the sky that had suddenly closed in like a cave, as if night had fallen.

"God knows I'll live to regret this," Don Diego Alcozèr murmured, slumped against one of the columns.

"Let's attack the picnic basket . . . and the last one in is a poor . . . weak . . . fool!" cried Gasparino Salvo, setting a good example.

They all helped themselves to the picnic basket except Don Diego, each one grabbing whatever first fell to hand. And the big drops of rain pelted down as if they were hail.

"Let's take shelter in some nearby farmhouse!" Don Diego begged. "Quick, quick. Let's run!"

They rushed from the temple: the rain suddenly turned torrential, as if the heavens were tipping over on them with extraordinary violence, as if, in fact, the floodgates of heaven had opened.

"May God have mercy!" Don Diego cried, pulling himself into the smallest compass possible under the lash of the storm.

Stellina and the six young men laughed. They went to the nearest house, but the iron gates before the entrance were closed. They knocked at the gate and cried for help. This wasn't a rain: it was a flood.

Fifo Garofalo took off his cloak and, with the help of the others, held it up as a palanquin over Don Diego and Stellina. Down, down, down the water came. Soon the cloak was sodden.

"Back to San Nicola!" Mauro Salvo cried, seizing Stellina by the hand and starting off at a run.

"To San Nicola! There's a roof there," the others agreed, following at their heels.

And they all started off up the hill that had become a veritable torrent.

Under the roof, Don Diego, as chilled as the rest, started to shake with cold.

"If we stay here, we'll catch our death! Cursed be the moment I agreed to leave the house.... I'll live to regret it! We're drenched.... Just feel how damp the air is!"

All of a sudden, the fury of the rains abated; it seemed as if the clouds might lift.

"Don't you believe it! It's still raining.... just take a look...."

The sheets of rain poured down thinner and fewer than before, but they kept up steadily. They decided that, drenched as they were, they'd be better off somewhere other than under the drafty roof of the church, and they started up the road again in search of better shelter.

"It's no use, Don Diego," Fifo Garofalo told the old man after having knocked at one more gate. "Today is Sunday. At this time of day the peasants are at mass in town. Let's resign ourselves to it and start out again! The rain has slacked off; let's hope it stops altogether."

"Let's get going, yes, let's," muttered poor Don Diego.
"But you'll see: I'll be dead when we get there."

Fear acted as a goad to gasping old age, and Don Diego
was the first up the hill. Soon the rain came down hard again.

"Give us a hand here! Let us carry you," Totò Salvo and
Fifo Garofalo told the old man.

"I'm dying, dying," Don Diego groaned, as he was carried
forward by the two young men who curvetted like horses,
leaping, straining, and tossing their heads joyously in the dren-
ching rain, amid the guffaws of laughter of those who followed them.

They reached town breathless, with their clothing stuck to
their bodies. Don Diego wanted to go to bed at once, as his
teeth were already chattering. He was trembling from head to
foot and in a frightening, piteous state.

"A doctor . . . a doctor . . . I'm dying. Send for Marcantonio
at once. . . ."

Fifo Garofalo sped in search of the doctor, while Pepè Alletto, at Stellina's bidding, went after Don Marcantonio. The
others went away, downcast and ashamed.

XIII

"Oh, blessed boy! What have you been doing out in weather
like this?" Raví cried as he saw Pepè, raindrenched from head
to foot.

Pepè told him quickly about the excursion and expressed
his own regret for the part he might have played in Don
Diego's illness.

"It's up to God!" Don Marcantonio commented, hastily,
scrambling into his topcoat. "So he dies! If he weren't a baptized Christian, I'd say it was high time, He had a high old
time with the young fellows, did he? Well, so be it! Don Pepè,
I'm not referring to you. This has nothing to do with you.
It's up to God! Rosa, my umbrella. . . . Let's go, Don Pepè."

They found Don Diego delirious, with a raging fever, and
Stellina weeping, frightened by the disconnected phrases that
Don Diego addressed to one or another of his previous wives,
asking them to cast up their accounts for the wrongs they had
done him.

"Are you my departed Luzza? Well, then, for God's sake, tell me what you want!"

His delirium lasted for days. Then Don Diego's haunting spirits foresook him, though he suffered on under a draining fever.

Stellina, Pepè, and Don Marcantonio watched over the sick man every night. In the utter stillness, Don Diego's chest started to wheeze.

"It's pneumonia, as I live and breathe!" Don Marcantonio said. And the three of them looked each other in the eyes by the dim light of the lamp.

On the morning after this vigil, the doctor stated that it was, indeed, pneumonia, and he declared Don Diego's condition dangerous.

The three of them—faced with death waiting there before them near the bed on which the slender frame of Don Diego lay buried under a mound of covers, his long strand of hair snaking over his pillow beside his swollen, bald pate—waited as though feeling secret remorse for their thoughts and the hopes that opened before them in the event of Don Diego's death. Pepè was the most acutely aware of this, Stellina the least. As for Don Marcantonio, he whispered in the silence, looking from his daughter to their friend: "Well, the time has come, children. The time has come...." All three of them sighed and bowed their heads as if awaiting a dire fate rather than a liberation.

They spared no pains during the long course of Don Diego's illness while the sick man clung to life by a thread—as a bush clings to the edge of a cliff. They vied with each other in their care and in the intensity of their devotion. As if their consciences were truly relieved and lightened by the efforts they deployed, each of them wished to assume the major burden in order to free the others. Thus, among them, they begged each other insistently to eat a trifle or to catch a moment's sleep.

Pepè spared himself least of all, but the strength with which he so gamely resisted weariness and fasting did not come to him from will power. He could really neither sleep nor eat, so buoyed up was he by the thought of his own imminent happiness. He was already in port, he had reached the eve of his good fortune, virtually kept going by the looks, the words Stellina addressed him, in the full certainty that she

loved him, after their days of close intimacy, and that she too
felt happy on the eve of a new life.

Don Marcantonio held them with a steadfast glance.

"They are aflame!" he said to himself, his mouth taut. And
one evening, passing through the hallway, he thought he heard
the sound of a kiss coming from the darkened sitting room.
He coughed. Later, he called Pepè aside and told him quietly:

"Dear Don Pepè, for God's sake be prudent! Be a man . . .
if God wills it, we have come to port. . . ."

Pepè pretended not to understand and asked him innocently:
"Why should I be prudent?"

"For no reason at all," snapped Don Marcantonio. "But
let me repeat, prudence! Take care, for her husband is still
on the spot. That fellow is quite capable of reviving, for he
seems to have nine lives like a cat. Then how would I look?
I'd look like nothing at all, Don Pepè! Two and two still make
four—either you behave with prudence and discretion or out
you go, I tell you. I'll have no monkey business."

XIV

Although Don Diego had already taken a turn for the
better, Pepè Alletto left his house one evening beaming with
happiness. When he reached the entrance to the Ràbato just
beyond Via Mazzara, he found Mauro Salvo, accompanied
by his brothers and his cousins, the Garofalos, blocking his
way.

It did not require much perception for Pepè to have noticed that Mauro Salvo was in love with Stellina, and
Pepè had perceived it from the first evening he had seen
her again in her husband's house. Besides, Stellina herself
had admitted the fact, laughing. So nothing to be feared on
her side. But Pepè well knew that Salvo was capable of
any act of violence whatsoever. For this reason, rather than
from timidity, he had sought to avoid any other compromis-
ing scene and had acted in such a way as not to offer Salvo
the least excuse. He felt himself further protected by the
friendly feelings of Mauro's brothers, Totò and Gasparino, and
of his Garofalo cousins, who disapproved of Mauro's attitude—if only for the fact that it might cause their being
turned away from Alcozèr's door where they spent pleasant

evenings in Stellina's company and where they had come to like her old husband.

But in the end the door had been closed in their faces because of Don Diego's illness, and they had made common cause with Mauro because of this, not because they shared his jealousy but because Pepè had continued to pass through that door. Pepè had already noticed a change in the attitudes of his friends and more than once he had sought to avoid them. But here they were coming toward him, with Mauro in the lead.

Mauro told him brusquely, stopping him: "Come with me. I want to talk to you."

"What for?" Alletto asked him, trying out a half-smile. "Why can't you talk to me here?"

"Too many people," Mauro replied crisply. "Get going."

Pepè thrust out his lower lip and shrugged his shoulders, to indicate that he had no idea what Salvo wanted of him with his threatening, mysterious air, and he said: "I was minding my own business ... if I'm not mistaken."

But Salvo cut him off, yelling with real violence, "Your own business? What business, you threadbare jackanapes!"

"Oh!" Pepè exclaimed. "Watch your language...."

"You are threadbare and a jackanapes. Yes, you are," Mauro repeated, turning and facing him down threateningly. "And don't you dare reply or I'll give you such a drubbing you won't know what hit you."

Pepè raised his eyes to heaven, his mouth open as if to say, "My patience is at an end!" Then he exploded with, "Listen, dear friend. I neither wish nor want to pick a fight with anyone. See?"

"Fine!" Mauro concluded hastily. "Since you want to act like a lamb, just take care that you don't set foot in Don Diego Alcozèr's house."

"What! Why not? Who's to stop me?"

"I'm here to stop you!"

"You? But why?"

"Because that's the way I want it! Since I can't go there, neither can you. Neither you nor anyone else. Understand?"

"That's just fine! And what if Raví takes me there with him?"

"You'll get to the door and then about face! If you don't, I'll make short work of it. I'll be on guard tomorrow evening and if I see you go inside, you just watch out! Not another word. Now, go home."

"Good evening," Pepè heard himself saying automatically in the stunned state in which Mauro's peremptory threats had left him.

XV

Hearing the doorbell, Donna Bettina did not fail to call out as usual:

"Clean your shoes!"

"I've cleaned them," Pepè answered as he came in. "I cleaned them on the pants of a few people who won't mind their own business."

His mother took fright: "Not another fight?"

"No ... but almost!" Pepè hastened to reassure her. "By a hair's breadth, I missed getting into my ... usual pickle."

"Pepè, my boy, not *more* dirty work?" Donna Bettina wailed, asking the question with the same loving tone she often used toward her son. She seemed to have aged ten years since Filomena's death. She had not wanted to show her bereavement by shedding tears, but it was clear that her sorrow—suffered in silence—still devoured her.

Pepè, shaking his fists in the air, cried, "But I'll settle their hash for them! I've already fought one duel! We'll see ... we'll just see...."

He started to pace the room like a young lion in its cage. Donna Bettina watched him with her mouth slightly open as if she were stunned. Then she pleaded, "For goodness' sake, Pepè, tell me what happened. Don't torment me!"

"Nothing happened," her son answered. "Certain friends of mine.... Are we having dinner this evening, Mama, or aren't we?"

"Pepè," his mother warned him, "I'm telling you I am no longer young and I can't stand these upsets ... I can't stand any more ... I can't stand any more.... You and you alone will be the cause of my death ... you alone, mind!"

"It's all right, it's all right, Mother ... we won't say another word about it!" Pepè said heartily, and sat down to table with a will, as if his body wished to make up for the insults his spirit had suffered.

"Just let him die, and we'll see . . . " he said to himself, turning over thoughts of Don Alcozèr in his mind.

Thus he had mentally decided to put off confronting Salvo until Alcozèr's death, in order not to bring his thoughts up short at the end of twenty-four hours when he would find his rival at Don Diego's door. Looking, instead, toward the future, he felt how much stronger his own position was than Salvo's. Yet this conviction did not comfort him completely in the face of tomorrow's ordeal.

He did not sleep a wink that night, thinking of what he might have said to his rival on the spot.

At the same time, Donna Bettina, in her small bed beside Pepè's, was having a strange dream. She imagined she saw Don Diego coming toward her, all smiles and good manners; he bowed, one hand on his heart; he kneeled at her feet; he took one of her hands and kissed it, sighing, "Oh, Bettina, in memory of our earlier love!" Then, in her dream, she burst out laughing, and Don Diego, wounded by her laughter, proposed these tardy amends: he would give up his wife, who was far too young for him, to Pepè on condition that Donna Bettina accept him as her husband. "The union of two old people in search of peace, the union of two young people burning with love. . . ."

At this point, she awoke and found Pepè, seated in bed with his shoulders supported by the fat pillow propped against the headboard, shaking one outstretched arm threateningly and declaiming between clenched teeth, "And I tell you I'll kill you!"

"Pepè," she quavered, "what are you saying? What's the matter?"

"Nothing . . . I'm thinking!"

"In the middle of the night? Tell me what's the matter!"

"I'm not sleepy; I'm thinking," Pepè replied, annoyed. "Go to sleep . . . go to sleep. . . ."

Donna Bettina was quiet for a few minutes and put her head down on the pillow. Then she asked in a hushed voice, almost as if she were embarrassed at her attempts to elicit a confidence from her son, "What are you thinking about?" Pepè did not answer. Only, after a moment, he shook his head and uttered a sigh audible in the silence of the big room.

"Threadbare . . ." he said.

"Forgive your father, Pepè. He was ruined by his own foolish ways," Donna Bettina concluded, sighing in turn.

And little by little, the sorrowing old woman once more drifted off to sleep.

XVI

Pepè did not even consider the possibility of not going to Alcozèr's house that evening. It would have been tantamount to ceding his every right over Stellina to Mauro Salvo and, worse still, to giving clear-cut proof of a fear he was later to admit even to himself. As the hour of his usual visit drew near, he went to Raví's house so that they might pay their call together: certainly Salvo would not have the effrontery to attack him, seeing him accompanied by Stellina's father.

But neither Don Marcantonio nor his wife was at home.

"They've been at their daughter's since noon," the maid told him. "Heaven knows what may have happened! I can speak frankly to you. . . . That poor girl has really been sacrificed!"

Once more out in the street, Pepè began to think over whether or not he should go to Alcozèr's. What would people say if they were to scuffle right beneath her windows? I'm not sure I could control myself. Yesterday I was prudent enough, but this evening, if I should run into him, on my honor I'm sure things would end badly. Besides, there are *five* of them. Small wonder if I prefer to be accompanied by someone else.

Turning over such thoughts as these in his mind, Pepè dragged his feet in the direction of Coppa's house. He was rather worried that his brother-in-law would force him into another duel—that was why he had decided the night before against going to his house, although he recognized that he would have been a firmer escort than Raví.

Ciro had not left the house since his wife's death. He told the many clients who sought him out:

"First I must expiate, gentlemen, far different wrongs. I regret that I cannot be of service to you," he muttered mysteriously.

The supposed wrongs he was expiating were the presumed defects his dead wife had shown toward their two children's education. Obsessed with the idea of making strong men of them, he made them do exercises attributed to ancient Rome: he had them run naked every morning for about half an hour around a deep pool in the garden and then dive into the ice-cold water.

"Sink or swim!"

Then he ordered:

"Dry yourselves in the sun!"

And, if it were an overcast day:

"There's no sun. I'm sorry. Dry yourselves in the shade."

No more school: it was better to be stalwart brutes than learned invalids.

"Just leave your training up to me."

Pepè found him in his study teaching the boys how to box.

"A little practice along these lines wouldn't do you any harm!" Ciro told him. "You look half dead ... why, you're a disgusting spectacle. Come here! Let me feel your muscle ... here, bend your arm."

He felt his biceps, then looked at him as if nauseated and asked him:

"Why don't you kill yourself?"

"Thanks for the greeting," Pepè answered with a sickly smile. "You even make the children laugh. What's more, you're right. I too would like to be like you, able to keep half a dozen hoodlums at bay. Courage, yes ... that's all well and good; but courage alone without strength isn't enough."

"Faulty education!" Ciro shouted, ruled by the *idée fixe* of the moment.

"Ah, yes ... education has a lot to do with it."

"A lot? It's everything!"

"You're right. .... But you will admit that there are a lot of people in our part of the world who don't know how to mind their own business."

"Have you been the butt of some other prank?" Ciro asked with a derisive smile. "Why, I can't understand, since you stink of a lily liver at twenty paces!"

"Not at all!" Pepè retorted, stung by his words. "Every-

body should know that I'm not afraid. I've known how to deliver a slap to whomever deserved...."

"By pure chance!"

"I've fought a duel, and a fairly decent duel, at that!"

"Couldn't avoid it...."

"But what if they're five to one?"

"Who are they?" Ciro asked, his brows puckered threateningly.

"Mauro Salvo...."

"Is that the clown whose eyes look as if they wore shutters?"

"The very one, with his brothers and his two cousins, the
Garofalo boys.... There are five of them, see? Mauro is
madly in love with Signora Alcozèr, Raví's daughter. You
know the one. Of course, she doesn't care a fig about him.
Otherwise, I'd ... well, what do you think of the situation?
He—Mauro—insists that no one can go into Don Diego's
house, neither I, nor he, nor ... anyone. He says ... well,
the long and short of it is that he says if I go there this
evening, I'd better watch out.... He'll be waiting for me
with his gang in front of old Alcozèr's front door."

"I don't understand," Ciro said menacingly. "He'd use
brute force?"

"Yes! Brute force.... Five against one, see?"

"And you, you dolt, you said you wouldn't go?"

"Not at all!"

"Meanwhile, you're here ... and you're afraid! I can read
it in your eyes: you're afraid! Ah, but you'll go, all right;
this very evening, right now.... Brute force, not even from
God! Come with me."

"Where?"

"To Alcozèr's house!"

"Now?"

"Right now! I need time to dress. What time do you
usually go?"

"At about six-thirty."

Ciro looked at his watch and then exclaimed, shocked,
"What a coward you are!"

"Why?" Pepè stammered.

"It's a quarter to seven.... Never mind, though. We'll find
them.... I'll be ready in five minutes."

He ran upstairs and came down less than five minutes later, struggling into his jacket.

"Wait, Ciro . . . let me fix your tie," Pepè said, straightening the knot.

"Foolishness! Worrying about a tie!" Coppa cried, standing back and trying to blast his brother-in-law with a look. Then he gave him a firm push. "March!" he said. "I'll straighten them out for you, and without any walking stick."

He started off with Pepè. As they walked, Coppa shook with rage and exclaimed every so often, "Oh yes? Well, just you wait. Now tell *me* that no one can go into Alcozèr's house. I'm going in. Ah, so you'd use brute force, would you? Well, just you wait!"

Pepè trotted along beside him like a pet dog. As they neared Alcozèr's house, he looked up and, turning pale, said quietly to his brother-in-law, "He's there. There he is, with the others."

"Pay no attention. Don't look at them!" Ciro ordered.

"All five of them . . ." Pepè murmured.

There was Mauro Salvo at his post, and a little farther off, his satellites—his four cousins and brothers. As soon as Mauro caught sight of Pepè accompanied by Coppa, he pushed himself away from the wall against which he had been leaning, took one hand out of his pocket, and came toward them slowly, looking at Coppa, whom he addressed when he had reached the middle of the street.

"If you'll excuse me, Counselor, I'd like a few words with Pepè."

Ciro moved toward him and stopped right in front of him, fixing him with his eyes. Coppa's brows were furrowed, and his jaws worked convulsively. He pulled at his lower lips with two fingers and then said, "I'm having a few words with Pepè myself for the moment, and I won't let anyone else talk to him. I'm telling you this and I'm also telling it to your relatives over there waiting for you. If you want to tell *me* your few words, I'm at your service."

"As you wish, Don Ciro!" Mauro replied, thrusting his hand back in his pocket and rising on tiptoe, as if he were obliged to stretch his utmost in order to accept Coppa's refusal in this fashion.

"It will keep for another time . . ." he went on, "at your

convenience. There'll be plenty of time." And he went on his way.

XVII

There were squalls, in fact quite a gale, in Don Diego's house that day. That morning Stellina had had an outburst of rage against her old husband, who had become unbearable, poor fellow, since his convalescence. She had sent a note to her father asking him to come get her right away or she would throw herself from the balcony. Don Marcantonio had rushed to her house together with his wife; he intended to insist that his daughter show the most respectful devotion to her husband and to tell Pepè Alletto that he must not visit his son-in-law's house anymore.

When Ciro Coppa and Pepè entered the sitting room, they found Stellina in tears, slumped against the back of the sofa. Donna Rosa was seated beside her, her eyes lowered, her lips tight shut, and her hands clasped over her little paunch. Don Marcantonio was walking up and down, his hands behind his back, yelling reproaches at his daughter so loudly that Don Diego could not help but hear them, though he was shut away in his bedroom. When he saw Coppa, he stopped yelling at once and went eagerly to greet him.

"Honored sir! Dear lawyer, what an honor. . . . You are welcome, Don Pepè. . . . Rosa, here is Lawyer Coppa come to call. . . . I'm sorry that my daughter . . . Stellina, come on, now, a little effort . . . see, here's our honored lawyer who has deigned to pay us a visit. . . . I do apologize, Dr. Coppa, that you've arrived just at a time when . . . well, you know what family troubles are . . . passing clouds. . . . Here, do sit down. Sit down."

Greeted by this tearful scene, Coppa said as he settled himself, "But if our call is . . . even accidentally . . . ill-timed, I hope Signora Alcozèr will forgive me."

"You? How could you be concerned?" Raví replied, smiling.

Ciro interrupted him, looking at him coldly: "Let us leave it up to the mistress of the house to answer that. She may know more about it than you."

Stellina, her eyes red from weeping, put down her handkerchief and looked at Coppa, at a complete loss for what to say. Then she stammered, "I don't know...."

"But not in the *least*...." Don Marcantonio made one more try.

"Let me make myself quite clear!" Coppa went on, irritated. "I relied on Pepè, and perhaps I was wrong. But it's a sure thing that I prevented a scene under the windows.... I could not imagine that I might be causing the Signora any distress by intruding."

Pepè, finally seeing through the misunderstanding in which his brother-in-law was caught, turned red in the face and, bouncing up and down on his chair, told him, "No, Ciro... this does not concern *us*.... It's entirely my affair."

"Let me set things straight, honored sir!" Don Marcantonio put in firmly. "You are not in question.... It's a bagatelle, a minor difference that took place this morning between husband and wife. You know how it goes: 'I want it this way...' and 'I won't hear of it that way...' Well, do I make myself clear? The fault is all my daughter's; she's clearly to blame.... Yes, yes, a hundred times yes! There's no point in your weeping, my girl! You can weep till tomorrow morning—I'm still your father and it's up to me to tell you right from wrong. Am I right, dear lawyer? It seems to me that, so far as I've gone, I'm right. And what I say is that prudent conduct and obedience make a good wife! Then, let's have a little consideration, for God's sake! Most respected Don Ciro, my son-in-law is just now recovering from a grave illness—the only reason he didn't die was that he didn't *want* to die yet. Now he's still in bed in there, convalescing, and he's a little hard to get on with, as you may imagine. But one should feel sorry for him."

"I'm not saying a word," Stellina sobbed, her face once more concealed by the handkerchief. "You go ahead, and who knows what people will think of me?... But if they only knew... Lord, oh Lord, oh Lord! I can't stand it any longer...."

At these words, Ciro Coppa got up, his face congested and almost exploding with irritation and rage.

Raví, on edge, yelled at his daughter, "Speak up, then. Speak.... Why don't you speak?"

"Because I'm not like you," Stellina answered, her voice broken by sobs.

"Not like me. . . . What am I, then, ungrateful girl?" Don Marcantonio burst out. "Have I been thinking of myself? What have I gained from all this, pray? Haven't I been thinking of what's best for you? Answer me!"

"Yes, yes . . ." Stellina sobbed. "People will know how you've been thinking of what's best for me when they come one day to pick up my shattered body under the windows!"

"Just listen to her, dear lawyer. Just listen to her. Are these things one should say to a father who has done . . . for her . . ."

"For me? What have you done for me?" Stellina interrupted him, pressing her two fists down on the sofa and finally revealing her tear-stained face. "You locked me up, on bread and water."

"I did?"

"You did, in order to force me to marry a man older than you. And my mother is right here to witness the fact. Mother, you tell them I'm telling the truth! And then there are the neighbors—lots and lots of mouths you can't shut up. . . . I've begged you every day to take me away from here. I don't want to stay here any longer. And if you don't take me away from here, you'll see what I'll do!"

"Don Pepè, just hear what she's saying!" Don Marcantonio protested, half-stunned. "This is my reward! You tell them . . ."

Pepè once more bounced up and down on his chair, looking most embarrassed. Meanwhile Don Diego from the nearby sickroom let go with two huge sneezes.

"Health and prosperity!" Don Marcantonio called out with a mock gesture of rage, adding in a lowered voice, "And may your gall burst!"

With the exception of Coppa, they could not help smiling at this strange outburst.

"Gentlemen and ladies," Ciro said ponderously, "without resorting to violence, there's a solution for everything: the law."

"What can the law have to do with this, honored sir?" Don Marcantonio exploded.

"I tell you, there's the law, and that's all there is to it!" cried Ciro, who would not allow himself to be crossed even in someone else's house.

"I know there's the law," Don Marcantonio persisted,

though humbly. "But these are minor family differences that are best settled within the family, dear lawyer. If not today, then tomorrow...."

"That is not up to you to decide," Ciro retorted.

"What do you mean, it's not up to me? I'm her father!"

"The law does not look with favor on fathers who exert force to oblige their daughters to marry against their will and inclination. If you are not aware of this, let me so inform you. Signora, if you wish to have recourse to my service, I herewith place myself wholly and entirely at your disposal. If you wish to do so, you may free yourself of the tie that seems odious to you and recover your freedom."

"What? Where?" Raví stammered, having for the moment lost the thread of the argument. "In my family? You're mad! A court case in my family? A public scandal? A stain on my good name? You're mad! I'd close my door in her face. Then she'd have all the freedom she wants to die of hunger!"

"In that case," Coppa thundered, "I'll see to it. No one will die of hunger ... and not even God himself will threaten me with brute force!"

"What has that to do with it?" Raví hazarded.

The doorbell rang at length as if pulled by a nervous hand. Don Marcantonio did not wait for an answer, and Stellina ran from the room, followed by her mother. Pepè, who had gone to open the door, found himself face to face with Mauro Salvo and his gang.

Raví was there to greet them.

"Gentlemen, please forgive me.... Do come in, if you wish ... but, you see ..."

"No, thanks, dear Don Marcantonio!" Mauro said. "We came to ask how Don Diego is...."

"Better ... better, and full of life!" Don Marcantonio answered hastily.

"We also wanted to greet Signora Stellina," Salvo went on. "But if we can't ..."

"You can't!" said Coppa in a tone that cut short all argument, as he looked Mauro Salvo in the eyes. "We are all about to leave and stop inconveniencing the household."

Then, turning to Pepè, he added: "Go see the lady of the house. Tell her that I'll have the honor of calling on her here tomorrow morning, and in your company."

Pepè did as he was told, and soon they all took their leave without so much as a goodbye to Raví, who stood on the landing like a tree rooted to the spot.

As soon as they were down by the main entrance, Mauro Salvo said, pointedly stressing every word, "Pepè, see you soon!" And he started off with his brothers and cousins.

Ciro Coppa loudly ordered Pepè not to answer them, speaking in a tone loud enough for the Salvos and Garofalos to hear.

XVIII

"Is Don Pepè at home?" Raví gasped, at first failing to recognize Donna Bettina, who had hurried to open the door.

"And who might you be?" Donna Bettina asked in her turn, irritated by the furious clangor Raví had set up when he had jerked at the bellpull. Now she looked him over from head to foot.

"Oh, forgive me, madam! I am Marcantonio Raví, at your service. Forgive me for coming so early.... Damn that dog! Just listen to him bark.... I have to talk to Pepè about very urgent business that concerns both him and me."

"Please come in," Donna Bettina said somewhat more warmly, though she was still clearly uneasy at the sight of this thick-set fellow, whose suit was not well brushed and whose shoes were dusty, entering her house. "I think he's still in bed.... I'll go call him."

Don Marcantonio started to walk up and down the room nervously. Soon Pepè arrived, rubbing his hands that were stiff from the cold, and with his face hastily washed and dried.

"Here I am."

"Dear Don Pepè, tell me what your brother-in-law intends to do. I'm up to *here* with rage. I didn't close my eyes all night. And I'm almost as annoyed with you."

"With me?"

"Yes, sir! Let me get it all out or I'll burst, I tell you. How did you ever get it into your head to introduce that devil, that self-righteous demon, into my daughter's household?"

"I?" said Pepè. "He wanted to go along with me."

"What for? To set fire to my house? Tell me at once what he intends to do."

Pepè protested that he knew nothing of Coppa's intentions. He said that he too was sorry about the things Ciro had said the previous evening at Alcozèr's house, and he added that he wanted to find some excuse to prevent his brother-in-law from returning to visit Stellina.

"Find it, Don Pepè," Raví exclaimed. "Just you find it, for God's sake! I took you for an ingrate and I'm heartily sorry. I thought you and your brother-in-law were in cahoots to ruin my daughter. I was wrong. Of course, it would ruin you as well. Let us speak frankly: Make it clear to that madman that it's a matter of your own interests . . . that are at stake. . . . My daughter needs no more than one more push such as she got last night to turn all our well-laid plans into a cocked hat, I can tell you. Her face lit up when she heard that the law could help her out and could give her back her freedom. . . . 'What freedom, you little idiot?' I asked her. 'What do you hope to accomplish? Where would you go?' I tried to get on her good side. I even went so far as to tell her that I knew who it was she liked and I begged her, for that person's happiness as well as her own, to be both prudent and patient. . . . A year or two . . . what's that out of a lifetime? If I was told, you must live the most wretched life—in chains—for two years, or five years, for that matter, and then as a reward you'll be rich and free, wouldn't I agree to it? Who wouldn't? That's no sacrifice! What I call sacrifice is when one never gets any reward. I made a sacrifice, for instance, when I married off my daughter to an old man, for her exclusive benefit. If my veins had run gold, I'd have bled myself white to make her rich and happy. But she, the ungrateful girl . . . well, enough of this. I told her, 'Daughter, how can you make your dreams come true if you don't do this? . . .' See how I've had to go about it, Pepè? And here you come along and play havoc with the whole plan by bringing that nosy know-it-all into the house. Now, however, *now* what's the situation? My daughter let it be understood that she's furious with you, too, since she suspects you were in on my deal to have her marry the old man. . . ."

"I?" Pepè exclaimed, blushing to the whites of his eyes. "How could I have been?"

"Oh, I stood up for you!" Don Marcantonio cut him short in order to reassure him. "I stood up for you, in general terms ... you see, I never mentioned you by name specifically, of course. ... I must have some heavy sins on my soul without knowing it, Don Pepè, for God to refuse me the grace of ridding this world of that seventy-two-year-old piece of rancid fruit! By the way, yesterday I ran into the doctor who took care of him and saved his bloody life for him. And I couldn't keep from telling him, 'That's some favor you did me!' Well, as I said, enough of all this. You and I understand each other, Don Pepè. I just came by to open your eyes to the situation: you be careful your brother-in-law doesn't wreck everything for you. Let me tell you again that you've got to let him know clearly how things stand. After all, what can I be accused of? Only of having wanted to assure first my daughter's financial independence and then her happiness. That's no crime. I'm a very god among fathers, at that rate. I'll be on my way, Don Pepè; see that you attend to it."

Alletto was left greatly troubled and secretly annoyed with Stellina. Didn't she love him any longer? Or couldn't she understand that, by rebelling as she was doing, her whole position would be destroyed? Was her hatred for her old husband really greater than her love for him? And if she did suspect that there had been an early, secret agreement between him and her father, wouldn't her love have turned to hate? Wasn't it clear that her rage would be turned against him, too? What could he do?

In all this confusion, he felt he was going mad and he thought, gloomily, she wants to free herself of her old husband! And how is she to go about it, since her father won't have her in his house under those circumstances and since my hands are tied? Is she thinking of another way of regaining her freedom? And can I truly advise her to be patient? If she really loved me, she would be giving herself that advice. ... Doesn't she love me any longer?

Yet, every day before yesterday. ...

Another thought popped into his head: in order to get even with him, could Mauro Salvo have written her, insinuating that there was an understanding between Pepè and Raví? That bully was capable of anything! Yes, yes, that must have been it. "I must absolutely clear myself and prove that the imputation is a calumny. I'll openly take a stand against Raví's position. I'll ask Ciro so insistently to help me find work that he'll get me a job, and then...."

He decided to go straight off to his brother-in-law's house, but then another thought detained him. Mauro Salvo and his gang, like a band of mad hunters, were supposed to be searching the town for him. He began to think of ways of getting to Coppa's house without running smack-dab into his rival.

XIX

He was still turning the question over in his mind when he beheld Ciro standing before him: Ciro Coppa in the Allettos' house!

Donna Bettina, on seeing him, had been rooted to the spot and hadn't been able to utter a word. Ciro had walked in without so much as a greeting.

"You here?" Pepè exclaimed on seeing him. "Who opened the door?"

"Your mother, and she's still standing there as if she'd seen a ghost," Ciro replied darkly.

"Well . . . you know, it's as if . . ." Pepè tried to excuse his mother.

Ciro interrupted. "She's an old woman, and I don't blame her; you, on the other hand, are an ass, and that's why you're surprised to see me. Well, that's enough of that. Why aren't you dressed yet? What are you waiting for? Go get dressed, and let's be on our way."

"To see Signora Alcozèr? Don't you think it's a bit early?"

"No. We're calling on business, not to pay a visit. Dress yourself in my presence: you're likely to take two hours, otherwise."

"Five minutes," Pepè protested. "All right. Let's go in my room."

They went into the bedroom, and Ciro could not suppress a giggle and a nod of the head at sight of the twin beds.

"Oh, I'm quite aware of it . . ." Pepè sighed. "But since mother. . . . Did you say we were calling on business? I didn't quite understand."

"Yes, business, business!" Ciro answered brusquely. "I thought about it all night long, and today . . ."

"You thought about Signora Alcozèr?" Pepè asked timidly, peeking out from his shirtfront as he slipped the shirt on.

"Not exactly about *her*. I thought about her case. This is an infamous injustice that must be righted at all cost."

"Of course. But . . . excuse me . . . how would you propose to go about it?"

"Finish getting dressed, will you? Don't waste any more time."

"All right, all right . . . but didn't you hear her father last night?"

"I don't give a damn about her father," Coppa replied. "I'll crush him like the rat he is. Legally."

"That may be," Pepè conceded. "But . . . if you don't mind . . . please tell me . . . would you like to have the marriage annulled?"

"That's my business. In any case, it's really up to the lady."

"True enough," Pepè agreed again. "But . . . what would happen then?"

"I tell you that's my business. Get dressed!"

Pepè was brought up short by an idea that struck him all at once, and he looked at his brother-in-law aghast. Then he started to throw his clothes on helter-skelter, in a manner quite contrary to his usual meticulous fashion. "Why not?" he said to himself. "He's quite capable of it. He's capable of anything, as he himself puts it, in order to get the satisfaction of crushing Raví and Mauro Salvo. He's decided to stand up for my interests? Then he'll defend me to the bitter end. He's not the kind of man who does things by halves. On the contrary—it's not enough for him to *win*, he has to triumph. Oh, God, in this fashion Stellina will at last be mine! And then . . . then he'll think about getting me some work. . . ."

As if in answer to Pepè's tacit thoughts, Ciro said, "Her father says he won't have her in his house? Small harm done! For the time being, there's that dim-witted sister of mine, Rosaria, who is the Mother Superior at the College at Sant' Anna, and she will be able to lodge her at the school until the case is settled. Then we'll see. If she's willing, there's always my house."

"Your house?" Pepè asked, smiling.

"Dear Pepè, if you don't like the idea, there's nothing I can do about it."

"Not at all ... not at all. ..." Pepè beat a hasty retreat. "Why should it offend me?"

"You're thinking of your mother, perhaps."

"Not at all. ... You'll see that Mother, poor soul, is quite used to accepting the exigencies of a situation."

"So much the better!" Coppa exclaimed. "I scarcely thought you had enough common sense to realize that I absolutely must have a woman in the house. As I was saying, I thought about it all night. ... I absolutely must have a woman in the house, if only on account of the boys. I can't be their governess for the rest of my life. My health is suffering from the strain already. Besides, I have to get on with my profession. This way, if she's willing, I'll kill two birds with one stone: I'll do an act of kindness and I'll look after my own welfare at the same time."

"Of course, of course," Pepè approved, beaming with joy. "Ciro, you'll see what kind of woman she is! How good she is!"

"So, you approve of the idea?"

"Why ever wouldn't I? But one more point ... dear Ciro," he added hesitantly. "I would like to ask you, afterward, to give a little thought to finding me a job ... so that I shouldn't weigh on you even the least bit. Then I'd be really happy."

"I'll think about it, don't worry," Ciro answered vaguely. "And now let's go."

This time, they found Mauro Salvo and Fifo Garofalo— those two representing their entire contingent—at Alcozèr's house. They had come far earlier than usual, on the pretext of paying a call on the patient. Thus Stellina could free herself of their presence, when Coppa and Pepè arrived, by ushering them into Don Diego's room.

"Here we are, by ourselves!" she said, smiling as she reentered the sitting room. "Please sit down, honored lawyer, and you too, Don Pepè. ..."

Ciro acted as if he had lost his tongue. He stared at Stellina, who seemed so different from the way she had been the evening before. Suddenly, he did not know what to do with his hands. They seemed to be causing him acute discomfort. First he thrust them into his trouser pockets, then into his vest pockets, and finally into his jacket pockets; then, bowing, he stammered a thank you and, once seated, he placed his hands on his knees and began to speak, his eyes lowered:

"Listen, Signora Stellina, I do not have the honor of know-ing what you think of me, of my character. The reputation I've made, believe me, in no way corresponds to my true nature: I seem overbearing to many because I will accept no overbearing behaviour by my peers toward me, nor will I bow to the provincial prejudices of the area or the individ-ual whims each man tends to develop on his own. I'll accept no show of brute force, not even from God. For these rea-sons, I may seem strange just because I want to be free in the midst of so many who are enslaved by others or by themselves—for instance, take my brother-in-law Pepè."

"Who, me?" Pepè exclaimed, almost as if shaken out of a dream in which he had been following the apparently ir-relevant intricacies of Coppa's discourse, the while admiring his mellifluous delivery.

"Yes, enslaved by yourself and by others," Ciro repeated, calmly, firmly, with tranquil conviction, while Stellina smiled. "One can be poor and yet free. Yet it seems that your father, madam, does not see it that way. Each of us un-derstands life in his own way. As for me, I repeat, I am not overbearing. I always do whatever I must do, and I always know what I'm doing. So much as a preamble to the state-ment that I was greatly moved by the scene I witnessed here last night and by your own words. I thought about the situation at some length, signora, and I considered every angle of your case."

"Thank you," said Stellina, bowing her head.

"You may thank me later," Ciro went on. "Meanwhile, let me repeat what I had the honor to tell you yesterday: that you may, whenever you wish, loose the bonds of this marriage to which you submitted by force. We can produce evidence. If I am not misinformed, there are many witnesses. Yet if we could not produce a single one, I think it would suffice to produce—if you'll forgive me—your good husband, incontrovertible proof of the coercion to which you were subjected. What you yourself said about him yesterday and what I have heard from Pepè permit me to speak in this fashion. In short, without the slightest hesitation, I guarantee a verdict of dissolution of marriage. And, after mature reflection, I place myself once more at your complete disposal. Do not let your father's threats discourage you. You may know that I have a sister who is the Mother Superior at the College of Sant' Anna. Well and good. You could seek temporary refuge with my sister at her school. Thus, when all's said and done, there's nothing more to it than saying the word."

Pepè nodded approval, looking at Stellina, who was listening thoughtfully, her eyes cast down.

"Naturally," Ciro concluded, "I could not expect an immediate reply from you. It would not be prudent on your part. Think things over and then, a month or more from now, when you'll have had ample time to consider the pros and cons of the situation, you will give me your answer—yes or no. Meanwhile, if you'll allow me, I will call on you accompanied by our Pepè, here. Or, if you prefer, you can send me a simple note, a short one saying no more than, 'Signor Coppa, yes,' and I will go to work on the case at once. Are we agreed?"

XX

So Ciro began to frequent Alcozèr's house in which the Salvo and Garofalo boys could now be found again. But Don Diego was no longer the same after his illness. The sad humors of age, which he had, for so many years, diluted in ambiguous smiles, now gave an almost poisonous savor to every word he uttered, and these in turn affected Stellina's nature so that she grew sadder day by day.

Coppa's presence had upset the old man's plan of defense. Pepè Alletto and Mauro Salvo had been pushed into the background by the person of this man who had entered his house and openly challenged his every right over his wife. Ciro frightened him and kept him in an unbearable state of distress, as if he were almost ashamed of himself —a feeling he had never known until now. Everything he had aimed at in these last years—and because of which he had remarried—was now lost to him: he could not enjoy life through the happiness of those around him.

"A foretaste of hell?" he asked himself. "No, no. What an idea!"

However, he could not foresee the end of this new state of affairs, nor could he see his way clear of the hedge of thorns that had come to block the end of his long, flowery way.

Ciro, meanwhile, watched over Stellina without seeming to do so. Every so often he would look at her, and she read in that glance that seemed so severe and full of good will not only his determination to wait patiently but his detestation and scorn for the presence and chatter of the young men. And she saw protection as well as patient waiting in his glance.

Pepè felt himself protected, too, although he was inwardly undecided as to whether he should give up Raví's secret support entirely—a prop he sensed was no longer strong enough to bolster the shaken structure of his shoes. But should he really rely entirely on the discretion of his brother-in-law?

"Ciro, you see ... well! ... enough of this, let's wait and see. ... "

Ciro, with his temper and unexpected outbreaks, did not, in truth, give him much confidence. "Except for the fact," he told himself, "that since he's been in this, he's stood firm. He seems like another person: controlled, prudent ... a little stiff, it's true, but who would ever have expected it? He's always civil, even friendly sometimes, especially with Fifo Garofalo. ... And I see he takes better care of his appearance: starched linen, new suit ... good for Ciro!"

The Salvo and Garofalo boys did not react in the same way, however, though they were determined to continue their visits to Don Diego's house. In the long run, Coppa's presence put everyone ill at ease, demanding as it did a circumspection and reserve that could not be tolerated indefinitely.

Stellina felt this and grew more fretful every day, suspended in what even she recognized as a precarious position and one she did not know how to resolve. Her very perplexity kept her in a state of perpetual agitation. Her fretfulness was further worked on daily by the exhortations and advice her father gave her; the increasingly sour reactions of her husband who, not having the courage to rid himself of all these hangers-on, insisted that she do it for him; and finally the fear she harbored that one day or another an outbreak—or worse—would take place between Coppa and Mauro Salvo, who nursed his resentment darkly and in silence.

Under such conditions and after another scene, more disgusting than usual, with her father and her husband, she told Coppa one evening that she was ready to seek refuge in the nunnery of Sant' Anna in care of a sister of his. She said she would go there forever, if need be, just to be quit of the hellish life she was leading, and asked him meanwhile to take whatever steps were necessary to rid her of her husband, if that were possible.

XXI

Three days later, Don Diego Alcozèr arrived at Raví's house, exclaiming, with his arms in the air:

"She's run away! She's run away!"

"Who? My daughter? Your wife?"

"Quondam, quondam . . ." he corrected Raví, accompanying his wry little smile with a gesture of protest. *"Quondam,* if you don't mind. . . . She's run away. And I'm delighted!"

Marcantonio Raví slumped into a chair as if he had been struck by lightning.

"Run away . . . with whom?"

"Only she knows," Don Diego answered happily, shrugging his shoulders. "It's all one to me whether she went off alone or in company. I brought with me the . . . whatsis . . . the . . . the *thing* from the court."

"Have we come to this already?" Raví exclaimed, struggling to his feet. "It's Coppa. It's all his fault . . . the scoundrel! He's ruined my daughter. . . . And you, you old fool, you let her run away!"

"My dear fellow, I'd have opened the door for her myself just so as to be left in peace."

"Rosa, Rosa!" Don Marcantonio called.

Donna Rosa appeared in the doorway, as placid as ever. "What's the matter?"

"It's . . . you see . . . your son-in-law here. . . ."

"Ex, ex. . . ."

"She's run away, Rosa! Run away!"

"Stellina?"

"Cover your face, old wife! We had to wait until we had turned gray for our daughter to cover us with shame!"

"I don't understand a word you're saying..." Donna Rosa said, stunned.

"Let me tell you all about it," Don Diego broke in. "This morning... Oh, Marcanto'—quiet down!"

"O God! O God!" Donna Rosa cried, rushing to the aid of her husband, who was furiously hitting his head as he stamped his feet and howled like a child.

"Leave me alone! Leave me alone! It's too great a dishonor! This is my reward! Ah, ungrateful girl! In court... in court..."

"Calm down, Marcantonio. This isn't the end of the world," Don Diego urged him. "Dissolution of matrimony. ... She has asked for it, and I agree a hundredfold. I'd agree to anything...."

"You, too?" Don Marcantonio cried, grabbing Don Diego by the arm and shaking him violently. "You too have the effrontery to drag me to court? You!"

"Excuse me, but..." Don Diego stammered, almost hiding his head between his shoulders, so afraid was he of Raví's ferocious look. "Excuse me, but she wanted it..."

"Wanted what?" Don Marcantonio roared, without letting go. "She can't *want* anything! Tell me where she's gone. At once!"

"I don't know...."

"D'you want me to go cut Coppa's throat?"

"Cut whosever throat you please, but let me go! It's none of my business.... It's simply fantastic! You're angry with *me!*"

"I'm angry with everybody. Just you wait, Don Diego. ... Things won't end like this.... We'll handle things right ... a proper dissolution... without dragging my honorable name, I beg you, in the mud..."

"A *proper* dissolution?" Don Diego asked timidly, hesitant. "But I... you know... how could I be left alone?"

"You mean you'd want to get married again?" Don Marcantonio thundered, grabbing his arm again. "Answer me!"

"I don't know..." Don Diego stammered, his back to the wall. "But... if your daughter..."

"I'll return her to your house at once! Just you wait. I'll
go see that assassin!"

"Please, Marcantonio!" his wife begged.

"Quiet, you!" Raví yelled at her. "I'll go armed with my
rights as a gentleman and a father: I am defending the hon-
or of my daughter."

"Marcantonio! Marcantonio!" Donna Rosa cried, rubbing
her forehead as she stood at the top of the stairs.

XXII

Urging himself on with imprecations of rage, Marcantonio
Raví hurried at breakneck speed to Coppa's house. When he
reached the door, he was out of breath.

Pepè Alletto came to open the door.

"You here?" Don Marcantonio cried. "Ungrateful wretch!
You, too?"

His yelling was interrupted by a terrible whiplash across
the desk in the office nearby, and a moment later Coppa
burst into the outer office.

"Who is it? Who dares raise his voice ..."

"Forgive me, honored lawyer!" Raví said, taking off his
hat.

"Out! Out of here!" Coppa said, pointing to the door with
his whip. "Out you go! Immediately!"

"No, sir! I came to ... I beg your pardon ... Don Pepè,
tell him for me ..."

"Get him out of here right away!" Ciro ordered his
brother-in-law.

"I am amazed, Don Pepè. You!" Raví pleaded, offended.
"I beg your pardon, Your Honor ... If you'll just let me
speak, I'll tell you on my knees."

And so saying, Don Marcantonio started to get down on
his knees. At this point, Donna Carmela Mèndola appeared
in the doorway. She was Raví's irritating neighbor, and on
seeing him, she pointed her finger at him and started to
yell.

"He's the one. Yes, sir, he's the one! He beat his daughter, yes, sir. I'll swear to it before man and God! I'm
not afraid. He's the one!"

"You keep quiet!" Coppa told her, furious. "And you,"

he added, grasping Raví by one arm, "you get out of here! I won't have scenes in my house!"

Don Marcantonio turned very pale and threatened Coppa with his eyes. He said, his voice trembling, "After all ..."

Coppa gave him a good push: "On your way!"

"I'm an old man!" Raví exclaimed, passing the hand he had raised threateningly over his hair.

"Ciro ..." Pepè begged his brother-in-law.

But Coppa replied sternly, "Out you go! Just remind yourself that you are an old man in case others, because of your own imprudence, forget it."

"Imprudence?" Raví said. "But I've come to . . ."

"Tell your reasons to the judges. In the meantime, get out of here!"

As soon as Raví had gone, Donna Carmela wanted to praise the lawyer for the way he had handled him.

"Not at all!" Ciro contradicted. "I behaved badly. But because of you! You shouldn't have come."

"Unnatural father ..." she went on.

"Not at all!" Ciro contradicted her again, more violently than before, and growing visibly angry. "He thought and still thinks he was acting for the good of his daughter. This in no way alters the fact that he has committed a crime. . . . Pepè, don't look at me with that idiotic expression on your face: you get on my nerves, I've already told you. Now, let's get back to work. Sit down and start writing."

Pepè had become Ciro's copyist and errand boy. His happiness in those days was only marred by the fear that he might not give his brother-in-law entire satisfaction. He was in a state of perpetual surprise. Coppa ordered him about sharply, but Pepè felt unbounded gratitude toward him, well recognizing the fact that he had taken up his cause less for his sake than out of a sense of correctness and justice. Pepè admired him, and rubbing his hands with joy, he repeated to himself Coppa's favorite expression:

"I won't take any bullying not even from God!"

But here he was paying no attention to business. "Get to work! Get to work!" He must think of nothing else until the case had been won and Stellina was his at last! Here, here, in this very house. . . . And Pepè, in an impulse of love, hugged himself and kissed his own hands as if they had been those of Stellina.

He had beaten the bush in Raví's entire neighborhood to gather witnesses to support the case Ciro had started. When at last nearly all the groundwork had been laid, Coppa asked him to call on Don Diego Alcozèr and ask him to a meeting.

"Most honored by the invitation," Don Diego told Pepè. "I'm quite ready. Be right with you."

Ciro greeted him very cordially, and Don Diego, glad of the welcome, wished to free his host from the possible embarrassment of asking certain difficult questions. He broached the subjects first himself.

"You gentlemen are young in comparison with me," he said, including Alletto in his glance, "and for that reason you could wait. But I am an old man, and I want to get out of this mess as quickly as possible. *Quonam pacto?* I am at your complete disposal, Your Honor. You tell me what you think I should do."

Ciro looked at him attentively for a moment, caught between surprise and suspicion. Then, in order to test his sincerity at once, he asked him:

"Well ... the solution ... you need make only a simple ... that is, if you are willing to do so ... a simple ..."

"Little statement?" Alcozèr prompted, accompanying the word with one of those cold little smiles Pepè knew so well. And he added, "One question. Will the case be heard in private session?"

"Certainly," Ciro replied. "If you wish it to be.... When you get right down to it, this is a slight enough sacrifice of vanity for a man who has been so fortunate as to reach your age."

"I have no vanity of that kind," the old man interrupted him sharply. "It would be ridiculous at my age. However, since this sacrifice you mention might, in some way, damage me for the future ... for those few days left me of the mad tomfoolery we call life ... I would prefer some other solution, if ..."

"This one," Ciro remarked, admiring the philosophic clarity with which Alcozèr dealt with the question and noting that he was ready to cede, "this solution is the surest, and the most rapid."

"Well," Don Diego concluded, shrugging his shoulders and smiling, "in order to get it over with...."

Since Alcozèr, who was, after all, the party most concerned, raised no objections, the case was soon placed on
the docket—thanks to Ciro's efforts and maneuvers—and,
when it was called, was tried behind closed doors.

A crowd of curious snoopers impatiently awaited the
judge's decision. Pepè Alletto had a fever and sat outside the
closed doors wringing his hands, despite the fact that the court
attendant on duty tried to cheer him up from time to
time: "You just listen to me. I know what I'm talking about:
the case is as good as won!"

Finally the door opened. Ciro, beaming, announced victory. Everyone applauded and exclaimed. Even Don Diego
Alcozèr clapped his hands, laughing. But Don Marcantonio
came out of the courtroom shaking his shaven head, his
teeth clenched, tears running down his flushed face: "My
daughter! My daughter! They've as good as killed my daughter for me."

Pepè wanted to embrace his brother-in-law, but Ciro, in
the excitement of his triumph amid all the applause, pushed
him away almost angrily.

The President of the Tribunal, ringing his bell, had the
corridor cleared, but as the crowd followed along in the
street and continued to applaud, Ciro spoke to them:

"Fellow citizens, those fathers were heroes who sacrificed
their daughters to propitiate the gods for some noble undertaking of the fatherland! But what words would describe
a father who sacrifices his own daughter to Mammon, for
his own ends?"

"Mammon! Mammon! Down with Mammon!" the crowd
cried, amid laughter and applause.

And from that day forth, Raví was known to the whole
town as Marcantonio Mammon.

XXIII

Pepè Alletto told himself that the reason Ciro had worked
so hard to win the case was a matter of strength of character. But when he saw that Ciro was busy getting rid of
his old furniture in order to make room for new things, he
began to question the accuracy of his own judgment.

"Can he be doing all this just for me?" He did not dare

ask him anything. After his triumph, Ciro, instead of becoming more cheerful, grew daily more and more dour.

"Pepè," he said one morning, taking him by the lapels of his coat and pulling him into a corner, "you have to tell me the truth: promise me, first. You *have* to tell me. If you lie, just look out for yourself!"

Pepè, who was relieved to feel some sort of understanding just around the corner—although an uneasy one—promised readily enough.

"I can't tell you how many days ago," Ciro went on, "I lost my peace of mind. You remember that you told me once how that idiot, Mauro Salvo, was paying court to Stellina. Was it true?"

"It was true enough, but she paid no attention to him," Pepè answered, trying with a smile to calm the threatening frown on Ciro's brow.

"Swear it!" Ciro demanded.

"What am I to swear to?" Pepè asked. "I know she didn't, and that's all there is to it."

"You know that Stellina never, never, paid the least attention to Salvo's attentions?"

"Yes, yes. I know she didn't."

"Swear it!"

"All right, I swear!"

Ciro started walking up and down his office, his chin drawn in and his hands in his pockets. His expression was gloomy, full of dissatisfaction.

"What are you getting yourself worked up about?" Pepè said. "You're worried without cause ... you're letting yourself be upset by something that has no basis in fact, I swear it again. ... When you come to think of it, I should know, if anyone does."

"You don't know anything!" Ciro roared, stopped in front of him, his eyes blazing.

Pepè shrugged.

"How should you ... I was there ..."

"Oh, you were there ..." Ciro broke in, his face contorted with rage. "You were there, were you? And a lot of other fools were there along with you! That house was open to everyone. ... And there was Stellina, smack in the middle of the group, while the old man was asleep. ..."

"It's true, we were all there," Pepè admitted. "But there

was no harm in that. . . . You're just jealous, so you can't understand. . . . We played innocent, harmless games, and we . . ."

"Innocence, you idiot, brings children into the world!" Ciro interrupted furiously. "There must be something behind it. Otherwise, how do you explain the fact that I've had to struggle till today to get her to agree to marriage? Explain that, if you can!"

"I explain it simply enough," Pepè said, seeking the right words, "by the fact that the poor girl . . . went through so much. . . . But, to tell you the truth, I wouldn't have expected it. . . . So, she didn't want to consider it?"

"She wanted to become a nun," Ciro answered darkly.

"But you've convinced her, now?"

"She convinced herself—with a little help from my sister. But tell me, now. Didn't you, with that foolish face of yours," Ciro went on, stopping to point a finger at Pepè, didn't you—tell me the truth, now—try to flirt with her?"

Pepè looked at him, stunned.

"What d'you mean . . . didn't I? I don't understand. . . ."

"Oh, come now. You know, it doesn't pay to play the fool with me!" Ciro said scornfully. "You, too, along with all the other idiots. . . . Well, enough of that. Now we've got to get the house in order. The furniture that's upstairs must be brought down and taken to the country to make room for the new things that are coming from Palermo. Then you'll go with me to City Hall. You'll be my witness."

"I'll be . . . your . . . what, what are you saying?" Pepè could scarcely manage to stammer. "I'll be your witness?"

"Do you mind?"

"What's going on here? Who's getting married?" He felt the floor give way beneath him and he pu. his hands to his temples, as if afraid they would explode. He closed his eyes to catch two tears that escaped, nonetheless, and ran down his ashen cheeks.

"It's nothing . . . nothing . . ." he said, almost to himself, his voice broken and his lips trembling. "You're right. . . . What a fool! How stupid! How could I have believed? . . . How could I have thought that you? . . .

"Have you gone mad? What are you permitting yourself to say?" Ciro cried. "Speak up! What got into your head?"

"Leave me alone, Ciro!" Pepè said, all patience gone, his tears flowing freely now.

"Oh, so you thought," Ciro inveighed, "you dared think that you would marry her! Had you come to an understanding? Speak up, damn you, or I'll strangle you...."

"I've told you, leave me alone!" Pepè cried, freeing himself from Ciro's grasp with the courage of desperation. "Isn't it enough for me to tell you that I've been a stupid idiot? Yes, yes, I was stupid enough to believe that what you did you did for me.... Now that's enough.... Marry her! What do you want of me? Hasn't she said yes?"

"But I want to know..." Coppa thundered, flinging himself on his brother-in-law.

Pepè tried to ward him off, then turned toward him with unusual daring. "Perhaps you didn't know? Or perhaps I didn't nearly get myself killed because of her? You didn't know that I've loved her all these years?"

"What about her?" Ciro babbled, his eyes aflame.

"Didn't she accept you?" Alletto repeated. "What more d'you want?"

"But between you two," Ciro went on, "tell me the truth or I won't answer for my actions. Between you and her... speak!"

"What do you want me to say?" Pepè groaned in Coppa's arms. "Leave me alone... you're hurting me...."

"Tell me the truth... what went on between you? I want to know...."

"There was a promise..." Pepè answered. "I was waiting for God to call the old man to his..."

"Then what?"

"Then you came on the scene.... She has accepted you. ...Now it's all over.... I don't know a thing, I can't do a thing about it... let me go.... It's all over...."

He took his hat from the rack, buffed it repeatedly with his sleeve, and went away, stunned.

Ciro stood there with his fists clenched against his cheeks, his eyes like those of a wild animal, and then he started to walk up and down the room.

XXIV

Don Diego Alcozèr saw Pepè Alletto on the street the day after Stellina's marriage to Coppa and called to him. As the young man drew near, his face troubled and his expression like that of a person about to faint, the old man spread his hand wide, applied the thumb to the end of his nose, and tried to waggle his four trembling fingers in the air.

"So much for you, Don Pepè! You were in such a hurry, dammit!"

"Don't bother me, you old fool!" Pepè broke out, shaking with rage.

Don Diego detained him by one arm.

"Now don't be so angry with me! Come here. . . . I, you and our ex-father-in-law should comfort each other. Come to my house. Marcantonio is coming along later, and this very evening, if you've no objections, we'll play a hand of cards together. . . . We'll keep each other company. . . ."

Pepè, wrapped in his own mourning, followed silently in Don Diego's footsteps. Alcozèr, staggering along on his wobbly old legs, chuckled to himself and turned around every so often to focus on his former presumptive heir.

"Forgive me for laughing, Don Pepè! But there are things in life to laugh at and things to cry over. I'm an old man and I haven't time to do both. I prefer to laugh. Besides, you'll do the crying for me. . . . Poor Don Pepè. You won't believe it, but I'm sorry for you! And to take you out of part of your misery right away, I might as well confess that I knew about it all the time: I knew you wanted to marry Stellina after my death, and that Marcantonio had agreed. That's why I said, 'our ex-father-in-law.' Well, what harm was there in that? I assure you I was mightily pleased over it, and d'you know why? Aside from your own qualities, I know that when someone desperately wants someone else to die, the 'victim' never dies. You were dear to me— like an amulet. Now, instead, what does it matter to you whether I live or die? But that time . . . remember? Tell me the truth: didn't you take me on that trip to the temples on purpose, the day it rained so hard? Heavens, Don Pepè, just think: you almost made it. . . . How maddening that thought must be! Bronchial pneumonia. . . . The good Lord made you enjoy my death and then snatched the enjoyment away from you, almost like seizing a piece of bread from between your very lips. Poor Don Pepè! And now. . . ."

Alletto stopped in front of Don Diego's door.

"If you want to go on talking like an idiot, I'll leave you here."

"No, no. Do come in, dear Don Pepè," Alcozèr said, once more taking him by the arm. "Come in! I'm sorry you won't find your future wife here anymore.... I'm only joking.... No one can hear us...."

Once inside the house, Don Diego led Pepè through the empty rooms, guessing most accurately what bitter pleasure the young man took in seeing once more those rooms Stellina had lived in. Alcozèr stopped in the dining room and, indicating one side of the bare table, said, as if to himself, "That's where she sat at dinner.... And over there, near the window, she would sit reading the novels Fifo Garofalo lent her...."

When they reached the bedroom, he did not point out anything special but, as he was changing into his lounging jacket, he spied Pepè looking at the double bed through the curtain. Don Diego snickered, then drew a long sigh and went to clap his young guest heartily on the shoulder.

"Ah, dear Don Pepè, day after tomorrow I'll be seventy-three.... If you had been less hasty.... Well, well, enough of this. I don't want to upset you.... There's the doorbell. It must be Marcantonio."

Raví did not expect to find Alletto in Don Diego's house. As soon as he saw him, his expression changed and he shouted, "Let me out of here!"

Don Diego held onto his coattails.

"Let me go," Don Marcantonio said, louder than ever. "I can't bear to set eyes on him."

"Come now, why ever not? Why?" Alcozèr asked, without letting him go. "Come back here. Let's all be friends again."

"It's he who ruined my daughter!" Don Marcantonio insisted.

Don Diego continued to work on him: "No, no. You mustn't say that. *Factum infectum,* and so on. He's more wretched than you, poor boy.... Come, come, now. Shake hands."

"Not even if Christ came down from the cross to ask me to," Raví protested.

"Come, now, Marcanto'! Give me your hand. Don Pepè, give me yours. That's it! Peace, once more. Don Pepè's only mistake—as I mentioned to him a moment ago—was haste! It's an understandable fault in a young man."

"No, sir!" Raví contradicted. "His mistake was bringing that archfiend into the house. I'll never recognize him as my son-in-law as long as I live. My daughter is dead to me! I'll not set eyes on her.... You've killed her for me, Don Pepè! Not another word ... let me weep.... You've killed her! Didn't I tell you he would be the ruin of both you and my daughter?"

"Pardon me," said Pepè, disturbed and touched by Raví's tears, "but wasn't I taken in and betrayed even worse than you? Admitting the fact that it was I who urged him to come here—which I don't—would I have done it if I had suspected or so much as supposed ..."

"Gentlemen, gentlemen ..." Don Diego interrupted them. "Do you want to listen to an old man? Don't give it another thought! That's the best advice we can have: recriminations are useless now.... Let's light the lamp, instead, and play a hand of cards...."

XXV

Every evening the three defeated men gathered at Don Diego's house to play cards. The conversation turned readily to Coppa, whom Raví, looking at Pepè, called "your brother-in-law."

"Brother-in-law, my foot!" Pepè answered. "My poor sister died, and it's he who made her die.... So let's call him your son-in-law."

"Son-in-law *if* I had recognized him," Don Marcantonio snapped. "Whereas you *have* recognized him as your brother-in-law. And you should still rue the day, as if you had murdered a brother."

Don Diego played the role of mediator during scenes like this, though inwardly he was exultant.

"Gentlemen, let's not exaggerate. Don't get excited.... Why do you always dwell on this subject, when you know it upsets you? Come, come ... let's pick up our hands! Let's not behave like young cocks in their cages who peck at each other instead of ... ah, giving each other reciprocal comfort. We've been wronged, betrayed, all three of us. Facts are facts, and we won't mention it again. Let's not judge a gallant gentleman by our case alone!"

"A murderer!" Raví shouted at this point, pounding his fist on the table.

"What, what! Did he murder your daughter?"

"Yes, *sir*! He did murder my daughter."

"Make up your mind how many people have murdered the poor girl. You used to say Don Pepè here..."

"Yes, he did!" Don Marcantonio went on. "He did, without intending to. With the hands of his brother-in-law."

"Your son-in-law," Pepè corrected him.

"What, again?"

And Don Diego hurriedly played a card. "I call you."

They played for a few cents a game and put their winnings aside to use for a dinner in town together. Raví wished in no wise to accept the repeated invitations of Don Diego, who would have wished to have him to dinner every night in order not to be alone.

"Forgive me, Don Diego, but I can't accept—oh, not because of you but because of the way people talk. They call me Mammon: I don't know what it means but, by God, you can yell it in the faces of those liars if I've ever asked for a cent, a wretched cent from you, even as a loan."

"Let them gossip!" Don Diego answered.

"No, sir! Let's play, and then we'll go to dinner. I'll pay for the meal since I've been losing more heavily than you two. Agreed?"

Pepè did not have the same reasons as Don Marcantonio to refuse Alcozèr's invitations, and he often stayed to supper with him, sometimes spending the night. He would share the double bed, the same one in which Stellina had slept. That was the chief reason that had induced him to stay in the first place—the voluptuous, bitter anguish of recalling her, of imagining her in that house.

Each evening, as soon as Raví had taken off, he and Don Diego would stand for a bit before going to bed on the little balcony that overlooked the countryside and, in the distance, the sea. They could see Coppa's country house from there, and Pepè, his head leaning on the iron of the railing, fixed his eyes on the light burning in the far-off house in the midst of the dark countryside. Over there, where the light was burning, there was Stellina! He could almost see her, almost follow her from room to room of that familiar house where his sister had spent so many unhappy years, and he asked himself, "What is she doing at this moment? What is she thinking? What is she saying?" And he felt destroyed within, swallowing in silence the tears that flooded his eyes as he fixed them on the distant light.

He let himself go and lost himself so completely in this vision that sometimes his head would slip from the railing little by little without his being aware of it, and almost fall.

"Don Pepè, are you asleep?" Alcozèr would ask.

And Pepè would shake his head to signify "no" so that his voice would not betray his tears.

"If you want to go to bed, I'm ready," Don Diego went on.

Pepè indicated by a gesture that he would like to wait another moment or two. He was certain that Stellina, like him, had been betrayed, tricked. Hadn't he heard from Ciro's own lips that she would have wished to stay on as a nun rather than consent to the unexpected betrayal of that marriage? Then she had given her consent, or, rather, she had had to bow her head, having understood that the one who loved her so much could give her no help and that her father would not take her back in his house. Further, she must have recognized that she could not even stay on in the nunnery under the direction of Coppa's sister.

And now, now she was there, there in the power of that overbearing man who had wrested her from Pepè's arms ... yes, wrested her with the brute force with which he was no doubt at this very moment forcing her to submit to his love —to submit with her body, but not, ah, *not* with her soul. ... Poor Stellina! He could only pity and commiserate with her....

Every day he worked on himself in this fashion, feeding his bitterness that led to self-deprecation, profound melancholy, and an awareness that he could do nothing to change matters. He had grown thin and pale, as if he had but now risen from a grave illness. If only he had not had to take care of that poor old mother of his ... if he had not feared to snap her thread of life....

On certain evenings, Don Diego annoyed him by talking of his terror-ridden fears, of the *spirits* that populated the vast deserts of his sleepless nights.

"I know that anyone who hasn't seen them doesn't believe in them. ... And those who have seen them, dear Don Pepè, don't speak of it for fear that at night the spirits will beat them. Because, you know, they beat people! To tell you the truth, I haven't felt the weight of their hands until now, but how many tricks they've played on me! They pull my covers off at night, turn the chairs upside down in the rooms, turn out my night light. . . . And I swear I've seen them with these very eyes. On certain nights, for instance, I've seen a head with curly red hair and its tongue sticking out peer around at me from behind the curtains of the alcove. . . . When my . . . let's see . . . yes, my second . . . or was it the third? . . yes, Luzza, my second wife, died—well, after a few days her spirit was present around me in this house. I heard her going from room to room every night, like the good housekeeper she was . . . blessed soul, if I say so myself. . . . And one night I saw her stick her head out of the doorway and look at me in bed. She smiled and waved at me, as if she wished to say, 'Enjoy the warmth of your bed; I'll see to the house.' Another night I heard a hellish row in the dining room. What was going on? Nothing. My other wife, the first one, Angelina, had turned up, too, and they were fighting between themselves. I tell you I heard them myself, with these very ears: each one was saying to the other that she was the true mistress of the household. . . . Then, *bang,* all of a sudden! I can't tell you how many plates fell to the floor. . . . What a racket! I jumped out of bed and went to the dining room—you can guess how afraid I was!— and there were all the broken dishes on the floor. . . . Say what you will! . . ."

"Couldn't it have been a cat?"

"Don Pepè, what cat could do a thing like that? Besides, I've never had a cat in the house. . . ."

"Perhaps a rat, then. . . ."

"Yes, or perhaps an earthquake! It's a question of calling them by one name or another. You call them rats, because you don't believe in them. And would you say they were rats when, for example, you hear their steps in the next room running about hurried and light-footed, with the heels going tap-tap-tap, or moving instead like a person who is trying to gather his thoughts? Are they cats or rats when you hear yourself called the worst names possible by four different voices? This has happened to me, and it's why I don't want to be alone at night, for then all four of my dead wives return to mistreat and revile me. Ah, Don Pepè, may you be freed of all such troubles!"

But it wasn't enough for Don Diego to talk about his spirits. Often, during the night, tormented by insomnia, he would wake Pepè because he thought he heard a sound in the silence of the house.

"Don't pinch me, for God's sake!" Pepè would cry. "Be quiet: I'm not asleep! For the hundredth time, let me tell you I don't want to be pinched. If you keep it up, tomorrow night you might as well get ready to sleep by yourself."

XXVI

No, no, Don Diego could not endure the threat of having to stay alone at night. In order to woo sleep and to spare Alletto the nuisance of his pinches, he drank a little more than the usual amount he had set himself many years before. But this solution did him little good: that extra glass tasted bitter, and he had to force it down.

"Don Pepè, my sleep medicine!" he would say at supper. "Let's hope that tonight it works."

In the beginning, it did work, but later—in the middle of the night—he would wake, and his old distress would be on him. Then, ever so quietly, a little pinch for Don Pepè.

"At it again! Can't you keep still?"

"Forgive me, Don Pepè. I wanted to ask you something."

"What 'something'? Go to sleep!"

"I can't, if you don't free me of a doubt I just had as I was thinking, a few moments ago. But you must tell me the truth! While I was ill, you were so good—or *seemed* so good—to me, remember? You were always here at the house, night and day. . . . Well, tell me the truth, now: in some idle moment, did you and Stellina? . . ."

"Are you out of your mind?" Pepè yelled at him.

"No. Be patient. It wouldn't mean a thing to me, at the moment. I'd simply transplant the horns of cuckoldry to Don Ciro's head. I've gotten rid of them. Tell me the truth!"

Pepè simply turned his back on him, not deigning to reply.

"I tell you, it wouldn't matter. . . . One rack of horns or another, after all. . . . I'm a philosopher, Don Pepè! Five wives, you understand! You can just imagine what a forest of horns

I must have on my head. Some evenings, while you are out there on the balcony dreaming and sighing away, I think about it, and I feel them growing and stretching, growing clear up to heaven . . . growing, growing. . . . I feel that if I should move my head I'd disturb the whole planetary system. . . . They should be like a flight of stairs for me when I die, a hundred years from now. My soul will run up those mammoth horns like a squirrel until it reaches Heaven, while all the bells on earth will ring a Gloria. . . . Don Pepè, are you asleep?"

The ingrate slept, or pretended he slept, and Don Diego fretted and fumed and flew into a passion. "Fine company he gives me!" And, to take his mind off his troubles, he began to think about a sixth marriage.

"The proverb says that he who wants too much ends up by having nothing. If I were to leave my money to some good work, divided into so and so many portions, it would benefit a number of people for a shorter or longer time, but in a very small way. For that reason, according to me, it would be better to leave it to a single person who would willingly earn it by a brief sacrifice, a sacrifice that in itself might be considered an act of charity: taking care of an old man like me. And for this person to have a just reward for her sacrifice, she must be young and in shape to enjoy her wealth and the years before her. What would an old woman do with my money? Besides, I hate old age. According to my plan, youth would be served. . . . You think the whole countryside would start laughing if I were to marry again? Well, people laugh so seldom nowadays that if they laughed at me I'd have done them another service. Let the whole town go with me to City Hall, all of them laughing their heads off. It would be a sign of good luck. . . . I've thought it over, and you'll see—I'll do it. I shan't say a word to Marcantonio about it for the moment, because I'm sure it would upset him. . . ."

And Don Diego was not wrong. In fact, the very evening Raví heard that his *quondam* son-in-law was about to take a sixth wife, he arrived at Don Diego's house in a rage.

"What! At your age, you're thinking of marrying again?"

"After all," Don Diego chuckled, "let me remind you, Marcantonio, that I'm only a year older than I was when I married your daughter."

"That's all well and good," Don Marcantonio said, swallowing bile, "but it *is* a year later, and then, think of the scandal. Do you discount that? A year ago your name was not on everyone's lips. ... I'm speaking in your own best interests. ... Don't expose yourself to ridicule, dear Don Diego, and to a sure refusal. ..."

"As to the refusal ... never fear ... all I have to do is make up my mind which one I want ..." Don Diego reassured him. "I've already had four or five proposals."

"What a townful of swindlers!" Don Marcantonio burst out. "Five proposals! You see? It was envy, pure and simple envy, that made them talk against me when I gave you my daughter. And to think they called me an unnatural father, a Mammon ... went around saying I sold my own flesh and blood. Swindlers! I was right all along!"

Raví did not know that, among the four or five proposals, there was one from the Mèndola woman, his implacable neighbor, offering Don Diego her daughter. But Marcantonio's outburst against the town served to calm him, and he settled down to play cards with his two companions.

"Young men who are in a position to get married are hard to come by these days," Don Diego said, between one hand and the next. "Besides, an old man in my position, dear Marcantonio, attracts others just as I attracted you. ..."

"Why, of course! It's obvious. No need to tell *me*," Raví said heartily. "But this time, Don Diego, I'd advise you to die soon after the ceremony. ..."

"Ha! Ha!" Don Diego giggled, making the sign of the horns with both his hands.

"I can wish you the same," Marcantonio exclaimed. "In fact, I hope you live a hundred years to torment all those who have spoken against me. However, I'd also advise you to change your tune. Don't have so many young people come to the house. Otherwise, you might have a repetition of what happened this time. ..."

Don Diego agreed and added:

"I'm sorry for your sake, Don Pepè, but this time keep away from me! But, since you're a good young man and you deserve it, I might advise my young wife in my will to pick you rather than someone else. ..."

Pepè took no part in the conversation. He smiled weakly

at Don Diego and suggested they stop playing cards for the
evening.

XXVII

"If you're really aware and sure that I love you, why are
you afraid of me?"

"Whoever told you I was afraid of you?"

"Your eyes."

Stellina quickly lowered her eyes.

"No! Look at me. . . . There! Those aren't the eyes of a
woman who feels sure of herself!"

"Perhaps not . . ." Stellina admitted timidly. "It's because I
haven't yet understood you and I'm afraid of displeasing you
unintentionally."

"Isn't it rather," Ciro countered, "isn't it rather because,
deep down, your conscience is troubling you about something?"

This thought was like a nail driven into his skull night and
day.

He had made a pact with himself not to set foot in town as
long as Alcozèr was alive. He felt he could not have stood
the sight of that mummy who had seen the woman who belonged to *him* in the intimacy of the night; that mummy who
could evoke for him the memory of those nights in which
Alcozèr had been by her side and soil them for him.

The peaceful countryside did not manage to calm his spirit.
He saw and heard nothing, absorbed as he was in his own
inner gnawing. He did not want Stellina to suffer from the depression that this new kind of jealousy for an old man caused
in him and from his remorse at having married her—a
remorse exacerbated by the strong love he felt for her.

To take his mind off the whole thing, he turned to violent exercise. He bought twenty horses from Tunis at a
horse fair and now set about training them on the heath just
as a circus trainer might do, whipping them up with all the
fury of the hundred devils raging in his flesh. Then, off with
them! All twenty of them he herded before him. He drove
them at a gallop, trampling the grain to shreds like a veritable
scourge of God. Off with them! Off, in a cloud of dust, and
running as far as the fountain.

"Whoa!"

And there he would water them.

On the way back, he was sometimes like the man who kept looking for the very beast he was riding. Then, what curses, what imprecations mingled with commands to halt:

"Whoa! Easy on, there! Whoa, damn you!"

And he would count them again. In the end, he would beat the poor horse he was on, as if it were to blame that he hadn't counted right in the first place.

Stellina, meanwhile, began to have some faint idea that her husband loved her in his own way. Still, she had no idea how she could go about returning his love, supposing she wanted to. She found no way to enter his heart and tame it. She would have liked to recognize and enjoy her own contentment—if not with the present state of things, then at least with the fact that she had escaped from her previous hateful situation. But on the one hand, this was prevented by the anguished perplexity, the unremitting anxiety about doing good or ill, into which Ciro's nature forced her; on the other hand, by the fear that he would discover what had taken place with Alletto—whose very memory she forced herself daily to erase. She was afraid that if even a fleeting thought of him crossed her mind, Ciro would be able to read it in her eyes.

In this frame of mind, poor Stellina, after five months of wordless torment, had a miscarriage and nearly died. Then it was that Coppa realized he must return to town.

XXVIII

"Am I out of my mind? Ciro Coppa jealous of an old man?"

As soon as he reached town, he felt a lightening of the great weight that had oppressed him for months in the country. And in this new frame of mind he wanted to test his own strength. He no longer feared rivals. What reason had he, Ciro Coppa, to fear Pepè Alletto, for example? What the devil!

Instead, he sought him out all over town and, having found him, called out to him, while Alletto, pretending not to have seen him, sped in the opposite direction.

"Pepè! Once I promised you a job. . . . Well, I've found one for you. Do you want to come to work for me?"

"For you?"

"Yes, in my office. I'm starting up my practice again tomorrow. You'll have a good many things to copy—so, better you than another. Just don't make any spelling errors. . . ."

Pepè stood there with his mouth open, looking at him.

"Come on, come on," Ciro insisted. "Understand?"

"I understand, all right," Pepè answered, not yet able to take in the whys and wherefores of Coppa's offer.

"Do you accept?"

"I? . . . Yes, why not?"

"I'll expect you, then, tomorrow at eight. We'll get together on terms. Bye-bye."

"Has he gone mad?" Pepè asked himself as soon as Coppa had taken off. "What can he want of me? Does he want to see if anything went on between Stellina and me? Does he want to find us out?"

He decided not to go, and he was sorry he hadn't known how to refuse. But now, having accepted the offer, he could not back down. No, no: he must turn up in order to give Coppa absolutely no reason to suppose that he, Pepè, had any cause to be afraid of him.

The next day, promptly at eight, pale, with his thoughts every which way, he presented himself at Ciro's office.

"Just take a look around! Everything's changed," Coppa said, showing him his new desk, bookshelves, and the chairs lined up against the wall where he had now placed his copyist's desk. "And my life too has changed, let me tell you! There comes a day when a strong man knows he must engage in a higher kind of struggle, no longer against others but against himself. One must win out, dominate one's own nature, conquer one's animal traits, and acquire absolute control over oneself."

So saying, Ciro nervously brandished a whip while Pepè, confused and muddle-headed, nodded hearty approval.

"You approve, but you don't understand!" Ciro went on, after having observed Pepè narrowly for a moment. "One can't grasp such a concept lightly."

"I really wasn't . . ." Pepè stammered, trying on a feeble, embarrassed smile.

"I know, I know! Let me explain, let me give you an example. Until today, I was at such a point that a weak man like you, Pepè Alletto, could tell *me*, Ciro Coppa, 'Ciro, I

say you're a coward!' (Don't laugh, you fool.) If you were to
say such a thing, I might turn pale, clench my fists to control
my temper, close my eyes, swallow hard. But then, having
overcome my rage, I would answer you calmly, even courteously, 'Dear Pepè, you think I am a coward? Let us discuss
your statement, if you don't mind.' What do you say to
that? And I won't stop there! Each day will mark a new con-
quest over my baser nature, over the beast in me. You can
be sure I will come out on top! Meanwhile, sit down—that's
your desk. There are papers to be copied. Mind you, a good,
clear hand! Be careful about your punctuation, and watch
your spelling. . . . Nothing else to say."

XXIX

From that day forth, a new life of unspeakable anguish
began for Pepè. Every morning he went to Ciro's office with
his mind in a whirl of suspense and anxiety, after having
spent the night trying to understand or at least to catch a
glimmer of what it was Ciro wanted from him.

Ciro walked up and down the study in front of the copyist's table.

"Mind your spelling . . . I beg you. Yesterday you wrote
prestige with two *g*'s."

Every so often, he would stop. Pepè, hunched over, and
intent on his copying, yet feeling Coppa's eyes on him,
would ask himself: "Why is he looking at me that way?"

On other days, Ciro did not walk up and down. Instead,
he would sit with his face hidden by his arms, which he
held crossed before him on his desk. Then Pepè would raise
his eyes and look at him.

"What's eating him, I wonder?"

Sometimes, not understanding some word in the transcript
he was copying, he found himself obliged to ask Coppa about
it. He would call him quietly. Ciro would not reply.

"Is he asleep?" Pepè would ask himself, and he would call
again, adding, "Aren't you feeling well?"

"No, I don't feel well. I am all worked up inside," Ciro
would answer dourly, without raising his head.

Pepè would pull a long face at this enigmatic reply, think
it over for a moment or two, then shrug his shoulders, leave

a blank for the indecipherable word, and go back to his copying.

One day, leaping to his feet, Ciro cried, "Curses!" And again, "Curses! Curses!"

"What's the matter with you?" Pepè asked him, frightened by the sudden outburst.

"Tell me I make you tremble!' Ciro howled, leaning with both arms over Pepè's worktable. "Tell me so at once! Admit that when you see me, your knees buckle under you!"

"Why should they?" Pepè faltered.

"Oh, you idiot, don't you know that if I were to lay these hands on you, I'd crush you. I'd snuff you out!"

"I know," Pepè said with a tremulous smile, his eyes full of supplication. "But there's no reason. . . . unless you've gone mad. . . ."

Ciro flung himself away from the table.

"All right. Go on with your copying. I've reached the point where I must put a whip in your hand and order you to beat me until the blood comes! And it's all because of my ungovernable temper. I should be beaten, and if you go at it quietly, she'll not even hear it. I make her . . . make her unhappy . . . poor girl. . . . Beat me, beat away! Beat me, I deserve it!"

Ciro himself had begun to be afraid he was losing his mind. Since he had had this new fixation about overcoming his baser nature, he scarcely ate, he slept little, he had not a moment's peace. He wanted to give himself the major proof of his victory: this proof would be to have Stellina come into his office when Pepè was there. Walking back and forth, he was tempted to use the speaking tube that was in a corner of the office near the copyist's desk in order to tell Stellina to come down. He stopped to observe Pepè almost as if to prove to himself how ridiculous, how unworthy of him was the jealousy he felt for this worthless wretch, as pale as a piece of straw. Yet he could not, not yet, approach the speaking tube that attracted him there in the corner. And he went to his desk to slump down, face hidden by his hands, torn asunder inside. Finally, he cried out, "Damnation!"

Nor did his internal struggle end there in his office. At the Tribunal, at the Court of Assizes, he would yearn to overcome his rebellious feelings at all costs. He would turn to Pepè seated there beside him and tell him to go back to the office to pick up some paper or other he needed.

"If you don't find it, go upstairs and ask my wife to look for it...."

But as soon as Pepè left the hall, he would run after him and call out in the staircase of the Courthouse:

"Pepè, Pepè, come back...I don't need that paper anymore."

One day, however, he was not quick enough to call him back. The court attendants frowned at him. The public prosecutor was about to conclude his summation, and Ciro could not leave the hall—he had to speak next.

"Silence! Silence, by God!" Coppa cried, transfigured, electrified. He leaped to his feet and pounded his fist on the bench, facing the king's prosecutor. "At this very moment I am winning a sublime victory over myself and I can no longer permit you to pull down about my ears—or about the ears of the jurors—the wretched debris of the edifice of good sense that, for the last hour, you have been trying to demolish with your blunt and rusty pick!"

All hell broke loose: his fellow lawyers rushed toward Coppa to make him sit down and shut up. The presiding judge rose to his feet, ringing his bell for order. The judges and jurors were stunned. The public—of two minds about what had happened—burst into imprecations and applause. Amid the general uproar and confusion, Ciro overheard an abusive phrase uttered by the king's prosecutor, and picking up the inkwell from the bench, he threw it at him like a stone. Then the carabinieri, stationed at the entrances to the courtroom, moved in. The presiding judge cried:

"Place him under arrest!"

Coppa and the carabinieri began a frantic tussle. Like a trapped bull, Ciro sought every means to get them to unhand him when, all of a sudden, the men who were holding him felt him slip heavily to the floor, senseless.

There was a quick reaction of horror and consternation in the hall. The courtroom that had been emptying gradually was filled anew with a crowd of pale, anxious, stunned faces. From the jurors' benches, from the judge's seat, from the places reserved for the spectators, everyone, standing, looked at Coppa, who was now slumped in a chair, his head bowed to his chest, his breathing heavy, his frame convulsed with apoplexy.

XXX

Toward midnight, Stellina, Pepè, and Marcantonio Raví found themselves gathered about the bed on which Ciro had just ceased his death rattle, much as they had stood about another bed at another wake.

This time, however, Stellina was weeping, with her face hidden in her handkerchief; and her tears irritated Don Marcantonio, as dark and taciturn as ever, and humiliated Pepè.

Seated on the bench at the foot of the bed, with his arms about the shoulders of Coppa's two children who sat silently beside him, their eyes bathed in tears and fixed on the lifeless face of their father, Pepè thought of his sister Filomena who had died in this very room. Then as now the room had been lit by four funeral candles at the four corners of the bed, and he seemed to see her there, stretched out beside her husband. Here were the two little orphans, the two young beings left in that house. Pepè held them close to him and felt, in an exaltation of grief, that Filomena was entrusting them to him from the world beyond the grave. His glance sadly fixed on Stellina, he waited and waited for her to raise her eyes from her handkerchief, see him embracing the children, and understand.

At a certain point, Don Marcantonio burst out, "This fellow who seemed such a lion is lying here dead! And that old fellow is hale and hearty! Day after tomorrow he's going to marry Tina Mèndola, your good friend. . . . Don Pepè, after all. . . ."

He did not finish the sentence.

"Give me a pair of scissors, daughter. Feel how those candles splatter? You have to keep your eye on everything in life . . . even on this. . . ."

THE BLACK SHAWL

"Wait here," Bandi told d'Andrea. "I'll go in and talk to her. If she still refuses to see you, come in anyway!"

Both were nearsighted and stood very close together as they faced each other. Tall, thin, about the same age and build, they might have been taken for brothers, especially in their straightlaced look revealing finicky natures bent on doing everything just so. When they talked together, one of them would usually adjust the other's glasses on his nose, straighten his tie, or, if nothing else, idly finger the buttons of his coat. But they talked little, and their uncommunicative natures showed clearly in their gloomy faces.

Raised together, they had helped each other with their lessons right up to the time they entered the university—one to become a lawyer and the other a doctor. Now, separated during the day by their professions, they met each sundown for a walk along the road which led from town into the open country.

They knew each other so intimately that a sign, a word, a look was enough for the one immediately to grasp the other's thought. Their walk usually began with a brief exchange of words and was followed by a long silence while they mulled things over. Walking along with heads lowered like tired horses, their hands clasped behind their backs, neither of them felt any desire to look in the direction of the low wall bordering the road where a view of the whole countryside opened out: hills, valleys, plains, with the sea in the distance, all aglow under the last rays of the setting sun. It was incredible that anyone could pass by such a magnificent panorama without giving it even a fleeting glance.

"Eleonora isn't feeling well," Bandi had told d'Andrea the day before.

"Would you like me to take a look at her?" d'Andrea asked, gathering from his friend's eyes that his sister's illness was nothing serious.

"She says no."

They both frowned, thinking almost with hatred of the woman who had mothered them and to whom they owed everything.

D'Andrea, still a child when his parents died, had been taken in by an uncle who was in no way able to provide for him. Eleonora Bandi, orphaned at eighteen and with a brother much younger than herself, was able to manage at first, with painstaking economy, on the small nest egg left by her parents. Then, by giving piano and singing lessons, she kept her brother as well as his inseparable friend in school.

Eleonora was enormous, but the gentle sweetness of her features gave her that seraphic look often seen in churches on the faces of marble angels in flowing robes. The expression in her beautiful black eyes, fringed with velvety lashes, and the harmonious sound of her voice softened the impression made by the size of her body.

She played and sang, not perfectly perhaps, but with much feeling. Had she not been born and raised among the prejudices of a small town and hampered by her responsibility for her little brother, she might have ventured into the theatrical world. It had been her dream at one time, but never more than a dream. Now almost forty, she was content with the tribute paid her musical talent by the townspeople and their admiration for her unswerving effort to secure the future of those two fatherless boys.

Dr. D'Andrea sat waiting in the little sitting room for his friend to come out and call him.

The room, flooded with light despite its low ceiling, with its worn, old-fashioned furniture, breathed an air of days gone by in the unchanging reflection of two large facing mirrors. Only Eleonora's piano, a baby grand, was new. The faces of the old family portraits hanging around the walls, the true occupants of the room, seemed to look down on it with a frown.

Finally, tired of waiting, the doctor got up and poked his head around the door into the hall. He heard crying in the next room and rapped on the closed door.

"Come in," said Bandi, opening the door. "I can't understand what makes her so stubborn."

"I tell you there's nothing wrong with me," Eleonora insisted through her tears.

Huge and pale, dressed all in black as usual, she sat in a big leather armchair, a strange look on her childlike face, perhaps more ambiguous than strange because of a certain hardness in her eyes—an almost mad fixity which she tried in vain to conceal.

"There is nothing wrong with me, I assure you," she repeated more calmly. "For pity's sake, leave me alone! Don't pay any attention to me."

"Very well," her brother concluded, in a ruthless, obstinate tone of voice. "Meanwhile, Carlo's here. You can tell him what ails you." And he went out, slamming the door furiously behind him.

Eleonora buried her face in her hands and sobbed.

D'Andrea looked at her with embarrassment; then he asked, "What is it? Can't you tell me, either?"

As Eleonora continued to sob, he went to her and gingerly tried to remove her hands from her face.

"Quiet down, now. Tell me what it's all about. That's why I came."

Eleonora shook her head, then suddenly seized his hand in both of hers and, her face distorted as if in pain, moaned. "Carlo! Carlo!"

D'Andrea leaned over her, feeling that his customary impassive behavior was being compromised.

"Tell me . . ."

She laid her cheek against his hand and pleaded desperately in a low voice, "Help me die, Carlo. Show me how. Have pity on me. I haven't the courage, the strength . . ."

"Die?" the young man asked, smiling. "Why do you say that?"

"Die, yes!" she repeated, choked by sobs. "Show me the way. You are a doctor. Take me out of this agony. Have mercy. I *must* die. There's no other way out. Only death."

He stared at her in bewilderment. She raised her eyes to look at him but quickly closed them, her face twisted again in sudden despair.

"Yes, yes," she said firmly. "Carlo, I am lost."

Instinctively d'Andrea withdrew the hand she was still holding in both her own.

"What . . . what are you saying?" he faltered.

Without looking at him, she put a finger to her lips and pointed to the door.

"If he knew! Don't tell him, I beg you. First let me die. Give me something. I'll take it just like medicine, believing it *is* medicine you have given me. Only let it be quick! I haven't the courage. For two months I've struggled in despair without finding the strength or the way of putting an end to it. What help can you give me, Carlo?"

"Help?" D'Andrea repeated, aghast.

Eleonora once more stretched out her hands to take his arm and pleaded, "If you won't help me die, can't you... save me in some other way?"

At this suggestion d'Andrea withdrew more than ever and frowned severely.

"I beg you, Carlo!" she insisted. "Not for myself, but so that Giorgio won't find out. If I've ever done anything for you, help me now. Save me! Is this the way I must end, after having tried so hard and suffered so much? Dishonored, at my age? What misery! What horror!"

"But, Eleonora, how did it happen? Who did it?" d'Andrea blurted out in appalled curiosity, finding nothing else to say in the face of the depth of her despair.

Eleonora again pointed to the door, covering her face with her hands. "Don't remind me! I don't want to think about it. But won't you spare Giorgio this shame?"

"How?" asked d'Andrea. "It's a crime! It would be a double crime! Think of something else."

"No!" she replied curtly. "Enough! I understand. Leave me now. I can't bear any more."

Her head fell back on the chair and she collapsed, exhausted.

Carlo d'Andrea, his eyes popping behind the thick lenses of his glasses, waited awhile in silence, unable to believe what he had heard or to imagine how this woman—a shining example of virtue and self-denial—could have been led astray. Impossible! Eleonora Bandi? In her youth she had had many proposals of marriage, one more attractive than the other, but she had refused them all out of love for her little brother. Why, then, now that her youth was gone—or was it perhaps just because of that?

He looked at her voluminous body and the suspicion in his eyes suddenly took on a lewd, ugly glint.

"Go, then," she said abruptly.

Without lifting her head, Eleonora could feel the change in his expression.

"Go! Go and tell Giorgio so that he can do as he likes with me and get it over with. Go!" she repeated.

D'Andrea went out stiffly. She raised her head a little to watch him leave. Then, as soon as the door had closed, she fell back into her former position.

II

After two months of mental torture, this confession of her plight gave her unexpected relief. It seemed to her that the worst was over. She no longer had the strength to struggle against this humiliation. She would have to abandon herself to her fate, whatever it would be.

Would her brother kill her when he came in? Well, all the better. She had no right to expect consideration or sympathy. Although she had done more than her duty for him and for that other ungrateful one, now all the hard-won fruits of her sacrifice were swept away.

She closed her eyes tight in a fit of revulsion.

In her conscience she blamed herself. Yes, she who had found the strength to resist the impulses of youth for so many years, she who had always had the purest, noblest sentiments, she who had given up everything for the sake of duty—now, in a moment, all was lost.

In self-defense she had only one explanation to give her brother, and what weight would that carry in his eyes? She could say, "Look, Giorgio, it was because of you that I fell." And yet that was the simple truth.

She had mothered her little brother with loving care, and in return for everything she had so willingly lavished on him, in reward for the dedication of her entire life, he had never given her the pleasure of even the slightest smile of satisfaction, and neither had his friend. Their souls seemed poisoned by silence and boredom, weighed down by stupid restraint. As soon as they received their degrees, like workhorses they threw themselves into harness with such relentless dedication that in no time they had managed to become self-supporting.

This haste to be free of their obligation to her, as if they could hardly wait to see the end of it, wounded her deeply. Almost overnight she found herself with no purpose in life. What was there for her to do, now that the boys were grown and no longer needed her, now that her youth was forever lost?

Even his first professional earnings had not brought a smile to her brother's face. Did he consider what she had done for him as a dead weight? For the rest of his life, would he feel obliged to repay her sacrifice?

She tried to speak to him straight from the heart: "Don't worry about me, Giorgio. My only wish is to see you happy and contented. Understand?"

But he broke in: "Hush! What do you mean? I know what my duty is. From now on I take the responsibility."

"But why take it like this?" she wanted to ask. But knowing his obstinacy, she did not insist. However, there were times when she felt that she could no longer endure this pall of gloom.

From day to day his professional earnings increased and he surrounded her with comforts, even insisting that she give up her music lessons. In the loneliness of this forced leisure an unfortunate idea occurred to her which, at first, had only made her laugh: *What if I should find a husband?*

Since she was already thirty-nine, any candidate would really have to be made to order. Yet it was the only way to free both her brother and herself of this crushing debt of gratitude.

Unconsciously, she began to pay more attention to her appearance, taking on a certain air of eligibility which she had never assumed before. The several young men who had proposed to her had long since married and had children. Although this had never mattered to her, she now felt resentful and envious of the lives her friends had made for themselves.

She alone was left like this.

But maybe there was still time; who could tell? Was her busy life to drag itself out in emptiness? Was the bright flame of her passionate spirit to be quenched under this shadow?

She was overcome with longing and bitterness which gradually altered her natural charm, her voice, her smile. She became biting, even aggressive, in conversation, and hated herself for this change in her disposition. Her body was repulsive to her, and she was harassed by unsuspected desires which deeply troubled her.

Her brother, meanwhile, had saved enough money to buy a farm and build a charming little villa. At his insistence she first went there for a month's vacation. Then, assuming that he had bought the farm in order to be rid of her occasionally, she decided to live there altogether. He would be left free, no longer burdened by her company or the sight of her, while she would slowly rid herself of this foolish idea of marrying at her age.

The first days went very well, and she saw no reason why this new life should not continue. She would rise at dawn and take long walks across country, stopping here and there to listen, enchanted, to the cocks crowing, calling from one farmyard to another in the surprising silence of the open meadows where the grass shivered in the coolness of the early morning, or to admire the green moss striping a rock, or the velvety lichen of the twisted trunk of an ancient olive tree.

There, close to the earth, she would soon have recovered her good spirits, thinking and feeling differently. She would have become like the good wife of the tenant farmer who was always ready to keep her company and teach her so many things about nature, simple things which suddenly revealed a new, unexpected, and deeper meaning to life.

But the tenant farmer was unbearable. He boasted of having "liberal" ideas, of having circled the world. He had been to South America, too—eight years in *Benossary*—and he did not intend his only son, Gerlando, to be a lowly peasant. Consequently, he had kept him in school for thirteen years. He wanted to give him a little *lettering,* as he put it, so he could send him to America, where no doubt he would make a fortune.

Gerlando was nineteen, and for all his thirteen years of study, he had not yet finished the third year in trade school. He was a big, uncouth boy, all of a piece. His father's ambitions were a real martyrdom for him. The citified ways he picked up unconsciously from his schoolfellows only accentuated his boorishness.

By dousing his bristling head with water every morning, he managed to comb his hair and part it on one side, but as soon as it dried, it rose stiffly, as if sprouting from his scalp.

Even his eyebrows shot out from under his low forehead, while the first hairs of a rough beard sprouted in little tufts beneath his lip and around his chin. Poor Gerlando! One could only pity him, so big, so dull-witted, and so shaggy, sitting before an open book. Some mornings his father had a hard time rousing him from his leaden sleep and getting him off, still stunned, steps weaving, eyes dulled, to his purgatory in the nearby town.

When Eleonora came to the country, Gerlando, through his mother, addressed himself to the signorina to persuade his father to stop tormenting him with school, school, school! He could not stand it any longer. Eleonora tried to intervene, but the tenant farmer would have none of it. With all due respect and regard for the signorina, he would be obliged if she would not meddle in his affairs. So then, partly out of pity, partly to have something to do, Eleonora started to help the poor young man with his studies.

Every afternoon she had him come to the villa with his class books and notebooks. He arrived feeling ill at ease and ashamed because he noticed that the lady found his stupidity amusing, but what could he do? This was what his father wanted. He knew he could not learn from books, but, by golly, when it came to felling a tree or an ox ... Gerlando raised his sinewy arm, and a tender, proud look came into his eyes as he smiled, baring his strong teeth.

Impulsively, from one day to the next, Eleonora stopped the lessons. She did not want to see him again! Her piano was sent out from the city, and for a while she did nothing but play and sing and read. One evening she noticed that Gerlando, suddenly deprived of her help, her company, and her little jokes, had come to spy on her, to listen to her playing and singing. Meaning to take him by surprise, she left the piano and quickly ran down the steps of the villa.

"What are you doing here?"

"I came to listen."

"Do you like it?"

"Very much, signora. I'm in heaven!"

At this she burst out laughing. Her laugh struck Gerlando like a slap across the face, and he seized her, jumping on her in the darkness behind the villa, beyond the shaft of light shining from the open door across the balcony.

Overcome by surprise, she had not been able to push him

off. She felt faint—she did not know why—under his brutal impact and had let herself go. She had yielded against her will.

That was how it had happened.

Next day Eleonora returned to the city.

Now why didn't Giorgio come in to humiliate her? Perhaps d'Andrea had not yet told him. Perhaps he was thinking of a way to spare her this shame. But how?

She hid her face in her hands to shut out the emptiness before her, but she found the same emptiness inside herself. There was no solution. Only death. When? How?

The door burst open, and Giorgio appeared, pale, hysterical, his hair in disorder and his eyes red from weeping. D'Andrea held him by the arm.

"I want to know just one thing," he said between clenched teeth, stressing each word. "I want to know *who* it was!"

Eleonora, her head bowed, her eyes closed, slowly shook her head and began sobbing.

"I'll make you tell me!" screamed Bandi, going up to her while his friend tried to hold him back. "And whoever it may be, you'll marry!"

"No, Giorgio," she moaned, lowering her head still further and twisting her hands in her lap. "It's impossible, impossible!"

"Is he married?" he demanded, threatening her with clenched fists.

"No," she said quickly, "but it's out of the question."

"Who is it?" screamed Bandi, trembling all over. "Who is it? Out with it!"

Feeling her brother's fury towering over her, Eleonora withdrew still further and whispered under his murderous look, "Giorgio, I cannot tell you . . ."

"His name or I'll kill you!" roared Bandi, raising his fist.

But d'Andrea interceded, pushing his friend aside. "Go," he said severely. "She will tell me. Go . . . go!" And he pushed him out of the room.

III

Her brother was inflexible.

Before the wedding, during the few days required for the

publication of the banns, he mercilessly pursued the scandal. To forestall the low jokes he anticipated from all sides, he deliberately set out to broadcast his shame in the crudest possible language. He appeared to be out of his head, and everyone felt sorry for him.

But he had a tussle with the tenant farmer to get him to consent to this marriage.

For all his liberal ideas, the old man at first refused to believe such a thing possible. Then he said, "Don't worry, Your Honor; I'll stamp him underfoot as we crush the juice from the grapes. Better still, I'll hand him over to you, bound hand and foot, and Your Honor can do whatever you like with him. I'll provide the lash for the whipping myself, and I'll soak it three days beforehand so it will cut all the harder."

But when he understood that this was not the gentleman's intention and that Bandi had something else in mind—marriage—he was again taken aback.

"What? What is Your Honor saying? A lady of her standing marry the son of a common peasant?"

And he flatly refused.

"Begging your pardon, the signorina is old enough to know what she is up to. She knows right from wrong. She should never have done what she did with my son. Let me tell you: she had him come to her house every day! Your Honor can understand . . . a big fellow . . . and at that age, they don't reason or pay much attention. Now is this the way I'm going to lose my son who cost me I don't know how much to educate? The signorina, with all due respect, is old enough to be his mother!"

Bandi had to promise to turn over the farm as dowry and to provide his sister with an income. So the bargain was struck, and the wedding was a big event for the little town.

Everyone seemed to enjoy repudiating the admiration and respect they had formerly shown Eleonora Bandi. Between their esteem, which she had now lost, and the derision with which they accompanied her to this shameful wedding, there seemed no room for compassion.

All the sympathy was for the brother, who, of couse, did not wish to take part in the ceremony. D'Andrea did not attend either, giving as his excuse that he must keep Giorgio company on this sad day.

An old friend of Eleonora's parents—a doctor from whom
d'Andrea had managed to filch a large part of his practice
—offered to serve as her witness. He brought another friend
along as second witness.

Eleonora rode with them in a closed carriage to the Town
Hall. Later they would go on to a secluded little church for
the religious ceremony.

The groom, sulking and gloomy, came in another carriage
with his parents. They were all dressed up and feeling very
superior because, after all, their son was marrying a real
lady, the sister of a lawyer, whose dowry would provide
them with a farm, a fine villa, and an income to boot! To
live up to his new status, Gerlando would now have to finish
his studies. The bride was a little old? All the better! An heir
was already on the way—and by the laws of nature, she
would be the first to die, leaving Gerlando and his offspring
rich and free.

These and similar considerations were being aired in a
third carriage occupied by the groom's witnesses, peasant
friends of his father, and two uncles on his mother's side.
Numerous other friends and relatives of the groom waited
at the villa, all in their best clothes—the men in dark-blue
suits and the women in new caps and gaily colored aprons.
The tenant farmer, with his "liberal" ideas, had ordered a
fitting reception—everything first class.

At the Town Hall, before entering the clerk's office, Eleonora had a crying spell. The groom stood to one side surrounded by relatives who urged him to go over to her, but
the old doctor begged him to stay away for the moment.

Before she had entirely recovered. Eleonora went into the
office, and when she saw the boy beside her looking gawkier
than ever because of his embarrassment, she had an impulse
to rebel. "No! No!" And she gave him a look as if urging
him to do the same. But a few minutes later they both said
their "yes," accepting their inescapable punishment.

The second ceremony in the lonely little church was hurriedly dispatched, and then the sad procession started off toward the villa. Eleonora did not want to part from her two
friends, but she was obliged to climb into the carriage with
the groom and her in-laws.

Not a word was exchanged between them the whole way.
The tenant farmer and his wife seemed dismayed, occasional-

ly stealing a glance at their daughter-in-law, then exchanging looks before lowering their eyes. Withdrawn and frowning, the groom stared out the window.

They were greeted at the villa by a loud salvo of firecrackers and by shouts of joy and applause. But the bride's expression and behavior chilled the guests, though she tried to smile at these simple folk who were celebrating a wedding in their own way, according to tradition.

She soon begged to be excused, but stopped short on the threshold of her former bedroom when she saw that a nuptial bed had been prepared for them there. "Here, with him! Never! Never!" Filled with disgust, she fled into another room, turned the key in the lock, and fell into a big chair, covering her face with her hands.

The voices of the jubilant guests reached her through the closed door. They were baiting Gerlando, congratulating him not so much on his wife as on the family he had married into and the beautiful property he had acquired.

Filled with shame, Gerlando leaned over the balcony, replying to their boisterous taunts with an occasional shrug of his heavy shoulders.

Yes, he was ashamed to be married to that woman. It was all his father's fault, he and his cursed ideas about school. The signorina had treated him like a big dunce, making fun of him and hurting his feelings. Then this had to happen! All his father thought about was the piece of property. But he—how was he going to live with this woman who made him feel so uncomfortable and who certainly blamed him for her shame and dishonor? What was worse, his father now claimed he would have to finish school! Imagine what fair game he would make for his schoolmates with a wife twenty years older than himself, a wife who looked like a mountain besides.

While Gerlando was tormenting himself with such thoughts, his mother and father were putting the final touches to the banquet. At last, triumphant, they came into the room where the table was spread. The table service, hired for the occasion, came from a restaurant in the city, which also provided a cook and two waiters to serve.

The tenant farmer came out on the balcony and said to Gerlando, "Go and tell your wife the banquet will be ready in a moment."

"Nothing doing. I won't go!" Gerlando grunted, stamping his foot. "Tell her yourself!"

"It's your place, jackass!" cried his father. "You're the husband! Go!"

"No, thanks! I refuse!" Gerlando repeated obstinately, protecting his head against an anticipated blow with his raised arm.

In a rage his father grabbed him by his coat collar and gave him a big shove.

"Blockhead! You got yourself into this mess in the first place and now you're ashamed! She's your wife!"

The guests came running to make peace and to coax Gerlando to go upstairs.

"What harm is there in that? Just tell her to come down and have a bite."

"But I don't even know what to call her!" cried Gerlando, exasperated.

Some of the guests burst out laughing, while others were quick to restrain the farmer, who wanted to strike his stupid son for spoiling the fine party he had prepared at so much expense!

"Call her by her baptismal name," his mother suggested softly. "Her name is Eleonora, isn't it? Call her Eleonora. She's your wife. Go, my son, go," she said, leading him toward the nuptial suite.

Gerlando rapped on the door. He rapped softly the first time and waited. Silence. What should he say to her? What a predicament! Why didn't she answer? Maybe she hadn't heard. He rapped again more loudly and waited. Silence.

Then, uneasily, he tried calling her by name in a low voice as his mother had suggested. But what came out was an Eleonora which sounded so ridiculous that quickly, as if to wipe it out, he said loudly, "Eleonora!"

At last her voice, coming from another room, asked, "Who is it?"

Frightened and stammering, he went to the other door, "I," he said, "I, Ger . . . Gerlando. It's all ready."

"I cannot come down," she answered. "Go ahead without me."

Gerlando returned to the dining room with a feeling of relief.

"She's not coming. She said she won't come ... she can't come."

"Hurrah for the blockhead!" exclaimed his father, who called him nothing else. "Did you tell her we were all at the table? Why didn't you *make* her come down?"

His wife interposed, trying to explain to her husband that it was perhaps best to leave the bride alone for the moment. The guests agreed: "The emotion ... the discomfort ... you understand."

But the farmer, who wanted to show his daughter-in-law that he knew how to do things right, sulked and gruffly ordered the waiters to serve dinner.

Although the guests were looking forward to the mouth-watering delicacies to come, they all felt ill at ease and dazzled by the extravagant number of glittering objects on the new tablecloth: four glasses of different sizes and shapes at each place, big and little forks, big and little knives, and then there were strange-looking feathers sticking out of small rolls of fringed paper.

Seated well back from the table, they perspired in their heavy Sunday clothes and stared at one another's hard, sun-burned, and uncommonly clean faces. They dared not lift their big hands, gnarled by hard work in the fields, to pick up a fork (the small one or the large?) or a knife, they were so intimidated by the waiters, who moved deftly around the table serving in white cotton gloves.

As the farmer ate, he looked at his son and shook his head, an expression of contempt on his face.

"Look at him! Look at him!" he muttered to himself. "What does he look like there all alone at the head of the table! How could a bride respect a big ape like that? She's right to feel ashamed of him! Ah, if I were only in his place!"

The meal ended in an atmosphere of general gloom, and the guests, with one excuse or another, soon took their leave. It was already evening.

"Now," said his father, when the two waiters had cleared the table and quiet descended on the villa, "what are you going to do? You'll have to get out of this by yourself."

And he ordered his wife to follow him to their farmhouse not far from the villa.

Left alone, Gerlando looked around him, frowning uncertainly.

He was conscious of her presence up there in that locked room. Maybe, now that all was quiet, she would come out. Then what was he supposed to do? Ah, how gladly he would have run back to the farmhouse to be near his mother, or would God he could sleep out in the open under a tree!

Suppose she was waiting for him to call her again? If she was resigned to the punishment her brother had inflicted on her, maybe she considered herself at her husband's disposal and was now waiting for him to—yes, invite her to . . .

He listened: all was silent. Perhaps she was already asleep. It was dark. The moon shone into the room through the open door of the balcony. Without bothering to turn on a light, Gerlando took a chair and sat out on the balcony overlooking the open country which sloped away toward the far-distant sea.

Large, bright stars shone in the clear night, and the moon cut a swath of silver across the water. From the vast fields of yellow grain the tremulous chant of crickets rose in a prolonged threnody. Suddenly, close by, an owl uttered a doleful "keewhoo," and from far off, like an echo, another replied.

Resting his arms on the railing of the balcony, he instinctively covered his ears to shut out those "keewhoos" calling to each other across the enchanted silence under the moon, and to escape from the wretchedness of his own uncertainty. Then, noticing the corner of a wall below which circled the entire farm, he thought that now all this land was his and the trees were his, olive, almond, carob, fig, and mulberry. His too the vines.

His father had every reason to feel content because from now on his son would be subject to no one. And, after all, it was not such a bad idea to continue with his studies. He was better off there in school than here all day long in his wife's company. He'd take care of any of his schoolfellows who tried to make fun of him. Now he was a gentleman, and it no longer mattered to him if he were expelled from school. But this would not happen. He proposed to study hard from now on, so that one day he could take his place among the gentry in town with no embarrassment, talking and discussing with them on equal terms. He needed only four more years to get his certificate from trade school, and then he would be an expert agronomist or an accountant. Then his brother-in-law, the lawyer—who seemed to think he had thrown his sister to the dogs—would have to tip his hat to him! Yes, indeed! And he would have every right to say, "What do you think you've given me? An old woman, that's what! I've completed my studies and now have a gentleman's profession. I can win a beautiful, rich young girl with a family just as good as yours."

With these thoughts he fell asleep, his head cradled in his arms, leaning on the balcony railing.

The two "keewhoos," one near, the other far, continued their voluptuous lament. The luminous night seemed to trail a rippling moon-veil over the earth, the fields trilled with crickets, and from afar a deep murmur arose from the sea.

Late that night Eleonora appeared, like a shadow, in the doorway of the balcony. She had not expected to find the young man asleep there. It both pained and frightened her. For a moment she paused, wondering if she should wake him to tell him what she had decided to do and ask him to withdraw from the balcony. But, on the point of shaking him, of calling his name, her courage failed her and she herself withdrew softly, returning to the room from which she had come.

IV

An agreement was easily reached.

The next morning Eleonora had a motherly talk with Gerlando. He would take charge of everything and would be free to do whatever he wished, as if no tie existed between them. She asked him only to leave her in peace, alone in that small room, waited on by the old family servant who had seen her grow up.

Gerlando, aching all over from the dampness, had come in from the balcony at an early hour and had fallen asleep on the couch in the dining room. Roused from sleep thus suddenly, he had a great desire to rub his eyes with his fists. His mouth hung open as he tried to knit his brows, not so much to show that he understood as to indicate his approval, and he kept nodding his head—yes, yes—to everything. But when his father and mother heard of the pact, they were furious, and Gerlando tried in vain to make them understand that it suited him perfectly, that he was more than happy with this arrangement.

To calm his father, he solemnly promised to return to school early in October. But out of pique his mother insisted that he take the finest room to sleep in, the best room to study in, the nicest room to eat in—all the best rooms in the villa.

"And *you* give the orders, understand? Crack the whip, or I will come myself to see that you are obeyed and respected!"

She swore she would never speak to that wheedler again, a woman who had slighted her son like that, and such a handsome young man, too, far too good for the likes of her!

Starting that very day Gerlando began to study for his examinations in October. It was already late, with only twenty-four days ahead of him, but by applying himself, who knows? Perhaps after all he would get that certificate he had been struggling for for the past three years.

When the anxious bewilderment of the first few days was past, Eleonora, on the advice of Gesa, her servant, began to prepare a layette for the coming baby. It made her cry that she had not even thought of it.

Gesa, who excelled at this work, helped her and gave her the measurements for the first little shirts, the first cap. Fate has reserved this consolation for me, Eleonora thought, and she had not realized it. She would have a little boy or girl to care for, to devote herself to entirely. She hoped that God would send her a boy. She was not young, and it would be difficult to leave a little girl in the hands of such a father were she to die—a little girl to whom she had imparted all her own feelings, her own thoughts. A boy would suffer less under the conditions which misfortune had brought him.

Tortured by such considerations and tired of working, she would pick up a book to divert her thoughts—one of the books her brother had sent her when she first came here. Every now and then, with a gesture of the head, she would ask the servant, "What's he up to?"

Gesa would hunch her shoulders, purse her lips, and reply, "Umph! His head's in a book. Who knows if he's sleeping or trying to think?"

Gerlando was thinking, all right. He thought that, all in all, his life wasn't very entertaining.

Here he was: he had a farm and he didn't have it; he had a wife and he didn't have her; he was on bad terms with his parents; he was furious with himself because he could remember nothing at all that he studied. Meantime his indolence left him prey to sneaking desires—among others, a longing for his wife because she kept apart from him. True, the woman was no longer desirable, but what kind of pact was this? He was the husband and, if anyone, he should be the one to decide!

He got up and went out of the room. As he passed her door, he caught sight of her, and all his vexation vanished. Snorting so as not to admit his lack of courage, he told himself that she was not worth it.

Then, one day in October, he came back from town defeated, having once more failed his examination for the first technical certificate. Now, enough! He was through! He didn't want to hear another word about it. He took his books, notebooks, drawing squares, boxes, pencils and carried them down in front of the villa to make a bonfire. His father ran up to stop him, but Gerlando was vicious.

"Let me be! Here, I'm the boss!"

His mother came running, too, and several farmers who were working in the fields. Wisps of smoke gradually thickened and rose from the heap of papers, amid the cries of the onlookers. Then, with a flash, flames crackled and blazed. The screams brought Eleonora out onto the balcony with her servant.

Livid, in his shirtsleeves, and strutting about like a turkey gobbler, Gerlando wildly hurled in the last books he was holding under his arm—the unwitting instruments of his long, futile torture.

Eleonora could hardly refrain from laughing at the scene and quickly withdrew from the balcony. But her mother-in-law had spied her and said to her son, "Your lady finds it amusing, eh? It makes her laugh."

"It will make her cry!" Gerlando shouted menacingly, going white as he glanced up at the balcony.

Eleonora heard his threat and paled also. She understood that the dreary peace she had enjoyed until now was over. It had been no more than a respite accorded by fate. What could that brute want of her? She was already spent. Another blow, however light, would finish her.

A moment later, dark and panting, Gerlando appeared.

"As of today, things are going to change around here!" he announced. "I'm fed up. I'm going to be a farmer like my father, and you will stop playing the lady. Away with all these baby clothes. This child is going to be born a farmer, too, and will not need these fancy frills. Dismiss the servant. Do the cooking and clean the house yourself, the same as my mother does. Understand?"

Eleonora rose, trembling with indignation.

"Your mother is your mother," she said, looking him proudly in the eyes. "I am myself, and your being a peasant does not change me."

"You are my wife!" screamed Gerlando, seizing her violently by the arm. "You will do as I say. I give the orders here! Is that clear?"

Then he turned to the old servant and pointed to the door. "Get out! Leave immediately. I won't have any servants in this house!"

"I go with you, Gesa!" cried Eleonora, trying to free her arm from his grasp.

But Gerlando would not let go. He held her even more tightly and forced her to sit down.

"No, you stay here! You are chained to me, understand? I've been the laughingstock of the countryside because of you. Now that's over and done with! You come out of your lair, see. I'm not going to be left alone to weep over my shame." He turned to Gesa once more. "Out with you!" And he shoved her toward the door.

"What have you to complain of?" Eleonora asked, her eyes brimming with tears. "What have I ever asked of you?"

"What have you asked? Not to touch you, not to have any contact with you, as if I were ... as if I were not good enough for an old woman like you! And you pay a servant to wait on me at the table instead of waiting on me yourself as a wife should."

"What difference can all this make to you?" Eleonora asked, disheartened. "I will serve you with my own hands from now on. Is that better?"

As she said this she burst into sobs and her legs gave way under her. Frightened, bewildered, Gerlando supported her with Gesa's help, and between them they put her into the big chair.

Toward evening her pains started.

Gerlando, repentant and scared, ran to call his mother. A farmhand was sent to town to get the midwife. Meanwhile, the tenant farmer, foreseeing the danger of losing his farm if his daughter-in-law should have a miscarriage, scolded his son:

"Blockhead! What have you done now? What if the baby dies? Suppose you don't have any more children? You'll be out in the street! What are you going to do? You left school and you don't even know how to handle a shovel. You're ruined!"

"What do I care?" cried Gerlando. "Just so long as nothing happens to her!"

His mother came running, her arms in the air. "A doctor! A doctor is needed right away! She's taken bad!"

"What's wrong?" asked Gerlando, white as a sheet.

But his father pushed him. "Run! Run!"

On the way Gerlando, trembling with apprehension, started to cry, but forced himself to keep on running. Halfway, he met the midwife returning with the farmhand in the carriage.

"Hurry! Hurry!" he cried. "I'm going for the doctor. She's dying."

He stumbled and fell heavily. Covered with dirt, he got up and ran on desperately, sucking at his bleeding hand.

When he returned to the villa with the doctor, Eleonora had almost bled to death.

"Murderer! Murderer!" muttered Gesa as she looked after her mistress. "It's all his fault! He dared lay a hand on her!"

But Eleonora shook her head. She felt herself slipping away little by little, her strength waning. Already cold, she was not sorry to die. It was sweet to die like this—a great relief after the torment she had endured. Her face like wax, staring up at the ceiling, she waited for her eyes to close softly of themselves, forever. She could no longer distinguish anything clearly. As if in a dream, she saw the old doctor who had served as her marriage witness and smiled at him.

V

While Eleonora lay between life and death, Gerlando never left her bedside day or night.

When she was at last able to get up and sit in a big chair, she seemed like another woman, transparent, almost bloodless. She saw Gerlando beside her, looking as if he too had come through a critical illness, and his parents next to him, full of kind attentions. Looking at them with those beautiful black eyes of hers, large and sad in her pale, thin face, she no longer felt any bond with them whatever. It was as if she had come back, new and different, from a remote place where every tie was severed—not only with them but with all her former life.

She breathed with difficulty, and her heart, beating wildly, jumped at the slightest sound.

Her head lolling on the back of the chair, her eyes closed, she regretted bitterly that she had not died. What had she to do here? Why was she condemned to see these faces around her again and look at all these things from which she felt so remote? Why this reconciliation with the depressing, sickening apparition of her past? A reconciliation which was more painful at times than others, as if someone had pushed her in the back, forcing her to see and feel the presence, the living, breathing reality of the odious life which was no longer hers.

She was convinced that she would never rise from that chair. She believed that at any moment she must die of heart failure. However, a few days later she got up and was able to take a few steps around the room. Then, with time, she even went downstairs and out of doors, supported by Gerlando and the faithful Gesa. She formed the habit of going at sunset to the edge of the embankment which was the southern boundary of her property. From this plateau a magnificent vista opened out over the sloping fields all the way down to the sea. At first Gerlando and Gesa accompanied her, as usual; then she went with her old servant; finally she was able to go alone.

Seated on a stone at the foot of a century-old olive tree, she looked along the whole coast, slightly curving in the distance. Its little inlets and bays seemed to be cut out of the sea which changed with the shifting winds. She saw the sun, like a great disk of fire, slowly drown in the slimy sea moss resting on the gray water to the west and fall in triumph behind the glowing waves in a marvelous pageant of blazing clouds. She saw the evening star appear, glowing softly and serenely in the vaporous sky; then came the limpid moon, barely lit. Her eyes drank in the melancholy sweetness of the impending dark, and she breathed deeply, accepting the still, the quiet, as a superhuman consolation penetrating to the depths of her being.

Meantime, in the nearby farmhouse the old tenant farmer and his wife had resumed their conspiracy against her, goading their son to look after his own interests.

"Why do you leave her alone?" his father asked craftily. "Don't you realize that, after her illness, she's grateful for all the affection you showed her? Don't leave her for a moment. Always try to get closer to her heart. Then ... then arrange it so that the servant doesn't sleep in the same room with her. She is well now and certainly can't need Gesa during the night."

Irritated, Gerlando shook his head at these suggestions.

"It's out of the question. It would never enter her head that I might ... not at all! She treats me like a son. You should hear the things she says to me! She considers herself old, finished, done with insofar as this world is concerned."

"Old?" put in his mother. "Certainly she's no longer a child, but she's not old either. You wait and see."

"They'll take away the land!" pursued his father. "I've already told you: you'll be dispossessed, out in the street! If your wife dies and there are no children, her dowry goes back to her family. Then what will you have? You'll have lost out at school and wasted all that time, without getting a thing out of it. Not so much as a fistful of flies! Think it over! Think it over while there's still time. Too much has been lost already. What else can you hope for?"

"Be gentle," his mother said sweetly. "You must win her over with kindness; talk to her like this: 'After all, what have you given me? I respected you as you wished, but now you should think about me a little. What am I to do? What can I do, if you leave me like this?' After all, dear God, there's no need to fight a war!"

"Then you can say in passing," his father pressed, " 'Do you want to please your brother who treated you the way he did and let him kick me out of here like a dog?' It's gospel truth. Just you wait and see. You'll be kicked out, lock, stock, and barrel, and your mother and I, poor old folks that we are, will go with you!"

Gerlando did not answer. His mother's words were almost a relief but, in their way, irritating, too. His father's forecasts stirred his bile. What was he to do? He saw the difficulty of the undertaking and he also recognized its urgency. In any case he would try.

Now Eleonora ate at table with him. One evening at dinner, seeing him staring at the tablecloth deep in thought, she asked, "You're not eating. What is the matter?"

Although he had been expecting this question for several days because of the way he was behaving, he did not remember for the moment what he had planned to say and made a vague gesture with his hand.

"What's the matter?" Eleonora insisted.

"Nothing," Gerlando replied impatiently. "My father, as usual . . ."

"School again?" she asked, smiling to get him to talk.

"No, worse!" he said. "He . . . he raises so many doubts in my mind . . . he worries me with thoughts of my future because he is old, he says, and here am I without a trade or profession. As long as you're here it's all right, but then . . . then . . . nothing says . . ."

"Tell your father," Eleonora replied gravely, half closing her eyes as if to shut out his blushing face, "tell your father that he does not have to worry about it. I have provided for everything, tell him, so he can be at rest. Since we are talking about this, listen: if I should die suddenly—after all, one is here today and gone tomorrow—you will find a yellow envelope in the second drawer of the bureau in my room. There is a document in it for you."

"A document?" Gerlando repeated, not knowing what else to say in his embarrassment.

Eleonora nodded and added, "Don't worry about it anymore."

Relieved, Gerlando told his parents the next morning everything Eleonora had said. But they, especially his father, were not at all convinced.

"A document? Tricks!"

What could that document be? A will leaving the farm to her husband? And if it were not drawn up in accordance with all the rules and regulations? It would be easily suspect, considering it was in a woman's handwriting and not drawn with the help of a notary. Then the following day wouldn't they have to deal with the brother, a man of law, a swindler?

"Lawsuits, my son! May God preserve you! Justice is not

for the poor. And that one there—in his rage he would be capable of making black white and white black.

"Besides, who knows if this document is really there in that drawer of the bureau? Or did she just say that to get you to leave her in peace?

"Have you seen it? No. Well, even supposing she showed it to you, would you understand what it was all about? For that matter, what would we make out of it ourselves? Whereas if you had a son, there'd be no need of documents! Don't let her make a fool of you. Listen to us. Flesh! Flesh and blood! Not paper!"

And so one day, as she sat under the olive tree on the hill, Eleonora saw Gerlando before her. He had come up stealthily.

She was wrapped in a large black shawl, for she felt cold, although the month of February was so mild that it seemed like spring. The vast slopes below were green with the new crops. The placid sea as well as the sky was rose-tinted, faded, but very soft, and the countryside looked like enamel as it lay dappled with shade.

Wearied by her admiration of that marvelous harmony of colors, Eleonora rested her head against the trunk of the tree. The black shawl was pulled up over her head, and only her face was revealed, even paler than usual.

"What are you doing?" Gerlando asked. "You look like Our Lady of Sorrows."

"Just looking," she said with a sigh, half closing her eyes.

"If you could see how . . . how well you look in that black shawl," he added.

"Well?" said Eleonora, smiling sadly. "I feel cold."

"No, I mean well in . . . in . . . in the face," he stammered, sitting down on the ground.

Eleonora, her head against the tree, closed her eyes and smiled to keep from crying, assailed by a wave of regret for her lost youth so miserably spent. Yes, at eighteen she had been very beautiful.

Suddenly, absorbed in thought, she felt herself shaken gently.

"Give me your hand," begged Gerlando, looking up at her with feverish eyes.

She pretended not to understand.

"My hand? Why?" she asked him. "I cannot pull you up. I haven't enough strength even for myself. . . . It's almost dark; let us go in." And she stood up.

"I didn't mean you to pull me up," Gerlando explained. "Let's stay here in the dark. It is so beautiful . . ."

As he spoke he quickly grabbed her around the knees, smiling nervously, his lips dry.

"No!" she cried. "Are you mad? Leave me alone!"

To keep from falling, she braced herself against his shoulders, trying to push him back. But as she moved her arms and leaned over him kneeling there, the shawl came loose and covered him completely.

"I want you! I want you!" he cried, wrapped in the odor of her body, clasping her tightly with one arm as he sought to slip the other up to her waist.

But with a great effort she managed to wrench herself free and ran to the edge of the bank. She turned to cry, "Don't move or I'll jump!"

At that she saw him rush headlong toward her and, leaning back, she threw herself over the cliff.

He caught himself with difficulty on the brink, his face white, his arms upraised. There was a sickening thud and, looking down, he saw a heap of black clothing lying on the green field beneath. The shawl, opening in the wind, fell softly a little farther on.

His hands in his hair, he turned to look toward the farmhouse, but his eyes met the large, pale face of the moon just risen above the dense grove of olive trees. He hung there terrified, staring as if he had been seen from the heavens and stood accused.

A MERE FORMALITY

IN the spacious offices of the Orsani Bank, the old clerk, Carlo Bertone, wearing a skullcap and with glasses clamped to the tip of his nose as if to squeeze little tufts of gray hair from each nostril, leaned on his high desk and worked over a difficult computation in a big ledger. Pale, hollow-eyed, Gabriele Orsani stood watching the operation over his shoulder, spurring him on from time to time when Bertone seemed to despair of coming to the end of the ever-mounting sum.

"Wretched glasses," complained the old man, impatiently flipping them off his nose with one finger.

Gabriele Orsani laughed. "What good do those glasses do you, my poor Carlo? They won't make things any clearer."

Annoyed, Bertone picked up the ledger and said, "Allow me to go into the next room. With you carrying on in here I can't accomplish a thing. It takes peace and quiet."

"Bravo, Carlo," Orsani mocked. "Peace and quiet ... with that maelstrom you have in your hands?" he said, pointing to the ledger.

He threw himself into an easy chair near the window and lit a cigarette.

The dark-blue curtains gave the room a restful half-light. They swelled occasionally with a light breeze from the sea. With the sudden glare of light, the noise of the surf could be heard breaking on the beach.

At the door Bertone suggested that his chief receive an odd character who was waiting in the anteroom. Meanwhile, he would try to unravel the intricate account.

"Odd?" Gabriele repeated. "Who is he?"

"I don't know, but he has been waiting half an hour. Dr. Sarti sent him."

"Then show him in."

A small man around fifty, with gray hair waved and parted artfully down the middle, was ushered into the room. He looked like a puppet whose strings were controlled by invis-

163

ible hands jerking his jointed limbs into bows and other comical gestures.

He had only one good eye, but seemed to think that, by wearing a monocle over the artificial eye, the defect would pass unnoticed.

He handed Orsani his visiting card:

LAPO VANNETI
Inspector
London Life Assurance Company, Ltd.

Subscribed Capital £4,500,000—Paid-in Capital £2,559,400

"Mozt exzellent zir," he began, and after that there was no stopping him.

Just as he used a monocle to disguise his glass eye, so he brought out an odd little laugh after every unfortunate "z" to hide the defect in his speech.

Orsani tried to interrupt him several times, but to no avail.

"While pazzing through thiz highly ezteemed provinze," the undaunted little man went on with rambling eloquence, "thankz to the meritz of our company, the oldezt, mozt reliable of itz kind, I have clozed a number of exzellent contractz covering all the zpecial combinations offered to our clientz, not to mention the exzeptional advantagez which I will briefly zum up for you...."

Gabriele Orsani felt limp; Signor Vannetti did all the talking, putting the questions and giving the answers himself, raising doubts only to swoop them aside.

"Mozt kind zir, I know you might object and zay to me, Yes, dear Vannetti, of course I have every confidenze in your company, but what can I do? (Zuppozition.) The rate is too zteep, or I haven't that much extra cash in the bank (everyone knows hiz own affairz bezt.) My dear Vannetti, you might zay, there iz nothing to dizcuss. But here, mozt kind zir, I will take the liberty of pointing out the zpecial advantagez our company haz to offer. Ah, I know, you zay—all the companiez offer them more or lezz. No, no, excuze me, signore, if I dare queztion your ztatement. The advantagez..."

Orsani, seeing him pull a batch of printed matter out of his briefcase, held up his hand as if to defend himself.

"Excuse me," he said hurriedly, "but I read something somewhere about a company insuring the hands of a famous violinist for I don't know how much. Is that right?"

Signor Vannetti was momentarily taken aback, then he smiled. "American nonzenze. We, of courze..."

"I asked you," Gabriele rushed in quickly, "because I also used to..." And he resorted to the pantomime of playing a violin.

Completely disconcerted, Vannetti seemed to think that congratulations were in order.

"Wonderful...wonderful...but really we don't go in for that kind of buzinezz."

"It's an idea, nevertheless." Orsani sighed, rising to his feet. "You might insure everything subject to loss or damage over an average lifetime—hair and teeth, for instance. And what about the head! One so easily loses one's head. As the violinist insured his hands, so a dandy might insure his hair, a sportsman his teeth, a businessman his head. Think it over. It has possibilities."

Crossing the room, he now pressed a button on the wall near his desk, adding, "Please excuse me for a moment."

Embarrassed, Vannetti bowed. He imagined that, in order to get rid of him, Orsani had made a most unkind allusion to his glass eye.

Bertone answered the bell, entering the room with a bewildered look.

"In the filing cabinet on your desk, under the letter S..." Gabriele began.

"The sulfur-mine report?" asked Bertone.

"The last report, after we built the shaft with the ramp..."

"That has already been taken into account," said Bertone, nodding.

Worried and frowning, Gabriele sought the old man's eyes and asked, "Well, what then?"

Bertone, ill at ease, looked at Vannetti, who at last realized his presence was an intrusion and ceremoniously begged to be excused: "With me, a zuggeztion iz enough: I catch on right away. I wizdraw. That iz, I mean, with your permizzion I will go negzt door for a little znack, then I'll come back. Pleze don't dizturb yourzelvez. I know the way. Goodbye!"

With another jerky little bow, he went out.

II

"Well?" Gabriele Orsani repeated as soon as Vannetti had gone.

"The expense of that last construction job, coming just when it did," Bertone said hesitantly.

Gabriele flew into a rage.

"God alone knows how many times you have said the same thing! What else was there for me to do? Cancel the contract? For my creditors that mine represents my last hope of solvency—I know it. And I know better than you that a hundred and thirty thousand lire have been sunk there without a cent of return. Don't make me shout!"

Bertone pressed his hands over his tired eyes a moment. Flicking imaginary dust from his sleeve, he said softly, almost to himself, "If only there were a way to get hold of enough money to set the machinery in motion—the machinery we still have to pay for. Then there are the notes about to fall due at the bank . . ."

Pacing back and forth, his hands in his pockets, Orsani frowned and stopped. "How much, all in all?"

"Ah . . ." Bertone sighed.

"Ah!" mimicked Gabriele furiously. "Give me a round figure! Tell me frankly—is this the end? Am I ruined? Praised be the blessed memory of my father! He pushed me into this, and I did as he wished. Let's wipe the slate clean and say no more about it."

"Don't give up now," pleaded Bertone. "Of course, the way things look at the moment . . . but let me explain."

Gabriele put his hands on the old clerk's shoulders. "What can you explain, my good friend? You're trembling all over. Now is not the time to get upset. You should have opposed my plans from the very beginning, with all the authority of your years of service. You knew how unfitted I was for this business and you should have advised me. Why do you put me off like this? I feel sorry for both of us."

"What could I have done?" Bertone asked, tears in his eyes.

"Nothing," replied Orsani. "And neither could I, but I must

put the blame on someone. Don't mind what I say. How has all this happened? How have I let myself be trapped here, in this business? I still don't know what my mistakes were—apart from building that shaft where I floundered like a drowning man. What other mistakes did I make?"

Bertone shrugged, closed his eyes, and raised his hands as if to say, What's the use of talking? "Better try to find a way out," he said tearfully.

Again Gabriele laughed. "A way out? What can I do? Take up the violin I used to play before my father wished this fine business on me? Go from door to door like a blind man, a beggar, to earn my children's bread? Is that what you suggest?"

"If I may say so," Bertone ventured, "all in all, if we manage to meet the payments as they fall due, and cut down on everything—excuse me, your household expenses included—I think that for the next four or five months, at least, we can swing it. Meantime . . ."

"*Meantime* is a word that can no longer deceive me," Orsani said sadly, shaking his head.

Bertone insisted that it could be done and started out of the office to finish the work on his balance sheet.

"I will show you just where we stand in a moment," he said over his shoulder.

Gabriele again slumped into the easy chair by the window. He clasp his hands behind his neck and started to think.

No one suspected the gravity of the situation as yet, although he himself had no more illusions. A few more months of desperate expedients and then the inevitable crash would come.

For almost three weeks now he had stayed in the office, as if there he might stumble across a solution in one of the pigeonholes of his desk or hidden away in one of the ledgers. Little by little his violent tension had relaxed, his will had weakened, and he now found his thoughts drifting away from this relentless torture.

He deplored his blind, spiritless obedience to his father's wishes which had cut short his studies of mathematics and music to plunge him into the maze of business. He still resented the wrench he had felt on leaving Rome to return to Sicily, bringing with him a doctor's degree in physics and mathematics, a violin, and a nightingale. Ah, blissful self-delusion! He had fancied he could study in his spare time.

Only once, three months after his return, had he taken his violin from its case, and then it was to enclose the embalmed remains of his dead nightingale in what he considered a fitting sepulcher.

He never understood why his father, so able himself, should fail to recognize how unsuited he was for business. Perhaps his reasoning had been clouded by a desire to carry on the old Orsani name in its established milieu, and he had been led to believe that, with time and the inducements of wealth, his son would adjust to this new life and grow to like it.

How could he blame his father now when he himself had never raised the slightest objection, accepting everything as though it were a pact concluded at his birth, the conditions of which were never to be reviewed? And then, to avoid the temptations of the very different life which had been his dream, he had agreed to marry the girl long destined for him—his orphaned cousin, Flavia.

Like all the women of this accursed region where the men, enmeshed in the intricacies of endless, risky business ventures, never found any leisure to dedicate to love, Flavia took up the modest role of housekeeper without bitterness, as if this were understood between them. When he came home exhausted from the mines, or the bank, or the beach where he sometimes spent the whole day under the hot sun supervising the loading of sulfur, she saw to it that he had every material comfort.

Before he had time to understand the business, his father suddenly died, leaving him to head the firm. Alone, without a mentor, he hoped for a while to sell everything and retire early. But it was not so simple. All the capital was tied up in the sulfur mines. He had to follow along in the groove and chose as his guide good old Bertone, whom his father before him had trusted implicitly.

He felt utterly confused by the weight of responsibility suddenly dumped on his shoulders, a weight rendered even more unwieldy by the fact that the future of his three children was at stake. Never before had he felt so like a blindfolded animal hitched to a bar, turning a millstone around and around.

Embittered by regrets over the life he might have had, he saw his wife and children as the living destruction of his ideal. His heart was burdened with resentment that found no release. Flavia, seeing him sad, brooding, silent, assumed that he was obsessed by business worries. She had never tried to draw close to him, wounded perhaps by his neglect of her, and she dared not remonstrate now with a man so beset by overwhelming responsibilities.

Some evenings he watched her leaning over the balustrade of the large terrace, looking at the sea as it slapped against the wall below. It was as if she stood on the quarter deck of a ship gazing off into the starstudded night, a night filled with the restless movement of that vast stretch of water. At times, the deep, hoarse whistle of a ship weighing anchor came up to them from the harbor. What was she thinking? Did the moan of the sea convey to her any obscure forebodings?

It never occurred to him to disturb her, convinced as he was that she could never enter his world. His eyes slowly filled with silent tears. Would it continue like this until death, with no hope of change? On such gloomy evenings his emotion was so intense that the static condition of his existence seemed intolerable to him. Sudden mad impulses flashed across his mind. With only one life to live, how was a man to continue along the same unhappy path forever? The thought of others eking out harder, more materially ungrateful lives did not soothe his sorrow.

He was sometimes brought back to himself by the familiar cry of one of his children. Flavia would stir, too, but it was he who would jump up, saying, "I'll go." He would pick up the child from its crib and, cradling it in his arms, walk up and down the room, quieting his own grief as well as the baby's unrest. After putting the child to sleep, he would stand for a moment by the window, looking up at the brightest star.

Nine years had passed like that. At the beginning of this year, just when his financial position took a turn for the worse, Flavia grew extravagant. She even asked for a carriage of her own, and he had not known how to refuse her. Now, here was Bertone pressing him to cut down all expenses, even those at home!

On the other hand, Dr. Sarti, his closest friend, had recommended a change for Flavia to counteract the nervous depression brought on, it seemed, by her monotonous life. Gabriele rose and began to pace back and forth, thinking of Lucio Sarti with mixed feelings of envy and scorn.

They had been students together in Rome. At that time it would have been impossible for either of them to get through the day without seeing the other. Until recently this bond had remained unchanged. But during the illness of one of his children, Sarti's concern for Flavia appeared excessive to Gabriele. It was no more than an impression because he had complete confidence in the loyalty of his friend and of his wife.

However, there was no denying that Flavia now agreed with whatever the doctor said. Lately she had taken to nodding her head when Sarti spoke—she who, as a rule, never opened her mouth about anything to him. He was annoyed. If she approved of such ideas, why hadn't she spoken out before? Why had she never discussed the children's education with him if she shared the doctor's more rigid opinions in preference to his own? He even accused her inwardly of not loving the children. What other conclusion could he draw if she disagreed with him and yet said nothing until a third person put her views into words?

For that matter, Sarti had no right to meddle. Gabriele thought that for sometime now his friend seemed to forget certain things—for instance that all, or almost all, he had was thanks to him.

Who, if not he, had extricated Sarti from the squalor in which he was born? Sarti's father, convicted of robbery, had died in jail. Then, when the boy was old enough to understand how his mother made her living, he ran away. Gabriele had found him working as a waiter in a third-rate coffee-house, and it was he who had wheedled a small job for him in his father's bank. He lent him his own books and classroom notes to study. It was solely through Gabriele's help that Sarti had been able to make a career. Gifted and a hard worker, Sarti had built up a secure position for himself without having to renounce his own dreams. Sarti was a man, while he—he now stood on the brink of disaster.

Two knocks on the door which led from the office to his private apartments now interrupted his thoughts.

"Come in," he said.

Flavia entered.

III

Her lovely figure was enhanced by a navy-blue dress which set off her blond beauty, and on her head she wore a smart but simple dark hat. She was buttoning her gloves.

"I wanted to ask," she said, "if you were going to use your carriage, because the bay cannot be hitched to mine today."

Gabriele looked at her, as lovely and flowerlike as if she had stepped out of a misty dream world whose language was unintelligible to him.

"What?" he asked. "Why?"

"It seems the poor thing has picked up a nail. He limps."

"Who?"

"The bay. Didn't you hear?"

"Ah," said Gabriele, rousing himself. "Too bad!"

"I'm not playing for sympathy," Flavia said resentfully. "I was just asking for your carriage. I'll walk."

And she started to leave.

"Please take it. I have no need for it," Gabriele hurried to say. "Are you going alone?"

"With Carlo. Ado and Tina are being punished."

"Poor little things." Gabriele sighed, almost unaware that he had spoken.

Flavia mistook his tenderness for reproof and asked him please to leave those decisions up to her.

"Of course, if they were naughty," he said, "they should be punished. I was only thinking that, through no fault of theirs, a much greater punishment will be meted out to them before long."

Flavia turned to look at him. "And what may that be?"

"Nothing, dear. Nothing heavier than your veil or one of the plumes on your hat. Ruin, that's all!"

"Ruin?"

"Poverty, yes—and possibly even worse for me."

"What are you talking about?"

"Does it surprise you?"

Flavia, deeply troubled, came up to him and fixed her eyes on his as if she doubted his seriousness.

With a smile, Gabriele answered her halting questions

calmly, gently, as though it no longer concerned him, until he noticed how upset she was.

"Ah, my dear!" he exclaimed. "If, in all these years, you had paid the slightest attention to me, if you had tried to understand how little pleasure this hypothetical business gave me, you would not be so shocked now. There is a limit to what a man can do, and when he is forced beyond his capacities——"

"*Forced!* Who forced you?" Flavia interrupted, noting the emphasis he had put on the word.

Gabriele looked at his wife as though her interruption and the defiance with which she now faced him were confusing. He felt a bitter taste rise in his throat, and his mouth went dry. Opening his lips in a grotesque exaggeration of the same nervous smile, he asked, "Did you think it was spontaneous?"

"I never forced you," Flavia shot back. "If it was for me, you might have spared yourself the sacrifice. I would have preferred a thousand times the most abject poverty——"

"Don't!" he cried, beside himself. "Don't say it. Since you can't know what you are talking about . . ."

"Poverty? What have I had out of life?"

"*You?* How about me?"

They faced each other, trembling with anger, almost frightened by their deep-rooted hatred which now flared up after smoldering in secret for so long.

"Why blame me?" cried Flavia. "If, as you say, I paid no attention to you, when did you ever pay any attention to me? You throw your sacrifice in my teeth, as if *I* hadn't been sacrificed, condemned to atone for the dream-life you gave up. Was this the life I was meant to have? Had I no right to dream of a different life? Who made you love me? Me, the chain that bound you to forced labor. Can anyone love a chain? Meanwhile, I was supposed to be content with your work and not expect anything more from you. I have never complained, but now you provoke me!"

Gabriele buried his face in his hands, repeating, "This, too, this, too. . . . Next," he broke out, "my children will throw my sacrifice in my face like a useless rag."

"You distort everything I say," she answered with a shrug.

"No . . . no," Gabriele went on with biting sarcasm. "I deserve no other recognition. Call them! I've ruined them, and they have a right to accuse me."

"No!" said Flavia, softening at the thought of her children. "Poor little things, why should they blame you?" Then with fluttering hands she cried, "How will they ever make out, brought up as they have been?"

"How?" snapped Gabriele. "Without a father's guidance, you mean? That's another thing they can taunt me with. Go and prompt them! And to cap it all, Lucio Sarti will blame me."

"What has Lucio Sarti to do with it?" said Flavia, stunned by his last remark.

"You repeat every word he says," Gabriele went on, very pale. "All you need to do is to put his thick-lensed glasses on your nose."

Flavia drew a long sigh and, half closing her eyes, said with undiguised scorn, "Anyone who has ever known us as a family could see——"

"Only he," Gabriele interrupted with increasing violence. "He alone! He grew up knowing how to take care of himself because his father . . ."

He stopped, regretting his words, and then continued: "I don't hold it against him, but it explains why he lives as he does—apprehensive, austere, mindful of every little thing, hoping people will forget the stigma of his parents. But why should I be a tyrant to my children?"

"Who said anything about your being a tyrant?" Flavia tried to cut in.

"Free . . ." he said, "I wanted my children to grow up free, since I was condemned to this torment by my father. As a reward, I promised myself the joy of seeing them free—the only reward I asked for my wasted life. All in vain . . . now."

Sobbing convulsively, he broke off and, raising his trembling arms, sank unconscious to the floor.

Terrified, Flavia called for help. Bertone and another clerk ran in from the bank. They lifted Gabriele to a couch, and Flavia, seeing the deathly pallor of his damp face, began raving incoherently: "What's the matter with him? O God, help me! Help! It's all my fault. It's all my fault!"

The clerk ran to call Dr. Sarti, who lived nearby.

"It's my fault . . . it's my fault," moaned Flavia.

"No, signora," Bertone said, gently supporting Gabriele's

head. "Since this morning—actually for some time now...
poor boy... if you could only know..."

"I know. I know..."

"Then what did you expect? It was bound to happen."

What could she do? Bathe his temples? Yes, perhaps
a little ether. Flavia rang a bell, and the butler entered.

"Ether. Get a small bottle of ether. Be quick."

"What a blow! Poor boy," Bertone murmured bitterly to
himself, gazing through his tears at Orsani's face.

"Are we actually ruined?" Flavia asked him.

"If he had only listened to me," sighed the old clerk. "But
he was never cut out for this business."

The butler hurried in with a bottle of ether.

"A little on a handkerchief?"

"No, it's better right from the bottle. Here," said Bertone.
"Put your finger like this and let him breathe it in slowly."

Lucio Sarti rushed in all out of breath, followed by the
clerk. Tall, his stern expression hardening the beauty of his
fine, almost feminine features, Sarti wore spectacles very
close to his myopic eyes. He hardly noticed Flavia's presence,
brushing past her to the side of the sick man.

"Please, let me examine him," he said, turning to Flavia.
"Don't carry on like that."

Opening Gabriele's shirt, he pressed his ear to the heart.
After listening for a moment, he stood up and felt carefully
over the entire chest as if he were searching for something.

"Well?" asked Flavia.

Taking up his stethoscope, he asked, "Is there any caffein
in the house?"

"No... I don't know..." Flavia said. "I have some
ether."

"That's no good."

He went over to the desk and wrote out a prescription,
handing it to the clerk.

"Here. And hurry."

Then he also sent Bertone to the pharmacy for an injec-
tion syringe which he had forgotten to bring with him.

"Doctor," implored Flavia.

But Sarti ignored her and went back to the couch. Before
auscultating the patient, he gave orders without looking
around: "Make arrangements for him to be moved upstairs."

"Go... go..." Flavia told the butler.

The man had hardly closed the door before she grasped Sarti by the arm and pleaded, looking him in the eyes, "What is wrong? Is it serious? I must know."

"I don't know myself yet," Sarti replied with enforced calm.

He placed the stethoscope on Gabriele's chest and bent down to listen, closing his eyes, his face contracted as if to shut out any distracting thoughts.

At one time he had set his heart on Flavia Orsani, who had been taken in by her uncle when she was orphaned. He did not know then how rich she was or that her father, at his death, had entrusted her inheritance to his brother. Sarti had worked hard to overcome the memory of his parents' disgrace and had counted on Flavia's sympathy as well as the affection which the Orsani family had always shown him. But soon after he returned to Sicily with his doctor's diploma and established himself in the community, Flavia became Gabriele's wife. Gabriele, in all the time they had spent together in Rome, had never given him the slightest intimation that he was in love with his cousin, but nevertheless he had taken her from Sarti without either making her happy or himself. It was a tragedy for all three of them.

Over the years, as if nothing had happened, he attended Gabriele's growing family as a doctor, trying to hide the distress he suffered every time he entered that loveless household. He sensed the wealth of affection locked in Flavia's heart which Gabriele, neglecting her as he did, probably never even suspected, and the fact that the children were left to grow up without a father's guidance. He wondered if Flavia had ever known he loved her. The answer came during a moment of supreme anguish when one of the children was critically ill. Painfully alone, almost delirious in her anxiety, Flavia had turned to him and opened her heart, saying she had always, always understood, right from the beginning.

And now, at this moment, with Gabriele unconscious before them, she turned to him. "I beseech you to tell me," Flavia insisted, unable to bear the suspense any longer. "Is it serious?"

"Yes," he said briefly.

"Is it his heart? It happened so quickly. Please explain."

"What good would that do? You do not understand the scientific terms."

But she was not content until he explained them.

"Then, is there no hope?" she asked.

He removed his glasses, blinking his eyes. "I would never have had it happen like this, believe me. I wish that I might give my own life to save his."

Flavia turned pale. She stared at her husband and made Sarti a sign to be quiet.

"I would like to say so many things," he went on, unheeding, "but then you understand me so well already, don't you? You know I will do everything I can, without thinking of myself or of you."

"Hush!" she said, terrified.

"Trust me! Why should we reproach ourselves? He never suspected the harm he did us, and he will never know. I will give him all the care of a devoted friend . . ."

Breathless, trembling, Flavia could not take her eyes off her husband.

"He has come around," she said.

Sarti turned to look at him. "No."

"Yes, he moved," she said softly.

They hung there a moment in suspense, eyeing him. The doctor bent down to take the patient's pulse and called to him: "Gabriele . . . Gabriele."

IV

Ashen and weary from the effort of holding himself in check for so long, Gabriele opened his eyes and asked his wife to leave the room.

"I'm all right now. Take the carriage and go for a drive," he said to reassure her. "I want to talk with Lucio. Go!"

Flavia did not wish him to suspect the seriousness of his illness, so she accepted his suggestion, urging him, however, to keep as quiet as he could. Then she said goodbye to the doctor and went out.

After staring at the door through which she had disappeared, Gabriele put his hand to his chest and asked, "Is it the heart? During the auscultation, a funny thing happened. It seemed to me that that little man—what's his name, Lapo? —yes, that little man with the glass eye had tied me up and I couldn't free myself. You laughed and said, 'Failure—' wasn't that it?—'failure of the aortic valve'?"

Sarti blanched when he heard him repeat the technical term he had explained to Flavia.

Gabriele smiled. " I heard you, you know."

"What . . . exactly what did you hear?" Sarti asked, a painful smile on his lips as he struggled for control himself.

"What you said to my wife," Gabriele replied calmly, staring before him with sightless eyes. "I saw . . . it seems I could see through closed lids. Tell me, please, without beating around the bush, without any silly lies—how long do I have to live? The less, the better."

Sarti observed him, astonished and frightened, especially by his extraordinary calm.

"What has come over you?" he asked.

"An inspiration!" Gabriele exclaimed, his eyes flashing. "Ah . . . by God!"

He pulled himself up and went over to the door leading in to the bank where he buzzed for Bertone.

"Listen, Carlo," he said as the clerk appeared. "If that little man who was here this morning should come back, have him wait. Better still, send someone or go find him yourself right away. He said he was going to the café next door."

He closed the door and turned to Sarti, rubbing his hands together as if in gratification.

"You sent him! Now I'm going to grab him by that wavy hair of his and plant him between us. I want to take out some insurance. Tell me just how to go about it. You are the company doctor, aren't you?"

Tortured by doubt as to how much Orsani had overheard, Lucio Sarti was taken aback by his sudden decision, which did not seem to make any sense. For the moment he felt relieved.

"What foolishness!" he exclaimed.

"Why?" Gabriele replied quickly. "I can pay the premiums for three or four months anyway. I know I won't live longer than that."

"You *know*?" said Sarti, forcing a laugh. "And who set this inflexible time limit? Go along with you!"

Somewhat reassured, he thought it was just a subterfuge to find out the truth about his condition. But Gabriele was quite serious and began to talk about his inevitable financial ruin. Sarti turned cold. He now saw that his sudden decision had a reason behind it and he felt cornered. Having sent the inspector to Orsani that morning, how could he in all conscience fail to approve Gabriele's application without betraying the gravity of the illness which had struck him so suddenly?

"But you can live a very long time, my friend, if you take the necessary precautions," said the doctor.

"Precautions? How?" Gabriele cried. "I've lost everything, I tell you! You still insist I can live a long life? So much the better. If that is true, there is no moral difficulty for you to approve."

"How about your own calculations?" asked Sarti, suddenly remembering what Gabriele had said. "If you can afford to honor the premiums only for the next three or four months? . . ."

Gabriele thought for a moment. "Take care, Lucio. Don't deceive me. Don't raise this question to try to dissuade me from an action of which you don't approve, something you don't want to be implicated in—although it would involve little or no responsibility on your part."

"There you are mistaken!" Sarti said before he could check himself.

Gabriele smiled bitterly. "Then it's true," he said. "Then you know I'm doomed, perhaps even before the time I've allowed. I heard you, you know. It's all a question now of trying to save something for the children. And I mean to provide for them! Don't worry, if there's any mistake in the timing, I'll know how to die, and no one will be any the wiser."

Lucio Sarti rose, shrugging his shoulders, and glanced around for his hat.

"Since you won't listen to reason," he said, "allow me to leave."

"Reason?" cried Gabriele, grasping him by the arm. "Come here! I tell you I'm going to provide for my children, understand?"

"But how do you mean to provide for them? Do you seriously think you can do it this way?"

"By my death."

"Nonsense! Excuse me, but do you expect me, as your doctor, to stand here and listen to such talk?"

"Yes," said Gabriele violently, still holding him by the arm, "because you are going to help me."

"To kill yourself?" asked Sarti wrathfully.

"No. That, if necessary, will be my concern."

"What, then? Cheat? Steal?"

"Steal? Steal from whom? We are dealing with a company which exposes itself to such risks. Don't interrupt. What they lose on me they gain from a hundred others. But call it stealing—it is still my concern, not yours. I'll make it straight with God. You don't enter into it!"

"You're mistaken," Sarti repeated emphatically.

"Will you benefit from this money?" Gabriele asked, staring pointedly at him. "It will be paid to my wife and three children. So what risk is there for you?"

Under Orsani's look, Lucio Sarti realized that his friend had really heard everything he had said to Flavia. Gabriele was now only controlling himself to accomplish his purpose, to place an insurmountable obstacle between his friend and his wife by making Sarti an accomplice to this fraud. Acting for the insurance company, he could not declare Gabriele in good health today and hope to marry Flavia if she was the beneficiary of this insurance. The company would most certainly suspect him. But why this intense hatred even beyond the grave? The things he had overheard should prove beyond a doubt that he had nothing with which to reproach either of them. What was the reason, then?

Sustaining Orsani's look, he determined to defend himself until the very last, but his voice wavered when he asked, "What risk do you mean?"

"Wait," said Gabriele abruptly, as though surprised by his own perception. "Don't forget I was your friend long before you became associated with this company. Wasn't I?"

"Of course . . . but . . ." Lucio stammered.

"Don't worry. I'm not going to throw anything up to you. I'm only trying to point out that you are not putting *me* first at this moment, but the company."

"But fraud . . ." said Sarti heavily.

"So many doctors make mistakes," Gabriele retorted. "Who can accuse you of anything? Who can say at this moment that I'm not perfectly fit? I'm the picture of health. I may die in five or six months, but what doctor could foresee that? In any case, so far as you and your conscience are concerned, you are duty-bound, as my friend, to deceive me."

Crushed, his head bowed, Sarti took off his glasses and

rubbed his eyes; then, in a trembling voice, he tried to make a last stand.

"I would prefer to find another way to accomplish what you call dutifully deceiving you."

"How?"

"Do you remember where and how my father died?"

Gabriele stared at him, bewildered, whispered to himself, "What's that got to do with it?"

"You are not in my position, so you cannot judge," Sarti went on, replacing his glasses, his jaw set. "Remember how I grew up and allow me to act decently now, with no regrets."

"I do not understand" said Gabriele coldly, "what regrets you could possibly have in insuring my children's future."

"At the expense of others?"

"I have no such intentions."

"But you know that will be the result."

"I know something else which means far more to me and should to you. There is no other way. Because of this scruple of yours which I cannot share, you would have me refuse an opportunity which you have laid at my door."

He went over to the door to listen, making a sign to Sarti to be quiet.

"There, he's come in."

"No. It's useless, Gabriele," Sarti cried in desperation. "Don't force me."

Orsani once more seized his arm. "Mind you, Lucio! This is my only chance of saving myself."

"Not this way," protested Sarti. "Listen, Gabriele: by all that's sacred I promise that your children ..."

"Charity?" he sneered.

"No," Lucio replied quickly. "I will only be repaying you what you have given me."

"By what right? How could you provide for my children? You? They have a mother. By what right? It's not only gratitude, is it? You lie! You refuse for another reason which you dare not admit!"

As he spoke he took Sarti by the shoulders and shook him, commanding him at the same time to lower his voice and asking how far his deceit had gone. Sarti, refusing to submit to violence, tried to free himself, to defend himself and Flavia.

"We'll see," Orsani said between clenched teeth.

He went to the door and called Vannetti in, masking his agitation with enforced gaiety.

"A prize! he cried as he returned with the ceremonious little man. "A big prize for our friend, Dr. Sarti, the company's most eloquent advocate. I was about to give up the idea, put it out of my mind, but he convinced me. He overcame all my doubts. Hand him the medical declaration to sign immediately. He is in a hurry. He has to leave. Then we'll work out the whys and wherefores between ourselves." And he clapped him on the back.

Vannetti, delighted, took a printed form out of his briefcase and handed it to Gabriele in a burst of congratulations, repeating, "A mere formality ... a mere formality."

"Here, sign this," commanded Gabriele, putting the form down in front of Sarti, who looked as if he were in a trance, his eyes riveted to the ridiculous, jerky little man—the personification of his unlucky fate.

FUMES

As soon as the miners came up from the bottom of the pit, dead tired and gasping for breath, their eyes sought the distant green of that hill which closed off the wide valley to the west.

Here, on these parched slopes of burned shale, not a blade of grass had grown for some time. Sulfur mines rose like ant-hills and seared the surrounding ground with their fumes.

The green hill soothed their eyes, smarting in the daylight after so many hours spent in darkness.

For those whose job it was to feed the furnaces or the huge melting pots with chunk sulfur, for those who watched over the molten sulfur, or for those who worked under the furnaces catching the slow-moving mass of burned sulfur which dropped into their hods of damp wood, the very sight of all that green in the distance eased the pain of breathing —the bitter curse of the fumes which clung to their throats, causing grim spasms of suffocation.

The little Sicilian boys let their loads fall from their bruised, skinned backs and sat down on the sacks for a breath of air. They were caked with slimy clay from the walls of the tunnels and the sides of the slippery stairs with their broken steps which led up from the "hole." Scratching their heads, they peered through the glassy sulfurous vapor, which shimmered in the sunlight as it rose off the melting pots. Sometimes they thought about life on those farms, a happy life in the open air without risk or drudgery, and they envied the farmers.

"They are blessed."

That far-off hill was a land of dreams for all of them. From over there came the oil for their lanterns which barely pierced the utter darkness of the mine. From there came their coarse, black bread which kept them going through the long day's grind. From there, wine, their only comfort—wine to give them courage and strength to endure this cursed life, if

182

one could call it life: underground they looked like ghosts at work.

The farmers on the green hill spat when they looked across the valley at those parched slopes.

There, in those devastating fumes, they saw their enemy. When the wind blew in their direction carrying the stench of burned sulfur, they gazed helplessly at their trees and cursed the fools who went on digging graves to bury their fortunes. Not content with drying up the whole valley, they were envious of the little spot of green, and wanted to destroy those beautiful farms with their pickaxes and furnaces.

For it was rumored that there were sulfur deposits under the hill. Those ridges of siliceous limestone at the top, with crystal outcroppings at the base, made it very plain, and mining engineers had often confirmed it.

Although courted by rich offers, the farm owners not only refused to lease their subterranean soil for exploitation but would not make the most superficial test, if only out of curiosity.

The country lay there spread out in the sunshine for all to see, subject of course to bad years but compensated by the good ones. As for the sulfur mines, they were blind holes, and woe to him who slipped and fell in. He is no wise man who will give up a certainty for an uncertainty.

Every landowner on the hill hammered the alternatives into the others' minds, like a pledge of unity against temptation. They knew that if one capitulated and a sulfur mine should rise in their midst, all would suffer. Once destruction began, other yawning mouths of hell would open and in a few years the trees and plants would die, poisoned by the "fumes." Then, farewell, green hill.

II

Among those most often approached was Don Mattia Scala, the owner of a little farm with a fine stand of almond and olive trees. His land was halfway down the slope of the hill, and here, to his disgust, all indications pointed to the richest deposit of minerals.

Several engineers from the Royal Mining Corps had come to study these outcroppings and make tests. Scala received them as a jealous husband would receive a doctor who came to his house to examine his wife for a secret illness.

He could not close the door in the face of men sent out by the government on official business. But he got his own back by shooing away others who came—either on behalf of rich mine owners or from mining companies—with proposals to lease the rights to his land.

"Lease! Nothing doing!" he cried. "Not if you offered me the riches of Croesus! Not even if you said: Mattia, scratch here with one foot like a chicken, and you'll find enough sulfur to make you as rich as—who shall I say?—as Midas with all his gold! I swear, I would not scratch!"

If they still persisted, he would shout, "Now, go away, or I'll call the dogs!"

He was obliged to repeat this threat quite often because the gate to his farm was on a *trazzera,* or mule track, across the hill, which was used as a shortcut by men who worked in the mines: miners, overseers, engineers, on their way to and from the valley. The engineers took pleasure in goading him, and if they caught sight of him in his garden, they would stop by the gate to call out, "Changed your mind yet?"

And Don Mattia, to scare them away, would call up his dogs.

"Here, Scampirro! Here, Regina!"

He too had had the sulfur mania at one time, but it had sucked him dry. Now the sight of sulfur, even at a distance turned his stomach.

"What is it? The devil?" they teased him.

"Worse! Because the devil may damn your soul, but if he chooses he can make you rich, whereas sulfur makes you poorer than Job and damns your soul into the bargain!"

Tall, lean, pale, with a white hat pushed back on his round head, he looked like a telegraph pole. He wore little gold rings through his ears, which stamped him as half middle-class, half peasant, a fact he took no pains to conceal.

He was liked by all the landowners on the hill.

They remembered that he had once been very rich and they were glad that, after losing almost everything, he had come there to live on those few acres bought with money he was able to realize on the sale of his house in town. For the town house had gone with all its furnishings, and he had

had to sell the jewels of his wife, who had died of a heart
attack. They remembered too that, at first, he had shut himself up in the four rooms of the little farmhouse and refused
to see anyone. Iana, a child of about sixteen then, lived
there with him, and they thought she was his daughter
until they discovered she was the young sister of Dima Chiarenza, the scoundrel who had tricked him and brought about
his ruin.

There was a long story behind it.

Mattia Scala had known Dima Chiarenza since he was a
boy. Both of his parents were dead, and his sister was much
younger than himself. Scala helped him, gave him a job, and
even made him his partner after he had leased a sulfur mine.
Scala assumed the financial burden of the operation, and
Dima Chiarenza was to stay on the job in order to direct and
supervise the work.

Meanwhile Iana (Ianuzza, they called her) grew up in
Mattia's house, with his only son, Neli, about her own age.
Mattia and his wife soon noticed that the attachment between
the two children was not one of a brother for a sister. Not to
keep the straw too near the flame, they wisely decided to send
Neli away for a while until he was at least eighteen. The
boy went to the sulfur mine to lend Chiarenza a hand and
to keep him company. They contemplated a wedding in another two or three years, if everything went on smoothly.

How could Don Mattia Scala ever have suspected Dima
Chiarenza, whom he trusted as he did himself, whom he had
taken in off the street and treated like a son? Dima Chiarenza
had betrayed him as Judas betrayed Christ.

That was the way it happened. Chiarenza was in league
with the chief engineer of the mine, he plotted with the overseers, made deals with the weighers and carters. He stole
with impunity from administrative expenses, from the sulfur extracted, and even cheated on the coal used for the en-
gines that pumped water out of the mine. And one night the
pit was flooded, completely destroying the ramp which Scala
had built at a cost of three hundred thousand lire.

Neli was on the spot that infernal night. He had helped in
the desperate, futile efforts to prevent disaster. Foreseeing his
father's hatred for Chiarenza, a hatred which might extend
to Iana, Dima's innocent sister, Neli thought that he too
might be held responsible for this havoc because he had not

denounced the thief who was soon to be his brother-in-law. He fled in panic in the midst of the furor and disappeared without leaving a trace.

A few days later, his mother died, devotedly nursed by Iana. Scala found himself alone, without funds, his wife and his son gone, too. Only the girl remained, almost out of her mind with shame and grief. She clung to him, refusing to leave, and threatened to jump out the window if he sent her back to her brother. Won over by her insistence, Scala swallowed his repugnance and agreed to take her with him to his little farm.

Gradually, as time passed, he emerged from his brooding silence. He began to exchange a few words with his neighbors, telling them about himself and the girl.

"So, then she is not your daughter?"

"No, but it's just as if she were."

At first he felt ashamed to say who she really was. He never mentioned his son; the pain went too deep. And, for that matter, what news had he to give? None! The police, after a long search, had found no trace of him.

Several years later, Iana grew tired of waiting hopelessly for her fiancé's return and decided to go back to town to live with her brother. He had married a rich old woman, a notorious usurer, and he too had turned moneylender. In no time, he became one of the richest men in town.

Scala lived on alone at the farm. Eight years went by, and outwardly, at least, he appeared to be himself again. He made friends with all the landowners on the hill, who often gathered at his place in the evening.

Nature seemed to be trying to make up to him for all he had suffered. He was lucky to acquire those few acres because Butera, a rich landowner on the hill, had taken it into his head gradually to acquire all the land. By lending money, he extended the boundaries of his domain. He had already swallowed half of Nino Mo's farm, and by advancing money on dowries for five daughters, had reduced Labiso's holdings to a corner of ground no larger than a handkerchief. He had eyed Lopes' land for some time, when the owner, after a series of bad years, took it into his head to sell off a piece at a lower price to a stranger—Don Mattia Scala.

In no time, by throwing himself into his work completely, trying to numb his sorrow, Don Mattia improved the land so much that his friends were amazed, and Lopes most of all. Actually he was consumed with jealousy. A slovenly man, his face florid and freckled, he wore his hat tilted far forward as if to avoid seeing anyone or anything. But occasionally from under the brim of that hat, an unexpected sidelong glance would flash out of his sleepy green eyes.

After a turn about the farm, the friends would come back to the little clearing before the house.

There Scala would invite them to sit on the low wall buttressing the steep slope on which the house stood. At the bottom of the slope behind the house rose a few tall, dark poplars, much to Don Mattia's annoyance. He could not figure out why Lopes had planted them there.

"What good are they? Tell me that. They don't bear fruit and they're in the way."

"Chop them down for charcoal," Lopes replied indolently.

But Butera advised, "Not so fast. First see if you can get someone to take them off your hands."

"Whoever would want them?"

"Woodcarvers, perhaps, for statues of saints."

"Saints? Oh, now I understand," Don Mattia concluded, "why saints no longer work miracles if they are made out of wood like this!"

Toward evening, those poplars were the meeting place of all the sparrows on the hill. Their incessant, noisy twittering disturbed the friends who lingered below to discuss the sulfur mines, as usual, and the havoc they wrought.

Nocio Butera generally opened the discussion. He was by way of being a big fish in that little pond because of his landholdings. He had studied to be a lawyer, but only once in his life had he exercised his profession—just after he had taken his degree. The poor young man had memorized his speech and believed he would be able to reel it off without a hitch for his first court case. However, in the middle of his address to the jury, he lost the thread of what he was saying and could not go on. Tears welled up in his eyes as if he were a baby, and before the whole court he shook his clenched fist in the face of Justice, standing aloft, scales in hand.

"And then what? Good God!" he groaned aloud in exasperation.

Sometimes they reminded him of that famous fiasco: "Eh, and then what? Good God!"

Nocio Butera pretended to chuckle with them, muttering through his teeth, "Yes . . . yes . . ." as his plump fingers scratched the black whiskers on his ruddy cheeks or adjusted the gold-rimmed glasses on his lumpy nose. He could have afforded to laugh wholeheartedly with them because, despite his bad start as a lawyer, he now carried the flag as farmer and property manager. But men are never content with what they have. Nocio Butera seemed to take delight only in other men's failures. When he came to Scala's farm, it was usually to announce the current or imminent downfall of this one or that one and to string off the reasons behind it, proving how such a thing could never have happened to him.

Tino Labiso, very tall and already gone to seed, drew a large red-and-black checked handkerchief from his pocket and blew a blast from his nose which sounded like a sea trumpet. Then, carefully folding the handkerchief again, he passed it several times under his nose before returning it to his pocket. Like a prudent man not given to rash judgment, he would hazard, "Could be!"

"Could be? Is . . . is . . . is!" Nino Mo burst out, unable to abide Labiso's apathy.

Lopes showed signs of life under the big hat tipped over his nose and mumbled, "Let Mattia do the talking. He understands these things."

But always, before Mattia would settle down to talk, he went to the cellar for a jug of wine to offer his friends.

"Here's some vinegar. Poison yourselves!"

He drank, too; then, sitting down and crossing his knees, he asked, "Well, what's the matter?"

"The trouble is that they're a bunch of fools," Nino Mo exploded as usual. "All of them together and each one separately."

"Who?"

"Those sons of bitches, the mine owners! They dig and dig and the price of sulfur goes down, down, down. Why can't they understand they bring about their own ruin as well as ours by pouring money into those pits—those greedy hellholes which will swallow all of us!"

"What's to be done?" asked Scala.

"Limit production," replied Nocio Butera calmly. "Restrict

the production of sulfur. As I see it, that's the only solution."

"Madonna! What nonsense!" Don Mattia exclaimed, rising to his feet in order to gesticulate more freely. "Forgive me, dear Don Nocio, but you're out of your mind and I'll prove it to you. Tell me, out of, say, a thousand mines, how many do you think are directly exploited economically by the owner? Barely two hundred. All the others are leased. Do you agree, Tino Labiso?"

"Could be," Labiso repeated guardedly.

And Nino Mo: "Could be . . . *is, is, is!*"

Don Mattia raised a hand to silence them.

"Now, Don Nocio, what is the tenure, do you think, that the greed and power of these mine owners—all as paunchy as yourself—allow in leasing a mine? Tell me seriously."

"Ten years . . ." Butera hazarded, with a condescending smile.

"Twelve," Scala conceded, "sometimes twenty. Now what can be done in that time? What profit can be dug out in so few years? However speedy and lucky they may be, there is no possible way of amortizing the costs of operating a mine even in twenty years. I'm saying this to show you that, given a slump, the owner-operator might conceivably slow down his production to steady the market. But for the short-term tenant-operator, that's impossible. He would only be sacrificing his interests for the benefit of his successor. Therefore he is bound to produce as much as he can under existing circumstances. Do you follow me? If he is caught short, as generally happens, he is forced to sell his sulfur for whatever he can get to keep going, because if he shuts down, you know, the owner can repossess the mine. The result of all this— as Nino Mo says—is that the price of sulfur goes down, down, down, as if it were no better than common gravel. For that matter, can you, Don Nocio, an educated man, and you, Tino Labiso, tell me what the devil sulfur really is and what it's used for?"

At these direct questions even Lopes gaped. Nino Mo thrust restless hands in his pockets as if searching for an answer. Tino Labisco again pulled out his handkerchief to blow his nose, taking his time like a cautious man.

"Oh, that's a good one!" exclaimed Nocio Butera, also embarrassed. "It's used . . . it's used for . . . for spraying the vines."

"And . . . and also . . . in making matches . . . I think," added Tino Labiso, refolding his handkerchief.

"*I think. I think,*" Don Mattia scoffed. "What do you think? That's just the point. Ask anyone you like. Those are the only two answers they will give. They couldn't tell you of anything else. Meantime we slave, we knock ourselves out digging for it and carrying it down to the sea where all the big ships are anchored—English, American, German, French, even Greek —their holds open and waiting to suck it in. Then they give a fine blast on their whistles and—farewell! What use do they make of it out there in all those countries? No one knows. No one bothers to find out. Our riches, or rather our would-be riches, are drained from the veins of our gaping mountains while we stand by like so many blind men or simpletons, our bones aching from toil, our pockets empty. And what do we have left? These slopes, which once were farms, now completely parched by fumes from the sulfur which has been carried away."

After this poignant account of the way industry and commerce, with all the attendant merciless quarrels and money clashes, were exploiting their treasure—a treasure bestowed on them by nature—the four friends were speechless, as if sentenced to perpetual misery.

Then Scala returned to his first subject and began to enumerate the burdens a tenant-operator had to bear. He knew them all only too well, after years of bitter experience. Besides the burden of the short-term lease, he had to pay a tithe, or share in kind, of the gross amount of sulfur extracted. The owner was not interested in knowing whether the deposit was rich or poor, whether the nonproductive zones were rare or frequent, whether the subterranean levels were dry or flooded, whether prices were high or low—in brief, whether or not it was a paying venture. And, besides the tithe, there were all kinds of government taxes to be paid. In the mine itself, not only ramps had to be built, but shafts for ventilation and for the evacuation of water, roads and huts, furnaces and melting pots—all that was pertinent to the exploitation of a mine. Then, at the expiration of the lease, everything became the property of the owner, who even demanded that it be turned over to him in good working order —as if he had been the one to bear the expense of all these installations! It did not end there. The tenant-operator could not mine the sulfur the way he deemed best, but was obliged to follow the dictates of the owner and to construct arches, supports, or trusses, often contrary to the specific requirements of the terrain.

One had to be desperate or out of his right mind to accept such conditions—presenting one's throat like that to the knife. Who were these tenant-operators anyway? A penniless lot of poor devils who, in order to operate their rented mines, had to incur more debts and submit to more abuse, soliciting loans from the sulfur traders down by the sea.

And when it was all added up, what was left for the operator? Could he possibly pay a more miserable salary to the poor wretches who slaved underground, constantly exposed to death? Life was a struggle—hatred, starvation, and poverty for all: the operators, the miners, and the young boys, crushed under their heavy loads, toiling up and down the slippery stairs and along the dark tunnels of the pit.

When Scala stopped talking and his neighbors rose to go back to their farms, the moon, high and seemingly lost in the firmament, appeared to belong to a time long past, after the recital of so much misery. Under its light the desolation of the valley looked more sepulchral, more evil.

Each was thinking as he went along that beneath those moonlit slopes, five or six hundred feet underground, people were breathlessly digging, digging. It made no difference to the poor miners buried down there whether it was night or day because, for them, it was always night.

III

Judging from Scala's words, everyone was convinced that he had all but forgotten his tragic past and no longer cared about anything save his little piece of land which he had not left in years, even for a day.

If someone brought up the subject of his son, lost in the great world somewhere, he eased his loss by speaking harshly of the boy's ingratitude and callousness.

"If he lives," he said, "he lives only for himself. For me, he is dead, and I no longer think about him."

He talked that way, yet in all the outlying district there was not a peasant leaving for America who did not receive a furtive visit from Don Mattia on the eve of his departure. He came secretly to entrust him with a letter for his son.

"Not that I think anything will come of it . . . but if you should, by any chance, happen to run into him or even hear tell of him over there . . ."

Many of those letters, crumpled, yellow, almost illegible, came back again when the immigrant returned four or five years later. No one had seen Neli or even heard of him, either in Argentina or in Brazil or in the United States.

Don Mattia would listen and shrug his shoulders: "What difference can it make, after all? Give it back to me. I don't even remember sending it . . ."

He wanted to hide his grief from strangers, deluding himself with the hope that his son was in America, in some remote place, and would come back one day to discover that his father had made a new life here in the country and was waiting quietly for his return.

Perhaps his land did not amount to much, but for several years Don Mattia had secretly nursed a dream of enlarging it. He had already come to an agreement with his neighbor, and a price was fixed on that adjoining land. There was no limit to the privations and sacrifices he made to accumulate the necessary funds. He fell into the habit of leaning on the balcony of his little house, letting his eye vault the low wall which separated his land from that of his neighbor, and regarding it as his own. The money was ready. All that was needed was for his neighbor to sign the deed and clear out.

It seemed like a thousand years to Scala, but unfortunately he had to deal with an eccentric, a good enough man, mind you, but odd. Don Filippino Lo Cicero was quiet, polite, and meek, but without doubt not all there in the head. He read Latin from morning till night and lived all alone with a monkey he had received as a present.

The monkey was called Tita. She was old and tubercular to boot. Don Filippino took care of her like a child. He caressed her, giving in to her whims without complaint. He talked to her and was convinced she understood him. When she was depressed because of her illness, she would perch on the canopy of his bed, a favorite spot of hers, while he sat in his armchair reading aloud passages from the *Georgics* or the *Bucolics*.

"Tityre, tu patulae . . ."

The reading would be interrupted from time to time by exclamations over a phrase, an expression, sometimes a single word of which Don Filippino savored the sweetness or appreciated the exquisite fitness. He would place the book carefully on his knees, half close his eyes, and repeat rapidly, "Beautiful, beautiful, beautiful," as he slowly sank back against the chair, swooning with pleasure. Then Tina would come down from the top of the bed and anxiously climb up on his chest. In his ecstasy Don Filippino would often embrace her and say, "Listen, Tita, listen . . . beautiful! Beautiful!"

Don Mattia Scala grew tired of waiting. He wanted that land. He was in a hurry and he was right. The price was set, the money ready, and Don Filippino needed that money. But, dear God, how could he ever find the same pleasure in reading the pastoral poetry of his divine Virgil in the city?

"Be patient, Don Mattia."

The first time Scala heard this, his eyes opened wide in astonishment.

"Are you joking or serious?"

Joking? Not in the least. Don Filippino was most serious. It seemed to him that Scala could never understand certain things. For instance there was Tita, accustomed to living in the country, who might not take to living in the city, poor little thing.

On nice days Don Filippino went for a walk with her. He allowed her to walk alone very, very slowly for a while before he picked her up in his arms and carried her like a baby. When he sat down on a stone to read under a tree, Tita would climb up through the branches and, hanging by her tail, swing back and forth trying to grab the tassel of his cap or snatch off his wig or whisk Virgil out of his hands.

"Be good, Tita! Please do me this favor, my poor Tita."

Yes, the dear little thing might die any day now, and Mattia Scala would just have to wait.

"Wait," Don Filippino told him; "wait at least until this little beast is no more. Then my land will be yours. Is that agreeable?"

Yet more than a year had passed, and the ugly little beast refused to die.

"Would you like me to give you a cure for her?" Scala asked one day. "I have an excellent remedy."

Don Filippino smiled apprehensively and asked, "Are you making fun of me?"

"No. Not at all. A veterinarian who studied in Naples gave me this cure, and he knows what he is talking about."

"Would to God, Don Mattia!"

"Well, then, take about a quart of good oil. Do you have *good* oil? Really good oil?"

"I'll buy it, whatever the price."

"Good. About a quart. Bring it to a boil with three cloves of garlic."

"Garlic?"

"Three cloves. Pay attention. When the oil comes to a boil, mind you, not just bubbling, remove it from the fire. Then take a good handful of flour from Majorca and throw it in."

"Flour from Majorca?"

"From Majorca, yes, sir! Stir it to a soft paste, the consistency of thick salve, and apply it while it is still warm to the chest and over the back of that ugly beast. Cover well with cotton, plenty of absorbent cotton, and bind with gauze. Understand?"

"Oh, yes. Absorbent cotton, then gauze. And after that?"

"Then open the window and toss her out."

"Ohooooooooo!" Don Filippino groaned. "Poor Tita!"

"Poor farm, I say! You take no care of it. And I'm forced to sit over there looking on from a distance and thinking, the vines are all but gone; the trees have been waiting ten years to be pruned; the fruit trees haven't been grafted, and suckers shoot up unchecked, draining life from them. On all sides, things seem to be begging for help. The olive trees now are only good for firewood. In the end, what will I get for my money? Can I afford to let things drag along like this?"

Don Filippino looked so depressed by these just reproaches that Don Mattia did not have the heart to add any more. What was the use of talking, anyway? The poor man did not live in this world. The sun, our sun, never rose for him; for him, the sun of Virgil's day never set.

Don Filippino had always lived on that farm, first with his uncle, a priest, who had left it to him when he died, then alone ever since. He had been orphaned at the age of three, and his uncle, a lifelong Latin and hunting enthusiast, had taken him in. But Don Filippino had never liked to hunt.

Perhaps this was due to his uncle's accident: the poor man shot off two fingers of his left hand one day while loading his gun. Don Filippino chose to devote himself entirely to Latin, content to swoon with pleasure several times a reading. Whereas his uncle, who had a fiery temper despite his calling, would leap to his feet in transports of rapture, his face flushed, the veins on his forehead bulging until they looked as if they would burst, and read Latin passages aloud. Then he would hurl the book to the floor or into the astonished face of Don Filippino, shouting, "Sublime, God damn it!"

He died of a stroke, leaving Don Filippino in possession of the farm, but it was possession in name only.

The uncle also owned a house in town which he willed to another sister's son, Saro Trigona. Taking into account his position as a hapless sulfur broker and ill-starred sire of a large brood, Trigona had hoped that his uncle would leave everything to him—house and farm as well. He knew, of course, that this would entail taking his cousin, Cicero, to live with him for the rest of his days. Although Cicero had been reared in the country by their uncle, he would never be able to run that farm. However, since his uncle had not shown this consideration and since Trigona had no legal right to the farm, he made every effort to profit from his cousin's inheritance, pitilessly mulcting Don Filippino. He took over everything the farm produced: wheat, beans, fruit, wine, and vegetables. If Don Filippino dared market any of it secretly, as if this were not his lawful right, his cousin Saro managed to find out about it and would descend on the farm in a rage, feeling cheated. Don Filippino would then humbly explain that he needed the money to pay the running expenses of the farm, but all to no avail. Saro would then demand the money.

"I'll kill myself. That's what I'll do!" he cried, pretending to pull a revolver out of his pocket. "I'll kill myself right here before your eyes, Filippino!" I can't go on this way. Nine children, Holy God, nine children all crying to me for bread!"

It was not so bad when he came to the country alone and made these scenes, but sometimes he brought his wife and string of children. This fairly drove Don Filippino out of his wits, accustomed as he was to living alone. Those nine boys, the oldest not yet fourteen, all supposedly crying for bread, took over the peaceful country house like unbridled demons.

They turned it inside out. The rooms shook with yells and screams in a wild stampede which inevitably ended in a collision and a terrible crash. Saro Trigona would then jump up and threaten, "I'll fix them!"

He ran off, chasing after the young rowdies. When he caught up with them, he distributed kicks, slaps, blows, and spankings. Their yells rose in every key as he lined them up according to height. That was how he "fixed" them.

"Hold still . . . ah, what a sight! Look, Filippino, aren't they a picture? What harmony!"

Don Filippino stopped his ears, closed his eyes, and stamped his small feet in despair.

"Take them away! They break everything; they ruin the house, the trees, everything! For pity's sake, take them away and leave me in peace."

Don Filippino seemed to forget that his cousin's wife never came empty-handed. She brought either an embroidered cap with a beautiful silk tassel—the one he was wearing, for instance—or slippers, those on his feet, which she had made herself. And his wig? A present from his cousin to prevent him from catching colds, to which he was exposed by his premature baldness. A wig from France! It had cost Saro Trigona a pretty penny. And what about Tita, the monkey? Was she not a present, too, from his cousin's wife, as a surprise, to amuse him and keep him company on his lonely farm?

"Jackass! Excuse me, but you're an ass!' cried Don Mattia Scala. "Why keep me waiting any longer? Sign the deed and free yourself of this yoke. With the money I'll hand over, you can live peacefully in the city for the rest of your days—given your simple needs and habits. Are you weak-minded? If you go on this way, you'll end by begging in the streets out of love for that Tita and your Virgil!"

Mattia Scala considered the farm as good as his and, not wishing to see it deteriorate further, made Cicero an advance payment.

"We will deduct so much for pruning, so much for the grafts, so much for manure, Don Filippino."

"Go ahead and deduct," Don Filippino sighed. "Just let me stay on here. In the city, with those nine devils close by, I'd be dead in no time. I'm not in your way here. You

are the master, dear Mattia. You can do whatever you please
and I won't say a word. All I want is to be left in peace."

"All well and good," Scala replied, "but meanwhile your
cousin enjoys all the benefits."

"What can that matter to you?" Cicero pointed out. "You
were to have paid the money in a lump sum. Instead, you
give it to me little by little, and in the end with one de-
duction today, another tomorrow, I will be the loser because
you will have paid for all the land and I . . . will have nothing."

IV

Don Filippino's reasoning was convincing, no doubt, but
meanwhile what security did Scala have for the money he
paid out? If Don Filippino should suddenly die—God forbid—
with no time for signing the necessary papers acknowledging
receipt of the money already paid against the sale, would
Saro Trigona, his sole heir, honor those payments and agree
to the sale?

From time to time this doubt arose in Don Mattia's mind,
but then he reasoned that, if he should try to force Don Filippino to give him possession of the farm, using the money already advanced as a lever, he might retort, "Who obliged
you to give me the money? As far as I'm concerned, the
farm might have stayed as it was; it didn't matter to me. You
can't put me out of my own house if I don't want to go."
Besides, Scala thought, he was dealing with an honest man
who wouldn't hurt a fly, and there was little danger of his
dying suddenly with the sober life he led. Healthy and vig-
orous as he was, he could last another hundred years. At
any rate, a time had been set: at the monkey's death. She
couldn't keep them waiting much longer.

It was such a piece of luck for him to get the land for
that price that he decided to be quiet and wait. Meantime,
he was glad to have a string attached to it, as it were, by
putting down small payments from time to time, whenever
he chose. He felt like the master and spent more time over
there than he did on his own farm.

"Do this . . . Do that . . ."

He gave orders and watched the farm improve. Meanwhile he had no taxes to pay on it. What more could one ask?

Poor Don Mattia! He might have been prepared for anything but that the cursed monkey, who had already given him so much trouble, would play such a final trick.

Scala had the habit of rising before dawn in order to supervise the preparations for the day's work, which he had laid out the previous evening with the farmhand. For example, if pruning was to be done that day, he wanted no running back and forth to the house for tools, ladder, or grindstone to sharpen a sickle, or a hatchet, water, or even lunch. The boy must leave, provided with everything he needed so as not to waste time.

"Got your jug and a bite to eat? Here, take an onion, too. And now get a move on!"

Thus before sunup Don Mattia was generally on his way to Cicero's farm. But that day, because he had to light a fire in the charcoal kiln, he was late. It was after ten when he arrived, and, oddly enough, Don Filippino's door was still closed. Don Mattia rapped. There was no reply. He rapped again— got no answer. He looked up to the balcony and found the shutters still closed as if for the night.

That's strange, he thought, going around to the farmer's house to talk to his wife. But her door, too, was closed. The farm looked deserted.

Scala put his hands to his mouth like a megaphone and called out to the farmer across the garden. He was answered a moment later from the bottom of the slope. Don Mattia called back asking the man if Don Filippino was with him. The farmhand replied that he had not seen him.

Alarmed, Scala returned to knock on the door once more, calling several times, "Don Filippino! Don Filippino!"

There was no reply. He did not know what to think and started pulling at his big nose. Only the evening before, he had left his friend in good health, so he could not now be so sick that he was unable to get out of bed. Perhaps he had merely forgotten to open the windows at the front of the house and had taken the monkey for a walk. Or perhaps he had closed the front door since there was no one at the cottage to look after the house.

Having reassured himself, Scala began looking for Don Filippino around the farm, stopping occasionally here and there to glance about with the watchful eye of an experienced farmer and make a mental note of any repairs that were needed. He called out as he went along, "Don Filippino! Don Filippino!"

In this manner he finally came to the far end of the property, where the farmer, helped by three hired hands, was digging the earth for the new vines.

"What's happened to Don Filippino? I can't find him."

The farmer looked stunned. He too thought it strange that the villa was still closed at this hour, and Don Mattia's apprehension returned. He suggested they all go back to see what had happened.

"This morning's starting off on the wrong foot."

"I don't understand," the farmer said. "It's not like him! He's always up so early!"

"Maybe the monkey is sick," one of the hired men suggested. "Maybe he's holding her in his arms and doesn't dare move for fear of disturbing her. . . ."

"Not even when he hears his name called the way I've been calling him?" said Don Mattia. "Not likely! Something must have happened."

When they reached the clearing in front of the house, the five of them, one after the other, called him but in vain. They took a turn around the house. On the west side they found one window with the shutters open.

"Ah!" said the farmer. "He has finally opened up. That's the kitchen window."

"Don Filippino!" shouted Mattia. "What's the matter with you? Do you want to drive us crazy?"

They waited, looking up, and they called again at the top of their lungs. Finally in desperation Mattia decided to investigate.

"Get me a ladder."

The farmer ran to his own place and was soon back with a ladder.

"I will go up," Mattia said, pale and distraught, pushing him aside.

At window level he took off his hat to cover his fist and smashed the glass. Then he opened the window and jumped inside.

There was no fire in the kitchen hearth. Not a sound could be heard through the house. It was like the dead of night inside, except for the light which filtered through the shutters.

"Don Filippino!" Scala called out. The sound of his own voice in that strange silence sent a chill down his spine.

Groping his way, he came to the darkened bedroom and stopped short. He saw, or thought he saw, in the dim light a shadow creep across the bed and disappear. His hair stood on end. He could not find his voice to call out. Rushing to the window, he threw it open and turned around. Aghast, eyes popping and mouth agape, his hands waving helplessly, he ran back to the kitchen window, trembling all over and cringing with terror.

"Up . . . up . . . come, come up. Killed! Murdered!"

"Murdered? What do you mean?" exclaimed the men below. They all rushed for the ladder, but the farmer, who wanted to go first, cried, "Mind the ladder now. One at a time."

Lying across the bed, his head thrown back and half buried in the pillow as though violently jerked into that position, Don Filippino lay with his throat ripped open. His hands were raised, those little hands which no longer seemed themselves, livid and grotesquely stiffened as they now were.

Don Mattia and the four terrified peasants stood staring. Suddenly, they were startled by a noise under the bed. They looked into one another's eyes before one of them stooped to investigate.

"The monkey," he sighed with relief, almost laughing.

Then the others bent down.

Tita was crouching under the high bed, her arms crossed over her chest. Seeing those five faces staring upside down at her, she took hold of the bed slats and sprang back and forth on her buttocks. Then she rounded her mouth and made a menacing noise: "khththth . . ."

"Look!" cried Scala. "Blood . . . blood all over her hands and chest! She killed him!"

Then he remembered the shadow he had seen move across the bed when he first came into the room, and he was convinced.

"Yes, she did it! I saw her with my own eyes! She was on the bed."

He pointed to the scratches on the cheeks and chin of the dead man.

"Look at that!"

But why in the world? The monkey who had been close to him for so many years, night and day...

"She may have rabies," one of the workmen cried.

At that, they all moved back from the bed.

"Wait! Get a stick!" said Mattia glancing around the room for something that could be used as a weapon.

The farmer picked up a chair by the back and stooped down, but the others, unarmed and defenseless, took fright.

"Wait! Wait!" they cried.

They picked up chairs, too, and the farmer then pushed his under the bed several times. Tita sprang out from the at the corpse and quickly averting his eyes at sight of that other side of the bed, swung herself up by the bedpost, and went to squat on the canopy. She peacefully scratched her belly as if nothing had happened and played with the corners of a handkerchief which Filippino had tied around her neck.

The five men stood there stupidly gazing up into the indifferent face of the beast.

"And now what's to be done?" asked Scala, looking down bloody throat. "Let's cover him with the sheet."

"No, sir!" said the farmer flatly. "We will leave him just as we found him. I'm part of this household and I don't want to get into trouble with the police. And you're all my witnesses."

"What's that got to do with it?" exclaimed Scala, moving toward the bed.

But the farmer insisted, putting out his hand to restrain him.

"You can never tell with the police. We're poor folk, the rest of us. . . . I know what I'm talking about."

"That may be," Mattia cried in exasperation, "but this poor fool died like a simpleton, a victim of his own stupidity. Meanwhile I'm even crazier and more stupid than he. I'm completely ruined! Ah, but all of you can bear witness to the fact that I poured my own money into this farm, and my own sweat, too. You can tell them. Now go and inform that fine gentlemen, Saro Trigona, and tell the magistrate and the police . . . let them come and see the doings of this— accursed animal!"

In a burst of temper he tore off the hat he was wearing and threw it at the monkey

Tita caught it in midair, examined it attentively, rubbed it across her face as if she were wiping her nose, then stuck it under her and sat on it. The four peasants burst into uncontrollable laughter.

V

There was not a trace of a will, not a mark in a ledger, not even a scrap of paper.

Because of the loss he had suffered, Don Mattia Scala was the laughingstock of his friends. In fact, Nocia Butera said he had easily foreseen that Don Filippino Cicero would wind up that way. He had known that the monkey would finish him off somehow.

So long as his cousin remained unburied, awaiting the certificates of the doctor and the magistrate, Saro Trigona refused to listen, on the excuse that his bereavement made it impossible for him to talk business.

"As if the monkey hadn't made him a present of that farm—in cold blood," muttered Scala, giving vent to his feelings.

He thought Trigona should have coined a gold medal in the monkey's honor instead of having her shot the next day, notwithstanding the pretty explanation given by the young doctor who came out with the magistrate to investigate the case. According to him, Tita, suffering from tuberculosis, probably had difficulty breathing. Then there was the handkerchief poor Filippino had tied around her neck which might have been too tight, and in trying to get it off, she might have pulled it even tighter. She had jumped on the bed, according to the doctor, in an effort to make her master understand that she could not breathe. Possibly she had taken hold of his throat to show him and, exasperated by her suffering, she could have tightened her grip—and the deed was done! After all, she was only an animal. She did not know any better.

Frowning, the magistrate approved the young doctor's rare insight by repeatedly nodding his big, sweaty, bald head.

Then, at last, with his cousin buried and the monkey shot, Saro Trigona put himself at the disposal of Don Mattia Scala.

"Dear Don Mattia, now we can discuss it."

There was little to discuss. Scala, in his jerky fashion, briefly explained his agreement with Cicero and how—waiting from day to day, from season to season, in the hope that the beast would die so he could take over the farm—he had spent several thousand lire on it, with Cicero's full consent, of course. This sum was to be deducted from the price agreed upon for the farm. Was that clear?

"Very clear," replied Trigona, listening attentively to Scala and nodding his head as the magistrate had done. "Very clear. And I, for my part, dear Don Mattia, am disposed to respect this agreement. As you know, I am a broker. These are hard times. To place a cargo of sulfur one needs the helping hand of God. Profits are swallowed up in taxes and portage fees. I tell you this because, with my professional responsibilities, I could not look after a farm; besides, I don't know a thing about it. Then, too, as you know, dear Don Mattia, I have nine sons all in school. One may be dumber than the other, but they all go to school. Therefore I must live in the city. Let's get down to ourselves. There is only one difficulty. Nine children, as we were saying: you can have no idea what that costs me in shoes alone. But there's no point in my adding it up for you. You'd go out of your mind. It's just to show you, dear Don Mattia . . ."

"For pity's sake, don't keep saying *dear Don Mattia*," Scala broke in, irritated by Trigona's interminable speech. *"Dear Don Mattia . . . dear Don Mattia . . .* Get to the point! I've already lost too much time with the monkey and Don Filippino."

"Well, then," Trigona said calmly, "I wanted to tell you that I've been forced to turn to a certain gentleman—God forbid—do I make myself clear? He has a knife at my throat, you understand? You know who the big moneylender is around here. . . ."

"Dima Chiarenza!" exclaimed Scala, jumping to his feet, very pale. He threw his hat on the ground and ran his fingers furiously through his hair. Then, his eyes wide, he pointed the index finger of the other hand like a gun at Trigona.

"You . . ." he said. "You went to that brigand? That cutthroat who devoured me alive? How much did you borrow?"

"Wait, I'll tell you," replied Trigona with agonizing calm. "Not I! Because that brigand, as you so aptly put it, would lend nothing against my signature . . ."

"Then what . . . Don Filippino?" groaned Scala, covering his face with his hands as if he wanted to hide his own words.

"And as security..." sighed Trigona, shaking his head sadly.

Don Mattia turned about the room, crying, "I'm ruined! I'm ruined!"

"Wait," said Trigona." Don't despair. Let's see if we can't remedy it. How much did you intend to pay Filippino for the land?"

"I?" cried Scala, halting, his hands on his chest. "Eighteen thousand lire, all told. There are about six acres of land, at three thousand an acre—spot cash. God knows how hard I worked to get the money together, and now I see the deal fall through, the very ground under my feet—ground I already considered my own!"

While Don Mattia unburdened himself, Saro Trigona frowned and counted on his fingers.

"Eighteen thousand...that is to say..."

"Easy..." interrupted Scala. "Eighteen thousand if the poor soul had turned over the farm to me then and there. But more than six thousand have already been spent on the farm, as you can see for yourself. I have witnesses: this year I put in two thousand American vine shoots; exorbitant! And then..."

Saro Trigona stood up to cut the conversation short, saying, "But twelve thousand isn't enough, dear Don Mattia. I owe that brigand more than twenty thousand. Just imagine!"

"Twenty thousand lire!" cried Scala. "Do you *eat* money, you and your children?"

Trigona drew a long sigh and said, giving Scala a slap on the arm, "My hard luck Don Mattia! Not a month ago I had to pay nine thousand lire to a merchant in Licata on the difference in price of a shipment of sulfur. Never mind! They were the last notes poor Filippino signed for me, God rest his soul!"

After many useless protests, they agreed to go to town that same day, twelve thousand lire in hand, and try to come to terms with Chiarenza.

VI

Dima Chiarenza's house stood on the main square of the town.

It was an old two-story house, blackened by time. English and German tourists who came to visit the sulfur mines used to stop in front of it to take pictures. The natives of the town stared at them with scorn and pity because, for them, the house was no better than a hovel, dilapidated and gloomy. It spoiled the harmony of the big square with the Town Hall opposite, all white, shining like marble, and so stately too with its eight columns forming a portico. Then there was the Mother Church here and the Commercial Bank there, with the imposing coffeehouse on one side and the Club on the other.

According to the members of the Club, the municipality should do something to make Chiarenza give his house at least a good coat of whitewash. It would do him good, too, they said. It would brighten his face, which had taken on the same color as his house. However, they amended, just to be fair, this house had come to him with his wife as part of her dowry, and perhaps, in taking his marriage vows, he had felt obliged to respect the antiquity of each.

Don Mattia Scala and Saro Trigona, standing in the dim light of the huge waiting room, found some twenty peasants, all roughly dressed alike in heavy suits of dark-blue cloth, big hobnail shoes of raw leather, and, on their heads, black stocking caps with pompons at the end. Several of them wore earrings, and since it was Sunday they were freshly shaven.

"Tell him I'm here," said Trigona to the manservant seated by the door before a little table, the top of which was all marked up with figures and names.

"Just be patient a moment," the man replied, staring stupidly at Scala, well aware of his enmity for his master. "Don Tino Labiso is inside."

"He, too! Poor fellow," murmured Mattia, looking at the waiting peasants who were as dumfounded as the servant to see him in this house.

After a while Scala could easily tell from their expressions which had come to settle their debts, which had brought only part of the sum due, and which already had in their eyes the plea they meant to turn on the moneylender to beseech his patience until the end of the following month. Then there were those who had come with nothing, not even a reasonable plea. They looked crushed beforehand at the prospect of starvation, knowing Chiarenza would ruth-

lessly strip them of all they possessed and throw them out
in the street.

Suddenly the door of the "bank" opened, and Tino Labiso,
his face flaming, almost purple, his eyes bright as if he might
have wept, ran off without seeing anyone, holding his red-
and-black checked handkerchief in his hand—an emblem of
his unfortunate prudence.

Scala and Trigona were shown into the "banking room." It
was dark, with only one window protected by iron bars
looking onto a narrow passageway. In full daylight
Chiarenza had to keep a light burning on his desk, covered
by a little green shade.

He was seated in an old leather armchair before a desk
with pigeonholes crammed full of papers. Chiarenza wore a
shawl over his shoulders, a skullcap on his head, and wool
mitts on his hands, which were cruelly deformed by arthritis.
Although he was not yet forty, he looked more than fifty. His
face was yellow, his hair gray and dry, and it hung down
over his temples like that of an invalid. His glasses were
pushed up on his narrow, wrinkled forehead, and he gazed
before him with almost lifeless eyes shadowed by heavy
lids. Evidently he had to make an effort to quell his agitation
and present a calm front before Scala.

The knowledge of his infamous reputation only inspired
him with hatred, a gloomy hatred against everybody but particularly against his old benefactor and first victim, Mattia
Scala. Chiarenza did not yet know what was wanted of him,
but he was determined to agree to nothing, not to appear in
any way to repent the crime he had always scornfully
denied, passing Scala off as a fool.

Don Mattia had not seen him in many years even from a
distance, and he was stunned by Chiarenza's appearance. He
would not have recognized him had he met him on the street.

God's punishment, he thought, frowning, because he immediately realized that the man, altered as he was, would
consider that he had expiated his sin and that no further
reparation was due.

His eyes lowered, his face stiff with pain, Dima Chiarenza
put one hand over his kidneys to hoist himself out of his
chair. But Saro Trigona insisted that he remain seated and
immediately launched into his habitual entangled phrases to
explain the purpose of their visit: he by selling the farm in-

herited from his cousin to dear Don Mattia, there present, would then be able to pay at once twelve thousand lire against his debt to *caro caro Don Dima*, who, in return, would then agree to take no judiciary action against the Cicero estate, as pending ...

"Easy there, son," Chiarenza interrupted at this point, pulling his glasses down over his nose. "I've already taken steps this very day to recall the notes signed by your cousin, now long overdue. One can't be too careful."

"How about my money?" Scala broke in. "Cicero's farm was worth no more than eighteen thousand lire. But now I've sunk more than six thousand into it, so if an honest appraisal were made, you would not get it for less than twenty-four thousand."

"Good," Chiarenza replied calmly. "As Trigona owes me twenty-five thousand, it means that in taking over the farm I stand to lose one thousand lire plus the interest."

"Twenty-five!" exclaimed Don Mattia, turning to Trigona, his eyes popping.

The latter twisted around in his chair as if it were an instrument of torture, and stammered, "How ... how is that?"

"Well, son, I'll show you," Chiarenza said calmly, again placing his hands over his kidneys as he rose. "Here are my ledgers. They speak for themselves."

"Leave the ledgers out of this!" cried Scala, starting forward. "It's a question of my money ... the money I put into the farm."

"How does that concern me?" said Chiarenza, hunching his shoulders and closing his eyes. "Who made you put it in?"

Furiously Don Mattia repeated the story about his understanding with Cicero.

"Too bad," Chiarenza remarked, scarcely breathing and again closing his eyes to hide his difficulty in controlling himself. "Too bad. I see that, as always, you know nothing about business."

"You dare throw that in my face!" cried Scala. *"You!"*

"I'm not throwing anything in your face, but good God, before laying out your money you should have had enough sense to find out if Cicero was in a position to sell his farm. He had already signed it away in notes that exceeded its value!"

"And so," continued Scala, "you'll also profit from my money."

"I don't profit from anything," Chiarenza was quick to reply. "It seems to me that I already pointed out that, according to your estimated value of the land, I stand to lose at least a thousand lire."

Saro Trigona tried to interrupt, flashing the twelve thousand lire Mattia had in his portfolio before Chiarenza.

"Money is money!"

"And how it flies!" retorted Chiarenza. "The best investment for money today is land. I will have you know, my friend, that notes are double-edged weapons. Interest rises and falls, but land remains stable."

Don Mattia agreed and, changing his tone and manner, told Chiarenza of his long love for the adjoining farm. He said that, after all the privations he had endured, he did not know how he could ever bear to lose it. If Chiarenza would be content, for the moment, with the sum he had with him, he would pay him the balance down to the last cent. He would give him the money, not Trigona, and he would hold to the price of twenty-four thousand lire, as though he had not already put six thousand into it. He would even go up to twenty-five thousand if Chiarenza would agree to wipe out Trigona's debt.

"What more can I say?"

Dima Chiarenza listened, his eyes shut, while Scala talked. Then he said in a solemn voice, "Listen, Don Mattia. I see that this land is close to your heart, and I would gladly let you have it if it were not for my health. But the doctors have ordered rest and country air. . . ."

"Aha!" cried Scala, trembling. "Then you would go there to live next to me?"

"Moreover," Chiarenza continued, "you would not be giving me half the amount I should have. Who knows how long I would have to wait for the rest of the money? Meanwhile, by accepting a small loss, I can recover both my money and my health by taking possession of the land. I want to leave everything in order for my heirs."

"Don't give me this talk!" Scala interrupted indignantly. "You speak of your heirs. You have no children. Are you thinking of your nephews? You're a little late. You never thought of them before. Tell the truth for once: Say, 'I mean to persecute you forever.' Isn't it enough that you ruined me, caused the death of my wife, and caused my only son to run away out of despair? Is it not enough that, in return for the good I did you, you made me a pauper? Must you now take this land away from me, land into which I have put my life's blood? Why, why this hatred for me? What have I done to you? When you betrayed me like a Judas, I did not open my mouth. I was too busy thinking of my wife, who was dying because of what you had done, and of my son, who fled because of you. Proof, material proof of your theft, to send you to jail, there was none. While the whole town with one voice cried, *Thief! Traitor!* I went quietly to that little farm. I said nothing. But there is a God, and he has punished you. Look at those hands—the hands of a thief! See how deformed, how rapacious they are! Ah! You hide them? You are dead . . . dead! Still you persist in doing me harm. But this time you won't succeed. I told you the sacrifice I was prepared to make for that land. Answer me: Will you accept my offer?"

Chiarenza, twisted and grim, shouted furiously. "No!"

"Then, if I can't have it, neither will you."

Scala turned to leave.

"What will you do?"

Scala raised his hand menacingly and looked him straight in the eyes.

"Burn you out."

VII

Once Don Mattia had left Chiarenza's house and had rid himself of Trigona, who sorrowfully tried to explain his good intentions, he first went to see a lawyer friend of his to consult him on this affair. He wanted to know if he could legally prevent Chiarenza from taking possession of the farm.

At first the lawyer could understand little or nothing from Scala's emotional account and tried instead to calm him, but without much success.

"In conclusion," he said, "you have no proofs, no documents?"

"Nothing at all."

"Then what the devil do you expect me to do?"

"Just a moment," Mattia said as he was leaving. "Can you tell me, by any chance, where Scelzi, the engineer, lives?"

When he had the address Mattia decided to go to him right away.

Scelzi was one of the engineers who passed Scala's villa every morning, going along the mule track to the sulfur mines in the valley. He had been the most insistent in nagging him to lease the rights to his land. How many times Scala had threatened him with his dogs to get rid of him!

Although it was Sunday, a day when Scelzi usually saw no one on business, he lost no time having this unusual visitor shown into his study.

"What wind blows you here, Don Mattia?"

Scala frowned; planting himself in front of the younger man and looked him squarely in the eyes, he said, "I'm ready."

"Ah! Excellent! You will lease?"

"Lease, nothing. I want to sell outright. What are your terms?"

"Don't you know?" exclaimed Scelzi. "I've repeated them to you so many times."

"Will you have to make more tests?" Mattia asked, gloomy and reckless.

"No! Look here," said the engineer, pointing to a geological map on the wall carefully marked by the Royal Mining Corps of the region. He put his finger over a place on the map, adding, "It's right here. No need to go any further."

"All right. Draw up the contract immediately."

"Now? Tomorrow . . . tomorrow morning first thing, I will talk with the Administration Council. Meanwhile, if you wish, we can write out an agreement now which will certainly be accepted—unless you want to insert other conditions?"

"I need to tie it up right away," Scala said abruptly. "Everything, all of it will be destroyed, will it not?"

Scelzi looked at him in astonishment. He had heard a little about this man's impulsive nature, but he was not prepared for this.

"The damage done by the 'fumes,'" he said, "is foreseen by the contract, and an indemnity is allowed."

"I know. I don't care, just so the farms are destroyed—all the farms."

"What . . ." Scelzi began, puzzled.

"That is what I'm after . . . that's what I want," Mattia went on, bringing his fist down on the desk. "Here, engineer . . . write, write. Neither I nor he. Everything will be burned up. Write. Pay no attention to what I'm saying."

about his son. He knew that a few months earlier he had

Scelzi sat before his desk and began to write out the agreement, after first slowly explaining the advantageous conditions which Scala had so often scorned. Now the farmer sat there frowning darkly and nodding his consent.

When the agreement was drawn up, Scelzi could not resist asking the reason for this unexpected right-about-face.

"Bad year?"

"Bad year? The year to come, you mean," said Scala, "when the mine opens."

Scelzi supposed that Don Mattia had received sad news made a petition to Rome through the consul asking that another search be made, but he did not want to bring up that delicate subject.

As he left, Scala again urged him to put the business through as speedily as possible. "At once," Don Mattia said, "and see to it that you tie me up well!"

But just the same it had taken two days for the deliberations of the Council, the writing of the contract by a notary, and the registration of the deed itself: two awful days for Mattia Scala. He neither ate nor slept, but followed Scelzi here and there as if he had lost his mind, repeating over and over, "Tie me up well . . . tie me up well."

When the contract was duly signed and witnessed, Don Mattia Scala rushed out of the notary's office like a man who has taken leave of his senses. He ran to the store on the outskirts of town where he had left his mare three days earlier, and rode away.

The sun was setting. An endless string of sulfur carts jolted along the dusty road toward the railroad station in endless succession. Astride his mare, Don Mattia looked with hatred on those springless carts loaded with sulfur from the far-off mines in the valley, beyond the hill which was not yet visible.

The wide road was flanked by two rows of prickly-pear cactus, their fleshy leaves dusted with sulfur from the carts in their incessant shuttling back and forth.

Don Mattia's aversion increased as he watched them. There

was nothing to be seen but sulfur in this place. The very air you breathed was laden with sulfur: it hurt your throat and burned your eyes.

At a turn in the road the green hill finally came into view, touched by the last rays of the sun.

Scala feasted his eyes on it and clenched his fist over the bridle until it hurt. To him the sun seemed to be kissing the green of that hill for the last time. Perhaps he himself would never see it again as he now saw it from the crest of the road. In twenty years, at this very turning, those who came after him would look upon a bare mound, dried and gray, pocked by sulfur mines.

And where will I be then? he thought with a feeling of bitter loneliness. This instantly brought his missing son to mind, roving the world somewhere, if he was still alive. Overcome with emotion, his eyes filled with tears. It was for the boy's sake that he had found strength to rise above the poverty into which Chiarenza had plunged him. And now his tormentor had deprived him of his farm.

"No! No!" he roared between clenched teeth. "Neither he nor I!"

He spurred the mare on as if he would fly there to destroy the farm which could never be his. It was evening when he came to the foot of the hill. The road followed around for a while before it joined the mule track. The moon came up, shining so brightly that it seemed like daybreak. The crickets all around wildly saluted this lunar dawn.

As Scala passed the neighboring farms, he was stung with violent remorse. He thought of his friends, fellow landowners, who were as yet unaware of his betrayal.

All those dear farms would go before long. Not a blade of grass would be left and he, he, would be guilty of laying waste the green hill. In his thoughts, as he drew near home, he was once more seated on his little balcony and was looking at the low wall that bordered his own small farm. He reflected wretchedly that his gaze should have stopped there ... and not leaped over that wall onto his neighbor's land. Without the freedom of that little field—and with his enemy living there beside him—he would feel like a prisoner deprived of air. No! No!

"Destroy it ... destroy it! Neither he nor I! Let it burn!"

He looked around at his trees, his throat gripped in anguish. The centuries-old olive trees with their mighty, gray, twisted trunks stood motionless in a mystical reverie under the moonlight. He imagined those living leaves, furled by the first biting fumes from the sulfur mine. They would soon fall. Then the naked trees would blacken and die, poisoned by the hot breath off the furnaces. Finally the ax. Firewood ... all these trees.

A light breeze came up with the moon's ascent. All the leaves stirred as if sensing their approaching doom, and their shivering rippled along Don Mattia's spine as he stood there bowed over the neck of his white mare.

THE FOOTWARMER

IN the wintertime, what good were those black oaks planted in a double row around the large square to give summer shade? After a rain, every little gust of wind shook water from the leaves onto the people walking below. And this dampness hastened the decay of Papa-rè's poor kiosk.

Apart from these difficulties in winter, the shade those trees gave in summer was surely a blessing. Well ... men take things for granted when they go right, accepting them as their due, but let the slightest thing go wrong and their tempers flare. Irritable, ungrateful beasts, men! Good Lord, why did they have to walk under those trees right after a rain anyway?

It was ironical that Papa-rè's kiosk was considered "im-summer shade in his kiosk either. Actually he could never enjoy it because, winter or summer, he was not there during the day. What he did and where he went were a mystery. He always came back along via San Lorenzo looking very tired, as if he had walked a long way. Although the kiosk was closed most of the time and Papa-rè hardly turned a penny there, he had to pay taxes just like everyone else.

It was ironical that Papa-rè's kiosk was considered "immovable property," when it was likely to walk off by itself at any moment, what with the termites that occupied the premises in place of the owner. But termites were no concern of the tax collector. If the kiosk had taken a turn around the square or ambled up the street, it would still have been taxed the same as any other piece of real estate.

In back of the kiosk was a self-styled music hall, built of wood. To be exact, it was a barracks painted with flowery ostentation where so-called singers held forth to the accompaniment of a honky-tonk piano. How they managed to perform, poor things, was a mystery, for they barely had breath enough to say, "I'm hungry." Yet, reeking of tobacco smoke, the place was jammed every night with customers in carnival mood. They were highly entertained by the clumsy antics of the poor girls, who, when their voices couldn't make it, waved their arms or, more often, their legs.

"Hurrah! Bravo! Encore!" the men shouted, taking sides for this girl or that, and applauding or booing so violently that the police had to come settle their brawls.

Every night Papa-rè waited until after one for these distinguished customers. Half dead of cold, he dozed behind his wares: cigars, tallow candles, matches, tapers, and the few evening papers left over from his usual rounds.

In the early evening he waited for his little granddaughter to bring him the big earthenware footwarmer. Taking it by the handles and holding it at arms' length, he waved it back and forth to fan the coals. Then he banked them with ashes kept in the kiosk for that purpose and, without bothering to lock the door, left the little stove smoldering there untended. Old and decrepit as he was, Papa-rè could never have withstood those cold nights without his footwarmer.

And without a good pair of legs and a shrill voice, how was he to go on selling papers? Years alone had not weakened Papa-rè, nor was it age that made his legs do foolish things, but rather the weight of so many misfortunes. It had all begun when the Holy Father lost his temporal power, and was followed soon after by the death of Papa-rè's wife, and then that of his only daughter—a disgraceful death in a miserable hospital, giving birth to this little girl for whom he went on living and toiling. Ah, if he hadn't the little one to look after . . .

Papa-rè wore an immense, battered old hat, much too big for him, which sank below his eyebrows. It seemed like a symbol of fate weighing on his old age. Who had made him a present of that hat? Where had he ever found it? Standing under it, there in the middle of the square, he seemed to say, "Here I am. If I'm to go on living, I must wear this wretched hat, which is so heavy I can hardly breathe!"

Go on *living!* But he didn't in the least want to go on living! He was bone-tired and hardly earned anything any more. He used to get hundreds of papers; now the distributor gave him a few copies out of pity—and then only after all the other newsboys had been supplied. They fought their way ahead of each other to be the first on the street with the news. Papa-rè now hung behind. He even waited until the women had theirs. When some roughneck shoved him aside, he bore it patiently, withdrawing into a corner, letting them all shoot by like rockets.

"For you, Papa-rè—have fun. Two dozen all for you tonight. Revolution in Russia!"

Papa-rè shrugged, blinked and picked up his pack. He was the last to leave. Then he too tried to run and strain his hoarse voice to a shout:

"Tribu-u-une!"

Then a notch lower:

"Revolution in Russia!"

And finally, almost to himself:

"Read all about it!"

Fortunately there were two porters in via Volturno, one in via Gaeta, and another in via Palestro, who were faithful and waited for him. The other copies he disposed of as best he could, wandering all through the Macao district. Around ten o'clock, tired and spent, he went back to his kiosk, where he waited, dozing, until the customers came out of the café. He was fed up with this godforsaken business. But when you are old, what choice is there? Rack your brains and you'll find none. The only alternative was to jump off the high wall of the Pincio.

At sunset, seeing his grandchild arrive almost barefoot and in rags, wrapped in an old woolen shawl given her by a neighbor, Papa-rè regretted the small cost of that fire which was so essential to him. He had no other comfort in life now but the child and the footwarmer. He smiled as he saw her coming and rubbed his hands together. He kissed the child's forehead and shook the little stove to stir up the embers.

But one evening—either because his hands were colder than usual or because he felt weaker and more tired—as he started to wave the footwarmer back and forth in the middle of the square, it flew out of his hands and broke into pieces. People passing by greeted the crash with howls of laughter, provoked by Papa-rè's expression when he saw the faithful companion of his cold nights fly from his grasp and by the simplicity of the child, who ran forward as if to catch the stove in midair.

Grandfather and grandchild looked dully into each other's eyes. Papa-rè's arms were extended as if they were still in the act of swinging the little stove. But this time he had swung it too far. The live coals hissed there among the shreds of pottery in a puddle of rainwater.

"Cheer up!" he said finally, rousing himself and shaking his head. "Laugh! Laugh, dear, and I will too. Go, my Nena, go on home. Who knows? Perhaps it's for the best."

And he went off to get his newspapers.

That evening he roamed the streets of the Macao neighborhood instead of returning around ten to the kiosk. He knew it would be deathly cold sitting in there. But soon he grew tired. Before going into the kiosk, he stopped at the place on the square where the footwarmer had shattered, as if he might still find a little warmth from its charred remains. The jarring sound of the battered piano came to him from the cafè, broken by scattered applause and catcalls from the customers. Papa-rè had turned the collar of his shabby overcoat up to his ears, and he clutched the few remaining newspapers tightly to his breast as he stopped a moment to look through the frosted glass door. Must be good and warm in there, with a little hot punch in your stomach! That west wind had started to blow again, lashing his face and whitening the cobbles on the square with frost. There was not a cloud in the sky; even the stars looked shivery-bright.

Papa-rè sighed as he turned to the dark kiosk under the black oaks; then, stuffing the papers under his arm, he was about to shoot back the bolt when a harsh voice called from within, "Papa-rè!"

The old man was startled, and leaned down to peer inside. "Who's there?"

"Rosalba. Where's your footwarmer?"

"Rosalba?"

"Vignas. Don't you remember me? Rosalba Vignas!"

"Ah," said Papa-rè, who had only a confused recollection of the names of the café singers, past and present. "Why don't you go in where it's warm? What are you doing here?"

"I'm waiting for you. Coming in?"

"What do you want with me? Let me take a look at you."

"I don't want you to see me. I'm in here under the counter. Come on in. We'll be fine and warm."

Papa-rè, bending down, went in through the low door and shut it after him.

"Where are you?"

"Here," the woman answered.

She could not be seen, hidden there under the counter where Papa-rè displayed his papers, cigars, boxes of matches, and candles. She filled the space where Papa-rè usually put his feet when he sat on his high stool.

"Where's the footwarmer?" she asked again from below. "Don't you use it anymore?"

"Hush! I broke it today. It slipped from my hands as I was swinging it."

"What a pity! You'll die of the cold in here. I'd counted on your footwarmer. Sit down. Let me warm you up, Papa-rè."

"You? Warm me up? How? I'm old, child. Go on with you. What do you want of me?"

The woman broke into a shrill laugh and took a firm hold of one of his legs.

"Now, be quiet," said Papa-rè, pushing her away. "You smell of liquor. Are you drunk?"

"A little. Please sit down. You'll see there's room for both of us. Up . . . up . . . on the stool, like that. Now let's warm up your legs. Want another footwarmer? Here it is."

She put a bundle on his knees. How nice and warm it felt!

"What's this thing?" asked the old man.

"My baby girl."

"Your baby. . . . You brought your baby here, too?"

"He turned me out of the house, Papa-rè. He left me."

"Who?"

"Him, Cesare. I'm out in the cold with this baby in my arms!"

Papa-rè got off the high stool, bent down in the dark toward the woman crouching there, and held out the baby.

"Take it, child, take it and go away. I have my own worries. Leave me alone."

"It's cold," said the woman hoarsely. "Are you going to throw me out, too?"

"You can't expect to live here," he said sharply. "Are you crazy or just drunk?"

The woman did not reply nor move. Perhaps she was weeping. The faint sound of a mandolin, titillating the silence, moved gradually closer from the end of via Volturno, and then suddenly turned and was gone, fading away in the distance.

"Please let me wait in here," the woman said.

"Wait. For whom?" asked Papa-rè.

"Him. I told you,—Cesave. He's here in the café. I saw
him through the window."

"Then go find him if you know he's in there."

"I can't with the baby. He's left me, I tell you. He's there
with somebody else. You know who? That Mignon! She
starts singing there tomorrow night. He's introducing her, fancy
that! He even had her take singing lessons from a teacher at
so much an hour! I just want to say a couple of words to
him as soon as he comes out. To him *and* to her. Ah, let me
wait here. I'm not in your way. Besides, I keep you
warmer, too. Papa-rè, with this cold outside and my poor
little baby. . . . It won't be long now, a half-hour, more or
less. Come on, be nice, Papa-rè! Sit down proper and take the
baby on your knees. I can't hold her under here. You'll both
be warmer. The poor mite's asleep; she won't be any trouble."

Papa-rè settled himself and took the baby back on his
knees, muttering, "Just look at the new footwarmer I've found
for myself. . . . What do you want to tell him?"

"Nothing. Just a couple of words," she repeated.

They were silent for quite a while. From the station nearby came the mournful whistle of an occasional train, arriving or departing. A few stray dogs crossed the big, deserted
square. On the other side two night watchmen passed,
wrapped in their cloaks. In the silence even the hum of the
street lamps could be heard.

"You have a grandchild, haven't you, Papa-rè?" the woman
asked, settling herself further under the counter with a sigh.

"Nena? Yes."

"No mama?"

"None."

"Look at my little girl. Isn't she pretty?"

Papa-rè did not answer.

"Isn't she pretty?" the woman insisted. "Now what is to
happen to her, dear little thing? But I can't go on like this
any longer. Someone will have to take her in. You see, I
can't find work with her in my arms. Where can I leave her?
Then, too, who would hire me? They won't take me on even
as a servant."

"Do be quiet!" the old man said nervously and began to
cough.

He remembered his daughter, who had left him a little
baby so like this one on his knees. He hugged the child to

him tenderly, but the caress was not for her; it was for his own grandchild, who had been small and good and quiet like this one.

A loud burst of applause and shouts rang out from the music hall.

"That bastard!" the woman cried through clenched teeth. "He's having a time for himself in there with that ugly monkey. She's as withered and dried up as an old stick. Tell me, does he still stop here every night like he used to for a cigar as soon it lets out?"

"I don't know." Papa-rè shrugged.

"Cesare, from Milan, you know him perfectly well! That blond, tall, big fellow with his beard parted on his chin. He's a handsome devil and he knows it, the rat. He makes use of it, too. Don't you remember last year when he took me off with him?"

"No," replied the old man dryly. "How do you expect me to remember if you won't let me see your face?"

The woman gave a laugh that sounded like a sob and said, "You wouldn't recognize me any more. I'm the one who used to sing duets with that fool, Peppot. You know Peppot? Monte Bisbin? Yes, that's the one. But it doesn't matter if you don't remember. I'm so changed. He finished me off, used me up in a year. And you know what? At first he even said he wanted to marry me. That's a good joke! Imagine!"

"Imagine," repeated Papa-rè, starting to doze off.

"Of course, I never believed him," the woman continued. "All I wanted was to stay with him because this little creature was on the way. I don't know how that happened; perhaps it was because I was so much in love with him that God wanted to punish me. Later on it was worse. So I had a daughter. Seems like nothing! Gilda Boa—you remember Gilda Boa? Well, she told me, 'Get rid of it!' How do you like that? He'd have agreed to get rid of it, all right. He had the nerve to say it didn't look like him! But look at her, Papa-rè—if she's not his spit and image! Ah, the brute! He knew very well it was his; I couldn't have made it with anybody else, because there was never anybody for me but him. I loved him so. I was like a slave to him. He beat me, and I didn't complain; he let me almost die of hunger, and I didn't complain. How I suffered, God knows, Papa-rè. But

not for me, you understand; for this little one here. I had no
milk for her unless I ate. Now . . ."

It went on that way a while longer, but Papa-rè was not
following. He was tired, and comforted by the warmth of that
little baby he had found there in place of his footwarmer, he
had fallen asleep as usual. He was roused with a start when
the door of the cafè opened and the noisy customers began
pouring out into the night while the last applause still rang in
the room. Where had the woman gone?

"Hey! What are you doing there?" Papa-rè asked sleepily.

She was hiding on all fours behind the legs of the high
stool on which Papa-rè was seated. She had opened the little
door with one hand and lurked there, panting like an animal.

"What are you doing?" Papa-rè repeated.

A pistol shot rang out just outside the kiosk.

"Lay low, or they'll arrest you, too!" the woman cried as
she rushed out, banging the door after her.

Papa-rè, frightened by the shouts, curses, and all the dread-
ful confusion around the kiosk, cowered there trembling as
he bent over the little one, who had jumped at the sound of
the shot. A carriage pulled up and soon after rattled off toward the Hospital of Saint Anthony. A knot of excited people
went past the kiosk, shouting and gesticulating, then disappeared in the direction of the Piazza delle Terme. There were
others who still stood about heatedly discussing the incident,
and Papa-rè strained his ears to listen. He didn't move, however, for fear the baby might start crying. Then one of the
waiters from the cafè came up to the kiosk to buy a cigar.

"Did you see what happened, Papa-rè?"

"I . . . heard . . . it . . . all," he stammered.

"And you didn't move?" said the waiter, laughing. "Always cozy in there with your footwarmer, eh?"

"With my footwarmer, yes," Papa-rè said, leaning over, his
toothless mouth open in a wan smile.

THE UMBRELLA

"And wittle boats, wittle boats," Mimi repeated, toddling along, trying to step out in front of her mother, who held her firmly by the hand under the umbrella.

Dinuccia, her elder sister, walked along as prim and serious as a little old woman. She held an old torn umbrella in both hands. It would be handed down to the maid as soon as the new umbrella was bought.

"Umbrella," Mimi went on, "two umbellas, two waincoats, four wittle boats."

"Yes, darling, little boats and all, but hurry," her mother urged impatiently, trying to move more quickly through the shifting mass of people who pressed along the sidewalk in the drizzling rain.

Suddenly the store lights flashed on with a low hum, a blinding contrast of opalescent, glowing red and yellow.

The hard-pressed little mother, as she hurried along, was thinking that seasons should never change—above all, winter should never come! Such an expense! Every year new books were needed for school, and new clothes to protect the girls against the cold, wind, and rain. Poor darlings, orphaned before the younger had had time to learn to say "Daddy!" How wretched she felt to see them going off mornings without the proper things to wear.

Having been accustomed to comfort all these years, she found this sudden reversal all the harder to bear. Try as she might, she could not stretch the meager pension left by her husband any further.

Now that Mimi was enrolled in kindergarten, tuition cost six lire more a month—and she could not bring herself to take Dinuccia out of private school. But tuition was the least of her worries. She had to keep up appearances in that school where all the other students came from well-to-do families.

But she did not lose her head. Now that her husband—who was almost twenty years older than she—had died unexpectedly, leaving her with two children to raise, she went back to finish her schooling. Armed with a diploma and availing herself of her husband's connections, she made the most of her unfortunate situation to get appointed to a new class in a supplementary school. But even her salary added to the pension was barely enough to make ends meet.

Had she wished—but she never bothered to dress well, and now, combing her hair hurriedly every morning and pulling on an old hat to go off to school, without glancing to right or left. . . . Still, had she wished—already two offers of marriage—and why did men turn to look at her, even tonight walking between the two children in this rain? What folly even to think that she would give Dinuccia and Mimi another father.

Meanwhile all those admiring glances—some impertinent, some languid and yearning—annoyed and irritated her, but deep within they excited her. They made her renunciation of worldly pleasures seem heroic. They made her daily sacrifice for the children seem light and beautiful.

Her pleasure was like that of a miser whose self-inflicted privations do not bother him so long as he knows he can have anything he wishes. But what if the miser's gold should lose its value from one moment to the next?

Some days, for no reason at all, or rather for no reason she cared to admit to herself, she felt restless and cross, taking advantage of the slightest pretext—and how many there were—to flare up. Dinuccia became the target of her ill humor. The serious, inquiring look on the child's pale face provoked her mother's outbursts. She felt a reproach in those large, pensive eyes.

"Goose!" she cried, turning on the child.

Why goose? Could the little girl understand the reason for this irritation when even her mother refused to comprehend it? Dinuccia was surprised to see her mother less lighthearted than usual. But it was not at all surprising, with all the demands and worries and difficulties plaguing her.

However, she used them as an excuse to hide her remorse for speaking harshly to the child and making her cry. Although her troubles were real enough, her refusal to admit the reason for her nervousness made her all the more depressed and upset.

Fortunately there was the little one, Mimi, who with that

winning way of hers performed the same miracle of restoring calm every time. She tried to put her simple, loving look into words, forming them with cherry-red lips.

"Pretty . . . Mama pretty."

Then she would bow with her hands behind her back, shaking all the black ringlets on her little head.

"You like?"

She never could manage "Do you like me?" but only "You like?" Her mother would open her arms and, almost before that little creature could fling herself into them, she would start to cry, hugging her close. Quickly she called Dinuccia and hugged her, too, very tenderly, especially after she had snapped at her. Her depression gave way to overwhelming joy at the thought of these two little girls to whom she was so willing to dedicate herself.

But this evening their mother was feeling gay.

"Come, Mimi, here we are."

The little one was staring wide-eyed into a dazzling shop window on via Nazionale. Pulled away by her mother, she went into the store, repeating, "Boats; first wittle boats."

"Yes, hush!" her mother told her as a clerk came over to wait on them.

"Boats . . . there, you see, you've made me say it, too! I mean two pairs of——"

"Boats," prompted Mimi.

"Show me some rubber boots for these children. The baby calls them 'boats.' It really *is* a nicer word than galoshes."

"Overshoes," corrected the clerk dryly, raising his eyebrows with an air of self-importance.

"Little boats is cuter."

"Me first, me first!" cried Mimi, clambering up on a chair and waving her feet.

"Mimi!" her mother scolded with a severe glance.

Dinuccia instantly noticed the change, and her grave eyes took on that questioning look which so irked her mother. Neither of them paid attention to Mimi's joy as the supercilious clerk tried on the first little boot: she wanted to get down immediately and walk, before the other one was put on.

"Sit still, Mimi, or we will go right home. It's too large; can't you see?"

The clerk would have liked to try this pair on the older child before going back to look for a smaller size, but Dinuccia warded him off, pointing to her little sister.

"Silly, what difference does it make?" said her mother, taking her roughly by the arms and lifting her onto a chair. To pacify Mimi, she told the clerk to go for another pair and meanwhile she would try these on the older child.

Dinuccia, with the overshoes on her feet, did not move from her chair. But as soon as she was fitted Mimi slipped nimbly down, clapping her hands and turning around and around like a top, uttering little squeals of joy. First she raised one foot and then the other to examine them. Dinuccia looked on, smiling wanly, but her expression clouded when she heard her mother exclaim, "Forty *lire!* Twenty lire a *pair!*"

"American-made, signora," the clerk replied, meeting the customer's astonished expression with the cool dignity of one who knows the value of his merchandise. "An indestructible article. Look, you can roll it in your fist."

"I understand . . . but . . . for such small feet, twenty lire?"

"We have only two prices, signora," the clerk retorted. "Twenty lire for the small size and thirty-five for the larger. A little longer or a little shorter makes no difference, you understand. It's the labor that counts."

"I was not prepared for anything like that," confessed the mother in distress. "I figured twenty lire for the two pairs at the outside."

"Impossible!" said the clerk, horrified.

"Look," said the mother, trying to bargain with him. "I have other things to buy: two raincoats, two umbrellas."

"We have everything."

"I know. That is why I came here. Will you allow me a discount?"

The clerk raised his hands in protest. "We have a fixed price, signora. Take it or leave it."

The mother gave him a wrathful look: it was all well and good to say *leave* it. But how was she ever going to get those little boats off Mimi's feet now without a tantrum? She should have asked the price first. But who would ever have thought they cost so much? She had counted on spending a hundred and twenty lire for everything, and no more.

"Show me the raincoats," she said. "How much are they?"

"Step this way, please."

"Dinuccia! Mimi!" she called, annoyed. "Now be good, Mimi, or I will take off your galoshes. Come here, let me see. Aren't they still a little too large?"

She would have liked to take them off her feet and try to find a cheaper pair somewhere else. She felt like slapping the clerk.

"No . . . not too big . . . pretty," cried Mimi rebelliously.

"Let me see."

"Pretty, no, pretty. *Very* pretty!" Mimi said again and again, scampering off. She waved her little arms, toddled about, and puffed out her cheeks to blow like the wind, pretending she was paddling through water in her little boats.

Even the clerk deigned to smile at this, although he would have done better not to. The mother mistook the smile for pity, and her blood froze. She thought of the hundred and thirty-five lire she carried in her bag, figuring that if raincoats cost forty lire each and forty for two pairs of overshoes, it left only fifteen lire—certainly not enough to buy two umbrellas. Maybe she could find one—a very cheap one.

But each child wanted to have an umbrella all her own, as well as the little boats. They were not at all interested in the heavy gray raincoats. When they found out that only one umbrella was to be bought, the fight began.

Dinuccia reasoned that, as she was the elder, the new umbrella should belong to her, but Mimi had been promised an umbrella, too, and would not listen to reason. The mother tried vainly to make peace, saying the umbrella would belong to neither one of them, but that they could both go to school under it.

"Then I will cawwy it," Mimi announced promptly.

"No, I will," protested Dinuccia.

"You will take turns," their mother said sharply. To Mimi she added, "You could never hold it straight anyway."

"Yes, I *can* cawwy it, too."

"But it's taller than you are. Look!"

And her mother stood the umbrella beside her. Mimi quickly grabbed it with both hands. This seemed unfair to Dinuccia, who tried to snatch it back.

"Shame on you!" cried their mother. "What a scene! What well-behaved children I have! There, the umbrella is for me. Neither of you shall have it."

Back again on the sidewalk, although they were now wearing raincoats and little boats, both children were silent, brooding with hurt, angry eyes, thinking only of the umbrella. Once they got home the fight would start again. It was all very well to own one umbrella between them, but who would have the privilege of carrying it to school? That was the whole point: to hold the umbrella and walk under it in the rain. Dinuccia felt sure that she should be the one to carry it. Wasn't she proving right now how well she could carry an umbrella in the street? Having carried the old umbrella all the way to the store, why wasn't she given the new one to carry now? Why had it been bought? For her mother to carry rolled up under her arm? Her mother was walking with Mimi under her own umbrella, and she was left to struggle with the ugly old one. It was Mimi, tyrannical Mimi, who deserved to be punished. She was too little anyway to carry an umbrella. Let her just try it once!

Thinking of her grievances, Dinuccia stole a glance from under her umbrella, careful not to tilt it and hoping her mama would notice how well she was carrying it. But she saw a dark scowl on her mother's face such as she had never seen before. The umbrella wobbled between her little hands. A shiver ran down her spine. She thought that not only Mimi but her mama, too, was bad. Carefully shielding Mimi under her own umbrella, her mother was paying not the slightest attention to her, leaving her with that awful old umbrella which leaked and was so heavy it made her arms ache. She wondered how much longer she could manage to hold it.

The mother, having left the store angry and humiliated, now struggled to put a wicked thought out of her mind—a terrible thought which she knew would leave an ugly mark if she allowed it to reflect on her conscience. But there were times when she was faced with hard reality that the same thought had occurred to her: if only she did not have Dinuccia—not that she should die, God, no!—but if she were not there, if she had never been born! Mimi was always so gay and natural. With only Mimi, she might have remarried. Mimi would soon find her way into the heart of a new father. She would put her little arms around his neck, shake all her curls, and ask, in that enchanting way of hers, "You like?" Who could resist her? But Dinuccia, with those serious, questioning eyes ... ah, she could imagine only too well those eyes turned pensively on a stepfather. No, never! With that child she could never marry again. It was out of the question.

She glanced down at Dinuccia and, as usual, a flood of remorse and anxious affection swept over her. There she was, walking along intent on proving just how well she could carry an umbrella. It made the mother smile. If only some passer-by would remark, "'Look at that little girl, how nicely she carries her umbrella!" That old umbrella, poor dear, how happy she would be if she could carry the new one. Yes, but Mimi ... Mimi always got her way. She should never have promised her one in the first place when she could not afford to buy two. Mimi was selfish. It was only right for Dinuccia, who could carry an umbrella so well, to have the new one instead of that old thing.

At this, she gave the new umbrella to Dinuccia, but the child did not welcome it with as much enthusiasm as her mother had anticipated. Could she possibly have guessed her guilty thoughts?

The new umbrella felt so much lighter that Dinuccia looked up with a grateful little smile, but this did not satisfy her mother, who turned immediately to Mimi.

"Stay close beside me like a good little girl, under my umbrella. Dinuccia will carry her own umbrella. What would people say if they were to see her with that old thing? 'Ah, how poor she is,' they'd say. 'She must be somebody's little housemaid.' You wouldn't want them to say anything like that about your sister, now would you?"

Mimi did not answer. She was busy with her own concerns. As soon as they got in the door, she was going to tell her mama, "Me umbella ... me cawwy umbrella upstairs."

Once in her possession, the umbrella would be safe! And when they reached the top of the stairs, she refused to surrender it, protesting that Didi had carried it for a long time in the street. Then the inevitable fight broke out. While their mother was in the next room taking off her things, Dinuccia tried to grab the umbrella away from Mimi, and it fell with a bang on the floor. Mimi screamed, and immediately the umbrella was restored to her. Dinuccia was punished and went without any supper.

Later, when her mother went to look for her, she found her

sound asleep, curled up on the floor in a corner beside the big wardrobe. She was burning with fever. Now her mother understood why she had not rejoiced when she gave her the new umbrella in the street, and why, always so patient with her little sister, she had made Mimi cry that evening.

"Oh, God, no," the mother cried in alarm, picking the child up in her arms. "My little Dinuccia . . . no . . . no . . . no."

She undressed her and put her to bed, sitting by her side drained of all feeling, as though in a trance.

That night it poured and all the next day. The rain came down without a let-up for six days in a row.

Mimi's first thought when she awoke the following morning was about the umbrella, which she had carefully placed beside her bed before going to sleep. She was delighted to see it was still raining so she could wear her little boats and her new raincoat, too. She would go to school with her feet in the boats and hold the umbrella proudly over her head in the rain.

No? She was not going to school today? Why not? Dinuccia was sick? Too bad, because it was such a lovely rainy day.

She wanted to ask her mother to send her to school with the maid, but her mother cried and paid no attention to her. She went to the kitchen to ask the maid, but found her about to rush out to call the doctor. She was in such a hurry she did not even turn around.

Mimi looked out the window for a while, watching the beautiful rain, then she put on her little boats and her raincoat before the looking glass. She pulled the hood up over her head and all the way down to her eyebrows. Then she opened the beautiful umbrella. It was a little difficult, but she managed, and she stood there looking at herself blissfully in the mirror, feet together, shoulders hunched as she laughed and shivered under the imaginary rain.

Every morning for five days Mimi rehearsed the same routine before the glass. Again and again she went back to look at herself before taking off the raincoat and overshoes and hiding the umbrella in a secret corner known only to her. Now the umbrella was hers, all hers, and she would never give it up, not even to Mama. What a pity all that nice rain was going to waste!

On the evening of the sixth day the maid took Mimi to the apartment next door occupied by two old ladies, friends of her mama. They had been in and out of her house these last few days, going back and forth between the bedroom and the kitchen, but she was too occupied with her treasures to pay much attention. She was glad her mama was busy with her big sister and did not bother about her, so that she could play winter as much as she liked.

That night she ate at the neighbors' house and played and chattered about all sorts of things with the maid before she finally fell asleep.

She was awakened with a start, very late. The whole house shook with a violent clap of thunder which gradually diminished to a low rumble. The child looked around in bewilderment. Where was she? This was not her home. This was not her bed. She called the maid two or three times before wriggling out of the covers in which she was wrapped. She found she was still fully dressed. The bed beside her was unopened—and suddenly she realized where she was: this was the room where the two old ladies slept. She had visited this room many times. Slipping from the bed, she crossed the dark room and found the front door open wide. Out on the landing, she was terrified by the noise the rain made drumming on the skylight and by the sudden flashes of lightning. The door to her own apartment stood open.

Mimi rushed in and ran straight to the bedroom, calling, "Mama! Mama!"

One of the old ladies sitting by the side of the dying child ran quickly to meet her at the door.

"Go, go, my darling," she said, a finger to her lips. "Hush! Mama is in there."

"Didi?" questioned the child as she caught sight of her sister's waxen face under the soft glow of the night light.

"Yes, dear," the old lady replied. "God wants to take her to Him. Didi is going up to Heaven."

"To Heaven?"

Mimi went away without another word. She stopped in the dark hallway, a little perplexed. Through the open door she could hear the rain beating against the skylight. A flash of lightning lit up the window, revealing the stormy sky. Mimi ran quickly down the long hallway.

A moment later the two old women watching by Dinuccia saw Mimi return with the new umbrella in her arms.

"Here, umbella . . . for Didi," she said falteringly. It's waining up in Heaven."

BOMBOLO

BOMBOLO sat in the café all day long, a red fez on his big, curly head, his legs, straddling the table base, one commanding fist on the marble top and the other on his hip. He would look around, not defiantly but with a stern expression that said flatly, "Make no mistake about it: here you deal with me!"

Landowners came one after another, not only from Montelusa but from all the surrounding countryside—even the old Marchese, Don Nicolino Nigrelli, who always carried an ebony cane and held the round ivory ball of the handle against his puckered lips as if he were playing a flute. Then there were Baron Don Mauro Ragona, Tavella, too—all of them respectfully baring their heads.

"Don Zuli, please do me a favor."

Before this deference, Bombolo would jump to his feet, pull off his fez, and stand at attention, head high, eyes lowered.

"At your service, Excellency," he would say.

The usual complaints, on the one hand, and exhortations, on the other, would soon follow. Nigrelli had lost four head of cattle on the hill; Ragona eight from the sheep fold; Tavella five from the stable. One came to tell him that the boy watching over his herd had been tied to a tree. Another said his cow had been taken and the newborn calf left to die of starvation.

Bombolo would at first show indignation over such outrages, exclaiming, "The villains!"

Then, lifting clasped hands, he would go on: "But, sir, we call them villains, yet in all conscience, how much do these poor villains earn a day? Three tari—one lira and a quarter! That's what they're paid, isn't it? And what's three tari for a man? One of God's poor creatures baptized like you—not like me, a heathen Turk, as you can see," he would say, pointing to his fez. "Tell me, sir, isn't it a moral crime to pay three tari a day to a man who wields a shovel and sweats blood from sunrise to sunset, without pause except at noon, when he takes time out to munch a crust of bread with saliva for a chaser, and then returns to work still chewing his last mouthful? Look at Cosimo Lopes. Since he's been paying his peasants three lire a day, has he had anything to complain about?" Quickly, he pulled a hair from his head and held it up as if it were a talisman. "Three lire, sir, is only right! Do as I say and if tomorrow *any*one mistreats you or your animals, you may come and spit in my face. I'll be here."

In the end, changing both his manner and tone of voice, he would ask, "How many head did you say? Four? Leave it to me. I'll go saddle my horse now."

For two or three days he would pretend to scour the countryside for the missing cattle, riding all night, or so he said, in the rain or under the stars. No one believed it, of course. He well knew that they didn't believe it. But when, upon his return, he would reappear before old Marchese Nigrelli, or Ragona, or any of the others, he was received with the usual exclamations: "Poor Zuli, what a hard time you've had of it!"

"Never mind, never mind. It was not easy, but I tracked them down. You needn't worry; the animals are stabled and well cared for. They are all right where they are. The cattle rustlers themselves aren't so well off. If their lives weren't so hard, you can be sure they'd never resort to this kind of thing. . . . Well, that's all there is to it. They're willing to return the cattle—but, as usual, you understand, in dealing with a gentleman like yourself through my good offices, without agreements or conditions, they leave it entirely up to your conscience. . . . Don't worry! Tonight, without fail, your animals will reappear on the hill, better looking than ever."

He would have taken it as an affront to himself as well as to the landowners had he so much as suspected that the rustlers might be ambushed by the police that night. He knew only too well that if the gentry appealed to him, it was because they had no faith in the authorities. They would never get their cattle back that way. But working through Bombolo, any thought of treachery was ruled out.

Bombolo received the money—five hundred, a thousand, two thousand lire, according to the number of animals sequestered—and every week on Saturday night he brought the total sum to the peasants of the League, who assembled in a store near the top of San Gerlando. There he saw that "justice was done." That is, by computing each peasant's wages at three lire a day, those who had worked for only three tari that week received the difference. Those who, through no fault of their own, had "sat it out" without work were paid seven lire for the week, or a lira a day. However, first of all deductions were made for the small weekly pensions allotted the families of three members—Todesco, Principe, and Barrera—who had been arrested one night by a scouting patrol and sentenced to three years in prison. They had not "sung." Another share was set aside as dues to the watchmen who cooperated by allowing themselves to be bound and gagged. If anything was left over, it was put aside as cash reserve.

Bombolo kept nothing for himself, not a cent. The rumors going around Montelusa were malicious lies. He really had no need for the money. He had made a fortune in the East, where he had lived a long time. No one knew exactly where, nor how, but it was certain that he had money and was not interested in the relatively small sums that passed through his hands. They said you could see what he was by that fez, by his lazily watchful expression, his colorful speech, and the special odor given off by his whole person—spicy, exotic—thanks perhaps to the little leather pouches and small wooden boxes he always carried about him or from the Turkish tobacco he smoked. Because tobacco was a state monopoly, the foreign leaf had to be smuggled off boats in the nearby harbor. Some said he was engaged in shady business. They saw him, they said, sitting there hour after hour with that bright-red cylinder on his head, looking out to sea for all the world as if he were waiting for a sail to appear off Punta Bianca.

He had married into the Dimino family, rich landowners, with holdings so vast you could walk all day and not come to the end of them. Even though their daughter had died four years after her marriage, old Dimino and his wife were so fond of Bombolo that, it was said, they would give him their last cent!

He was a kind of Robin Hood working for justice, happy in the respect, love, and gratitude of the peasants, who looked on him as their king. He held them all in the palm of his hand. Experience had taught him that open meetings, in protest against the tyrannical avarice of the property owners, would only be broken up by the police and the ringleader carted off to jail. That was the way they had always administered justice in Sicily. Even the landowners took no stock in it. But in the store up there on San Gerlando, Bombolo meted out justice in his own way.

If those gentlemen-farmers insisted on paying no more than three tari a day—well, what they didn't give freely, they would have to give by force. Peacefully, without bloodshed or violence, and with all due regard for the welfare of the animals.

Bombolo had a notebook in which he listed all the proprietors of the district, their names, the extent and location of their lands, as well as their livestock, large and small. Each week he would call a secret meeting of his most trusted henchman to decide, from the open notebook, who would "pay the tax" and which peasants were to make the raid. They would be chosen because of their familiarity with the place, their friendship with the watchmen, or their daring.

"A small touch never hurt anyone" was one of his favorite sayings.

But he went wild when one of the members of the League was reported for leeching, or idling. He would go after him and shake him with both hands so violently that the culprit's beret would fly off and his shirt and pants would part company.

"Snake in the grass!" Bombolo would shout. "What do you take me for? A champion of thieves and vagrants? Down here you must sweat blood! Down here on Saturday nights you must report with your back breaking with fatigue, or this will quickly become a den of thieves. If you don't work, I'll crush you underfoot. I'll tear you apart! *Work is the law!* Only by work do you win the right to lead a beast by the horns from the stable of its owner and proclaim, 'Until I am paid what I have rightfully earned by the sweat of my brow, I will keep this animal.' "

In those moments he was frightening. Everyone in the dark store would listen, silent as shadows, staring at the flame of the candle butt melting over the dirty table. After such violent outbursts, Bombolo would gasp for breath, his mighty chest heaving and croaking like an old frog. If one of them had dared look up, he would have seen real tears of rage glisten in Bombolo's eyes. At those moments he saw his austere concept of justice abjectly compromised. He felt the weight of responsibility and a certain scorn and bitterness for his undertaking. The peasants did not seem to appreciate the salary of three lire a day which he had managed to wring from the landowners by harassing them day after day.

It fed his pride to hear the farm gentry themselves say that they had never seen the peasants work harder or more willingly. This alone, in his eyes, purified and exalted the task he had set himself. For him, all those who heeded his constant preaching and granted a fair wage were sacred, and he wanted them to be just as sacred to every other member of the League. When money was needed and he could not turn up a name in his notebook to "pay the tax"—all those listed having already paid up—Bombolo would turn white with rage if a member timidly suggested one of the sacred few. They were untouchable.

Then what?

"Then," Bombolo would explode, tossing the notebook into the air, *"then* we bleed my father-in-law."

Two or three peasants would be assigned to go to the Luna domain, under cover of darkness, and to make off with six or seven big animals owned by Dimino—one of the first landowners to pay his men the equitable three lire a day.

By bleeding his father-in-law, Bombolo was robbing himself because his son was Dimino's only heir. But he preferred to rob himself or his son rather than to go against what he knew was right. And what torment it was for him every time his father-in-law—dressed "old style" in knee breeches, black stocking cap with a pompon on the end, and little gold chains through his ears—sought him out and said, "What's the matter, Zuli? Is this the way they respect you? What's come over you? Have you lost your hold on them?"

"Spit in my face," replied Bombolo, eyes closed, drinking down the gall of Dimino's rebuke. "Spit in my face. What else can I say?"

He was only waiting until the three League members—Todesco, Principe, and Barrere—were released from prison to dissolve the League itself. There were days when those three years seemed to him like a million.

When the day finally came, there was a big celebration in the store on top of San Gerlando. They drank and they danced. Bombolo beamed when he got up to make the final speech. He recalled their deeds and sang their praises. As a reward—the highest reward for those three who had suffered imprisonment—an honest wage had now been firmly established throughout the area. His task was accomplished, he said, and he could retire in peace and contentment. He brought down the house when he added that he had sent his red fez to his father-in-law, who had never been able to stomach the "crown." In giving up the fez he gave up his reign and hereby declared the League dissolved.

Two weeks had not passed before the old Marchese, Don Nicolino Nigrelli, sauntered by the café as usual with the white ivory ball of his ebony cane held to his lips.

"Don Zuli, please do me a favor."

Bombolo went white as the marble table top and turned to look at the poor Marchese in such stupefaction that Don Nicolino backed away in fright and fell into a chair.

Bombolo stood over him, roaring between clenched teeth, "Again?"

Half fainting, although he was trying to smile, the Marchese lifted four fingers of his trembling hand and said, "Four, yes, as before. What's so new about that?"

Bombolo snatched the new hat off his head and tore it to shreds. Trembling, he moved between the tables, banging into them and upsetting the chairs. Then he turned on the Marchese, who still sat among the astonished customers, and cried, "Don't give them a single lira. By the Blessed Virgin! Don't give them *any*thing. I'll have to think this thing over."

Couldn't those three—Todesco, Principe, and Barrera—be content with that "highest reward" of which Bombolo had boasted at the last meeting of the League? If Bombolo himself, toward the end, had allowed them to bleed his own father-in-law, known to be among the first to concede the higher wage, then why couldn't they, in all fairness, continue to bleed the other landowners?

That evening, when Bombolo found them on San Gerlando after an all-day search, he attacked them like a wild beast. They let him strike them and knock them about. They even said he could kill them if he cared to: they would not lift a finger to defend themselves, out of respect and gratitude for all he had done. However, if he did this, he would be killing them unjustly, for they knew nothing at all about the theft. Their consciences were clear. League? What League? There *was* no more League! Hadn't he dissolved it? Ah, so he threatened to denounce them? What for? For their past? Then they were all in it, and he the ringleader. As to a raid on Marchese Nigrelli, they knew nothing about it. But they might well scout the countryside for two or three days and question the brigands, as he had done before them, riding all night in the rain and under the stars.

Hearing them talk like this, Bombolo bit his hands in rage and frustration. He said he would give them just three days. If at the end of that time the four head of cattle had not been returned without a lira of ransom—well, what would he do? He didn't yet know.

What could Bombolo do? Even the landowners themselves —Nigrelli, Ragona, Tavella, and all the others—tried to convince him that there was nothing he *could* do. Where did he come in? Hadn't he always acted as a disinterested party? What was so different today? Why did he now refuse to help anyone? Go to the police? Where would that get them? The police would not bring about the return of their cattle, nor would they find the guilty party who had made off with them. The proprietors themselves said it was simple-minded to expect the cattle to be returned without compensation. They had to make a deal, they said—without agreements or conditions. Just so long as Bombolo would act as go-between!

And from the tone in which these things were said, Bombolo understood that they mistook his present indignation for playacting, just as before they had misinterpreted his sympathy for the peasants.

In rage and despair he shouted that they should go back to paying the peasants three tari a day; they could at least do him that favor. Word of honor, they didn't deserve more than three tari! Shameless thieves! Dogs! Jailbirds! What then? Was he to burst his liver as well as his gall bladder because of these buzzards?

He sent his son to his grandparents up at the big Luna estate to ask them to return his red fez. Turk he was and Turk he would remain!

Two days later, bag and baggage, he went down to the harbor and boarded a Greek ship for the Levant.

THE WREATH

DR. CIMA paused before the entrance to the public gardens which rose on a hill on the outskirts of town. He lingered a moment, looking at the rustic gate, an iron bar suspended between columns. Two melancholy cypress trees loomed behind them, melancholy despite the rambler roses twining in and out of their dark branches. A steep path led from the gate to the top of the hill where a pergola stood out among the trees.

Enjoying the warmth of the early sun, he waited lazily for his inertia to pass so that he could stroll in that old deserted garden. In the cool shade of the northern slope of the hill the air was heavy with the mingled fragrance of mint, sage, and wild plum; the birds twittered incessantly in the nearby trees, welcoming the return of spring. The doctor gratefully breathed in the scented air, then started slowly up the path. New green bursting from all the plants, white butterflies fluttering over the flower beds—all gave a misty, dreamlike turn to his unhappy thoughts. How beautiful it was, this peaceful garden where few if any ever came to stroll!

If it were only mine, he thought, and this yearning was echoed by a prolonged sigh.

How many, like himself, had come here to walk and to sigh, If it were only mine? It is fate that whatever belongs to everyone never belongs to anyone in particular. At every turn a sign was posted: DON'T WALK ON THE FLOWER BEDS. DON'T DAMAGE THE PLANTS. DON'T PICK THE FLOWERS. You could take a look in passing! Ownership means "I" not "we," and only one person could say "I" here: the gardener. In a sense he was the true proprietor, and for this he was paid, given a house to live in, and allowed to pick the flowers which belonged to everybody and to no one, some of which he sold for his own profit.

The singing notes of one particular bird, soaring high above the others, suddenly reminded the doctor of a long-ago vacation he had spent on a dairy farm lost among trees in open country near the sea. He had been only a small boy, but how he loved hunting! Who could remember how many little birds he had shot and killed that summer!

The everyday cares and problems of his profession were set aside for the moment, but not the fact that he had turned forty his last birthday. For him, he thought, the better part of life was over, and unfortunately, he could not say he had ever really enjoyed being young. There were so many wonderful things in life! It could be so beautiful. A radiant morning like this made up for many sorrows, many disappointments.

An idea suddenly occurred to him, and he paused: Should he run back to the house for his young wife? They had been married seven months now, and he would have liked to share this enchanting walk with her. But after a moment's indecision he continued slowly along the path. No. This enchantment must be for him alone.

His wife might have felt it had she come here to walk by herself and without his having suggested it. Together, the charm would be lost. Even, as he thought about it, some of the radiance had faded. A bitter taste of sorrow, vaguely sensed before, rose in his throat.

He could not reproach his wife for anything, poor dear; certainly she was not to blame for the gray hair at his temples and streaking his beard. She was all goodness. But she was only twenty-two, eighteen years younger than he. He hoped the affectionate regard she had shown for him during their brief engagement would naturally turn to love once they were married, and she realized how much he loved her—like a young man despite his gray head. She was the first; he had never loved another woman.

Idle dreams! Love, real love, he had never been able to awaken in his wife—and never would, perhaps. She smiled when he appeared and she showed in many thoughtful little ways that she liked him, but this was not love.

His pain might have been less poignant were it not aggravated by an incident in his wife's life which he was unable to treat with the same gentle indulgence he usually showed for most other things.

With all the fervor of her eighteen years, she had fallen in love with a young student who had died of typhus. He knew this because he had been the doctor called to the boy's bedside. And he also knew that she had almost lost her mind, locking herself in her room in the dark, refusing to see anyone and never leaving the house. She even wanted to become a nun. Everybody at the time talked of nothing else but the sad fate of those two young lovers parted by death. The boy had been popular for his easy wit and charming, polite manner, while she who wept unconsolably after him was considered one of the most beautiful girls in the town.

A year passed before her family was able to persuade her to attend a few gatherings. Everyone was moved by her demeanor, her sad expression and soft smile—especially the men. To be loved by her, to rouse her from her obsessive loss, to restore her to life, to youth, became the dream, the ambition of all of them.

But she clung to her mourning. Malicious rumors began to circulate that, for all her modesty and humility, she must take a certain pride in her grief, realizing the love and admiration it inspired. But this was idle talk, prompted by jealousy and resentment. That her feelings were genuine was proven when, within a few months, she refused four or five offers of marriage from the more eligible young men.

But two years after the tragedy, by which time no one dared present himself because of the certainty of being refused, Dr. Francesco Cima proposed and was immediately accepted.

After the first surprise, however, everyone tried to explain his victory: she had said yes because the doctor was no longer young, and no one would imagine that she had married him for love, true love; she had said yes because, as a rational man, he would not expect to be loved like a young man and would be satisfied if she accorded him affection, devoted respect, and gratitude.

He soon found out how true this was, and it hurt. He had to check himself constantly to keep from blurting out some remark which might betray his suffering. It was torture to feel young and not to be able to express his passion for fear of losing her esteem.

He had been young for only one woman: his old mother, who had died three years before. She would have shared his joy in this beautiful morning, and he would have run to get her without giving it a second thought. That blessed old woman! He would have found her huddled in a corner, rosary in hand, praying for all the sick under his care. Dr. Cima smiled wistfully, shaking his head as he climbed the path up the hill. In praying for his patients his saintly old mother had shown little confidence in him or his training. Jokingly he accused her of this once, and she was quick to reply that she was not praying for his patients at all but was simply asking God to help him care for them!

"So you think that without God's help . . ." he began, but she did not let him finish.

"What are you saying? We need God's help always, my son!"

And so she prayed from morning until night. He almost wished he had had fewer patients, so as not to tire her so much. His smile returned. Remembering his mother, his thoughts resumed the airy unreality of a dream, and the enchantment of the day was restored.

Suddenly his train of thought was interrupted by the new gardener, weeding up above in a grassy plot.

"I'm here, *Signor Dottore*. Have you been looking for me long?"

"I? No, really . . ."

"It's ready—ready and waiting ever since eight o'clock," the gardener said, stepping forward, cap in hand, his forehead pearled with sweat. "If you want to see it, it's right here in the pagoda. We can go there now."

"See what?" asked the doctor, halting. "I don't know . . ."

"But Signor Doctor—the wreath!"

"Wreath?"

The gardener looked at him, equally astonished.

"Excuse me, but isn't today the twelfth?"

"Yes. What of it?"

"You sent your maid day before yesterday to order a wreath for today. Remember?"

"I? For the twelfth? Ah, yes, yes," said the doctor, pretending to remember. "I . . . yes, I sent the maid, of course."

"Violets and roses, don't you remember?" the gardener said, smiling at the doctor's absent-mindedness. "It's been ready since eight this morning. Come and see it."

Fortunately the gardener walked ahead, so he was unaware of the sudden change in Francesco Cima's face as he followed along mechanically, dazed and distressed.

A wreath? His wife must have secretly ordered a wreath. The twelfth, of course—the anniversary of that boy's death. Still such grieving, after three years? She wanted to send a wreath in secret, even now that she was married to him! She who was so timid, so modest, and yet so bold! So she still loved that boy! Would she carry his memory in her heart for life? Why had she ever married him? Why, if her heart belonged to that dead boy and always would? Why? Why? Why?

He raged inwardly as he walked along. He wanted to see the wreath, yes, see it with his own eyes before he was willing to believe his wife capable of such deception, such treachery.

When he saw it on an iron table propped against the wall, it seemed as though it were intended for him, and he stood there a long, long time gazing at it.

The gardener, in his own way, mistook his silence for admiration.

"Beautiful, heh? All fresh roses and violets, you know, picked at dawn. A hundred lire, Doctor. Do you know how much work it is to put all those little violets together one by one? And the roses. They're scarce in winter, and as soon as the season comes on everybody wants them. A hundred lire is very little. It's really worth at least another twenty."

The doctor tried to speak, but he had no voice left. His lips parted in a pitiful smile and finally he managed to get out, "I'll pay you for it. A hundred lire—too little. Roses and violets, yes. Here are a hundred and twenty."

"Thank you, Signor Doctor," said the gardener, quickly taking the money. "I think it's well worth it."

"Keep it here," the doctor said, putting his wallet back into his pocket. "If the maid comes, don't give it to her. I will return for it myself."

He went out of the pagoda and down the winding path. As soon as he was alone and unseen, he stopped and clenched his fists, his face twisting into a sobbing laugh. "And I'm the one who paid for it!"

What should he do now? Take his wife back to her father's house without, of course, saying anything to hurt her? That was what she deserved. Let her go off and cry for that dead boy at a distance without playing unfairly with the heart of an honest man whom it was her duty to respect, if nothing else. Neither love nor respect? She refused the younger men and accepted him because to her he seemed old, and she was sure he would not dream of claiming her love. With that grizzled beard, he would shut an eye, even both eyes, on her consuming sorrow. An old man couldn't object to anything. So she had planned to send a wreath on the sly. Now that she was married, at least she had not thought it fitting to go herself. Yet, however old her husband might be in her eyes, this was carrying things too far. She had sent the maid to order the wreath in proof of her undying love, and the maid would then have taken it to the boy's tomb.

How unjust the death of that boy had been! Had he lived, had he grown to be a man and become familiar with all the little deceits of life and had married his dear, loving girl, she would soon have discovered that it is one thing to make love from a window at eighteen and quite another to face stern, everyday realities when the first ardor cools and the tedium of daily living leads to quarrels. That's when a young husband grows bored and first considers being unfaithful to his wife. Ah, if only she had known such an experience with that young man, then, perhaps, this "old" one ...

He clenched his hands so hard that the nails dug into his palms. Looking down at his white, trembling hands, he got hold of himself. The first shock had passed. He stood there staring; then, seeing a bench not far off, he went over stiffly and sat down.

After all, wasn't this "old" man proposing to act like any young blood—make a scene, create a situation? And all those who had so readily pieced together her reasons for accepting him would then exclaim, "For shame! What on earth for? A wreath of flowers? Why not? She always sent a wreath to the cemetery on the twelfth, but the new gardener didn't know that. This year, too, she remembered, naturally, because the doctor has not been able to make her forget. It was wrong of her, no doubt, but one cannot reason with the heart. And after all the boy is dead!"

That is about what it would amount to.

Then what should he do? Let it go? Pretend to know nothing about it? Go back to the gardener and tell him to give the wreath to the maid, the wreath Cima had intended to keep there to confront her with?

No. Not that. He would then have to get his money back from the man and take him into his confidence.

Well, what then? Go back to the house and demand useless explanations? Face his wife with her poor subterfuge? Punish her? How contemptible all that was! How distasteful!

It was serious, and it went deep—serious because of the ridicule it would cause were his wife's true feelings for him to become known. He must control himself and realize that it did no good to feel young as long as everyone considered you mature, almost on the shelf. A very young man might have made a scene, but at his age he must win his wife's respect another way.

He got up, perfectly calm now, yet with a feeling of list-lessness. The birds continued to twitter gaily in the garden, but where was the enchantment of a moment ago?

Francesco Cima walked out of the garden and started home. When he came to his own front door, his calm vanished. Suddenly breathless, he wondered how he had ever managed the steps on such shaky legs. The idea of seeing his wife again now.... She must be feeling sadder than usual today, but she would probably know how to conceal her sorrow. He loved her—oh, how he loved her! And deep within himself he knew that she deserved to be loved because she was good, just as good as the perfection of her delicate features showed her to be, and the depth of her velvety black eyes, the pallor of her lovely face.

The maid opened the door. The sight of her disconcerted him, for the old woman was in on the secret, a sort of accomplice. She had served his wife's parents for many years and was now devoted to her, so it was likely she would not talk. And certainly she would not be able to assess, or even to understand, what he was about to do. In any case she was an outsider. He wanted this to be a secret between his wife and himself.

He went straight to her room and found her combing her hair before the mirror. Between her raised arms he caught sight of her face, reflecting a look of surprise to see him home at this hour.

"I came back," he said, "to invite you to come out with me."

"Now?" she asked, turning around without lowering her arms, smiling faintly, with that lovely mass of soft black hair piled loosely on her head.

Her pale smile upset him almost to the point of tears. He imagined it held a profound pity for him, for his love of her, as well as her own sorrow.

"Yes, now," he replied. "It is so beautiful out of doors. Hurry. We'll go to the little garden, then farther on, into the country. We'll take a carriage."

"Why?" she asked almost unconsciously. "Why today?"

At that question he feared his expression would surely

betray him. It was already a struggle to keep his voice calm.

"Wouldn't you like to go today?" he said. "It will do you good. Hurry! I want you to come with me." He went to the door and turned. "I'll wait for you in the office."

In a short time she was ready. For that matter she always did as he wished except where her heart was concerned, and there he had no power. She had put up that timid opposition: *Why today?* Yet even today, despite the sadness she must be feeling, she had obeyed him and was ready to go for a ride in the country, wherever he wished.

They went out and walked awhile through the small town; then he hired a carriage and ordered the driver to stop at the little garden. He went up alone, asking his wife gently to wait for him there a moment.

Dismayed when she saw him coming down the path followed by the gardener with the wreath, she almost fainted. But he encouraged her with a look.

"To the cemetery!" he said to the driver, jumping into the carriage.

As soon as they started off, she burst into tears and covered her face with her handkerchief.

"Don't cry," he said softly. "I didn't want to speak about it at home, and I don't want to say anything now. Please don't cry. It came about by accident. I had gone for a walk in the garden, and the gardener, thinking I had ordered the wreath, mentioned it. Don't cry anymore. We will go and leave it there together."

She kept her eyes hidden in the handkerchief until the carriage came to a stop at the gate of the cemetery.

He helped her down, then picked up the wreath and walked in with her.

"Come," he said, taking the first path to the left and looking at the graves, one by one, along the row.

It was the next to the last grave along that path. He took off his hat to lay the wreath at the foot of the grave, then stepped back quietly and withdrew to give her time to say a prayer. But she stayed there, silent, with the handkerchief still pressed to her eyes. She had not a thought, not a tear, for the dead boy. As though lost, she suddenly turned and looked at her husband as she had never looked at him before.

"Forgive me! Forgive me, Francesco! Take me home," she cried, clinging to his arm.

THE ROSE

THE little train moved on through the darkness of the winter evening at a pace that left little hope of its arriving on time.

Signora Lucietta Nespi, Loffredi's widow, bored and tired as she was from the long trip in that dirty second-class carriage, was in no hurry whatsoever to arrive at Peola.

She thought and thought.

Though she was being carried along in the train, her thoughts were still back there in the empty rooms of the house in Genoa. Stripped of the handsome furniture which, almost new, had had to go for a song, the rooms had suddenly seemed very small. What a disappointment! She needed so much, on that last visit, to see them as big and grand, so that when she was poor she could say proudly, "The house I had in Genoa . . ."

She would say it anyway, but the insignificance of those bare rooms would haunt her always. She thought about the good friends to whom she had not even said goodbye at the last minute because they, too, had let her down, though they had pretended to outdo one another in helping her. They had helped all right, by bringing around all those honest buyers whom they had tipped off to the opportunity of picking up for a pittance things that had originally cost a small fortune.

Signora Lucietta tightly closed her beautiful eyes on these unhappy thoughts, then opened them wide again as she lifted her forefinger to pass it along her pert little nose in that unconscious, pretty little way she had.

She was really very tired and would have liked to sleep. Her two fatherless children, poor dears, were sleeping soundly, the older one stretched out on the seat under a coat, and the baby curled up beside his mother, his blond head on her lap. She might have slept, too, if only she could have found a way of resting her head on her hand without waking the child pillowed on her knees.

The seat opposite was still marked where he had propped his little feet until the man had chosen to sit in that place—with all the empty seats in the other carriages!—a big man around thirty-five, dark and bearded, with light-green eyes—big, intense, sad eyes.

Signora Lucietta took an immediate dislike to him. For no reason his large eyes gave her the feeling that no matter where she would go the world would always remain alien to her. She would be lost, vainly calling for help among eyes like those now looking at her, veiled with sorrow but essentially unconcerned.

To avoid them, she kept her face turned toward the window although nothing could be seen outside. There was only the reflection of the oil lamp in the carriage, its little red flame wavering high among the shadows, smoking up the curved glass chimney. The reflection looked like another lamp suspended outside in the night, following after the train with difficulty and giving both comfort and fright.

"Faith," the gentleman murmured.

Signora Lucietta turned to look at him in astonishment. "What?"

"The light that is not there."

Brightening, she looked at him and smiled, pointing to the lamp hanging from the ceiling of their compartment. "But there it *is!*"

The man nodded, then added with a little smile, "Yes, like faith . . . we kindle a light here and we also see it there, without realizing that when it is put out here, there will be no light there either."

"You are a philosopher!" exclaimed little Signora Lucietta.

He raised a hand from the knob of his cane in a vague gesture and sighed. "I observe."

The train halted for a long time at a small junction. Not a voice could be heard. When the rhythmic noise of the wheels stopped, the unbroken silence seemed eternal.

"Mazzano," the gentleman murmured. "Usually there is a wait here for the through train."

Finally, they heard in the distance the plaintive whistle of the other train arriving late.

"Here it comes."

In that oncoming train, rolling over the same tracks on which she would soon pass, Signora Lucietta could hear the voice of her fate condemning her to be lost for all the rest of her days with her two little ones.

She shook off this moment of despair and asked her traveling companion, "Are we far from Peola?"

"It's more than an hour away," he replied. "Are you going to Peola, too?"

"Yes, I am the new telegraph operator. I passed the State examinations. I was fifth on the list, so they assigned me to Peola."

"Oh, yes. You were expected last night."

Signora Lucietta brightened up. "As a matter of fact," she started to say but remembered the sleeping child on her lap. She opened her arms, indicating the two children with a look. "You see how tied down I am ... and alone, with so many things to take care of at the last minute."

"You are the widow Loffredi, aren't you?"

"Yes." Signora Lucietta lowered her eyes.

"Did they ever find out anything more about it?" he asked after a short, weighty silence.

"Nothing. But there are those who know," Signora Lucietta said, her eyes flashing. "Loffredi's real murderer was not the hired killer who struck him in the back and then fled. They tried to imply that there was a woman involved, but I know better. Reprisal! It was political vengeance, pure and simple. Loffredi had no time to think about women. The one he had already took up too much ... what I mean is, I was all he needed. Just imagine! He married me when I was fifteen."

As she said this, Signora Lucietta's face turned bright pink and her restless eyes lit up as they darted back and forth; finally she lowered them as before. For a moment the man watched her, impressed by the rapid change from animation to sudden embarrassment.

How could anyone take this show of feeling seriously? Although the mother of two children, she looked no more than a child herself—a doll. She was ill at ease probably because she had stated so emphatically that, with a wife as young and sparkling as herself, Loffredi had no thought for other women.

She must realize that no one, seeing her and knowing the man Loffredi was, would believe her. No doubt she was influenced by him while he lived, and perhaps still was, in her memory. She could not bear for anyone to think that Loffredi had not cared for her or that, for him, she had been just a doll. She wanted to be sole heir to the sensation stirred up in all the Italian newspapers about a year ago over the tragic end of this fiery, irrepressible journalist.

Silvagni felt well pleased that he had guessed her character so exactly when, after a few well-placed questions, he succeeded in getting her to talk and unconsciously to confirm everything he had surmised.

He had a tender impulse toward this little meadowlark hardly out of its nest and just learning to fly who fancied it was already free, self-reliant and confident in its knowledge of life. No, no, Signora Lucietta would never be at a loss! To think that she had not lost her head through all the horror of that tragedy! She had run here, run there, done this and that, not so much for herself as for those little ones— and, yes, a little for herself, too. After all, she was only twenty—and at times she did not even look that! Her age was another obstacle for her, perhaps the most vexing of all. Everyone seeing her first rebel and then despair laughed as though she had no right to do either. The more furious she became, the more they laughed, each one promising her one thing or another, all of them wishing their offer might be coupled with a little caress which they dared not give. Well aware of their motives, she soon grew tired of their game and, in order to get away, applied for a civil-service job as a telegraph operator.

"Poor signora." Her fellow traveler sighed, smiling—he too!

"*Poor*. Why poor?"

"Ah . . . because . . . you'll see, it is not very amusing in Peola."

And he told her a few things about the town.

Boredom was always visible and tangible in all the streets and squares of Peola.

"How is it visible?"

"In the endless number of sleeping dogs stretched upon the cobblestones. They do not even wake up to scratch themselves; they do it in their sleep.

Anyone opening his mouth to yawn in Peola must beware —it might stay open for five yawns at least; their ennui took that long to come out! If there were anything specific to be done, everybody in Peola closed his eyes and said with a sigh, "Tomorrow . . ."

Because today and tomorrow were one and the same—and tomorrow was as good as never.

"You will see, there is nothing to do at the postoffice," he concluded. "No one ever goes there. Take this little train; it moves along like a stagecoach. Well, even a stagecoach would mean progress for Peola. Life in Peola goes by at the pace of a wheelbarrow."

"Heavens, you frighten me!" said Signora Lucietta.

"Don't be frightened," he said, smiling. "Now I'll give you some good news. In a few days, we're going to have a ball at the Club."

"Ah . . ."

Signora Lucietta looked at him with the sudden suspicion that even this gentleman wanted to make fun of her.

"Do the dogs dance?" she asked.

"No, the good citizens of Peola dance. You must go. It will amuse you. The Club happens to be right on the square, near the postoffice. Have you found a place to live?"

The signora said she had, in the same house where her predecessor had lodged.

"And, excuse me, your name is? . . ." she asked.

"Silvagni, signora. Fausto Silvagni. I am secretary at the Town Hall."

"Oh, really! It's a pleasure."

"Ahem . . ."

Silvagni lifted his hand in a weary gesture and smiled bitterly at her deference, a smile which reflected the melancholy of his large, light eyes.

At last the train greeted the little station of Peola with a plaintive whistle.

"Are we here?"

II

Peola lay ringed within a vast range of blue hills, cleft here and there by valleys of mist, darkened by oaks and firs, brightened by chestnut trees. The little town with its clusters of red roofs and its four bell towers, its uneven squares and narrow streets sloping between small old houses and a few

new and larger ones, now had the thrill of welcoming the
widow of Loffredi, the journalist whose tragic and mysterious death was still referred to in the country's leading newspapers. It was an uncommon privilege to hear directly from
her mouth many things no one in the big cities knew, but it
was almost enough just to see her and to be able to say,
"When he was alive, Loffredi clasped that little thing there
in his arms."

The good folk of Peola were very proud of her presence.
As for the dogs, they would have gone on sleeping peacefully, stretched out in the streets and squares of the town
unaware of this honor, had the rumor not been circulated
that their torpor made a bad impression on the signora. Everyone, particularly the young men but the older ones too, began
disturbing them, chasing them off with kicks or by stamping
their feet and clapping their hands.

The poor animals got up from the ground more surprised
than frightened and cast sidelong glances, barely cocking an
ear. Some of them, tripping off on three legs, the fourth
benumbed and drawn up, went elsewhere to stretch out.
What had happened? They might have understood had they
been less dulled by sleep. They had only to glance at that one
little square where no dog was allowed to lie, or even to run
past.

The postoffice stood on that square!

They might have noticed—had they just a little more
wit—that all who passed there, especially the young men
but the older ones too, seemed to breathe a different air,
more stimulating, which quickened their gait and their move-
ments. The men's heads turned as if a sudden rush of blood
made them uncomfortable in their starched collars, and their
hands busied themselves pulling down vests and adjusting ties.

The square crossed, they behaved as if they were intoxicated, hilarious and nervous. And at the sight of a dog:

"Get along with you!"

"Out of my way!"

"Off with you, ugly little cur!"

They even threw stones at them. Kicks were no longer
enough.

Fortunately, there were those who sided with the dogs. A
window would fly up and a woman, her eyes flashing, her

fists raised, would cry out furiously, "Ruffians! What do you have against those poor animals?"

Or else: "You too, Signor Notary? With all due respect, aren't you ashamed of yourself? What a treacherous kick! Poor little beast! Here, here, doggie. Look at his little paw! You've crippled it, and off you go with a cigar in your mouth perfectly unconcerned. How shameful! And you a decent family man!"

In no time a close bond of sympathy was established between the ugly women of Peola and the dogs, mercilessly persecuted by their men: husbands, fathers, brothers, cousins, fiancés, and, by contagion, all the riffraff of the town.

The women, a little more alert than the dogs—some of them at least—immediately noticed a new air about the menfolk that made their eyes shine and stare into space. The red, moss-covered roofs were brightened, and every corner of the sleepy old town was exhilarated—or so it appeared to the men, at least.

Yes, life so filled with worries, troubles, bitterness all of a sudden had smiled. God, how it smiled, for no reason at all! If, after days and days of fog and rain, a ray of sunlight shines through, doesn't it cheer the heart? Doesn't it draw a sigh of relief from every breast? No more than a ray of sunshine, and yet all life was suddenly changed. The heaviness lifted, the darkest thoughts brightened, and those who had not wanted to leave the house were out of doors again. Smell the good aroma of the damp earth. As good to breathe as the odor of fresh mushrooms. Plans for the future suddenly seemed so simple and easy. Everybody shook off the memory of bad moments, realizing that they had been given too much importance. Courage! Chin up! And up with the mustache, too!

That was the effect of the ray of sunlight which had abruptly pierced the clouds hanging over Peola, brightening the postoffice on the little square. Besides persecuting the sleeping dogs, husbands began to ask their wives, "Dear, why don't you arrange your hair better?"

Never, certainly not for years and years, had the citizens of Peola hummed so much without realizing it—at the Club, in their houses, or walking along the street.

Signora Lucietta saw and felt all of this. Such obvious desire flashed from burning eyes following her every move, voluptuously caressing her with a look, enveloping her with such warmth of feeling that she too became quite intoxicated.

It didn't require much doing because Signora Lucietta was already aquiver, simmering inside herself. What a nuisance they were, those little curls on her forehead, tumbling down every time she bent over to follow the ribbon of dotted paper running through its little ticking machine on the office table! She shook her head and almost jumped with surprise as her hair tickled her neck. What sudden blushes and catchings of breath, ending in a tired little laugh. Oh, but she cried, too. At times she wept without knowing why. Hot burning tears, brought on by a strange longing which ran through her whole body. She could not control those tears, and then, out of the blue, she would laugh again.

She determined to pay strict attention to her work in order not to dwell on anything else, not to let her fancy fly after every amusing or dangerous idea that came to her, not to lose herself in certain unlikely prospects. She must take hold of herself firmly with both hands, so that everything would proceed according to rules and regulations. She must always remember that her two poor little orphans were at home in the care of that stupid old bumptious servant. What a worry that was! Two children to raise all alone, by her own hard work and sacrifices. Today here, tomorrow there, adrift with them—and then, when they were grown and had a life of their own, maybe all the hardships she had suffered would be forgotten. No, now they were still very little. Why imagine such ugly things? She would be older then, her first youth past in any case, and when one is old, it is easier to smile even over sad memories.

Who was talking like that? She was, but not because such gloomy ideas came to her spontaneously. *He* passed the office every morning, that gentleman she had met on the train, and sometimes in the evening, too, when he came from the Town Hall. He would stand in the doorway a moment, or before her counter, talking of different things, even amusing things. For instance, they laughed together about the war on the dogs and about the ugly women rising to their defense. But she read mournful, depressing ideas there in his eyes, those large, clear eyes, and they remained with her long after he had gone.

It was he who had started her worrying about her children

—who knows why?—and without even asking about them or referring to them at all.

She felt annoyed, and repeated to herself that they were still so small—why allow herself to be discouraged? She should not and would not! Courage! She was still young, very young, and then . . .

"Can I help you, sir?" Yes, count the words of the telegram and then add two cents more. Would you like a telegraph blank? No? Well, I just asked. I understand. Good day, signore. Don't mention it.

How many came into the office just to ask silly questions! It was hard not to laugh. They were so comical, those Peola gentlemen. And the delegation of young men, members of the Club who came to the postoffice one morning with their nice old president to invite her to the famous ball Signor Silvagni had spoken of on the train. What a sight! They looked eager, ready to eat her up, and seemed to marvel that, at close range, she had such and such a nose, with eyes and a mouth like that—to mention only her head! But the most impertinent were also the most embarrassed. None of them knew how to begin.

"Would you do us the honor . . ." "It is a yearly custom, signora . . ." "A little *soirée dansante* . . ." "Oh, quite unpretentious, of course . . ." "A family affair." "Let me speak . . ." "What are you trying to say? If you would be so kind as to do us the honor . . ."

They fidgeted, wrung their hands, and stared at one another in an effort to get their words out, while the president, who was also mayor of the town, fumed, turning purple with rage. He had prepared a speech, and they did not even give him a chance to deliver it. He had also carefully arranged the long strand of hair over his bald pate before sticking it down and had worn yellow gloves, inserting two fingers of his right hand between the buttons of his vest.

"It is our custom every year . . ." he began at last.

Although she could hardly keep from laughing, she blushed at these pressing invitations, expressed more clearly in sly looks than big, uneasy words. At first she tried to get out of it: she was still in mourning, as they knew, and then there were the children . . . she could only spend evenings with them . . . she did not see them all day . . . she always put them

to bed ... and there were so many other things she had to
do ...

"Come now, just for one evening." "You could come after
they were in bed." "Isn't the servant there?" "For one
evening ..."

One of the boys, in his enthusiasm, went so far as to
say, "Mourning? What nonsense!"

Someone gave him a sharp poke in the ribs, and he did
not dare utter another word.

Finally Signora Lucietta promised she would go, or rather
that she would do her best to go. Then, when they all had
left, she stood there looking at her little white hand against
her black dress and at her finger on which Loffredi had
placed that gold ring when he married her. Her hand had
been so delicate then, the hand of a child, and now that
the fingers had filled out, the ring was too tight. She could
no longer take it off.

III

In the bedroom of her little furnished apartment Signora
Lucietta was telling herself that she would not go, cradling
in her arms—bye-bye—her blond angel dressed in black—
bye-bye—the smallest one who wanted to fall asleep in her
arms every night.

The older child, undressed by the heavy-handed old
servant, had gone to bed by himself, and, yes, the darling
was now fast asleep.

Very lightly, careful not to waken the sleeping baby in
her lap, Signora Lucietta now undressed him. Very softly,
first one, then the other shoe; the socks, one, two, and now
the little trousers along with the underpants, and now—ah,
now it was more difficult to slip the arms out of the sleeves.
Up, very carefully, with the help of the servant—no, not like
that; here, that's right ... there! Now the other side ...

"No, my darling ... yes, right here with your mama. Mama
is here. I will do it alone, then. Please turn down the bed?
There now."

But why so slowly, all this?

Did she really want to go dancing, a short year after her
husband's death? No, and perhaps she would not have gone

had she not seen—all of a sudden, as she came out of the bedroom into the little hallway in front of the closed window —a miracle.

She had been in that rented apartment for days and had not noticed the old wooden flower box standing there in front of the window. In that flower box a beautiful red rose had just opened—a miracle at this time of year.

She stood there astonished, looking at it as it bloomed between the drab gray hangings of that dirty little entrance, and her heart quickened with joy. In that rose she saw her own burning desire to enjoy herself for at least one night. Suddenly freed from the dilemma which made her hesitate— the specter of her husband, the thought of the children—she picked the rose and, looking into the mirror over the console, pinned it in her hair.

Yes, there! With that rose in her hair she would go to the ball—and with her twenty years, too, and her joy, dressed in black.

IV

It was rapture, delirium, madness!

When she appeared, just as everyone had given up the hope of seeing her, the three dark rooms of the Club, divided by large arches and badly lit with oil lamps and candles, suddenly seemed ablaze with light. Her face, a little drawn from inner excitement, was flushed, her eyes shone, and that red rose in her hair proclaimed her joy for all to see.

The men lost their heads. Throwing convention to the winds and taking no further notice of jealous wives, sweethearts, pining spinsters, young girls, sisters, cousins, they rushed over and crowded about her, with the excuse of welcoming their guest. The dancing had started, and without giving her time to look right or left, they nearly came to blows squabbling over her in their wild enthusiasm. Fifteen, twenty arms were offered, elbows crooked, all for her! But which one first? One at a time—she would take a turn with each of them. Make way, make way! What about the music? What were they doing, those musicians over there? Were they also lost in a spell of admiration? Music! Music!

And she was off, stepping out for her first dance with the old mayor and president of the Club, in full dress.

"Excellent!"

"Look at him go!"

"Oh, the tails of his coat. How they fly!"

"Great!"

"Heavens! His hair is coming unglued."

"What? Why, he's already leading her to a chair."

Again fifteen, twenty arms with elbows crooked appeared before her.

"With me! With me!"

"One moment!"

"She's promised me."

"No, I'm next."

What a sight! It was a wonder they didn't tear each other apart.

While waiting their turn, the unlucky ones wandered off dejectedly to ask other ladies to dance. The uglier ones accepted sulkily, but the others, furious, refused indignantly with a curt, "No, thank *you!*"

The women exchanged baleful looks, and some of them abruptly made a great show of leaving, signaling to their friends to follow.

"Come, let us go. Never have I witnessed such indecent behavior!"

Some cried tears of rage; others trembled with vexation, unburdening themselves to inconspicuous little men who sat stiffly in suits polished by long use and smelling of pepper and camphor. Not to be caught up in the swirl, these shy creatures clung to the wall like dried leaves sheltered by the honest silk skirts of their wives, sisters-in-law, or sisters— fancy dresses indeed, puffed and flounced, in violent shades of green, yellow, red, or blue, gowns which hermetically preserved their wearers' sullen provincial modesty in the musty smell of venerable wooden chests and which comforted both their nostrils and their consciences.

The heat of the rooms became stifling. A kind of haze rose from the steaming sensuality of the men. Panting, burning, their faces flushed purple, they took advantage of the brief pauses between the dances to paste down and smooth their wet and bristling hair, by slipping trembling hands over their heads, along their temples or necks. Their animal natures rebelled out of all reason against propriety. The ball came only once a year! What harm did it do? Let the women quiet down and stay put!

Fresh, light, filled with a joy that brushed aside any vulgar contact, laughing and escaping with a quick gesture, amusing herself, intact and pure in that moment of folly, an agile, flickering flame among those dark, burning, senseless logs, Signora Lucietta, triumphant, whirled like a top, dancing without seeing anything or anyone. The arches dividing the three rooms, the furniture, the yellow, green, red, and bright blue dresses of the ladies, the men's black clothes and white shirt fronts—all spun around in flashing streamers. As soon as one dancer wearied and started to pant heavily, she broke from his arms to throw herself into those of another, and off she went again, swirling around and around in a frenzied confusion of lights and colors.

Seated in the last room, against the wall in a dark corner, Fausto Silvagni, his hands on the knob of his cane, watched her for two hours, his large, light eyes warmed by a friendly smile. Only he understood the purity of that mad joy and delighted in it, as though his tenderness had made her a gift of this innocent exultation.

His tenderness? Still only tenderness? Wasn't this throbbing of his heart more than tenderness?

For many years Fausto Silvagni, his eyes intent and sad, had looked at everything as if from a long way off. To him all things were but fleeting shadows, even his thoughts, his feelings.

Misfortune and heavy obligations had doomed him to failure. His youthful dreams, kindled with so much spirit, had petered out and were now remembered only with bitterness. He fled reality, choosing to lose himself in painful isolation.

Now, in that exile, a feeling had come over him, an emotion he wanted to hold at bay, as yet unwilling to accept it but equally unwilling to reject it completely.

Perhaps, since they could not appear to him in any other form, this dear, mad little creature, dressed in black with a flashing rose in her hair, had brought the living incarnation of those long-lost dreams for him to clasp—living and breathing—in his arms. Could he not check her flight, hold her, and, at last, return through and with her from his remoteness? If he did not stop her, who knows where and how she would end. She too needed help, guidance, advice, lost as she was in a world not of her choosing but which, alas, she wanted to enjoy. That rose said so, that red rose in her hair.

For a while Fausto Silvagni had looked at that rose in dismay. He didn't know quite why. There it lay like a flame in her hair. She shook that foolish little head of hers so often, how was it that the rose did not fall? Was that what he feared?

Meanwhile, deep within him, his trembling heart was saying, "Tomorrow, tomorrow or one of these days, you will speak out. Meanwhile, let her dance on like a wild little sprite."

By now most of her partners were ready to drop and breathlessly declared themselves bested as they looked about for their wives who had left. Only six or seven obstinately held out, among them two old men—who would ever believe it?—the mayor and the widower notary. Both were in a sorry state, perspiring, faces flaming and eyes popping, ties crooked and shirts rumpled, pitiful in their senile frenzy. They had been nudged aside by the younger men all evening and now came forward for a couple of turns only to collapse on chairs like empty sacks one after the other.

It was the last lap, the closing dance.

Signora Lucietta found herself surrounded by all seven of the survivors, aggressively exuberant.

"With me!" "With me!"

The sensual overexcitement in their eyes alarmed her, and the thought that her innocent gaiety could arouse such passion disgusted and shamed her. She wanted to flee, to escape from them. At a startled fawnlike movement of her head, her hair, already loose, slipped down and the rose fell to the floor.

Fausto Silvagni was pulled to his feet by a strange presentiment of danger. The men fell all over one another in an effort to pick up the flower. It was the old mayor who retrieved it, but not without having his hand scratched.

"Here!" he cried, running with the others to offer it to Signora Lucietta, who was putting up her hair in the next room. "Here it is! Now you"—he was so out of breath that his head wobbled—"now *you* must make a choice. Here . . . offer it to one of us!"

"Hurrah! Wonderful idea!"

"She must choose . . ."

"Who will it be?"

"The judgment of Paris!"

"Hush! Wait and see!"

Breathless, holding the still-lovely rose high over her head, Signora Lucietta looked around at her pursuers like an animal at bay. She knew instinctively that they wanted to compromise her at all costs.

"To one of you? My choice?" she cried unexpectedly, a light in her eyes. "Very well, I will. But first step aside. Everyone stand aside. I will offer it to . . ."

Her eyes flew from one to another, as if hesitating in her decision. The awkward men stared at her uncertainly, their hands outstretched, their coarse faces grotesquely reflecting undisguised supplication. With a quick feint, she slipped by the last two on her left and ran toward the farther room. She had found a solution! She would present the rose to one of those who had sat quietly looking on all evening, the first one she came to.

"I will give it to . . ."

Her glance met the clear eyes of Fausto Silvagni. She turned pale and hesitated, trembling and confused.

"Oh, God!" she breathed, "have pity." Quickly recovering herself, she held out the flower, "Here, for you, take it. Take it, Signor Silvagni."

Fausto Silvagni took the rose and turned with a wan smile to look at the seven men rushing after her.

"No! Why to him? Why not to one of us! You must give it to one of us!"

"That's not so!" Signora Lucietta said impatiently. "You said to *someone*, that's all. And so I offered it to Signor Silvagni!"

"But that's an out-and-out declaration of love!" they protested.

"What?" exclaimed Signora Lucietta, her face crimson. "Not at all! It would have been a declaration had I offered it to one of you. But I gave it to Signor Silvagni, who hasn't moved from here all evening and who certainly would not interpret it as that! And you mustn't see it that way either."

"We do. We certainly do. After all, you chose him deliberately."

She was completely upset by their persecution. It had long since ceased to be a jest. Resentment showed in the men's eyes and mouths, and their sly winks and knowing grunts clearly referred to the visits Silvagni had paid her at the postoffice and to all the attention he had shown her since she had arrived. Meanwhile his own pallor and uneasiness, heightened their malicious suspicions. Why did he blanch and fidget? Did he too think that she.... Impossible! Why should he? Perhaps because the others chose to believe it. Why did he not protest? Why did his eyes reflect such suffering?

With a pang she suddenly understood everything. In her perplexity she was still confronted by the defiance of those insolent, thwarted men, however, as they screamed in unbridled rage around her.

"There now, you see! *You* say it doesn't mean a thing, but he doesn't utter a word!"

"What do you mean?" she cried, allowing her scorn to dominate her feelings to the contrary.

Trembling from head to foot, she turned to Silvagni. Looking him straight in the eyes, she asked, "Do you seriously think that in offering you this rose I have made a declaration of love?"

Fausto Silvagni looked at her for a moment, a pale, sad smile on his lips.

Poor little fairy, she was forced by their crude insistence to flee the magic circle of her joy, the innocent delirium in which she had whirled all evening like a little fool. Now, to safeguard the simplicity of her gift of a rose from the relentlessness of the men—all the purity of her joy in a single evening—she was asking him to give up a love which would last a lifetime and to make a reply which would wither the rose in his hand.

Looking coldly at the men, he said, "Not only do I not believe it, but you may be sure, signora, that no one else will ever think it. Here is the rose. Throw it away yourself because I cannot."

Signora Lucietta took the flower with a not too steady hand and tossed it into a corner.

"Thank you," she said, knowing full well what it was she was throwing away forever with that rose of a moment.

YESTERDAY AND TODAY

WAR had broken out only a few days before.

Marino Lerna, a volunteer in the first special course of Officers Training School, had received his commission as second lieutenant in the infantry. He spent a week on leave with his family and then left for Macerata to join his regiment, the 12th Casale Brigade.

He expected to spend a few months there training recruits before being sent to the front. However, three days after his arrival his name was called out in the courtyard of the barracks. Going upstairs, he found eleven other second lieutenants from different platoons who had all come to Macerata at about the same time.

"What's up? Why? Where?"

"Upstairs, in the colonel's office."

With his comrades Lerna stood stiffly at attention before a massive table cluttered with files and papers; he understood from the colonel's first words that they had been ordered to the front. Still dazzled by the June sunlight in the courtyard, he could distinguish nothing clearly in the dark room except the shining emblems on the collar of the colonel's uniform, the long, flushed, horse face barred by a large mustache, and the confusion of white papers scattered over the table.

His thoughts ran riot, and the colonel's military jargon, snapped out in a hard, clipped voice, made no sense to him. But by listening attentively he soon discovered that he had guessed right: they were scheduled to leave the following evening.

It was common knowledge around the barracks that the 12th Brigade held a tough position near Podgora, where many young officers had already been wiped out in several unsuccessful attacks. Now they were rushing men forward to replace those casualties.

When the colonel dismissed the twelve young men, their tension relaxed and for a few minutes they felt a kind of spurious hangover. This was quickly replaced by a show of nonchalance as each tried to impress the other with his *sangfroid*.

They all decided to go to the telegraph office and wire their families, bravely announcing their departure. That is, all except one—the very one out of eighty officer candidates in Rome who had been assigned with Marino Lerna to the 12th Regiment, a man named Sarri. It was Lerna's luck that Sarri would be paired off with him—the only one of his comrades he disliked.

Sarri had no one to whom he could telegraph the news of his departure. In the three days the men had spent together in Macerata, Lerna had come to feel less hostile toward him, although he had not radically changed his opinion. Perhaps this was because, when they were alone, Sarri dropped the contemptuous attitude which had made him so unpopular with all his comrades in Rome. It was now Lerna's opinion that this haughty manner was prompted by Sarri's determination never to appear to share his feelings with anyone else. To this end, he felt obliged not only to take a different stand from the others but exactly the opposite, without caring what people thought of him. He was proud of the antipathy he inspired, more because of this need for detachment than because of a cantankerous nature. He could get away with it because he was rich and all alone in the world.

He brought a young woman along with him to Macerata whom he had been keeping in Rome for the last three months. All the members of the platoon knew her well. Sarri, too, had counted on staying there a month or more during which time he had wanted, he said, to gratify his appetites, or at least the simpler one for the opposite sex. He was convinced he would be killed at the front, and, besides, the idea of living after the war in the wake of a countryful of heroes was intolerable!

"Aren't you coming?" Lerna asked when Sarri did not make a move to follow the others to the telegraph office.

Sarri shrugged.

Lerna, embarrassed, tried to cover up his mistake. "No . . . that is . . . I want to ask your advice."

"Really? Why mine?"

"I don't know. You see, three days ago, when I left Rome, I promised my father and mother——"

"Are you an only son?" asked Sarri.

"Yes. Why?"

"I pity you."

"Oh, I know, it's hard on them. I assured them I wouldn't leave for the front for a couple of months, and that before leaving I would go back and say goodbye . . ."

He was about to say "for the last time," but caught himself.

Sarri understood and smiled. "Go ahead, say it: 'for the last time.'"

"No. Let's hope not. I'll keep my fingers crossed. To greet them, let's say, once again before leaving."

"Good. And then?"

"Wait! My father made me promise that if my leave were canceled, I would let him know in time so that he could come here with Mama and say goodbye. Now we are leaving tomorrow at five."

"But if they caught the ten-o'clock train tonight," Sarri suggested, "they could be here tomorrow morning at seven and spend almost the whole day with you."

"Is that what you advise me to do?" asked Lerna.

"Not at all!" Sarri protested. "Here you have the good luck of being able to leave without tears . . ."

"No, for that matter, Mama has already cried."

"Isn't that enough for you? Do you want to see her cry again? Wire you're leaving tonight and say goodbye now. It's better for you, and for them, too."

Seeing that Lerna was still undecided, Sarri added, "So long. I'm going to tell Nini we're leaving. That'll be a laugh. She loves me, but if she cries, I'll slap her."

And he left.

Still wondering whether or not to follow Sarri's advice, Marino Lerna walked to the telegraph office. He found that all his comrades had sent their farewells, so he decided to do the same. Then, as he thought it over, it seemed like a betrayal of his poor father and mother, so he sent another telegram marked *urgent*, explaining that if they took the ten-o'clock train they would arrive in the morning in time to see him off.

Marino Lerna's mother was an uncompromising little woman of the old school whose like can now be found only in the provinces. Erect in her whalebone corset, a little stiff and angular without being thin, overanxious, she wavered between doubt and suspicion, her mousy little eyes darting restlessly to and fro.

She adored her only son to such a point that, not wishing to be separated from him during his university days, she had forsaken the comforts of her old home, with all the hereditary customs of village life in the Abruzzi, to go to live in Rome, where for the past two years she had felt completely lost.

The following morning she arrived in Macerata in such a state that her son quickly regretted having told them to come. She was hardly off the train before she started protesting, "No, no, no . . ." and she hung on his neck, crying against his chest.

"Oh, don't tell me, Rinuccio . . . don't tell me."

Meanwhile, his father's face was grave as he patted him on the shoulder. He was a man, and men do not cry.

Just before leaving Rome he had had a conversation with an unknown gentleman whose eldest son had been on the field of battle from the first day of the war, and he still had two younger sons at home. A conversation between fathers—that's all. "Without tears."

However, his effort to restrain his tears at all costs—an effort which showed clearly in his feverish, gleaming eyes—gave his thin, small, well-cared-for person an air of ridiculous solemnity, more pathetic perhaps than the uncontrolled grief of his wife.

He was evidently wrought up, alluding to that mysterious conversation with the unknown gentleman as if he had something to hide. The effect on him was curious: it made him aware of his own agitation under his mask of calm; this both annoyed and humiliated him when confronted by the frank, strong, silent emotion of his son, who was upset by his mother's tears and tried to reassure her more with caresses than with words.

It was just as Sarri had foreseen—a useless ordeal.

After taking his parents to the hotel, Marino Lerna had had to rush off immediately for the barracks, where he was kept until noon. He just had time to eat lunch with them in their hotel room—his mother's eyes were too red and swollen to go down to the dining room and she was barely able to stand—before bolting back to the base for his final instructions. His parents did not see him again until just a few minutes before the train left.

Alone with his wife in their room, the father embarked on a beautiful speech, a long, logical speech in which, swallowing frequently and passing a trembling little hand over his lips, he said she should not cry like that, because nothing indicated that their Rinuccio—God forbid—so many things could happen. The regiment might even be sent back to the rear lines, since as everyone knew, it had been at the front from the first day of the war. Then if all the soldiers were to be killed at the front. . . . Was it likely? They were more likely to be wounded. Some little wound—in the arm, for example. God would look after their son. Why put the evil eye on him with all those tears? She must remember that it was bad for Rinuccio to see her carrying on like that—surely it upset him.

But his wife said that it wasn't her fault. Her eyes . . . her eyes . . . what could she do? It was the effect of her son's words, everything he did—a cruel sensation of *remembrance*.

"Each word, you understand, has the effect not of being said now, but of *having* been said. It remains stamped there as if he were already no more. What can I do about it? O, God!"

"Isn't that an ill omen?" asked her husband.

"No! What are you saying!"

"I say it's a bad sign! As for me, I'm going to laugh. You'll see, I'm going to *laugh* when he leaves."

If it had gone on like that much longer, there would have been an argument. Their anxiety became even more acute with their son's prolonged delay. God! Why couldn't his superiors understand that these last moments belonged to his poor mama and papa?

Their impatience reached the breaking point when Marino's comrades began to arrive, one after the other, running into the hotel, leaving the carriages waiting outside for their luggage, ready to set off immediately for the station. An orderly carried out a dressing case; another was loaded down with a knapsack, an overcoat, and a dress sword. Then they all climbed in, and the vehicles rolled off at a great clip.

Marino, the last to leave the barracks, ran to the shoe-

maker's to pick up a pair of hobnail boots he had ordered
the previous day. And so he was late.

It was more than a separation; it was a wrenching apart,
with hysterics at the last moment. In fact, Marino arrived
with his parents just as the doors of the train were being
closed. He leaped into a carriage where his comrades hung
out calling to him to hurry, and the train began to move
amidst the hubbub of voices, tears, goodbyes, with handkerchiefs flying, hats and hands waving.

Signor Lerna waved his hat until the train disappeared. He
was annoyed with himself that he had not had time to do it
properly. When he turned around to his wife, he couldn't
find her. They had carried her away to the waiting room
in a faint.

Now the station was calm and deserted. In the dazzling
light of the long, drowsy summer afternoon there were only
the shining rails and the distant monotonous scraping of the
locusts.

All the carriages had gone off to town with people who
had come to the station to say goodbye. When Marino
Lerna's mother finally came to and could be taken back to
the hotel, there was not a single conveyance left. A station
attendant kindly offered to run over to the garage nearby to
see if the bus had returned from its trip to town.

At the last moment, when Marino's mother had been
helped, almost carried, to a seat in the bus and it was about
to start, a blond young girl ran up out of nowhere and
climbed in. She was wearing a large straw hat covered with
roses, a very low-necked dress; her eyes and lips were
painted. She was weeping as though her heart would break.

A beautiful young girl.

In one hand she clutched a small, blue, embroidered
handkerchief, and the other, sparkling with rings, she held
over her right cheek to hide the burning red mark of a slap.

It was the same Nini who had come to Macerata with
Sarri three days before. Marino Lerna's father knew what
kind of girl the little blonde was, but his wife did not. Seeing another woman in tears like herself, she couldn't resist
asking, "Are you a wife, signora?"

Holding the doll-sized handkerchief before her eyes, the
girl quickly shook her head.

"Sister?" the mother insisted.

But at this point her husband intervened, giving his wife a discreet nudge with his elbow.

Perhaps the young girl noticed his maneuver; in any case, she knew that the old lady would soon find out about her and she did not reply. But she also sensed something else which made her cry even harder: she knew that the old woman would stop crying now because she would be ashamed to mingle her tears with those of a girl like herself.

But *her* tears were real, too, she thought—and tears shed from a sorrow were more unusual than the everyday, natural tears of a mother. In Rome, toward the end, Nini had gone not only with Sarri but with many of his comrades as well—perhaps even with this boy for whom the old woman wept.

Today, at noon, she had sat with ten of the boys at table —a tableful of devils! They teased the life out of her like a bunch of giddy fools, and she let them have their way—poor boys leaving for the front. They insisted on baring her breasts right there in the restaurant. Her little breasts were famous among them, looking almost virginal with those up-turned nipples. Like idiots, they had wanted to christen them with champagne. She let them do whatever they liked—touch, kiss, press, pull, and fondle her—so that they might have a living memory of her flesh, made for love, out there where one by one all those handsome young men of twenty might be killed. She had laughed with them so much and—yes, dear God!—had kissed each of them for the last time and . . . Sarri was the one who had slapped her when her eyes had filled with tears, yet she didn't hold it against him.

So now why couldn't that old mama let her cry her heart out without taking offense? Of course the old lady did let her cry, but she stopped crying herself and there was no telling how badly she needed to cry, poor old soul.

So the young girl tried to hold back her tears to allow the mother's to flow freely, but all in vain. The more she tried to stop crying, the more uncontrollably her tears flowed down her cheeks. She was depressed too by the disapproval she felt. At last, unable to bear the scowl on the face of the old woman who stared at her with all the jealous hatred mothers feel for such girls, she burst into sobs.

"Have pity," she moaned. "I can't help crying, signora. They are *my* tears. I can cry, too. You for your son, and I . . . well, not really for your son, but for one who left with him and who slapped me because I was crying. You cry for one, I for all of them. I *can* cry for them, even for your son, signora. All . . . all of them."

Lerna's mother was so stricken over her son's departure that she needed to quiet her nerves, but this girl disturbed her and was offensive as well. The thought that her son would not be exposed to danger for another two days had given her a respite, so now she could be hard, and hard she was! Fortunately, the distance from the station back to town was not great. When the bus stopped, she got out without so much as a glance at the girl sitting there.

The following day, on their way back to Rome, Signora Lerna stood beside her husband when the train stopped in the station at Fabriano. As they leaned out the window of their first-class carriage, she recognized the young girl of the bus running along the platform with a very young man and looking for a place in the train. She was laughing, and in her arms she carried a bunch of flowers.

Signora Lerna turned to her husband and said in a voice loud enough to be heard, "Look, there's the one who was crying for 'all of them.'"

The girl turned, without anger or scorn, and her eyes seemed to say, "Poor foolish old mama, don't you understand that is the way of life? Yesterday I cried for one, so today I must laugh for another."

SUCH IS LIFE

REFLECTIVE silence, floors smelling of wax, spick-and-span muslin curtains at the windows: Signora Leuca's house had been like that for the past eleven years. But now a strange suspense hung over those rooms. Was it possible that Signora Leuca had agreed after a separation of eleven years to let her husband return to live with her?

The measured ticking of the big clock in the dining room was disturbing as it echoed through those voiceless rooms— as if time itself could continue to flow as evenly and serenely as before.

Yesterday, in the little sitting room with the highly sensitive floor, the small silver and crystal objects had tinkled. It was almost as if the teardrops of the gilded candelabra over the mantelpiece and the little liquor glasses on the tea table were shuddering with fear and indignation after Lawyer Arico's visit—"the old cricket," Signora Leuca called him to her friends.

"Ah, life . . . life . . ." he kept repeating after his long harangue, hunching his shoulders, half closing his large eyes in his sallow face, and painfully stretching his thin neck.

All those crystal and silver objects hung there in suspense, waiting for Signora Leuca to protest at least by a shake of her head. But no, she stood tall and erect, fresh and pink-and-white as ever, her spectacles high on her aquiline nose, as she faced the little man who twisted all over at one more leave-taking and went on repeating in the doorway: "Life. . . . Ah! Life. . . ."

Was life really like that—a burning shame too great to confess, an agony to be suffered by hunching one's shoulders and squinting one's eyes, or a hard, bitter pill to be swallowed by stretching the neck? Was it not life, after all, that Signora Leuca had spent here in this spotless, demure house for eleven years, receiving occasional visits from her good friends, the ladies of the Charity Society, the learned priest of Sant' Agnese, or the organist, Signor Ildebrando? Had she not enjoyed a life of unending peace, spotless order, and silence marked only by the slow, even ticking of the big clock indolently striking the hours and half-hours inside its glass case?

Signorina Trecke, an old maid, ran like a frightened dove to the parish house of Sant' Agnese to sound the alarm.

"Signora Leuca . . . Signora Leuca and her husband . . ." she panted.

Her anxiety turned to amazement, her amazement dissolved into a vague smile before the unruffled nod with which the priest received her news, which he already knew.

Long-legged, short-waisted and stooped, Signorina Trecke was still blond at sixty-six. She was half Russian, half German, yet perhaps more Russian than German. She had been converted to Catholicism by her brother-in-law, God rest his soul, and most zealous. Her eyes in her pale, flabby face were as blue as when she was eighteen, like two clear lakes obstinately reflecting the smiling, innocent skies of her youth, though who knows how many storm clouds had since passed to darken them. But Signorina Trecke went on feigning ignorance. She did not wish the gall of dismal experience to eat away at the fixity of her new faith, so she appeared completely naïve, to the great annoyance of her friends.

Melting into that empty smile of hers, she asked uneasily if Signor Marco Leuca really deserved to be forgiven, something she had never questioned because—perhaps it was slander, since His Reverence approved a reconciliation—but didn't Signora Leuca's husband have three children, three little girls with a . . . how do you say it? . . . by another woman? And what now? Would he abandon them to become reconciled with his wife? No? Then what? The wife here, another woman there, with three—how do you say it—three *natural* daughters?

"Nothing of the kind!" the priest tried to reassure her, his usual serenity tinged with a mildly protective air.

Though there were catacombs under Sant' Agnese and even a gloomy, solemn, subterranean church, the parish house stood in the open, surrounded by soft, leafy green amid plenty of air and sunlight. One could see in the priest's limpid eyes and hear in his warm voice the good effects of this environment not only on the body but the soul!

"My dear Signorina Trecke, it is not a question of two households or of abandonment either; it is not even a question of an out-and-out reconciliation. We will have, God willing, a simple, friendly relationship, a few brief visits from time to time, and that is all ... to bring a little comfort."

"To him?" asked Signorina Trecke.

"Of course to *him!*" the priest said. "To relieve the burden of his guilt, a kind word to soothe his gnawing remorse. He asks nothing more, and for that matter our excellent Signora Leuca could not grant anything less. Now, don't worry!"

The priest placed his words like beautiful little porcelain vases on the table before him, there, there, and there—each one graced with an artificial flower with green tissue paper twisted around the wire stem, charmingly effective at no cost whatsoever. But the organist, that good Signor Ildebrando who also acted as secretary, should have been told not to approve every word the priest said with honeyed smiles and little nods. It virtually turned Signorina Trecke's stomach.

Signor Ildebrando had never been able to forgive his long-dead parents for imposing such a sonorous name on him, most unsuitable for his slender, frail body as well as his temperament. He disliked ruddy, aggressive, noisy men who cocked an eye, hanging one thumb in the armhole of their vests like the great *I am!* His nature was tepid, mediocre, colorless, and whenever possible he hung back, clinging to the shadows. He thought that Signorina Trecke, drab as she was, should do the same, instead of putting herself forward in the thick of things, meddling where she was not directly concerned.

"Well, in that case," she was now saying to the priest, "I could invite him to my house for supper, couldn't I?"

"Of course not!" said the priest, taken aback. "What have you to do with it, Signorina Tecke?"

"Well, if he is to be pitied—my niece says she knows him," she haggled, widening her mouth in a bland smile.

"You will do well, my dear signorina," the priest replied severely, "to keep closer watch over your niece."

"I? But how can I, Father? I really don't understand these things, as I've just proved to you ... absolutely nothing," she said, opening her arms wide and bowing to take her leave, with a stupid smile still on her face and her childlike eyes clouded because of the hopeless ignorance with which she was afflicted.

Three days later Signor Marco Leuca, accompanied by Arico, the lawyer, paid his first visit.

Disheveled, shabby, blushing for shame, he looked bewildered in that impeccable house so delicately furnished, so jealously chaste. Trembling all over like a wounded animal, he could not utter a word. Then, in desperation, he dropped mutely to his knees before her. Signora Leuca was distressed and frightened by his appearance, aged and shockingly coarsened after eleven years, and she backed away in panic before his helpless gesture, although her first impulse had been to help him up.

"Oh, no. God! No!" she moaned.

Then, when he almost came to blows with the lawyer, who turned on him angrily, loudly commanding him to be calm and not to make a scene, she wanted to run out of the room. He made a furious lunge to shove Arico aside, determined to present himself before her in all his abjection and despair. Hanging his head, he was mortified that his theatrical gesture had misfired; he had fervently hoped she would place her hand tenderly on his hair, not as a caress, but in forgiveness.

How in heaven's name could Signora Leuca have done that? He might have known it was impossible. Pity, patience, even compassion she had, not only for him but for all poor wretches with the same insatiable penchant for vice.

Ah! Life . . .

It was violently marked on his loose face with the telltale sag of the lower lip and the dark pouches around his sad, troubled eyes. But, as the lawyer said, he could at last perhaps enjoy the peace and sweetness of a home—now that his hair was gray and hers completely white . . .

"The sweetness of a home, did you say, Lawyer Arico?"

Signora Leuca knew very well that her house no longer had sweetness, only great calm. She did not say it depressed her, only that she was accustomed to it. She read, busied herself working for the poor, took up collections with the other ladies of the Charity Society, went to church or to the dressmaker—for she liked to dress well—and, when necessary, made calls on Arico, the lawyer, who was in charge of her affairs. All in all, she never had an idle moment. She was content this way, since God had not blessed her life with more intimate joys. At times, in the silence between one stitch and the next on the little shirt she was knitting for a poor child of the neighborhood, or between one line and the next of the book she was reading, she would suddenly sink into a timeless mood where thought seemed vain and comfortless. She would stare, then, at a familiar object in the room as if seeing it for the first time and as if it had no significance for her. She regretted the things she had never known and suffered that her own heart should have deceived her into supposing she could have been happy by marrying a man who—well, a man. Now Signora Leuca did not even despise him anymore.

Yes, life.

It was not as her young girl's heart had dreamed. It was even wrong perhaps for her to speak of her revulsion for that physical contact which sullied one. Although difficult, it was also to be pitied since the price of pleasure had later to be paid in bitter tears.

It was in answer to the priest's exclamation, "In God's name, whoever said compassion was easy?" that she had let herself be persuaded to receive her husband briefly from time to time.

Her charity work, she knew, was really another way of passing the time. True, she did more than she really was able to do and exhausted herself going up and down stairs, or working late into the night for the poor. She threw off this fatigue by sheer will power. A good part of her income went to the needy, and she deprived herself of many things which, for her, were not entirely superfluous. But she could not say that she had ever made a real sacrifice, such as overcoming the recoil of her flesh at the thought of an insufferable contact or risking the harmony of her neat, orderly life. She was afraid she could never do it.

The same impulses sprang up in her as in everyone else, but where others surrendered blindly she was wary. Her natural instincts were too guarded, her life too hushed, rarefied to a point where ordinary things no longer had substance. She would suddenly notice new, strange aspects of them which disturbed her, as if for the fraction of a second she could penetrate a hidden reality different from that commonly attributed to them. At such times she feared she was losing her mind.

It should have annoyed her, therefore, that others thought her life so undisturbed and considered her the picture of serenity. Instead it pleased her. She wanted to believe it, convinced that she rejected every longing as soon as it arose within her because of her instinctive aversion for a soiled life. To be sure, she worked at her charities in the midst of sordidness, but she could not have mingled freely with the poor had she not felt herself immune. The only sacrifice she could make, after all, was to expose and eventually to conquer her own squeamishness. It was little enough. She did even more in subduing her own body, her own flesh and all that takes place in intimacy—even involuntarily—and which one never dares confess.

Meanwhile Signorina Trecke, with her usual air of feckless innocence, brought her niece to call and to hear the latest news. Other friends, Signora Marzorati, her daughter, and Signora Mielli, were already there. Urged to talk, Signora Leuca tried to say as little as possible about her husband's first visit.

Signorina Trecke exclaimed, "Ah, so he did come!"

Annoyed, her niece snapped back, "Why pretend not to know it, when you do?"

"I knew? I knew only that he was coming, not that he had come."

Her niece shrugged and turned away to talk to young Signorina Marzorati. The girl's mother bridled, not at all pleased to see her daughter talking with Signorina Trecke's niece, who was a scandal, not only because of her manner of dress, but because of all the gossip that raged around her.

Only Signora Leuca understood that it was not entirely the niece's fault but was partly due to what went on every day between her aunt and herself. They were engaged in a dangerous conflict, the aunt refusing to see any harm in the younger woman's behavior and the niece doing her utmost to shock her aunt out of her hypocritical pretense. There was no telling where this might lead. What was to be done when Signorina Trecke, who saw harm in the most harmless things, refused to recognize evil when it was flung in her face?

Here, for example, she had expected Signora Leuca to be distraught after her ordeal and instead found her calmly discussing her husband's visit as if nothing out of the ordinary had happened.

"But really nothing did happen," Signora Leuca said, smiling. "He stayed for about fifteen minutes with Lawyer Arico."

"Ah! I'm glad it was with the lawyer!" signed Signorina Trecke. "I was so afraid he would come alone."

"But why were you afraid?" asked Signora Leuca.

"My niece told me he was so fiery. Nella teaches in the school where he brings the oldest child every morning—goodness, even though they're not legitimate, I suppose they should be called his daughters, shouldn't they? Although they don't bear his name! Nella, what did you say their name was?" she asked.

"Smacca!" replied her niece sharply.

"Probably their mother's name," observed Signora Mielli, who always seemed to have dropped from the clouds when she did happen to say a few words.

"Yes, probably," Signorina Trecke went on. "Imagine! Right in front of my niece, he gave his daughter a—a slap one morning, and so hard it knocked the poor child down. Her cheek was quite scratched by his fingernail. When he saw how he had hurt her, my niece says he started to cry. Oh, I suppose he did some crying here, too!"

As the other two ladies turned, expecting a reply, Signora Leuca felt obliged to say yes, that he had cried.

Although the niece was deep in conversation with Signorina Marzorati, she followed every word the women were saying, and now she flashed out at her aunt, "No harm done! Her husband's tears never hurt Signora Leuca at all. I'm telling you this so you won't pretend to be shocked!"

Signora Leuca could not help noting the contemptuous tone of the girl's voice, but she did not quite understand the reason for it, unless the niece meant to offend her aunt by ridiculing her attitude. A look of chilled amazement passed between her other two friends, Signora Mielli and Signora Marzorati. She herself smiled sadly, trying to enlist their sympathy for poor Signorina Trecke, who, as usual, chose to find nothing amiss.

"He must have changed a lot," Nella Trecke confided in Signorina Marzorati's ear, "but I'll wager Signora Leuca's husband was *something* in his day!"

Signora Marzorati was obviously more and more upset

by her daughter's interest in whatever it was that that terrible girl was saying to her. The daughter wore glasses and had bulging breasts; her alarming naïveté was sometimes stormed by secret thoughts which made her blush crimson, because she feared she would no longer be taken for the overgrown child everyone considered her.

All this was clear to Signora Leuca, but it gave her no satisfaction that her eyes could see through things so plainly, completely aware that she was not deceived. Then there was Signora Mielli with that air of never knowing what she was doing or saying, as though in a dream, so that in a pinch she might always exclaim, "Really? Did I do this? Did I say that?"

When her five friends finally left, Signora Leuca felt tired and depressed. She looked at the empty, displaced chairs in the sitting room whose disorder seemed to ask what had been the reason for this visit and whether or not it had been really necessary. Yes, it seemed so, for one must look into others' lives to see what was going on in them, what others thought and what they had to say. This curiosity satisfied a desire in human beings to see beyond themselves, to vary the monotony of every day. It was a diversion from the irritations and difficulties of life. It helped pass the time. A misfortune? A scandal? And they would all run to see and hear about it. Who? Why? No, really? Impossible! When nothing happened, there was boredom and the agony of watching daylight slowly fade and die, as Signora Leuca was now doing through the windowpane.

The priest and the lawyer arranged that Marco Leuca would never come alone to visit his wife, that his visits would always be short, and that they would not exceed two a month. However, a few days after the first visit, he returned, alone this time and with the pitiful look of an unwanted dog expecting a kick.

Signora Leuca was annoyed, but concealed her agitation as she led him into the little dining room. He buried his face in his big hands and started to sob as soon as he sat down, but without dramatics this time. She looked at him and realized that it would take no more than an understanding word from her to dry his tears.

And then?

No. No. It was already too much that he had returned so soon and alone. Were she to encourage him with kind words, it would be tantamount to accepting his visits every day and asking for who knows what else, then farewell to the conditions of their agreement. No. He would have to stop crying of his own accord and find enough courage to say why he had come, giving a specific reason if he had one.

Dear God! After two hours of torture, Signora Leuca sat there stunned, trembling in every fiber of her body. He had come, he said, to confess. In vain she had reiterated that it was unnecessary, that she already knew everything, that Lawyer Arico had told her all. He had still wanted to confess.

He found the courage ruthlessly to expose his life and seemed to enjoy debasing himself more and more, that she might trample on him and that her foot might be sullied in the mire with him.

Signora Leuca was stupefied by certain unheard-of obscenities. The outrage of it all held her gaze fixed on his clear portrayal of every loathsome detail. Her cheeks burned. She was conscious of the queasiness with which she held a hundred-lire note between her fingers, which he quickly snatched out of her furtive hand as if to hide it from himself also.

Although she had given him the money to rid herself of him, afterward she wondered whether this had been the real motive of his visit. Perhaps not. In all conscience she had to admit that he had not asked for it, at least not directly. He had said, to move her, no doubt, that he had turned over to Lawyer Arico for his children the small sum remaining from his inheritance and had instructed him to pay that woman only the interest for household expenses. She was so stingy, he said, that she did not give him a cent to buy a cigar or even a cup of coffee if he felt like standing at a café bar. How could he possibly have asked his wife for anything after that confession, accusing himself of a weak character, a prey to all temptations, dumping all the blame on that woman's back? He had beseeched her, with hands joined as if in prayer, to help him overcome his weakness if only by letting him see her.

After that it was evil of her to have given him money just to get rid of him. She had played on the very weakness he had implored her to combat. Signora Leuca's humiliation only increased as she thought that perhaps he had felt no compunction whatsoever in accepting the money.

She turned to the window to look out at the bright green of the vacant lots for sale across the way. A row of cypress trees and a few pines were the sole survivors of the princely old villa which had fallen into decay and disappeared. The azure sky on that clear day filled the silent house with light.

"Dear Lord," Signora Leuca cried, covering her face with her hands. "The evil we do . . . the evil that is done unto us!"

Her face still hidden, she recalled the candid look of an old English minister that summer in Ari at a boardinghouse which stood on top of the hill like a castle. How green! How sunny! And that swarm of young girls flocking around her every time she stopped to admire the broad valley!

"Marzietta di Lama . . ."

That was her name . . . the girl with the piercing eyes . . . the one with the rippling laugh as she raised her arm to show the Signora a little scratch on her nose. If only she could have been a mother, how much it would have meant . . . but even that joy had been denied her.

Glancing at her hands, she saw her wedding ring and felt an impulse to throw it out the window. A symbol of her married state, it now reflected all the ignominy of that man's confession, she thought, as she twisted her hands in her lap.

Still, if she had been governed by her flesh, fascinated and led astray by insatiable desires, she too would probably have fallen headlong.

As she glanced about the dining room, the furniture seemed to draw back as if waiting for her to return to the quiet of her orderly life. But in her turmoil she hardly noticed; the disturbing violence of that man's body had entered here to challenge the stability of all she had sought to build around and within herself—her conscience, her whole house.

But who had advised and influenced her, and how far was her charity supposed to go, sinking into contact with such hidden shame? Everyone's shame, perhaps more so for those who did not show it because they managed to hide it from themselves than for that poor fiend who wore it blazoned across his face.

Was this, then, her punishment? Punishment for what? Did they suppose that she was to blame for not knowing how to hold him when he left the house eleven years ago to wind up in such degradation?

It was not true: she had never denied him anything which, as her husband, he had the right to expect—and not only out of duty. No. She had always tried to be honest with herself, however painful the truth might be, so that now she was forced to consider how her body had consented, knowing full well that duty would be no excuse to ease her conscience when it later awoke with disgust after all love and respect for the man had gone.

No, she had not sent him away; he left her when she no longer satisfied him.

Having succeeded in freeing herself of all desire, Signora Leuca wanted indignantly to ask those who advised her to show this "difficult proof of a charitable spirit" if that were not a bit too simple. If, on the contrary, it were not more mandatory to pity those who had struggled to resist passion? She wanted the proud satisfaction of being pitied, but in quite a different way. She wanted pity, not admiration! After all, she was not made of marble and was tired of insipid admiration. What did they think, that her deliverance had cost her nothing?

For the first time the shining order of her house annoyed her. She was bored with it all and, jumping to her feet, she shook her head and cried, "Hypocrisy!"

Marco Leuca walked away from his wife's house reeling with satisfaction. It seemed to him, as he swelled out his chest to breathe, that the road opened before him, making a way between the houses and the trees. By God, he was free! And to prove it he had only to thrust one hand into his pants pocket and crumple that note between his fingers. He was free of all those tiresome restrictions laid down by the priest and the lawyer who boosted him up the stairs of redemption to his wife's house.

She had placed a barrier between them when she had slipped him that hundred-lire note*—she stood on one side, he on the other, and there would be no more passing over. On his side he could befoul himself as much as he pleased.

* When this story was written, around 1930, one hundred lire were equivalent to about $12.50. [Translator's note.]

What a relief! What joy! And let her not dare presume, with her grand manner, that he no longer needed charity.

A hundred lire! Drink! Drink yourself drunk!

He laughed and glanced around, a mad gleam in his eyes. How well he had played his part! In return—one hundred lire! Almost a lire for every tear. He had enjoyed seeing her blench at certain descriptions; her eyes were troubled but gaping wide behind those glasses set on the bridge of her nose. When one hits on a way to reveal certain secret things, although they may be shocking, they also magnetize. Revulsion itself, shrinking like meat over a fire, with alarmed "whys," thirsts for more detail—but always from a distance, not close enough to touch! Here, come here and risk one little touch—it will not hurt. It will entice you . . .

He let out a loud guffaw, and people turned to stare at him. Nice, those girls over there by the fountain of Sant' Agnese! Cute! If only he could stroke them, under the pretense of taking a drink of water. But no, he wanted wine— and in a first-class place, like a gentleman! Besides, those girls lacked zest. It was the others, with flanks like mares and caverns which so completely seized one with pleasure, from whom it was impossible to break away.

[The revision begun by the author in the autumn of 1936 comes to an end here, although he intended to continue the development of this, his favorite work. In fact, among his papers, notes were found outlining three new chapters:

(I) *Coming out after the visit and the confession with one hundred lire to spend for a spree.*

Degradation, wine, women, the bodies of women with flanks like mares.

It was no good anymore.

(II) *This woman:*

She ran away once and then came back. Doubts about the last child.

The mediocrity of Sandrina and Lauretta. Elodina, the musician's orphan . . . a delicate stem, a rare flower.

(III) *Nella Trecke at home, seduction before our eyes*].

She said that whether they cried or not, the children's hair had to be combed; or else with all the dust and filth ...

Or else, what?

Lice! That's what. Then every morning there would be more tears, getting rid of them with a fine-tooth comb—if that would suffice! Sometimes it was necessary to take a razor and shave off all the hair ... then wouldn't they look pretty, the three of them, with shaved heads!

O God! Why did she have to pull their hair so hard? Plaited that tightly, it curled against their necks, like little pigs' tails, the ends tied off with string. It hardly looked as if they had any hair, soaked with oil as it was and parted clear down the back, just two pigtails, and yet Sandrina's hair was very thick.

Walking past the Villa Borghese, he glanced back at the tight little braids on her shoulders and felt tempted to stop and undo them. They took the shortcut through the park to save time, also because he wanted to prepare his daughter for the visit they were about to make. It was a long way from Via Flaminia to Sant' Agnese where his wife lived, and he wondered if it was not too far for the child to walk.

Poor Sandrina! It wasn't only her hair. With that dress on, that hat and those wretched little drawers showing below her petticoat, she seemed to feel ungraceful and walked along like a little old woman. But lately, whenever he had complained at home about the way the children were dressed or tried to loosen their braids, *she* had threatened, "Beware, or I'll kiss them!"

For a few months now she had had a swelling on her lip which had grown until it was as round and hard as a pea and almost black.

It could not amount to much because, even when she pressed it, it did not hurt her. They advised her to see a doctor, but she said that was nothing compared to other things: headaches, constant fatigue, and always a little fever toward evening. She did not need a doctor to tell her what was wrong—it was the terrible life she had to lead.

However, she stopped kissing the children. But she kissed him at night all right, laughing wildly and holding his head between her hands so that he could not move. She planted those kisses on his mouth ... there ... there ... and there because, just in case what the neighbors said was true, she wanted him to catch it in the same place. It was a wicked joke, but a joke nevertheless because she knew what they said was not true.

He didn't believe it either, or rather it seemed unlikely anyone could die from a little lump which was not even painful. Also he dared not believe it because it would be such a wonderful stroke of luck. So he laughed resentfully under those kisses she intended as poisonous stings. But one day he stopped before a mirror in a shop window to examine his lips carefully, passing a finger slowly across them and stretching the skin to make sure there was no crack. He, too, now refrained from kissing the children or, at most, he kissed the hair of the smallest one whose adorable little ways and sayings were hard to resist.

The other two, Sandrina and Lauretta, always had a dazed look on their faces as if in constant fear of something. The violent quarrels they witnessed almost every day had left them terrified. But when their father and mother locked themselves in their room, it was even worse. Screams came through the door, crying, slaps, blows, kicks, running and falling and the noise of flying objects crashing to bits.

There had been a fight last night, and he was now wearing a handkerchief wound around his right hand to hide a long scratch—if it was not a bite. There was another long scratch on his neck.

"Are you tired, Sandrina?"

"No, Papa."

"Would you like to sit over there on that bench to rest a little while?"

"No, Papa."

"Well, we'll take the streetcar on Via Veneto. Tell me... would you like to go to a beautiful house?"

Sandrina looked up from under her hat with an uncertain smile. She had already noticed that he spoke in a different tone of voice. It pleased her, though she did not know what to make of it. She nodded her head.

"To see a lady... whom I know," he went on. "But you..."

He stopped, not knowing how to put it. Sandrina quietly grew very attentive, waiting for him to go on, but as he said nothing more, she risked a question.

"What is her name?"

"She's . . . your aunt," he told her. "But be careful not to mention this at home to your mama, and not to Lauretta or Rosina either. Nobody at all, understand?"

He stopped to look at her. Sandrina glanced up at him but quickly lowered her eyes.

"You understand?" he repeated roughly, leaning down to look squarely in her eyes.

Sandrina hurriedly nodded her head several times.

"To no one!"

"No one."

"Do you know why I don't want you to tell?" he asked, walking on. "Because your mama . . . and this . . . this aunt have quarreled. If she ever found out I'd taken you there . . . well, you saw what happened yesterday? It would be even worse! Do you understand?"

"Yes, Papa."

"Don't say a word to anyone . . . or there will be trouble."

After all these instructions and threats, Sandrina stole a look at her father's gloomy face and no longer felt any pleasure at going to the aunt's beautiful house. She understood that her father was not going there to please her, after all, but because he wanted to go even at the risk of another fight if his visit were found out—certainly not through her . . . but suppose her mother asked her where they had gone? Frightened, Sandrina immediately turned to her father.

"Papa . . ."

"What is it?"

"What shall I tell Mama?"

He jerked her hand violently and pulled her arm.

"Nothing . . . nothing, I said. You musn't say anything at all!"

"I know, but if she asks me where we've been . . ." Sandrina pointed out, more dismayed than ever.

He regretted his roughness and leaned down to caress her.

"Sweet, my little sweet," he murmured. "I didn't understand . . . of course I'll tell you. I'll tell you just what to say if she asks where you've been. Now, perk up! Show me one of your pretty smiles. Quick, a little smile like the one you had when I took you to the puppet show."

His tenderness was more for himself than for the child. It made him feel he was being *good*. His heart swelled with joy as he caught the approving smile of a lady who happened to be passing as he bent solicitously over his daughter. He wanted Sandrina to give him a better reward, but although she tried obediently to smile, her cold, sad little face seemed to plead with him to accept it: the smile was the best she could do.

Sandrina was hardly ten, but she knew she would have to protect herself first from her father, then from her mother and sisters as well. Her face was pale and too thin to be pretty; the perky little nose did not match her eyes, which were grim and serious and, when fixed attentively or glancing slyly to either side, did not have a sweet expression.

He sensed his daughter's secret hostility and straightened up resentfully, thinking that he was a fool to expect anything from the children of such a mother.

For quite a while Signor Leuca had been thinking that it would be a good thing if his wife were to agree to raise his three children. Should their mother die—although he did not believe it likely—or should he take off one day, his rich wife could help these children as she did so many others. If it was not right to bring children into the world and then cast them off, at least he would have taken a step to insure their future. So this time Signora Leuca's husband came to visit her with a little girl.

He was afraid his wife would see through his scheme, as she had before when she suspected his visits of another motive than the need for moral comfort. Also he was not quite sure if, in her eyes, it would not seem brazen to bring this living proof of infidelity into her house.

He came in very dobutfully but brightened when he noticed her delight at sight of the child. He opened his arms wide and quietly let out a huge sigh of relief, smiling tremulously.

Signora Leuca welcomed the little girl tenderly, and Sandrina looked up at her with wide, bewildered eyes.

"Ah, look who is here! What is your name? Sandrina? That's a lovely name. You're the oldest, aren't you? And do you go to school? Oh, already in the fourth grade! Would you like to take off your little hat? We will put it here. Come, sit down beside me."

"Perhaps she doesn't know who I am?" she asked, turning to her husband who stood there tearfully looking on.

"My aunt," Sandrina supplied promptly.

"Yes, darling, your aunt," Signora Leuca agreed; surprised and touched by this answer, she leaned down to kiss the little girl's hand.

Many little children called her "aunt," affectionately prompted by their mothers to show their gratitude. But she felt especially pleased that he had suggested it, even though certainly for a different reason.

Very well, since she was her aunt, this little niece was to have a special treat: chocolate, cookies, and bread-and-butter spread with jam. Seating the child on a cushion at the table, nice and high like a grownup, she tied a little napkin around her neck.

"Ummm, it's good like this," Signora Leuca said as she prepared a slice of bread, first with butter, then with jam. "Now a spoonful of jam all by itself, to put in your mouth! Would you like that? Yes, I think you would."

Sandrina looked at her and smiled happily as though it were all too good to be true.

When she smiled, that ugly little dress and the way her hair was skinned back distressed Signora Leuca. Poor little thing! As soon as she had finished eating, they went into the bedroom to undo those miserable braids and make one large loose plait, tied halfway down with a satin bow. She then arranged Sandrina's hair becomingly over her forehead to soften her thin face, now pink with pleasure. How her eyes shone! Sandrina looked so entirely different that, seeing her own image in the mirror surrounded by the reflection of all the beautiful things in the bedroom, she did not know herself.

Signora Leuca was mystified by her husband's worried frown when she brought the child back, her face glowing and looking so changed.

Possibly this transformation in his daughter gave him the same feeling she herself had had while she combed the little girl's hair, but she did not want him to mistake her affection for regret that this little girl was not her own. Why, she had even forgotten he was waiting there in the next room while she was busy fussing over the child!

When they left, Signora Leuca went to the window to watch that lovely tassel of hair hanging down her back. After waiting for a while and not seeing them come out the door, she tiptoed to the head of the stairs, curious to see what was keeping them. Then she understood why he had been so dismayed. Her mind at ease, she could not help smiling.

There he was sitting on the steps below, intently trying to do up those two horrible little pigtails again. He had slipped the handkerchief off his hand, and from above Signora Leuca saw the long scratch and an even worse one on his neck.

She was sorry that she had so thoughtlessly put him in this predicament, and remembering the two pieces of dirty string lying on her dressing table, she realized he could never tie off the ends without them, or manage to pull the hair tightly enough with his clumsy hands. If that horrid woman who scratched him like that was not to know about this visit, the child must go home with the same pieces of string. Quickly she ran back to her room and then hurried down the stairs.

"Wait, wait!" she called out. "Let me do it. I'm sorry. I didn't think. You're prefectly right."

As he got up, very embarrassed, she quickly took his place and plaited the braids. Then she bent over Sandrina to kiss her. He slyly took her hand, and before she could snatch it back, she felt the revolting contact of his lips upon it.

A long time afterward, in her little dining room, Signora Leuca sat, still rubbing her hand.

Three weeks, a month went by, and her husband did not return. Signora Leuca had expected him to come with the other two children as he had said he would. Maybe that woman had found out about the last visit and had made a scene, or perhaps after his promise he was ashamed to come alone. She supposed he was ill, or possibly one of the children was sick, or even the woman herself. Maybe he was still embarrassed because she had discovered him on the stairs ... and she smiled over that. Or had he perhaps noticed her disgust when she had pulled her hand away?

Signora Leuca supposed so many things. Her friends of the Charity Society, stopping in to see her at that time, observed in a roundabout way that she supposed too much: if it was painful to receive her husband occasionally for short visits, then she should be happy that of himself he had spaced them out. To tell the truth, they said, those visits had grown rather frequent and were not, it would seem, any too brief either.

Finally she agreed that she did suppose too much but that she was still curious to know why he had not returned. It never occurred to her to question the reason for her concern. She said that she wanted to know if something had happened to him—not that it made any difference to her if he no longer came to see her.

Finally it no longer mattered. Everything seemed remote, even the closest things; as soon as she was conscious of them for an instant, they vanished. Curiosity was a thing of the past. She accepted, even welcomed, suffering, but it never touched her deeply. She seemed now to be immune to all the unhappiness life had to offer.

Then one day, instead of her husband, Lawyer Arico and the old priest came to see her. There could be no more doubt: something had happened. But what?

It was difficult to say whether the news was good or bad. The woman was dead . . . that woman.

"Dead?"

She had died suddenly of pneumonia. But the doctor who treated her said she had a cancer on her mouth and would not have lived very long in any case.

At this, Signora Leuca became suspicious. She asked the lawyer and the priest if they had known about the woman's condition when they suggested her husband's visits. Both protested—the priest before God and the lawyer on his word of honor.

"And did he?" Signora Leuca questioned.

"Did he what?"

"Did he know it?"

"Ah, that, yes," the little lawyer had to confess, twisting on his chair. "He said that . . . he had vaguely . . . vaguely suspected it, he said."

Seeing Signora Leuca frown, the old priest asked, "Do you suppose he foresaw her death? I don't think so."

"Oh, Father," Signora Leuca burst out, "for pity's sake, don't misunderstand me. If you only knew how humiliated I feel! Believe me, my charity does not depend on the washing of a dirty child's face. I'm afraid you do not think very highly of me, Father."

"Not at all! Not at all!" the old priest protested, smiling and blushing a little.

"I'm sorry, but it is true," Signora Leuca insisted.

Seeing how deeply upset she was, the priest grew serious.

"Let us take care not to sin out of spiritual pride, my dear signora."

"I?"

"Yes, you. One sins through pride in many ways. If, for example, you disparage the object of your charity by a suspicion of this kind and so make your act more commendable before God, or rather before your own conscience, your charity changes and becomes something different."

"My own conscience?"

"Yes, signora."

"Away from God."

"Yes, signora. I am warning you: for some time now I have noticed this tendency of yours and I am sorry to have to say it. I mean this searching for reasons . . . this suspicious questioning of every motive. You must guard against it."

Signora Leuca bowed her head sadly and covered her face with her hands, regretting her outburst.

"Yes, it's true," she murmured. "I am like that."

Then Lawyer Arico, always impatient of discussions that did not come straight to the point, ventured to say, "So now, signora . . ."

"No, wait, Signor Arico." She looked up and quickly cut him off. "It is bad, very bad, what you reproach me of, Father, and I thank you. But believe me it is not out of pride. Quite the contrary . . . "

"To disparage the object of one's charity?"

"No, myself, myself, Father! I would be more prone to disparage myself if I have had a wicked thought. In that case I think he would be helped by someone worse off than he— if it is true that he had no ulterior motive. Perhaps I don't express myself clearly. I mean that, even though he became reconciled with me knowing this woman might die, I would still have done all I could for his children and for him. Wait! Wait! Let me finish. Because it seems more natural to me that way, more humane, even more merciful, without any appearance of . . . of exaltation or false grandeur . . . because, well, we are like that . . . and if he is not, then all the better. That is all I wanted to say."

"Well, now . . ." the lawyer quickly put in, seeing that the priest was satisfied with this explanation, smiling and nodding his approval.

But he had no luck with the blessed woman—very noble and all that, but a nuisance for a man with a lot of work to do. There she was, turning around again.

"No, please wait, Lawyer Arico."

What more could she have to say? Now she wanted to strip herself of all merit for her charity. Ah, dear God! Whatever had made that priest talk of spiritual pride? Just listen to that! She said it would not be charity but a real pleasure for her to take three children into her home, educate them, and look after them like a mother. Fine! Now, that was that. If it was a pleasure for her . . . that was more than they had ever hoped to achieve by this visit. There was nothing left to do but thank her and go.

But that was not all . . . no, indeed! It could not be that simple! Now she wanted to know what price they thought she would have to pay for the joy of being a mother to those three little ones.

Lawyer Arico stared at the priest and felt annoyed when he appeared to understand the hidden meaning of that question—he even appeared to be confronted by a case of conscience which had never occurred to him: Yes, with those three little ones there was also the question of the husband. . . . If he were to come back again to live under the same roof with her . . .

"Oh, so that's it!" exclaimed Arico, scratching his neck with one finger. "Never mind, signora, I'll speak to him myself. His Reverence will speak to him, too. He certainly can't expect the impossible."

"And then?" she asked curtly.

"Then what?"

"Signor Arico, you can speak to him as much as you like, but you will never change him. We know him, dear God, and we must accept him as he is. He will promise, he will swear to both of you, and then . . . then the moment will come when he will forget his promises. Well, given the inevitable outcome . . . I say this for *me,* mind you, not for him!"

"How do you mean . . . for you?"

"For my responsibility in this, Signor Arico. I must foresee what is bound to happen, knowing as I do the man I am taking back! You will see. He will leave the children and go off, blaming me again and saying that I opened the door with my own hands to throw him back into his former life."

"But not at all, signora . . ."

"Don't be so quick to deny it. Wait and see if it does not turn out just as I have said."

"Well, in that case it'll be just too bad for him! You're already doing too much, taking in those children. If he wants to behave like a—forgive me, it almost slipped out—that's his responsibility, not yours by a long shot."

But Signora Leuca was not looking at the indignant little lawyer but at the silent priest. She knew from his silence that he no longer thought her conscience had strayed away from God. It meant that she must look to Him for inspiration—that the final issue was up to life, life as it is and always shall be.

Farewell, reflective silence, spotless order, calm.

Signora Leuca's house was turned inside out to allow for more guests than it could hold: four must be accommodated by pulling all the rooms apart and putting them together again—eliminating the little sitting room and the dressing room, piling up furniture, and carrying pieces off to the basement to make space for three little beds and other new furnishings yet to be bought.

Signora Leuca would give up her own room to the three little girls, and she would sleep in what had been the sitting room, relinquishing her wardrobe with its three-way mirror because it would not fit. Her husband would have to make do with the dressing room, large enough but rather dark.

She did not regret her comforts or all the beloved objects which now had to be discarded. She was gay in the midst of these scrambled rooms—so lonely before in their undisturbed order and now seemingly full of life because of their very confusion.

The new arrangement of the rooms, more practical than beautiful, nevertheless gave her pleasure. It represented another way of life to her. With old things in new places and new things arriving little by little, all her former uncertainty disappeared.

Meanwhile she saw herself going about these unfamiliar rooms, meeting her responsibilities and problems as they arose.

She wanted everything to be new for the children's room and spent whole mornings shopping: three little iron beds, enameled white—if there had been only one to buy she would have preferred to have it in wood, but three wooden beds were out of the question now that she had to economize. Everything must be white: chests of drawers, chairs, the little wardrobe with its mirror, and the writing tables with shelves to one side. Perhaps it was not practical to have white desks, with the risk of spilled ink, but she wanted to teach them to take care of their things, and when they did their homework, she would supervise—not to protect the desks but to see to it that the girls worked well. Beside each bed was a little pink rug, and the curtains at the windows were pink, as well as the coverlets on the beds. The whole room was pink and white.

That nasty old cricket, Arico, said she spent too much and that it would have been a saving to bring the beds, chairs, and tables from the other house for their use. She would not hear of it. She wanted nothing from there, not so much as a nail. But what if she were the only one to feel this aversion? What if he and the little ones wanted something familiar to keep? Without more ado she decided to visit the house on Via Flaminia.

"What!" cried Arico. "After you've gone and spent all that money?"

The neighbors in the house, friends and acquaintances of the dead woman, all leaned out of their windows or ran to stand in the old, dilapidated doorway to see her step down from the carriage—tall, erect, and elegantly dressed, a veil over her face. And what comments there were as soon as she walked into the vestibule and turned to the right, up the steps leading to a kind of terrace where two French doors opened out.

"Did you see her white hair?"

"Yes, but she looks young. What age would you say ... forty!"

"A real lady ..."

"And all for that old brute in there!"

"Still, it looks as if she's come to take him back!"

"Yes, he's probably good for something after all."

"Say what you like, for me a woman with glasses ..."

Whether it was because the day was overcast, or because

she had just come from outside, at first Signora Leuca could not make out a thing. Then, as she began to discern the poverty and filth around her, her heart ached that he had been reduced to living in such a place. A rank odor of stale flowers and medicines still lingered about the room.

"Where is he?"

Sandrina came in her petticoat to open the door. Her thin arms were bare, her hair uncombed, She was surprised by this unexpected visit of her beautiful aunt with the rich shining house, and said that her father was lying down and that the dressmaker had come.

"Ah, good!" Signora Leuca smiled and lifted her veil to kiss the little girl. "The dressmaker, did you say? We'll go in. Are you glad to see your aunt, dear? My poor child. Now that I am here ... perhaps it would be best if I spoke to the dressmaker. Has she taken your measurements?"

"Everything is finished."

"What! Already?"

Holding the child's hand, Signora Leuca started toward the back room—and there he was, disheveled, his shirt open on his hairy chest, hurriedly pulling on an old black coat.

"You—here! Come in. The dressmaker ... for ... for their mourning clothes ..."

His voice betrayed his distress, and he seemed to be hurrying her, either in an effort to hide his emotion or because he was ashamed of his dirty surroundings.

But before looking at the mourning clothes, she wanted to get acquainted with the other two children. Oh, just look at that little one, what a love! Her chubby legs were bare under her little skirt and her arms were raised to lift the rumpled mass of jet-black curls at her neck. What eyes! Wasn't she a little headstrong, Signora Leuca wondered?

"Rosetta? Is that her name? What a darling!"

"No, Rosina," corrected Sandrina.

Rosina? Rosetta would be better suited to her roundness. But neither Rosina nor Rosetta really, with that black hair and those black eyes—dear God, how penetrating they were —and that bud of a mouth, a fiery bud, and a little nose that was hardly a nose at all....

Was she five or not quite? Certainly one of those black dresses could not be meant for her. She should have a white one with a black satin sash. But later on she would attend to all that. . . .

"And this is Lauretta?"

Try as she might to sound affectionate, her voice was cold. It seemed as if she had already met this child in Sandrina—the same afflicted look, the same set, serious eyes in a long, pale face, the same miserably straight hair.

It was clear at a glance that the two older sisters had nothing in common with this little one, born a few years later. Lauretta was already over eight, fourteen months younger than Sandrina.

Signora Leuca checked a suspicion which rose in her mind, knowing about her husband's jealous fights with that woman. But now she was dead, and it was obvious the littlest one . . .

To conceal her doubt, she quickly turned to the dressmaker and exchanged a few words about the horrid dresses; then she told her husband the purpose of her visit. He agreed with her that nothing need be taken from the house. He would sell whatever he could and distribute the rest among the neighbors. He only wanted to take his clothes and whatever the children could still wear.

Signora Leuca had turned toward the bureau to look at the children's clothes when she spied her husband's gesture to restrain her and immediately saw the reason for it. On top of the dresser stood a photograph in a cheap copper frame. She realized it must be of that woman and pretended not to notice it. She told him there was no hurry about the girls' clothes; whatever they could not use should be given to the needy.

Then she asked Sandrina if she would like to go with her. Sandrina clapped her hands with delight, and Lauretta wanted to go, too. Why not the little one, then? They could all go with her this evening because their room was ready.

But the baby refused to budge. She would not be separated from her father. Without her father she would not leave, and he had to stay on a few more days to liquidate his sorry past.

That evening Signora Leuca returned home with two little girls dressed in black.

"This is your room. Do you like it?"

Sandrina and Lauretta were spellbound.

"You will sleep here," she told Sandrina, "and Lauretta there. Rosina will sleep in the smaller bed between you."

Then she showed them the little desks where they would do their homework, assigning a desk to each one.

"Both desks are exactly alike," she pointed out, "each one has a little shelf."

She explained that they would attend another school, close by in via Novara, and that she hoped they would study well, behave nicely, and be neat. As for their clothing, for the moment—they would keep the things they had until new frocks could be bought, pretty dresses to go walking in and others to wear at home with protective pinafores.

Meanwhile she bathed them, combed their hair, and showed them through the house—where their father would sleep, where she would sleep. Finally she seated them at the table with her for supper.

There were so many things the little girls needed to be taught, but for this evening it was best to allow them to do everything their own way. They were in a trance. They didn't know how to take up a glass or hold the small-scale knives and forks bought especially for them, but they would learn in time. And she too must learn not to spoil them by overindulgence.

She kept them with her after supper, talking, although she was careful not to let her curiosity about many things lead her into questioning them. However, nothing would induce Lauretta to speak; she sat watching her sister Sandrina, who was at ease, having been there before.

When Signora Leuca put them in bed, she discovered that they had not been taught to make the sign of the cross before going to sleep. She explained this to them as best she could and persuaded them to repeat a short prayer after her. Then, for the first time, she heard the sound of Lauretta's voice.

A little later, listening at their door to find out if they were asleep, she heard a terrible fight going on. They sounded like cats, pulling each other's hair, kicking and clawing. What was she to do? Open the door? Surprise them? If they kept their voices so low, it must be because they had misgivings and did not want her to hear them. Then Lauretta tiptoed back to bed, and there was silence, except for Sandrina's sobs half muffled under the covers.

That night Signora Leuca stayed awake a long time. She wondered what these children had for her that the others she had helped before did not have—all those children she could no longer afford to comfort. She had never before spent so much money for charitable work nor gone to so much trouble, and never once had she dreamed of taking one of the others into her home.

Was it because they were her husband's children? And for that matter, who knew if they really were, even one of them? No, that was not it. She had taken them in to fill the emptiness of her life, in spite of all the worry and difficulty this would mean for her . . . and certainly not only because of the children themselves.

So this was what it amounted to: She was the object of her own charity, to the detriment of those poor unfortunates whom she would no longer have time to care for and think about. It hardly seemed right. Even though it was impossible to do as much for them as for the two sleeping in there, already in a sense her own, she would feel conscience-stricken if she did nothing at all—at least for some of them: that little sick girl in via Reggio, and—oh God!—the little orphan, Elodina, in via Alessandria! She could not abandon them to their wretched fate when everything here was pink and white—beds, rugs, coverlets, and when she considered the pleasure she found in just thinking of things she wanted to buy for them—dainty underclothes, pretty shoes—and all the pains she would take to have them becomingly dressed. No! No! It was too unfair. And why, after all? Who were these children, really?

Tomorrow would she feel gratified to be praised for her generosity because she was taking in her husband's three children by another woman? And by a woman like that one? No. The very thought that such praise was inevitable made her regret what she had done. Were these children to be rewarded for their mother's shame and their father's guilt, "generously" forgiven by her? She had nothing to forgive, having suffered no more from her husband's actions than she suffered from so many other wrongs—for instance, the wrong she herself was now doing by excluding so many poor children because these three were more vital to her.

Ah! She would atone for her wrongdoing!

Suddenly she was aware of the slow, distinct ticking of the

clock across the same gaping silence as before. It must be very late. Hovering and forlorn, she saw all her thoughts, her deeds, every feature of her life, more painfully than ever before.

And there, peering through the shadows in the luster of its cheap copper frame, sat the picture of the dead woman on the dresser. What was he doing alone at this hour in that horrible house? And why did she imagine him standing in front of the dresser with the child, looking intently at that photograph?

Her fault lay in having climbed all the way to the top of a high mountain—not for the vainglory of climbing. What glory was there in that? Or should she consider it a punishment . . . or fate . . . rather than a fault?

She well knew the chill, the silence of the summit, from which everything appears small and distant, blurred by a mist of solitary sorrow which perhaps does not exist below, at close range, but which here, aloof and apart, forms a cloud between the viewer and day-to-day reality.

Three days later her husband arrived, the little one clinging around his neck like a wild, scared kitten. Exasperated by this untamed child and the weight of the two heavy suitcases he carried, one in each hand, he was indifferent to the happy, affectionate greetings of Lauretta and Sandrina and blind to their completely new appearance.

The two little girls, who were expecting their father to admire their good behavior, their rosy cleanliness, their well-combed hair, their new black pinafores with white lace collars and cuffs, their dainty stockings and shoes, were disappointed and hurt.

It was a miracle that he did not curse, strangled as he was by Rosina's plump arms viciously gripping him tighter and tighter. Finally, unable to make her let go, he wrenched her off violently and threw her into a chair.

"There, be quiet or I'll let you have it!"

At this the frantic child rolled over on the floor, screaming and kicking, hiding her face in her arms, her hands clutching her hair. Infuriated, he turned his back and strode to the window.

"I can't stand anymore!" he cried, facing his wife. "For sixteen days I have been shackled like this!"

As the baby crawled after him, howling like a wild thing, he added, "There! You see! You see!"

And just as Rosina was about to grab his leg, he lifted it up. Sandrina and Lauretta began to laugh.

"Oh, don't laugh!" Signora Leuca admonished them. "Shame on you, when your little sister is crying like that! Go, bring the toys we bought yesterday."

"Toys! Do you hear?" said her father, picking up the child.

The little one was somewhat mollified in his arms, although still convulsed with sobs. But as soon as Sandrina and Lauretta came back with the toys and she heard the tinkle of tiny cymbals struck by a mechanical clown, she buried her face in her father's neck, not to see or hear.

Signora Leuca had the impression that this clinging child was a bedevilment of the dead woman, tethering him to all she had represented for him in life: misery, vulgarity, and bondage.

She realized the impossibility of taming the little creature, who was as dark as if impregnated with the vice from which she had sprung, and whose blood, she sensed, was a savage mixture. Signora Leuca did not even attempt to take her from her father or persuade her to play with her sisters. She knew it was useless and might even make things worse.

She showed her husband to his room as if apologizing because it was not better, but immediately realized that this was the wrong attitude. In fact his reply, synchronizing with her thoughts, affected her strangely.

"Not at all! What are you trying to say?"

He frowned when he saw the single bed, having slept in a double bed until now, and asked, pointing to the child, "What about this nuisance?"

"She has her own bed in the girls' room," Signora Leuca told him. "Come, I'll show you."

He stood in the doorway admiring the lovely pink-and-white room with its three little beds. He was pleased and touched but ill at ease because he found it difficult to tell her that, since the death of that woman, the baby had taken her mother's place at night and might now refuse to sleep alone.

"Well, we shall see this evening," Signora Leuca replied. "If we manage to put her to bed in here, you might stay with her until she goes to sleep. Otherwise, we can move her little bed into your room and she can sleep there."

As she spoke, she saw that Sandrina and Lauretta would be only too happy to have this lovely room all to themselves. They had quickly adopted an air of well-brought-up little girls since they had come into her house, but their little sister clearly did not want to change. Their father was not too welcome either in the older girls' room in this lovely house where they were so happy, enjoying a new life with their "aunt."

In truth, their gloomy, unkempt father did not look as if he would ever adjust to these surroundings but must always feel a stranger, not daring to look about him, not knowing what to say, confused, embarrassed, repeating hoarsely, "It's too much, too much!"

He now asked permission to go to his room to unpack his bags, as though he were afraid someone might do it for him.

"Auntie, why are we in mourning for Mama when Papa isn't?"

Signora Leuca, who had not noticed the color of her husband's clothes, stared at the child and did not know what to reply; not that it was so difficult to think up an answer, but she suddenly realized that he was not wearing black out of regard for her, unwilling to parade his mourning for another woman before her eyes.

It saddened and upset her. How he must have wept for that woman! The horrible things he had confessed were still vivid in her mind, and she knew that, although he might have hated her for enslaving him, he probably would give much to have her back, now that she was gone, and who knew how deep and lasting his grief would be. Unless...

Signora Leuca broke off this supposition which had troubled her for many days. She was more than ever convinced that her prediction would come to pass, if not today or tomorrow, then as soon as his first embarrassment had passed and he regained his old self-confidence.

Her agitation mounted as she began to notice ways of his, familiar gestures and expressions, which should, on the contrary, have reassured her. His humility and the patience and the affection he had for the children were all but unbelievable ... so many things which aroused her sympathy for him in his position—sympathy more real than she had been prepared, out of duty, to show him.

She was impressed at dinner, as they were discussing the little lawyer, to see him lift one eyebrow and contract the other in an intelligent frown—an all-but-forgotten trait of his which had always pleased her. His natural good manners at table impressed her also. He was self-conscious only when she looked at him; then he would glance aside. His air of quiet good breeding came as a surprise to the two older girls, who stared as if they did not recognize him. However, Signora Leuca, to her delight, saw him fall into the spontaneous, charming manner she had known long ago.

Wine! What torture! She had to wrench her eyes from the bottle every time, though it remained almost untouched. Her eyes betrayed her, and it was useless to try to hide the fact that she knew about his habit of getting drunk every night. It must be hard on him now to drink hardly anything, yet he did not show it. Tonight was the first time in many years that they had sat together at table. Who knew if tomorrow, at lunch or at dinner, he would still be able to control himself?

After dinner, a tender, paternal smile moved his discolored lips under the graying mustache as he silently called her attention to the sleeping child in his lap. He asked quietly if it would not be better to undress her there before putting her to bed in the room where the other children were sleeping.

As she leaned over the child, her shoulder brushed his chest and she felt his breath on her hair. She touched him several times as she undressed the little one on his lap, but her apprehension disturbed her more than the actual contact. She was anxious lest her hands betray her nervousness.

Finally, when the child had been carefully put to bed and they both had tiptoed from the room, the dangerous moment was at hand, the moment when they were alone together in the intimacy of the house.

Yet, nothing happened. The door of the children's room was hardly closed before he sighed with relief and smilingly told her that he would now have peace until morning because Rosina never waked during the night. Then humbly and quietly he wished her good night and went to his room.

Signora Leuca lay in her bed turning many things over in

her mind. She was especially irritated with herself because
of her apprehension, the more unjustified when confronted
by his withdrawn attitude. He dared not look at her and certainly never dreamed of drawing closer than she would allow, for the moment.

What was it she feared then? She had locked the door behind her as soon as she entered her own room. This precau-
tion now made her angry. She was tempted to jump out of
bed and unlock the door.

The priest noticed it, he said, after the last meeting of the
Charity Society in the parish house. Her friends, Signora
Mielli and Signora Marzorati, had of course noticed it; and so
had good Signorina Trecke, impossible as it might seem.

Signora Leuca's zeal had cooled: she had not attended the
meetings of the Charity Society for two months now. Not only
that, but she had skipped Mass for several weeks. And she
treated her friends with indifference as if she suspected them
of being partly responsible for the state in which she now
found herself—with those three children in the house and that
man who, for all the respect he showed her, must weigh like
a stone around her neck.

There could be no question that the three children gave
her a lot of work, but if this was so—and no doubt it was,
since they had not even known how to make the sign of the
cross when they first came to her—then all the more reason
to attend Mass regularly every Sunday. Her attitude was in-
comprehensible, especially at the very time of the Novena
in preparation for the Feast of the Immaculate Conception
of the Blessed Virgin Mary.

Signora Mielli remarked that their friend, always so careful
about her appearance, had begun to neglect herself. Her hair
was badly combed, if at all, as if she no longer looked at herself in the mirror. Of course, she had *four* children to care
for, not three, and all the worry of the house, but she could
still have found time to groom herself properly had she
wanted to. Evidently, with the serene, unruffled life she had
led before, she did not know what a struggle it was to bring
up children. But merit lay in conquering difficulties, not in
going slack under their weight.

Too bad she had had to part with the devoted servant who
had been with her so many years. But it was only natural. She

should have taken in someone to help, for one person alone could not possibly do all the work now with three children and a man in the house.

"She hired another maid, yes, she certainly did!" said Signorina Trecke. "But had to discharge her on the spot, because it seems that her husband . . . well, I don't know . . ."

"What? Her husband!" exclaimed Signora Marzorati making a wry face.

Signorina Trecke opened her mouth in one of her usual smiles. She didn't quite understand what it was Signora Leuca had discovered, but her niece had laughed her head off when she heard it.

"She laughed like a fool. I can't think why."

"Of course," mused Signora Mielli with a faraway look in her eyes, "Now surely, that man . . ."

"Dear God!" cried Signora Marzorati. "If Signora Leuca . . . of course she's right, poor woman. In her place as a wife, I'd rather put up with . . . I don't know what! I mean, you understand, Signora Mielli . . . well, *out*side the house, at least!"

When the two ladies had exchanged a few words, heavy with innuendoes, Signorina Trecke remarked angelically that Signor Leuca did go outside the house—every evening, as a matter of fact.

"I happen to know this," she said, "because he comes to my house."

Surprised, Signora Marzorati scowled at her.

"To *your* house! What for?"

"To see my niece," replied Signorina Trecke.

There could be no harm in Signor Leuca's visits now that he was reconciled with Signora Leuca and the priest himself had favored this reconciliation.

"What reconciliation?" Signora Marzorati exploded. "Do you know, at least, what your niece and Signor Leuca talk about when they are together?"

Signorina Trecke lowered her aging eyelids with roguish cunning over her cloudless blue eyes.

"They talk about the Republic of Ecuador," she said.

"About the Republic of Ecuador!" gasped Signora Mielli, not so far off for once.

"Yes," explained Signorina Trecke. "Because an expedition of big industrialists has left for the Republic of Ecuador. Everything is still to be done there: bridges, roads, railroads,

electricity, schools . . . my niece knows a member of the expedition. She says that soon an even larger group will go:
workmen, farmers, engineers, even lawyers and teachers. She
says that she will go, too—my niece, that is—to this Republic
of Ecuador! That's all they talk about."

Signorina Trecke looked so stupid as she told them this
news that Signora Marzorati and Signora Mielli were annoyed and, restraining their curiosity, changed the subject,
turning away to discuss other things between themselves.

It was all over.

Signora Leuca, contrary to all her expectations, was hurt
not so much by what had actually happened as by what she
suffered within. It was because the harm she had foreseen,
feared, and awaited had failed to materialize that she now
endured this torment.

She was certain, despite the scorn she felt for her own
flesh, that she would not have yielded if her husband had
seized her one of those nights in the silence of the house, but
would have pushed him away. She would have been deaf to
the promptings of her conscience which made her realize
that, if she rejected him, she only gave him a fresh excuse to
fall back once more into that horrible life. She had to admit
that she would never have relented even though later her remorse would not be denied.

Yes, but it was equally certain that, if this had happened,
her suffering would have been less cruel than what she now
endured because it had not occurred.

For little by little her horror of his body, aroused by all
those indelible images with which his confession had seeded
her mind, had become a horror of her own flesh. Every evening when she closed her door—without locking it—she
looked at her body in the mirror and wondered if it was
really so undesirable that it did not even merit a sidelong
glance from a man like that, who had found pleasure until
recently in such a vulgar woman.

She was still beautiful and she knew it, thanks to the
glances of men who turned to look at her in the street when
she least expected it. Her hair, turned white as snow before
the age of thirty, brought out the youthful freshness of her
skin and gave an ambiguous grace, like an innocent lie, to
her smile everytime she said, "Now, I am old . . ."

Her smooth throat rising like an unblemished column from her shapely bosom, her . . . God! How frightful this intimate analysis of her whole body was in its vain attempt to reassure herself that she was still beautiful, still desirable! Her former assurance was, after all, the reason why she had so clearly forecast for the lawyer and the priest what demands her husband was sure to make on her, in consequence of which she would have been obliged to put him out of the house.

She had lost interest in her appearance as she became progressively convinced of her husband's indifference—although he continued to show her every polite consideration. Refusing to admit the reason to herself, she pretended she had no time to dress her hair properly, what with the two older girls to look after and get off early to school.

And when, by accident, she had found that awful woman's picture in his dresser drawer, how greedily her eyes had devoured it! What a disappointment it was, after having imagined that she was so beautiful! Provocative, yes, but in fact quite ugly, with a mad look in her eyes, and she was common. But it was only natural that he would have been attracted to that type of woman.

However, Nella, the vivacious niece of Signorina Trecke, certainly was not common in appearance, and she clearly pleased and attracted him. Sandrina had been in her class two years ago when she first began to teach near the Porta del Popolo. What a coincidence that she should find her former pupil at the school in via Novara where she was now teaching! She had walked home with her after class, Sandrina's father holding one hand and she the other. But now that it was all over, Signora Leuca did not want to complain even about the Trecke girl's betrayal. She had always felt an instinctive aversion for her and had recognized her as an enemy.

Considering his past reputation there should have been little need to seduce him, yet that is what Nella Trecke did under Signora Leuca's eyes, using her pupil as an excuse to come to the house nearly every day. She felt, no doubt, that a lady like Signora Leuca would not deign to notice, or would at most feel a little more scorn for that wretched man she had taken in—along with his daughters—out of charity.

Signora Leuca had accepted the challenge at first and

closed her eyes to the young girl's smiles and blandishments, not wanting to admit the obscure, hidden jealousy they awakened in her. However, when she could bear it no longer, she had forbidden the girl to come to the house. But, afraid of betraying her own distress, she had not warned Nella's stupid aunt or the old priest, and thus had abetted their scheme.

Then the scandal broke.

The priest and the ladies of the Charity Society blamed Signorina Trecke for having given the pair the opportunity to meet every evening at her house and plan their flight together to the Republic of Ecuador.

Signorina Trecke wept inconsolably not so much over the disgrace that her niece had brought on her as over the fact that she was still quite unable to see the evil she had fostered and which had now brought down so many reproaches on her head—all well deserved, of course. Unfortunately, no healthy suspicions were ever to cloud her childlike eyes, which would now be red from crying because her ungrateful niece had left her.

To crown it all, even Signora Leuca found herself accused of doing things by halves, always, of course, because of that overniceness which had so often hindered her from giving free rein to her charitable instincts, especially in the difficult task she had attempted this time.

Heavens! Having taken her husband back into her house, why could she not have accepted the role of a wife in every sense? One has crosses to bear, but virtue lies in resignation.

Signora Leuca let them talk; she even let them think it was her fault. The wound was too deep: let their words fall into it like so many drops of acid. She did not mind—the more it stung, the better.

She smilingly received Lawyer Arico's compliments—which he saw fit to present to her privately—on having freed herself of that lecherous brute, an offensive encumbrance in her house, no matter what the priest said about it. She herself had only objected to *his* return, the lawyer recalled, but hadn't she said that the children would be a pleasure? Well, now he was gone, and what's more she had not had to drive him out; and she had the children.

"What could be better?" he concluded.

In fact, what could be better?

Was she to confide to Lawyer Arico that suddenly, as soon

as she had heard of her husband's flight, the pleasure of having the children in the house had vanished as if by magic and a heavy burden of responsibility had settled on her shoulders, making the children seem strangers to her?

Signora Leuca did not even want to admit this to herself. She showered more attention and more affection on the three abandoned orphans than ever—but Signora Leuca felt a change come over her feelings for the little one, that savage little creature. She knew why only too well, but would not name the reason.

"Do you love me?"

"Ess!"

Kneeling in her lap, Rosina would stretch her little claw-like hands up to her neck, wrinkle her tiny nose, and purse that rosebud of a mouth.

"Oh! Not like that! My goodness! You look ugly that way!"

"*You* ugly!"

Signora Leuca had won her over to the extent that she now allowed herself to be picked up and cared for—but at the price of scratches, kicks, and even spittings in the face!

The other two stood by, watching a little enviously. They thought it unfair for their aunt to take such trouble with Rosina in front of them—Rosina, who was downright naughty while they were always good as gold.

Only once had Sandrina, evidently speaking for Lauretta, too, asked her, "Where is Papa?"

They must have understood something vaguely either from gossip at school or from the priest's words when he had come, very upset, to announce the elopement; or perhaps the copious tears Signorina Trecke had shed the following day, when she begged forgiveness for her niece, had told them more clearly than words.

"Papa has gone away, but he will come back," Signora Leuca answered calmly, and they were satisfied.

But would he come back? Signora Leuca was certain that he never would. In any case, even if he did turn up one day or another, what could it now matter to her?

It was all over.

Her spirit sadly on guard under its mask of candid serenity, Signora Leuca was inwardly torn by a distress no one suspected; she was left with the three children to care for and bring up, but what was more, she bore an ever-present tor-

ment, not for herself alone, who was perhaps better off than
many others, but for all things, all earthly creatures as she
saw them in the infinite anguish of her love and pity, in that
constant painful awareness—assuaged only by fleeting peaceful moments which brought relief and consolation—of the
futility of living like this. . . .

ESCAPE

THIS fog is the last straw! Bareggi thought as its icy needles stung his face and neck. Tomorrow I'll feel it in all my bones—head heavy as lead, eyes swollen shut between watery bags. It's enough to drive a man out of his mind.

Signor Bareggi, worn out by nephritis at fifty-two, squelched along the avenue with his cheap cloth shoes oozing as if there had been a downpour. His feet were so swollen that if a finger were pressed to them, it took a full minute for the skin to come smooth again, and the pain in his kidneys never let up.

Morning and evening, wearing the same cloth shoes, Signor Bareggi trudged from home to office and from his office, home. (Hadn't his doctor told him to exercise "within reason"?) As he dragged himself along, moving slowly because of those tender, aching feet, he nursed a dream: he would run away some day, run away to hide from it all, run away forever.

His home life drove him to desperation, too. The thought of having to go back day after day to that house—on its remote cross street off the long avenue where he was now walking—had become unbearable. It was not the distance he minded, though with his feet it was no small matter. Nor was it the isolation, which, in fact, he cherished. The cross streets were little more than lanes with no streetlamps, and as yet there were few signs of "civilization." There were only three small houses to the left, and, on the right, a country hedgerow shielded vast truck gardens. In the middle of the hedge was a weatherbeaten sign reading LOTS FOR SALE.

His was the third little house, with four dark rooms on the ground floor. There were shutters at the windows. In addition the glass panes had been screened to shield them from the stones thrown by the hoodlums in the neighborhood. But on the upper floor there were three small cheerful bedrooms and a little veranda with a view over the truck gardens, which was his delight in good weather.

As soon as he entered the house he was plagued by the anxious attentions of his wife and daughters, a fluttering hen followed by two peeping chicks. They ran here, flew there, getting his slippers or his cup of milk with the egg yolk in it. One of them would be down on all fours untying his shoes, another asking, in a whining voice, whether he was soaked from rain or sweat, according to the season—as if he could be dry when he had walked all the way home without an umbrella, or as if in mid-August he would not be bathed in perspiration!

All this coddling would be the ruination of his stomach. They only treat me this way so I can't give free rein to my feelings, he thought ruefully. How could he complain before those eyes melting with pity, before those eternally ministering hands?

And how he yearned to complain—about so many things! He had only to turn his head to the left or right to find a reason for complaint, a reason they never even dreamed of. Take the big old kitchen table, for instance. They all ate there, and with his diet of bread and milk, its smell of good raw meat and beautiful onions in their golden skins was a downright offense! Could he chide his daughters because they ate meat which their mother prepared deliciously with those onions? Or could he reproach them because they did the laundry at home to save money and threw the water, reeking of strong soap, out the door, thus spoiling that breath of fresh green from the vegetable gardens he so enjoyed in the evenings?

How unjustified such a reproof would seem to them who drudged all day long, stuck away there like exiles, little dreaming that, in other circumstances, each of them might have led a far different life.

Fortunately, his daughters were a little simple-minded, like their mother. He pitied them, but, seeing them reduce themselves to the state of old dish rags, his pity turned to sour vexation.

For he was not good-natured. No, no. He was not even good, as those poor women—and for that matter most everybody else—seemed to think. He was bad. At certain times the bitterness he felt deep inside must have burned in his eyes. It would come out as he sat alone at his desk in the office, unconsciously toying, perhaps, with the blade of his penknife. Insane impulses, like slashing the canvas sheathing of his desk top or the leather of his armchair, would almost overcome him. Instead, he would spread out his swollen hand, fingers splayed on the desk, and look at it while tears welled up in his eyes. With the other hand he would pluck furiously at the reddish hairs on the backs of his distended fingers.

He was bad, yes, but he was desperate, too, for he would probably wind up one of these days in a wheelchair, paralyzed down one side, completely at the mercy of those three tiresome women. It was this longing to escape while there was yet time that drove him wild.

That evening, as he was nearing the house, the longing suddenly rushed into his hands and one foot before it reached his head. His foot rose automatically to the step of the milkman's cart and his hands went to the seat, as it stood there untended at the corner of his lane.

What! Signor Bareggi, a serious man, sedate, respectable, a professional man, on a milkman's cart?

The impulse came over him when he had spied the cart through the thickening fog as he had turned off the avenue into the cross street; when his nostrils had caught that fresh odor of hay in the feedbag and the goaty smell of the milkman's coat thrown across the seat; when smells of the distant countryside far, far beyond Casal dei Pazzi—vast and free—had assailed him.

The horse, stretching his neck and cropping grass at the roadside, wandered a step at a time away from the three little houses at the end of the lane. The milkman tarried, as usual, to chat with the women, well knowing that his horse would wait patiently before their door. Tonight, when he came out, empty bottles in hand, and didn't find the horse in its usual place, he started to run toward the corner.

Bareggi's eyes were fever-bright. He tingled all over with pleasure and apprehension. Whatever happened, he no longer cared about the consequences for himself, the milkman, or his womenfolk. In the confusion of his troubled mind, all was dismissed as he seized the reins in one hand, the whip in the other, gave the horse a mighty slash on the rump—and they were off.

The startled horse looked old, but he wasn't. Bareggi had not counted on the beast's flying leap, which set up a din of clattering cans and jugs, racks and bottles, in back of him. The reins flew out of his hands when he tried to brace himself after the jolt, and his feet were knocked off the shaft as he was thrown backward. He scrambled to his feet again and recovered the reins, but scarcely was one danger over when another loomed. He held his breath as the maddened beast launched out on a wild race through the fog which had closed in with the coming night.

No one ran up to head them off or called out to anyone else to waylay them, even though all those milk cans banging around must have made a frightful racket. Perhaps there were no longer any people on the avenue or, if there were, their cries were not heard above the din. The streetlights must certainly have been lit by now, but Bareggi could not see them through the dense fog.

He let go of the whip and reins to hang onto the seat with both hands. The horse was either as fear-crazed as himself or not accustomed to the whip. Then again it might have been joy at the quick end of his evening's rounds that set him off, or his relief at no longer feeling the restraining reins. He neighed and neighed. Signor Bareggi was terrified by the violent backward thrust of his flanks in that race that seemed to gain momentum with every lunge.

The risk of crashing into something as they turned off the avenue crossed his mind, and he tried to retrieve the reins, but when he let go of the seat to stretch out a hand, he was thrown forward and banged his nose. Blood now spurted over his mouth, chin, and hands, but he had no time to stanch it. He could only clutch the seat and hang on for dear life. God, O God, how that milk was swishing and sloshing around in those overturned cans, splattering all over his back! Blood before and milk behind! Signor Bareggi laughed aloud as his bowels twisted in terror. He was laughing wildly at his own fear, instinctively rejecting the certainty of imminent disaster and hoping that, after all, this might turn out to be a magnificent joke—a mad prank to tell at the office tomorrow. He went on laughing desperately as he tried to recall the calm of the farmers watering their vegetable gardens while he watched them from his little balcony across the street. He thought next of things like the patches peasants wear on their clothes, as if to say, Yes, poverty covers my buttocks, knees, and elbows, as bright and defiant as a flag. Meanwhile, beneath such thoughts, the threat of turning over at any moment lay vivid and terrifying. At any moment the cart would surely crash into something and scatter all over the place.

They flew past the Nomentana gate, past the Casal dei Pazzi, on and on into the open country, dimly visible through the fog.

When the horse finally stopped in front of a small farmhouse, the cart was battered and not a can or jug was left inside.

Hearing the horse pull up unusually early, the milkman's wife called out a greeting. When no one replied, she went to the door with an oil lamp and saw the wreck. Again she called her husband's name. Where could he be? What had happened?

But these were questions which the horse, still panting and happy after his wonderful gallop, was unable to answer. Snorting and stamping, his eyes bloodshot, he could only shake his head.

THE SOFT TOUCH OF GRASS

THEY went into the next room, where he was sleeping in a big chair, to ask if he wanted to look at her for the last time before the lid was put on the coffin.

"It's dark. What time is it?" he asked.

It was nine-thirty in the morning, but the day was overcast and the light dim. The funeral had been set for ten o'clock.

Signor Pardi stared up at them with dull eyes. It hardly seemed possible that he could have slept so long and well all night. He was still numb with sleep and the sorrow of these last days. He would have liked to cover his face with his hands to shut out the faces of his neighbors grouped about his chair in the thin light; but sleep had weighted his body like lead, and although there was a tingling in his toes urging him to rise, it quickly went away. Should he still give way to his grief? He happened to say aloud, "Always . . ." but he said it like someone settling himself under the covers to go back to sleep. They all looked at him questioningly. Always what?

Always dark, even in the daytime, he had wanted to say, but it made no sense. The day after her death, the day of her funeral, he would always remember this wan light and his deep sleep, too, with her lying dead in the next room. Perhaps the windows . . .

"The windows?"

Yes, they were still closed. They had not been opened during the night, and the warm glow of those big dripping candles lingered. The bed had been taken away, and she was there in her padded casket, rigid and ashen against the creamy satin.

No. Enough. He had seen her.

He closed his eyes, for they burned from all the crying he had done these past few days. Enough. He had slept, and everything had been washed away with that sleep. Now he was relaxed, with a sense of sorrowful emptiness. Let the

314

casket be closed and carried away with all it held of his past life.

But since she was still there ...

He jumped to his feet and tottered. They caught him, and with eyes still closed he allowed himself to be led to the open casket. When he opened his eyes and saw her, he called her by name, her name that lived for him alone, the name in which he saw her and knew her in all the fullness of the life they had shared together. He glared resentfully at the others daring to stare at her lying still in death. What did they know about her? They could not even imagine what it meant to him to be deprived of her. He felt like screaming, and it must have been apparent, for his son hurried over to take him away. He was quick to see the meaning of this and felt a chill as though he were stripped bare. For shame—those foolish ideas up to the very last, even after his night-long sleep. Now they must hurry so as not to keep the friends waiting who had come to follow the coffin to the church.

"Come on, Papa. Be reasonable."

With angry, piteous eyes, the bereaved man turned back to his big chair.

Reasonable, yes; it was useless to cry out the anguish that welled within him and that could never be expressed by words or deeds. For a husband who is left a widower at a certain age, a man still yearning for his wife, can the loss be the same as that of a son for whom—at a certain point—it is almost timely to be left an orphan? Timely, since he was on the point of getting married and would, as soon as the three months' mourning were passed, now that he had the added excuse that it was better for both of them to have a woman to look after the house.

"Pardi! Pardi!" they shouted from the entrance hall.

His chill became more intense when he understood clearly for the first time that they were not calling him but his son. From now on their surname would belong more to his son than to him. And he, like a fool, had gone in there to cry out the living name of his mate, like a profanation. For shame! Yes, useless, foolish ideas, he now realized, after that long sleep which had washed him clean of everything.

Now the one vital thing to keep him going was his curiosity as to how their new home would be arranged. Where, for example, were they going to have him sleep? The big double bed had been removed. Would he have a small bed? he wondered. Yes, probably his son's single bed. Now he would have the small bed. And his son would soon be lying in a big bed, his wife beside him within arm's reach. He, alone, in his little bed, would stretch out his arms into thin air.

He felt torpid, perplexed, with a sensation of emptiness inside and all around him. His body was numb from sitting so long. If he tried now to get up, he felt sure that he would rise light as a feather in all that emptiness, now that his life was reduced to nothing. There was hardly any difference between himself and the big chair. Yet that chair appeared secure on its four legs, whereas he no longer knew where his feet and legs belonged nor what to do with his hands. What did he care about his life? He did not care particularly about the lives of others, either. Yet, as he was still alive, he must go on. Begin again—some sort of life which he could not yet conceive and which he certainly would never have contemplated if things had not changed in his own world. Now, deposed like this all of a sudden, not old and yet no longer young . . .

He smiled and shrugged his shoulders. For his son, all at once, he had become a child. But after all, as everyone knows, fathers are children to their grown sons who are full of worldly ambition and have successfully outdistanced them in positions of importance. They keep their fathers in idleness to repay all they have received when they themselves were small, and their fathers in turn become young again.

The single bed . . .

But they did not even give him the little room where his son had slept. Instead, they said, he would feel more independent in another, almost hidden on the courtyard; he would feel free there to do as he liked. They refurnished it with all the best pieces, so it would not occur to anyone that it had once been a servant's room. After the marriage, all the front rooms were pretentiously decorated and newly furnished, even to the luxury of carpets. Not a trace remained of the way the old house had looked. Even with his own furniture relegated to that little dark room, out of the mainstream of the young people's existence, he did not feel at home. Yet, oddly enough, he did not resent the disregard he seemed to have reaped along with the old furniture, because he admired the new rooms and was satisfied with his son's success.

But there was another deeper reason, not too clear as yet, a promise of another life, all shining and colorful, which was erasing the memory of the old one. He even drew a secret hope from it that a new life might begin for him, too. Unconsciously, he sensed the luminous opening of a door at his back whence he might escape at the right moment, easy enough now that no one bothered about him, leaving him as if on holiday in the sanctuary of his little room "to do as he pleased." He felt lighter than air. His eyes had a gleam in them that colored everything, leading him from marvel to marvel, as though he really were a child again. He had the eyes of a child—lively and open wide on a world which was still new.

He took the habit of going out early in the morning to begin his holiday which was to last as long as his life lasted. Relieved of all responsibilities, he agreed to pay his son so much every month out of his pension for his maintenance. It was very little. Though he needed nothing, his son thought he should keep some money for himself to satisfy any need he might have. But need for what? He was satisfied now just to look on at life.

Having shaken off the weight of experience, he no longer knew how to get along with oldsters. He avoided them. And the younger people considered him too old, so he went to the park where the children played.

That was how he started his new life—in the meadow among the children in the grass. What an exhilarating scent the grass had, and so fresh where it grew thick and high. The children played hide-and-seek there. The constant trickle of some hidden stream outpurled the rustle of the leaves. Forgetting their game, the children pulled off their shoes and stockings. What a delicious feeling to sink into all that freshness of soft new grass with bare feet!

He took off one shoe and was stealthily removing the other when a young girl appeared before him, her face flaming. "You pig!" she cried, her eyes flashing.

Her dress was caught up in front on a bush, and she quickly pulled it down over her legs, because he was looking up at her from where he sat on the ground.

He was stunned. What had she imagined? Already she had disappeared. He had wanted to enjoy the children's innocent fun. Bending down, he put his two hands over his hard, bare feet. What had she seen wrong? Was he too old to share a child's delight in going barefoot in the grass? Must one immediately think evil because he was old? Ah, he knew that he could change in a flash from being a child to becoming a man again, if he must. He was still a man, after all, but he didn't want to think about it. He refused to think about it. It was really as a child that he had taken off his shoes. How wrong it was of that wretched girl to insult him like that! He threw himself face down on the grass. All his grief, his loss, his daily loneliness had brought about this gesture, interpreted now in the light of vulgar malice. His gorge rose in disgust and bitterness. Stupid girl! If he had wanted that—even his son admitted he might have "some desires"—he had plenty of money in his pocket for such needs.

Indignant, he pulled himself upright. Shamefacedly, with trembling hands, he put on his shoes again. All the blood had gone to his head, and the pulse now beat hot behind his eyes. Yes, he knew where to go for that. He knew.

Calmer now, he got up and went back to the house. In the welter of furniture which seemed to have been placed there on purpose to drive him mad, he threw himself on the bed and turned his face to the wall.

SELECTED BIBLIOGRAPHY

Compiled by Eric Bentley

The following is a complete list of Pirandello's plays with the date of the first Italian performance. When a play has been published in English in the U. S., the English title is also given.

La morsa (The Vise), 1910
Lumíe di Sicilia (Sicilian Limes), 1910
Il dovere del medico (The Doctor's Duty), 1913
Se non così, 1915
Pensaci, Giacomino!, 1916
Liolà (Liolà), 1916
Così è (se vi pare) (It Is So!—If You Think So *or*,
   Right You Are), 1917
Il berretto a sonagli, 1917
La giara (The Jar), 1917
Il piacere dell'onestà (The Pleasure of Honesty), 1917
Ma non è una cosa seria, 1918
Il giuoco delle parti (The Rules of the Game), 1918
L'innesto, 1919
La patente (By Judgment of Court), 1919
L'uomo, la bestia, e la virtù, 1919
Tutto per bene, 1920
Come prima, meglio di prima, 1920
Cecè (Chee-Chee), 1920
La Signora Morli, una e due, 1920
Sei personaggi in cerca d'autore (Six Characters in Search
   of an Author), 1921
Enrico IV (Henry IV *or*, The Emperor), 1922
All'uscita (At the Gate), 1922
L'imbecille (The Imbecile), 1922
Vestire gli ignudi (Naked *or*, To Clothe the Naked), 1922
L'uomo dal fiore in bocca (The Man with the Flower
   in His Mouth), 1923
La vita che ti diedi (The Life I Gave You), 1923
L'altro figlio (The House with the Column), 1923
Ciascuno a suo modo (Each in His Own Way), 1924
Sagra del Signore della nave (Our Lord of the Ship), 1925
Diana e la Tuda (Diana and Tuda), 1927
L'amica delle mogli (The Wives' Friend), 1927
Bellavita, 1927
Scamandro, 1928
La nuova colonia (The New Colony), 1928
O di uno o di nessuno, 1929
Lazzaro (Lazarus), 1929
Come tu mi vuoi (As You Desire Me), 1930
Questa sera si recita a soggetto (Tonight We Improvise), 1930
Trovarsi (To Find Oneself), 1932

Quando si è qualcuno (When One Is Somebody), 1933
La Favola del figlio cambiato, 1934
Non si sa come (No One Knows How), 1935
Sogno (ma forse no) (Dreams, But Perhaps Not), 1936
I giganti della montagna (The Mountain Giants), 1937

The following is a list of books by Pirandello currently (1964) in print in the United States.

The Mountain Giants and Other Plays. (The New Colony, When One Is Somebody.) New York: Crown Publishers, 1964.
Naked Masks: Five Plays. Edited by Eric Bentley. (Liolà, It is so! [If you think so], Henry IV, Six Characters in Search of an Author, Each in His Own Way.) New York: E. P. Dutton (Everyman), 1952.
Plays. (Lazarus, The Life I Gave You, The Rules of the Game.) Baltimore: Penguin Books, Inc., 1959.
To Clothe the Naked and Two Other Plays. (The Rules of the Game, The Pleasure of Honesty.) New York: E. P. Dutton (Everyman), 1962.
Short Stories. New York: Simon and Schuster, 1959.

> *As You Desire Me*
> *Diana and Tuda*
> *No One Knows How*   Published in
> *The Wives' Friend*   separate volumes
> *To Find Oneself*   by Samuel French, Inc.
> *When One Is Somebody*   New York.

The following is a list of books published in the United States and wholly or in good part devoted to Pirandello. Each of these contains bibliographical data, as does *Naked Masks* (above).

McClintock, Lander. *The Age of Pirandello.* Bloomington, Ind.: Indiana University Press, 1951

Starkie, Walter. *Luigi Pirandello: 1867-1936,* second edition. New York: E. P. Dutton & Co., Inc.; London: John Murray, 1937.

Vittorini, Domenico. *The Drama of Luigi Pirandello.* Philadelphia: University of Pennsylvania Press, 1935.